CW00588645

Jennifer Lane lives in Wellington, _ _
husband and daughters, and feels equally at home in New
South Wales, Australia, where she was born and *Miracle* is set.
Her debut novel *All Our Secrets* (Rosa Mira Books) won the
Ngaio Marsh Award for Best First Novel in 2018.

Praise for *All Our Secrets*

"A hugely enjoyable mash-up of small-town horror
and coming-of-age story."
New Zealand Herald

"Coongahoola and Gracie's family home are rich,
warm, alive places in Lane's rendering."
Landfall

"The star of the book is brave, funny Gracie, who carries the
story on her often-embarrassed shoulders.
Highly recommended."
NZ Listener

"A compelling read … the feeling of menace is excellent."
Radio New Zealand

jenniferlane.co.nz

MIRACLE

JENNIFER LANE

CLOUD
INK

Published by Cloud Ink Press Ltd
PO Box 8988
Symonds Street
Auckland 1150
www.cloudink.co.nz

First published 2022

Copyright © Jennifer Lane 2022

The moral rights of the author have been asserted.

ISBN 978-0-473-62935-9

A catalogue record for this book is available from the National
Library of New Zealand.

Cover design by Janine Murray – jayyninety9@gmail.com
Internal design by Adrienne Charlton – www.ampublishingnz.com
Printed in New Zealand by Benefitz Ltd – www.benefitz.co.nz

For Mum

1

27 June 1986

Remembering that knock at the door still makes me shudder.
It wasn't actually a 'knock'. A knock is the gentle *tap tap tap* of
your aunty dropping off a still-warm cottage pie she's cooked
for your tea, or your nana if she's driven all the way from
Sydney for the weekend without dying from a stroke. This was
a *bash bash bash* that made my whole body jolt as if I'd just run
smack-bang into an electric fence, a *bash bash bash* that left my
skin all shivery and bumpy.

By the time I reached the hallway, Mum had fumbled
through all the locks and was holding the front door open, her
hand gripping its edge so tightly her knuckles were white.

'Is James Jamieson home?' a man's voice asked. I knew who
it belonged to before I saw the black boots on the doormat, one
shiny, one splattered in grey mud. I somehow knew this was
a cop's voice, even though I couldn't remember hearing one
in real life before. The legs of the cop it belonged to were two
inches longer than his navy blue trousers, and his bald head,
glistening under the porch light, was as round as a ping-pong
ball. Under his arm was a hat with a silver badge.

'Jim's here, yes. Why? What do you want Jim for?' Mum
held her dressing gown tightly around herself with one hand.

Her other hand still clung to the front door, as if she was ready to slam it.

Dad must've heard the cop's voice. The bedroom door squeaked open and Mum and I turned to see him emerge. Trudging along the hallway, he looked less like Dad and more like a man who'd done something really bad. His face was grey in the dull hall light, his hair was flat on one side and his crumpled work shirt hung halfway to his knees. I wish he'd bothered to put his trousers on. For some reason, his legs – thick, pale, hairy – made him look guilty.

'Mr Jamieson?' the cop said.

'Jim,' Dad answered. 'Jim Jamieson. We've met. Nigel, isn't it? What can I help you with?'

'It's Constable. Constable Kelly.' The cop's breath was coming out all foggy. 'You can help by coming with me to the station, Mr Jamieson.'

Although I should've known all this was about to happen, Constable Kelly may as well have pulled his gun out of its holster and shot me dead on the spot. I opened my mouth to speak, but there was too much to say. Constable Kelly looked down at his too-short trousers, probably feeling bad about taking Dad away.

I can't remember what happened next. Did Dad go back inside to put his jeans on? Surely he didn't go to the station in his blue undies. It was so cold I'd forced two tracksuit tops on over my nightie. Did Dad call out a goodbye to Julian? Not that Jules would've heard – he would've been hiding under his bed with his fingers jammed in his ears. Did he mess up my hair, kiss Mum's cheek? It's all a blur. All I can remember is him following Constable Kelly across the one, two, three, four stepping stones that joined our front veranda to our driveway. And thinking, *I've really done it now.*

2

Four months earlier

'Hey, what's Jimbo doing here?' Katie turned around and tapped her pen on my Spanish folder.

I felt the blood rush to my face. There were many ways to walk to the school office; what were the chances of him cutting through A Block? But sure enough, Dad's nose appeared at the window, the rest of him following approximately three centimetres later: thick curly hair, the silvery-grey of the scourer that sat, a crumby lump, in our kitchen sink, and a permanently sunburnt face, a souvenir from his long career as a postie. He wore a grey suit that must've belonged to someone who'd been twice his size before dying centuries ago, and a look on his face that suggested he was on his way to a meeting with Bob Hawke rather than our principal, Miss Jones. It was practically forty degrees too; he must've been sweltering! I felt a twinge of sadness. Poor Dad.

'Dunno.' I glanced at my watch: 2.15. Well, at least my plan had worked. I'd tricked him. I'd tricked my poor old dad.

'Forgot to kiss him goodbye this morning?' Katie asked, smirking at Oli, who sat at the desk next to hers. Oli was left-handed, and Katie right, so as they wrote down the answers to our ten-minute quiz, their elbows touched. Sometimes I'd

3

torment myself by counting how many times their elbows met. The record was thirty-three (double maths, C Block, 6 February 1985).

Katie had a big mouth, but I resisted the urge to tell her to shut it. Even though she was my best friend, she'd always thought she was better than me. It wasn't something we ever talked about, but I was pretty sure that my dad being a postie and her dad owning half of Boorunga had something to do with it. As well as bossing everyone around at Heller's Plastics – a gigantic factory painted in rainbow colours, presumably to compensate for turning the sky above it a dull grey with smoke – Reginald Heller owned the nearby Twirly Swirl biscuit factory (the Twirly Swirl biscuit itself – two vanilla wafers with yummy cream stuffed between them – was named by Katie when she was three). Reginald dressed in proper suits that hadn't been worn before him by men of different sizes and from different eras, and drove a sparkling white car with a sunroof, which he never used because, thanks to Heller's Plastics, Boorunga's air mostly stank like a dead thing lying at the bottom of your water tank.

'He's telling Miss Jones he's taking me out of here,' I said, trying to be calm, trying to pretend that my classmates weren't elbowing each other and pointing to my dad.

A month had passed since Dad's boss at the post office had handed him a typed letter, not for him to deliver, but to open and read himself. I could still see the look in Dad's eyes as he passed it to Mum. It was a look of shame.

'Ten weeks' pay for ten years' service,' Mum had read out loud. 'That's downright robbery! What about all those days you worked sick? When you had pneumonia? You risked your life making sure Martha got her *Reader's Digest* every Tuesday!'

Oli turned to face me, snapping me out of my thoughts. His eyes were so beautiful in real life, an even deeper brown than in the picture of him I kept in my mind for when he wasn't around. I had to force myself to keep breathing. *In out. In out. In out.*

'You don't look like him,' he said.

It was a compliment, I guessed. I wasn't as pretty as Katie, but nor was I one of the 'fuglies' who sat in a sad bunch near the tech block. My dirt-coloured hair permanently looked as if I'd just had an afternoon nap, even after dragging my comb through it, and my freckles, which thankfully hibernated in winter, made my face look like a giant dot-to-dot in summer. Granny Holmes'd promised me they'd disappear when I grew up, but at fourteen I remained as freckled as ever, so I wondered whether she'd just written that in my eighth birthday card to make me feel better. With a brother as picture-perfect as Julian, people always felt like they had to compliment me on something. 'You've got lovely cheekbones,' was the best Aunty Harriet could come up with. That, or 'You've got the legs of a ballerina.' At least I didn't inherit the gene responsible for Dad's nose.

Oli's comment suggested he'd never seen Dad before, that he didn't used to come to our house after school and force me to play 'classic catches' until the tennis ball disappeared into the night sky. Was he embarrassed on Dad's behalf too?

I couldn't blame Oli. Dad now appeared to be talking to himself: not just muttering under his breath like a normal mental person, but opening his mouth wide and making elaborate gestures with his arms, like someone who should be locked up for life. He was rehearsing his conversation with Miss Jones, I realised, just as he did at home in front of the hall mirror before all his job interviews. *Bloody hell, Dad!* I wanted to climb under my desk, bury my face in my hands.

'Is *everyone* in your family demented?' That came from Seth, Oli's best friend. He was sitting on the other side of Oli, next to Pheebs, his girlfriend since double art on Monday.

I was about to choke on the stuffy classroom air. I knew Seth was talking about Julian. Julian is seventeen months older than me but, while I survived the Boorunga earthquake unscathed despite being born smack-bang in the middle of it, he wasn't so lucky. I wiped my slippery, sweaty hands on my school tunic.

'Is everyone in your family a psychopath?' I glared at Seth.

Seth ignored my question, making me wonder whether I'd actually said it out loud; I was much braver inside my head than outside it.

Then Oli said, 'I reckon he looks like a hitman. Hope he's here to take out Jonesy.'

'Is he going for Petey's job?' Seth asked.

Petey was the caretaker who'd just been sacked, supposedly for having sex with Susan Singleton among all the balls, hoops, rackets, bats and wickets in the PE shed.

'He might get you a new mum, one of those hot Year 12s,' Seth was saying. 'One with half a –'

'What's the answer to 10d?' I asked. I didn't even know what the question was, I just wanted Seth to shut his mouth. Dad wouldn't be like Petey. Petey was only twenty-one. And Dad would always stick with Mum. Wouldn't he?

'Miracle? You obviously have a lot to say today,' Mr Healy announced from the platform. 'Perhaps you can tell us the events that triggered the Spanish Civil War.'

I looked up, my face burning. Yes, I am called 'Miracle'. That's another thing I can blame on the Boorunga earthquake. The quake measured 6.2 on the Richter scale, one of the biggest ever recorded in Australia, and I was born approximately thirty seconds into it, moments before the glass in the birthing suite's only window exploded. My real name – the name printed on my birth certificate – is Deborah. I could never understand why my parents chose a name with 'bor' in the middle of it.

But it didn't really matter anyway because once Dad and the midwife'd climbed out from under Mum's bed, Dad looked at me and said, 'It's a bloody miracle!' Thank God the 'bloody' part didn't stick.

'Can't remember, sorry,' I said to Mr Healy.

'Well, if you bothered to listen, maybe you would.' Mr Healy snapped a piece of chalk.

I usually paid attention. I got top of the class, sometimes tying with Oli. Admittedly, I only chose Spanish as an elective because I knew Oli was taking it and I wrote all the words on flash cards just to impress him, but it'd become my favourite subject too.

'Anyone else?' Mr Healy asked.

Big Bobby Sanson raised his hand. I don't know what he said, I just remember seeing his giant, pink arm waving in the air. After Big Bobby died, I'd lie awake trying to assemble all my memories of him. This, as dull as it was, is one of them.

'There goes your dad again,' Katie whispered. 'Reckon Miss Jones gave him the wooden spoon?'

I looked through the window, smeared by the faces, fingers and God knows what else of generations of Boorunga High kids. Dad was shuffling towards us, head bowed. He glanced up briefly, but didn't see me. His face was redder than usual and glimmering with sweat. He no longer looked as if he was on a mission to save the world. Instead, he seemed shrunken, his face as saggy and sad as his old-man suit.

'God, he must be a good hitman,' Seth said over his shoulder. 'Didn't make a sound.' He turned his hand into a pistol and pointed it at Pheebs's head. 'Pow!'

The others laughed and I forced a smile to pretend I could take a joke. Oli shot me a look that could've meant either a) I'm sorry you're such a loser or b) I'm sorry Seth is such a dickhead. I settled on b.

Katie and Oli picked up their pens, and started writing down whatever Big Bobby was saying, elbow brushing elbow for at least the twelfth time. But at that moment I didn't care. My plan had succeeded – Dad's face said it all – but I wasn't proud of myself. As I watched him disappear down the corridor, I felt like the worst daughter on the planet.

What had I done? I felt sorry for Dad, but more than that, I felt guilty.

Even so, on that stinking hot afternoon in February, I had no idea of the chain of events I'd set in motion. How could I? I wasn't psychic. It wasn't until months later that I realised, if I hadn't interfered, everything would've turned out much differently – not just for Dad, but for all of us.

3

'Here's one, Dad.' I circled an ad in *The Boorunga Times* with one of Julian's pencils. It was another hot, sticky afternoon, a few days after Dad's visit to school, and the air in our living room was thick with disappointment. 'Floor Manager at Twirly Swirl. We could eat free biscuits for breakfast, lunch and tea!'

To be honest, the thought of Katie's dad being Dad's boss made my stomach churn – she already looked down on me through her expensive contact lenses – but I was desperate to make up for what I'd done.

'That was Mick's job!' Dad said. 'Until he gave Bob a black eye for calling his wife a … something not very nice starting with 's', and was sacked on the spot! No, I couldn't take Mick's job. It's too soon.'

I drew a cross through the ad and flicked back to the front page. 'RISE IN ILLNESS "UNPRECEDENTED", DOCTORS CLAIM', yelled the words above a photo of the new hospital. I glanced over at the couch where Julian lay sleeping, his breathing loud and raspy, his head buried under a cushion.

A new Tears for Fears song was playing on Radio B1. 'Everybody wants to rule the world,' they sang. Not everybody, I thought. Dad would be happy with just a job, a reason to make his sandwiches each morning, to brush his teeth, throw his satchel on his shoulder and charge out the front door.

'I liked being a postie – my role of messenger, of bringing news,' Dad was saying.

'Half of it was bills,' Mum muttered, rearranging Mr Jackson's brown trousers on her ironing board. 'Most people dreaded the "news" you brought! Anyway, forget about the post office. If they valued you, they would've kept you on instead of hiring that young boy with the ridiculous earring in his nose.'

The last thing Dad needed was to be reminded about Jonno Peters. Dad reckoned Jonno only got the 'Fastest Deliverer of the Year Award' because he'd shove a whole street's worth of mail into the first letter box he came to. No one dared complain because Jonno looked like he'd just stepped out of the TV show, *World Championship Wrestling*. And he knew where everyone lived.

'There's heaps of other jobs,' I said. 'Mr Olsen goes on and on about it. We're even a case study in our economics text book. Boorunga is booming!'

I wasn't just saying that to make Dad feel better. I heard the word 'booming' all the time. It made me imagine our whole town – people, dogs, cats, teachers, and all – being stuffed into a cannon, and fired off into the sky. Boom!

Apparently everyone'd thought the earthquake would be the end of Boorunga. It'd just crumble away into a ghost town and eventually be swallowed by an even bigger quake. Haunted by aftershocks that rattled the town for months, most of our neighbours put their houses (or the pile of bricks that slumped in their place) on the market, loaded their broken furniture into their station wagons and sped off in search of stable ground.

But the population soon began climbing again. Word got around about our cheap land, and men in black suits surveyed Jackson and Armfield Streets, armed with clipboards and cameras, their shiny shoes coated in dust. Next came the bulldozers and more men, these ones with sunburnt faces, orange overalls and Blundstone boots.

Where Joe's Emporium and the Kitchen Warehouse used to be, the Twirly Swirl biscuit factory appeared, the smell of baking wafting out onto the streets, sweetening the stench of smoke erupting from Parsons Cigarettes and the plastics factory that later became Heller's Plastics. Smaller businesses opened too, and people moved to Boorunga from other towns to snap up the new jobs. Fourteen years after the earthquake, our town was twice its original size.

What the textbooks didn't mention though was that the earthquake left a curse on us. Either that or we were cursed already and that's why the earthquake struck. Earthquakes hardly ever happened in Australia; the faultline under Boorunga had kept itself a secret until 1972. Theories about a curse were always floating around school, but were particularly popular after Joanne Nelson in Year 10 died the same month as two kids from Boorunga Primary. I kept quiet whenever the quake was mentioned, or pretended I was busting to go to the loo or needed something from my school bag. I knew it couldn't have been my fault, despite Dad saying I was so full of life that as I forced my way out of Mum, 'the whole world trembled'. But to draw attention to myself would've just been asking for trouble.

I flicked back to the Classified section and scanned the page again, my fingers smudging the ink. 'What about this one, Dad? Crematorium Assistant?' I feel dumb about it now, but even as I was saying the word, I wasn't thinking about what a 'crematorium' actually was. I just noted the 'assistant' part and the 'no experience needed'.

I caught a whiff of the oily stink of our garage as Dad peered over my shoulder. With no mail sack to strap to his back, no neighbourhood dogs to placate with Meaty Bites from his pocket, and no letters to stuff into letter boxes, he spent his mornings in the garage, sawing, hammering, sanding and varnishing wooden toys – go-karts, cars, doll's houses – that Julian and I were years too old to play with.

'Interesting,' Dad said, but the flatness in his voice suggested otherwise and he sat back down.

'I'll cut it out.' I searched the table for the scissors.

'Thanks, Miri, but if I can't get a job looking after school grounds, who's going to employ me to … um … take care of people?'

'But they'd be *dead* people, Jim.' Mum's words floated out of a cloud of cigarette smoke and iron steam. After years of ironing other peoples' clothes, Mum could smoke hands-free. I'd watch in fascination as the ash tip grew longer and longer, threatening to fall onto a blouse or skirt, before, just in time, she'd whip the cigarette out of her lips and tap it on the KB beer ashtray on the windowsill. It was probably a skill that grew out of necessity: Mum ironed for up to five hours non-stop on a 'good' day. On a 'bad' day she could barely summon enough energy to light a cigarette, let alone lift the iron.

'How could you go wrong?' she was saying. 'They're hardly in a position to complain if you make a mistake! Besides, you would've got that job at the school if you'd turned up on time.'

The mention of the job at my school made my stomach sink. I dreaded that Dad would, once again, say he was certain he'd written down the right interview time, and question the health of his mind. How much longer could I resist the urge to confess, to yell out: *It was me! I rubbed out the 1! I turned 12.15 into 2.15?*

But wouldn't anyone have done what I did? Who else's dad mops up the piss on the floor of the boys' toilets? Or takes over from a twenty-one-year-old who slept with a Year 12 girl? What if Dad fell for a girl too? The thought practically made me gag. I couldn't imagine it; Dad wasn't like that. But he wasn't entirely innocent either. *Playboy* calendars had hung on the back of our toilet door for as long as I could remember. I had the sulky-faced, naked-except-for-high-heels ladies of January through to December to thank for my first lessons in puberty, but did I really need to know that stuff when I was five? It was obvious Dad liked looking at women who weren't Mum, women whose faces were less lined, bodies less saggy. Some girls at school weren't much younger than Miss April or May. Chloe Shriver owned a pair of high heels. And that new girl, Livvy – she looked like a model and Katie'd told me she'd been with at least four boys at our school. I shook my head to remove the thought.

I snipped out the ad, still not thinking about the word 'crematorium', about what Dad'd be required to do to a person, albeit a dead one.

'Here.' I handed it to Dad. 'It says to call Greg.'

'I guess it's something a bit different.' A sliver of hope lit up his eyes. 'Wonder what the lads would make of it!'

'Give it a go, Dad.' I wanted to be free of the guilt that'd kept me awake until long after he turned the TV off each night and the sound of his heavy feet disappeared along the hall. As long as he didn't get a job at the school. Or at the supermarket. What a nightmare that'd be: Dad being bossed around by sixteen-year-old boys with pimples and forced to wear a 'JIM' badge on his chest so Seth, Oli and the others could chant his name while he was stacking shelves.

Dad headed for the kitchen, squinting at the clipping in his hand. When he reappeared a few minutes later, a giant smile lit his face. 'I think I might have myself a new job,' he said. He winked at me, a signal that the old Dad was back.

'Shhh, don't wake Jules,' Mum said, before carrying on in her usual loud, husky voice. 'Don't get too excited. You don't know the first thing about the crematorium.'

'I know it's that new joint way out in the bush, past Hargrave's place.' Dad spoke softly, with one eye on the

13

couch where Julian lay. 'It's copped a bit of flak since opening – Greg was straight up with me – but that's because Raymond's Funerals was so popular. You know what small towns are like. Small town, small mind. Greg thinks people will come round.'

I was so relieved I almost threw my arms around Dad, but I was too old to hug my parents and I didn't want to make them suspicious. A great thing about Dad – the old Dad, anyway – was his optimism. He provided enough light for us to see through the dark, smoky cloud that surrounded Mum.

I was six and a half when I opened the pages of the battered diary under Mum and Dad's bed and saw the word for the first time. *Depression*. I remember pulling it apart in my head – *deep press shon* – and thinking it had something to do with all the ironing Mum did. Jill was always bringing her trousers to be 'pressed' (she called them 'slacks' but no one else called them anything so posh), her shirts, dresses and skirts (thankfully Mum drew the line at Jill's silk 'smalls'). She was paid money for it, sometimes as much as twenty dollars, but what was it about ironing that left her slumped on the couch in front of the TV, her mouth a silent line, her eyes closed to Dad's whispered offers of cups of tea?

One morning I decided to examine the iron for clues. Dad was on his postie run and Mum was still in bed, the only sound I could hear was the *drip drip drip* of the kitchen tap. I don't know where Julian was, maybe sitting at the table, lost in his drawing; when he was drawing it'd take a nuclear explosion to lift his eyes from the page. Or perhaps the smell of chicken curry, his favourite food, but a nuclear explosion was probably more likely in our house.

I'd always been forbidden to touch the iron; to me it was as deadly as a gun. My heart hammered as I lifted it with trembling hands. Was it the weight of it that weakened her?

Did its steam, thick as the cigarette smoke that poured out of her mouth, seep deep into her skin? Or was it the electricity (another thing I'd learned to be terrified of), shooting out of the wall, snaking down the cord, and zapping the life out of her? I couldn't tell – I wasn't brave enough to actually turn it on – but as I carefully placed it back on the ironing board, I promised myself I'd wear wrinkled clothes for the rest of my life. I wasn't going to spend my adult days sitting half-dead on the couch staring at *Wheel of Fortune*.

'It's my brain,' she replied, when I pleaded with her to let Dad take the iron to the dump, blaming it for flattening the energy she needed to attend my school Christmas pageant.

I still didn't really get it, but from then on, whenever she buried herself in her bed, burrowed deep down like a wombat, I pictured her poor sick brain, dry and shrivelled up inside her head.

Once when she really lost it with me – she'd spotted the *I love OH* scratched into the kitchen table – she said her depression was my fault. She'd never recovered from the trauma of my birth.

'I had nothing left, but you just kept wanting.' She held her head in her hands. 'And then … then Julian …'

But after Mum'd gone to bed that night, Dad promised me that her dark days came from a time long before either of us was born. One of the things that first attracted him to her was her big, sad brown eyes. 'They were begging for someone to love.' He treasured his memory of the first time he'd made her smile – 'a big one that showed off all her lovely teeth' – more than that of their first kiss. (I, too, preferred the image of Mum showing off her teeth to one of my parents pashing.)

Anyway, with Dad – the old, happy Dad – around I felt like everything was going to be all right, regardless of the shrivelled-up thing inside Mum's head.

'By all means give it a go.' Mum squashed her half-smoked cigarette into the ashtray. 'But if Greg's copping flak, you probably will too.'

'I can handle it.' Dad held up an arm and flexed his bicep, as if checking he hadn't over-promised. 'But someone's got to take care of the ... of those who've left this world, and no one's stepped up to take over Raymond's business. Have they?'

'No, but if you believe Jill, and I think she knows what she's talking about for once, the owner of the crematorium – this *Greg* – is in cahoots with Reginald Heller.'

But Dad'd moved on. 'It beats making biscuits ... or plastic bags! What a meaningless existence that'd be, though I'd do a better job than those dopes at Heller's. I'd make bags that take less than ten bloody minutes to get open!'

'They don't just make plastic bags, Dad.'

'I know, they make all the stuff you peel off and dump straight in the bin. Imagine that – making rubbish for a living!' Dad was on a roll. He leant back and put his feet up on the footstool, both big toes poking out of his socks. 'I'm sure my new job would beat working as a school caretaker too.'

'For sure. Year 10s are pigs.' My voice was calm, casual. If Dad got this job I'd be able to sleep again, life would go on as it had before. I could erase the image of my family cramming into a one-bedroom fibro house at the estate near the prison.

4

'Staying on at school wasn't an option for me.' Dad was telling the hall mirror the next morning, his deep frown matching his serious, down-turned mouth. 'So I don't have any qualifications to speak of. Or even any not to speak of.' He smiled. 'But no one can deny I'm a hard worker.'

Dad'd decided his second-hand suit brought him bad luck. So for this interview he'd chosen his white shirt, blue tie, and a pair of brown trousers that looked a lot like the ones Mum had ironed for Mr Jackson the night before.

'Good luck, Dad,' I said.

'Luck's got nothing to do with it, Miri.' He winked at me in the mirror. 'Greg Parker said I was the only applicant so far. Think that's a coincidence? I reckon this job was made for me. And you helped me find it.'

I crossed my fingers behind my back, hoping he wouldn't be disappointed, hoping that at last I'd be able to close my eyes at night without seeing his crumpled face and that lost look in his eyes.

'We're here!' Aunty Harriet followed her chirpy voice along the hall and into the living room, Julian lagging behind. 'Hello, Miracle, Henrietta.'

'Hi.' I was always happy to see Harriet. Her cheerfulness was as catching as a yawn on the school bus; a whiff of her warm, vanillary perfume was enough to lift me out of a bad mood, even when I had my period. But she seemed to have the opposite effect on Mum. At the sound of Harriet's voice, Mum rolled her eyes, lit a cigarette and sucked so hard she nearly swallowed it. A conversation with her sister was something to be endured.

One of Mum's many gripes was that she was one of two. A twin. The fact that their mum, Granny Holmes, gave her and Harriet 'dressed-up' boys' names irked her even further. Granny Holmes had grown up a mouse-sized girl in a house full of boys – her five brothers were 'great lumbering lumps of lads' – so throughout the long, hot months of her pregnancy, she couldn't envision producing anything other than a boy. She'd already decided to call 'him' Harry after the man she wished she'd married instead of Grandad (a long story she'd often tell while drinking sherry) so she 'near passed out with shock when not one boy, but two girls came sliding out (a detail that always made me wince), one after the other – whoosh, whoosh.'

I'd known without asking that the first 'whoosh' was Harriet. One of Mum's other gripes was that she was the second twin, that ever since she'd followed Harriet into the world, she'd been her shadow.

Aunty Harriet was a teacher at Julian's school – Huxley – a school for 'handicapped children', or 'spastics', 'spazzos', 'mongys' or 'retards' if you listened to the kids at my school. But Julian wasn't a spastic, spazzo, mongy or retard, despite what Seth and the others said. According to Mum, he'd been the most beautiful baby in Boorunga, or maybe even Australia (she couldn't verify that though, because she got carsick on long drives, so her research omitted all babies north of Newcastle, south of Bega, and west of Coongahoola). She said most newborns look like shrivelled up old men (me included, she sheepishly admitted when I probed), but not Julian. Whereas many come out not-quite-ready, he was born perfectly complete. He looked like an angel – the faded photos in his baby album confirm it – his smooth skin pale and flawless and his cheeks full and round. Even at sixteen, he still looked like he'd stepped out of a book about Jesus. His hair had darkened to a browny-blond, but his eyes were still bright blue and his skin was as smooth and soft as our five-year-old cousin, Worm's.

But then, the earthquake. At the exact moment the earth was shaking me out of Mum, Julian lay sleeping in the cot Harriet had set up for him in her spare room. Harriet had nodded off on the La-Z-Boy in their dining room. The first tremors jolted her awake, but before she could make sense of what was happening, she found she was lying on the carpet, inches away from the upended TV. She climbed to her feet, dazed. As the house continued to sway like a swing bridge between two cliffs, she clambered over books, records, the antiques she'd bought on a ten-day spree in Sydney, limped out of the dining room (a large ceramic vase had shattered the bone in her left ankle), and into the spare room. By the time she clutched Julian's limp body to her chest, he was unconscious.

Baby Julian didn't wake until three days later, by which time he lay hooked up to a machine twenty times his size in the temporary hospital set up in the scout hall. Dad blamed the wooden train he'd made Julian while Mum was packing her bag to go into hospital. Painted red and blue, and with tiny faces smiling out of each of its windows, it sat on the shelf by Julian's cot before the quake forced it to the floor. But Julian was examined by all of Boorunga's doctors and none found any sign of head injury. They were baffled, said it must have been the shock that put Julian into a coma and insisted he'd come right. But Dad said all you had to do was peer into the baby's vacant blue eyes to know something had happened to him during the quake and he'd never be the same again.

Julian did recover. To an extent. If you saw him walk past, you'd just marvel at what a perfect-looking boy he was, without guessing at the less-than-perfect goings-on inside him. It was only when you got up close that you'd notice his right arm quivering. Then you'd realise he'd never stopped shaking since the earthquake.

Now Julian was sitting on the couch, kicking off his KT-26s. Shoes had always made his feet feel 'stuffy'.

'I don't suppose you've heard from Jim yet?' Harriet asked. 'Worm's at soccer so I thought I'd pop in to see how his interview went.'

'Must've stopped off at the pub.' Mum examined the clock above the TV. 'That could either be good or bad news.'

'Mind if I make a cuppa?' Harriet walked into the kitchen before Mum answered. The kettle technically belonged to her anyway. She'd bought it from Kmart after our old one gave her an electric shock.

'Julian amazed me again today,' Harriet said from the doorway. 'Show them your picture, Jules.'

Julian suddenly snapped out of his dream world and looked up, blinking. He dug his sketchpad out of his backpack and flicked through the pages.

He opened it to a drawing of an old woman, her hair pulled back tightly and her face creased with fine lines.

'I don't look that old. Do I?' Mum touched her forehead. 'I hope that's not me.'

Mum's face actually bore as many lines as a street map of Boorunga, not that any of us would tell her. She probably still saw Harriet's smooth, well-cared-for face as her mirror image.

Julian shook his head.

'If that was you, we'd both be getting ready to shuffle off to

Jackson House.' Harriet placed Mum's tea on the coffee table. 'Unless Miracle is planning to take care of us herself?'

I shrugged. I didn't want to think about Harriet and Mum being like those half-dead people propped up on Zimmer frames, dresses absentmindedly tucked into stockings, slippers having long replaced real shoes. Besides, when they were that old, I'd be an adult. What if I ended up like Mum, with all her problems and fears, watching the Olympics on TV with a can of beer being the highlight of my year? And how could Julian ever possibly be an adult? He hadn't finished growing into a boy.

Just then Dad bounded through the back door, bringing the stink of the pub with him.

He handed Mum a white rose before digging around in his pocket and presenting Julian and me with a mushy chocolate frog each. He then removed a brown paper bag from his old leather postie satchel.

'Harriet.' He nodded at my aunty. 'If I'd known you were going to be here, I would've bought you a gift too.'

'Don't be silly.' Harriet's cheeks flushed pink. 'I'm just hiding out here while Worm learns how to kick a ball. I also couldn't wait to hear your news.'

'So it's *good* news, then?' Mum sniffed the rose. 'Or is this flower for your funeral?'

'Start Monday!'

'Congratulations!' Harriet said. 'So it's called Caring Cremations is it?

'Compassionate Cremations.'

I think that was the moment I really thought about where Dad was going to be working. Compassionate Cremations. A place where they burned people. Still, anything was better than a job at my school, wasn't it?

'Well, congratulations.' Mum kissed Dad's cheek; a gesture so rare I felt my face glow. I looked down at my bare feet.

'That's wonderful, Jim,' Harriet said. 'Must be a big relief.'

'Let's just say, I'll enjoy this drink.' Dad handed Mum a beer before lowering himself onto the couch next to Julian and ripping the ring off his own can.

Julian squished the chocolate that once resembled a smiling frog inside its wrapper. My brother was unusual in lots of ways but his ability to not stuff chocolate in his mouth the minute it reached his hand was one of the most baffling.

'What will you be doing exactly?' Mum was asking Dad.

Dad waved her question away. 'Details, details. We just talked about me – about whether I was the right man for the job. And I was!'

'Of course you were, Jim,' Harriet called from the kitchen. 'Did he say why he started up in Boorunga?'

'He said he saw a niche in the market. *Niche*. Don't you like that word? Sounds French or something.'

'Sounds like a fancy way of saying he heard about what happened to Raymond Miller.' Mum lifted the gold can but stopped before it reached her lips. 'Did he say you were the only person willing to apply?'

Dad ignored her last comment. 'Miller's Funerals left a hole. Someone had to fill it.'

'But how did Greg know?' Harriet asked. She placed a vase holding Mum's flower in the centre of the table, and sat down, cradling her tea. 'Have you seen the way he *walks*? You can tell he's from Sydney.'

'He's from Randwick.' Dad nodded. 'But he and Reginald Heller go way back.'

'So it *is* true.' Mum opened her packet of Parsons and dug out a cigarette.

'Heller might be an okay bloke, deep down,' Dad said. 'You can't believe what everyone says.'

'He's a crook!'

'Hen, that's a bit harsh.' Harriet glanced at me.

But I was used to Mum talking about Katie's dad like that. It was probably true. He was hardly ever home when I visited their place, and when he was, he just pretended I wasn't there, as if I was too unimportant to waste words on. He was a big, grumpy man with moon-coloured flesh and deep, dark stains under small angry eyes. Katie said he'd been grumpy as long as she'd been alive. Her mum Annette'd died while giving birth to her, so he blamed Katie as well as himself and the rest of the world for his loss. I suppose I was meant to feel sorry for him, but I couldn't. I just wondered why Katie's mum married him in the first place; how could that gravelly voice ever have said 'I love you'?

'I know they say that, but why?' Dad was still talking. 'Cause he's the only bloke in town who wears a suit?'

'Why else do people move here from Sydney?' Mum pursed her lips. 'They think they're better than us. I've heard all his staff hate him. Susan Hill's heart was fine until he promoted her to Canteen Manager.'

'They're called "entrepreneurs" and they come here for the cheap land,' Dad said.

'Thanks to the big bloody fault line under the ground!'

But Dad was on a high. 'Anyway Greg's business is quite separate. Our focus is on people. It's our mission to help ease the suffering of those who are left behind.'

'Our? We?'

'Greg Parker and me,' Dad said.

'You're pretty sure of yourself for a man who hasn't even started yet.'

'He's doing a good thing, Hen,' Harriet said. 'I think you'll be great, Jim. You've got a good heart.'

'Hope it's stronger than Susan Hill's heart!' Mum said.

'I think it's great too, Dad,' I said.

'Thanks. I've got a feeling about this. I've got a feeling my life's about to change.'

'Yeah, me too.' I smiled at him, not knowing just how right we both were.

5

By the time I got up on Monday morning, Dad was fully dressed and his wet curls were combed flat against his head. I wondered when Mr Jackson was expecting his trousers back, and whether Dad was deliberately trying to look like Dracula now that he was working in the death industry. Every day would probably feel like Halloween. He was standing in the hallway, trying to impress the mirror again.

'Good morning, Ma'am.' He turned to me, holding out his right hand. A folded red-chequered hanky poked out of his jacket pocket. Did he put it there to make himself look important, or to keep handy in case a dead man's wife needed to blow her nose?

'My name is James,' he said. 'I'd just like you to know I'm here for you.'

I let him shake my hand gently, then bolted for the kitchen in case he expected me to cry and pretend 'my loved one' had just died. Drama was my least favourite subject at school.

I was surprised to see Mum, not just out of bed, but holding a bread knife, spreading margarine onto thin slices of white bread. I stuffed a peanut butter sandwich into my school bag, even though it was destined for the bin outside the school gates. For Year 9 girls, eating at school was even less cool than wearing a jumper. I'm not sure why or how these rules were made, but questioning them would be even more uncool than breaking them, so I kept quiet. I did wonder, though, whether I was the only one who needed to devour eight Weet-Bix the second I got home.

Mum complained that she'd have no one to make her a cup of tea before *Wheel of Fortune*. But her tone was light and her eyes were clear. I knew she was as happy to see the old Dad as I was.

'Let me make it now – and you just bung it in the microwave later.' Dad packed three cheese and pickle sandwiches and a thermos of International Roast into his satchel. 'I could line up a few cuppas for you.'

'Don't worry, I'll just scream for help when I'm ready,' Mum said. 'I bet Joan can make a decent brew.'

Joan was Mrs Jensen-from-across-the-road, an ancient lady who spent most of her days a short, round shadow behind her net curtains, watching the street. Back then, we didn't know who or what she was waiting for, and what she'd do if she actually saw anything (I could run to the shop and back in the time it took her to retrieve *The Boorunga Times* from her front lawn), but knowing she was always on lookout gave our family an extra sense of security.

Normally I wouldn't be seen dead walking with Dad, especially when he had both satchel straps over his shoulders like a kindergartner. But on his first day I made an exception. Besides, we lived on the trashy side of town – anywhere south of Boorunga Bridge was 'squalorsville', according to my friends – so I wouldn't be spotted by anyone who mattered. Dad and I walked to the end of Burgess Road together and, as he waved goodbye from his bus stop, I had to squeeze my eyes to hold back the tears. Dad had a job again. No one could call him a dole bludger, or tell me I belonged in one of those falling-down fibro houses near Boorunga Prison. Everything was going to be okay.

The painfully slow squeak-click of the front door closing behind Dad that evening told me I'd got my hopes up too soon. I peered down the hallway and saw him leaning against the door, eyes shut. When he shuffled into the dining room his face looked as it had when he'd trudged through the Science block at school. At least his curls had sprung back into action, the only part of him still looking lively. My chest tightened. What had I done?

'So, Mr Crematorium Assistant, how was your first day?' Mum spoke gently, sensing his mood. She, Julian and I sat squeezed together on the couch, one of Mum's ideas for cutting heating costs.

'It was …' Dad sighed.

'Okay? Great? A complete bloody disaster?'

'I just thought … I imagined that …' Dad sank down into his chair and fiddled with his tie. I noticed the faint smell of something like Dettol.

'It'll take a while to adjust,' Mum said. 'It's a bit of a jump from stuffing letters in boxes to shoving people into them, and –'

'Hen!' Dad winced. 'It wasn't the work. There was a crowd outside. Protesters, you could call them. I felt like a crook entering the front door. Not the best introduction to a new career.'

'Protesting?' Mum said. 'About you deserting me for a new job? Or about your ridiculous tie?'

Dad ignored her. 'They were waving "Where's Raymond?" signs about and chanting his name – "Raymond, Raymond, Raymond" – over and over again. They were quite worked up.'

Raymond Miller. The old funeral director with hairy earlobes. Why would anyone care that he'd gone?

I imagined Dad slinking past a group of angry protesters, all men because women wouldn't kick up a stink about an old man leaving town, which is probably sexist, but this is Boorunga and protesting isn't something Boorunga people do. Jill Boston, Seth from my class's mum, often ranted in *The Boorunga Times* about the dangers of kids riding skateboards in the supermarket car park or the 'disgraceful' state of the lawns on our side of Boorunga Bridge, but I'm sure she wouldn't bother to walk the streets holding a sign or chanting about some old bloke in a suit. She had aerobics classes to go to and people to bad-mouth.

'Did your boss call the cops?' I asked.

Dad looked up, loosening his tie. 'He told me to ignore them, which I did. Greg arrived *after* Raymond'd left town, so they're definitely barking up the wrong tree. But still … a welcome like that is a bit of a turn-off.'

'There are other jobs, Dad,' I offered. Securing our family's future was harder than I'd thought. I saw the fibro houses, yards littered with beer bottles and rusted car parts. Could I walk to school from there without anyone knowing?

'And then, the pub.' Dad shook his head. 'I'd mentioned my job when I stopped off on Friday and we had a good laugh. I thought, you know, we were mucking about. But *they* – Ray, Ted and Stu – thought I was having them on. As if I'd make a joke out of my own career. My livelihood! So today, I turn up for a quiet schooner after a hard day, and they refused to sit with me. Even Ray moved stools. And Ted! Get this! Ted said he had to go home because Judy was making a roast!'

'So?' Mum asked.

'So, everyone knows Tuesday is her roast day!'

'Perhaps she wanted a change,' Mum said, as if this was the obvious answer. I didn't really know what a roast was; I couldn't remember Mum ever cooking one.

'But Ted *hates* Jude's roasts! The lamb is always too dry.'

'You're overthinking this, Jim.'

'They called Greg a *murderer*. They even blamed him for Bryce George's death. Said Bryce was "good as gold on Monday, dead as a doorknob on Friday".'

Bryce George had swum freestyle at the Commonwealth Games when he was a teenager, earning him a position as one of Boorunga's biggest celebrities. After he died of a lung disease, we held a special assembly at school and the netball courts were named the 'Bryce George Courts', since the school didn't have a pool.

'Leave if you want,' Mum said. 'We'll get by.'

'Thanks, love. But I'm sticking with it.' Dad tried to untangle his tie. 'I'm no quitter.'

'No, you're not. Why else would you still be married to me? Anyway, what about the actual job? What do you *do* exactly?'

'I don't want to talk about it. Not in front of the kids.'

Julian was busy in his own mind, so Dad needn't have worried about him, but his words made my skin prickle. There were plenty of things I didn't want *him* to know about: the two cigarettes hidden in my undies drawer, the $6.80 I'd stolen from the coin jar, those warm, sour sips of VB I'd snuck when getting him another beer, reading his painful attempts at poetry to Julian (Dad still thought poems had to rhyme), but now we'd switched positions. Dad was doing something he didn't want me to know about.

Things started going wrong at school the day after Big Bobby's funeral. Our Social Science class had filled the last two rows in St Mary's Church, all of us too stunned to even nudge each other or point at the tears running down Miss Jones's face. Even though Big Bobby hadn't been my friend, that morning I'd woken with the sense that something was missing, something was wrong. I'd had to force myself out of bed; I didn't have the energy to cope with being picked on.

Somehow everyone now knew about Dad's new job. I'd assumed that as long as he wasn't working at school, winking at the Year 12 girls or waving a handful of paddle-pop wrappers at me through my classroom window, no one would care about his chosen career path. But not only was he working in a crematorium, it was a crematorium half the town wanted to close down. How stupid was I?

Seth Boston started it, out of the blue, in Social Science: 'Miracle's old man smokes people!'

The others followed his cue:

'Compassionate *terminations*.'

I stared at the classroom door, willing Mr Lawson to walk in. Where was he?

'Heard there's a barbecue at Miracle's on the weekend? No one leaves alive!'

Even the Mormon girl spoke: 'Does your dad wear gloves?'

I lifted my desk lid and rummaged through the scraps of paper and exercise books, pretending not to care, forcing back tears. Where was Mr Lawson when you actually needed him? He was always in the classroom waiting to pounce on us for being late. Sometimes I wondered if he slept under his desk so he could say 'You're late!' when we drifted in for first period.

'… pours lighter fluid on them.'

'Shoves gunpowder up their bums and explodes the mother-fuckers. Boom!'

'That boom sets her crazy bro off! He starts frothing at the mouth.'

Even though the last comment came from Seth, it hurt more than the others. It hurt more because Oli was doubled over, shaking with laughter, his forehead resting on his desk. I'd thought Oli liked Julian. He knew he wasn't crazy. Surely he hadn't forgotten all the afternoons he'd spent at our house when we were in the same class at Boorunga Primary. He'd even lied for Julian and me when Mum busted us burying her cask of wine in the dirt-pile in our backyard. I can still see Mum, hands on hips and face blotched with anger, and Oli climbing onto the mound of dirt so he could look straight into her bloodshot eyes. He stood there, bare feet sinking into the soil, dirt pasted to the sticky patch around his Milo-y mouth, and said, in his brave, seven-year-old voice: 'It was my idea!' even though it was mine. I remember the dull ache in my heart.

I could handle the other kids, even Katie, but seeing Oli laugh knocked the wind out of me. He may as well have kneed me in the stomach. I hid my head in the desk as I tried to get my breath. Oli and I'd stopped being friends in Year 4 when I was in Mrs Avery's class and he had Mrs Gibbs, and I'd started pretending I shared the other girls' repulsion of 'boy germs'. And now he was Katie's boyfriend. She'd given him a twenty-dollar box of Darrel Lea 'English Toffee' chocolates on Valentine's Day in Year 8 and they'd acted as good as married ever since. But I hadn't stopped hoping.

I glanced up. Now that he'd run out of words, Seth was humming, his hands drumming along the wooden desk. It was the theme song to *The Addams Family*, just in case anyone was unaware that I belonged to a family of freaks. More laughter. I wanted to disappear.

'Shut up, Seth!' Katie said, elbowing Oli to get him onside. 'What happened to Julian was tragic. He's a gorgeous boy.'

'How can you tell?' Seth said. 'He never stands still.'

Katie flashed me an apologetic look, but both she and Oli were fighting back smiles.

I pretended to read my Social Science notes. Seth was just teasing; he teased everyone. This was about my family, not me. I couldn't let my eyes water. Crying at school was even poorer form than eating lunch. I searched the depths of my mind for a suitable comeback, but my thoughts had fled in panic.

Seth walked over to my desk, as the class watched the free entertainment.

'You know I'm joking. Don't you?' He patted my shoulder. 'Your brother's all right.'

I felt hot and tingly – not because Seth showed promise as a masseur, but because Oli was watching.

'Julian's an artist.' This was Oli, with no trace of laughter or sarcasm. 'He's really talented.'

Seth nodded, but I could tell he didn't agree. Or didn't care.

'Yeah, he is.' I took courage from Oli's words. 'He'll be a much a more successful artist than you'll be a comedian, Seth.'

Oli, Katie and the others smirked at that, so I felt like I'd redeemed myself, if only slightly.

Then I noticed the angry purple bruise on Seth's neck. I'd seen the new girl, Livvy, and some other Year 12 girls comparing similar ugly welts at the bus stop. Hickeys, they called them, and acted like they were trophies.

'What's that?' I pointed at his neck.

Seth stepped back, stung. He clasped his neck and tripped on his chair leg as he returned to his seat.

'What?' Pheebs frowned at me, confused. 'Show me, Seth.'

'Leave it,' Seth muttered. It was his turn to dig around in his desk.

By the time Mr Lawson burst through the door, red-faced, our classroom was silent. Most kids were writing in their workbooks, maybe even doing real work. Mr Lawson raised his eyebrows, puzzled but obviously pleased. I felt like hugging him, even though he looked like Bert from Sesame Street and I could smell his BO from the second back row.

The few times I looked up, Oli and Katie's elbows weren't touching and I saw that Pheebs had moved her desk away from Seth's. But I didn't feel any satisfaction. I felt flat.

I was still naïve, oblivious to what was going on around me. Perhaps it was trying to process what'd happened to Bobby that stopped me from seeing things clearly. I couldn't comprehend how someone could be sitting behind a desk one day, raising his big flabby arm, and lying in a morgue the next. Had there been fewer thoughts whirling around my head, clouding my mind, I might have realised that being teased at school was the least of my problems.

6

When Seth 'joked' about my family, I was grateful that at least he only knew half the story. What he did know, he must've heard from his mum, Jill, who Dad said had the 'loosest lips' in Boorunga. But there was no chance Seth would ever rock up to our front door (an embarrassment in itself – when Dad'd made it he'd obviously had other things on his mind – wind whistled through the gap at the top, while the gap at the bottom was so wide you could practically see the toes of the person on the other side), so there was no danger he'd glimpse Mum scuttling down the hallway, dressing gown billowing behind her, to hide in her bedroom. If Seth had ever had the opportunity to peer through the frosted glass that separated my family's world from the normal one, he probably would've organised a special Year 9 assembly to declare the extent of Mum's (and by default, my) weirdness.

Mum suffered from more than just depression. She went through periods of being too scared to leave the house. 'Agoraphobia' was yet another term I misunderstood. When I was little I took it to describe the way she yelled at the TV whenever Malcolm Fraser said something on the news (I later realised there's no condition she can blame going 'aggro' on). She was practically the opposite of Mrs Jensen-from-across-the-road, who spent her days at the window, transfixed by the outside world; Mum liked to pretend there was nothing beyond our house's mouldy walls.

On her worst days, even a wink of light from between our heavy living room curtains could snatch her breath, leaving her grey-faced and panting. Once, when I lost control of my billy-kart and smashed head-first into the garage door, she appeared before me like a ghost, my screams having forced her shaky legs to step, one after the other, out the front door, down the path and onto the front lawn. Mrs Jensen-from-across-the-road called an ambulance, which Mum and I shared, lying side by side, me with a bloody gash in my forehead, Mum gasping into a plastic mask.

Pre-quake, Mum was Women's Wear Manager at Grace Bros. Post-quake, she ironed the skirts, blouses and dresses she'd once sold to her customers, later extending her service to include the shirts and trousers of their husbands. Even now, I have trouble remembering her in any other setting than our living room, or lit by anything other than the dull yellow hanging bulb and the soft glow of our black and white TV.

Our house didn't always hold her captive. As suddenly as her agoraphobia arrived, it'd disappear, sometimes during her sleep. Then, after spending a few minutes psyching herself up – *Out you go, Hen. You've got this* – she'd slowly unlock the three locks, open the front door and stand there blinking in the sunlight. I know she was at my Grade 6 farewell because in the photo she's standing between Dad and me, though she looks like she's been superimposed: her face is colourless, and her eyes are closed as if she was wishing she was somewhere else.

Anyway, this is why I agreed to go with Mum to check out the crematorium one afternoon, even though it was the last place on earth I wanted to visit. Mum was dressed – in perfectly ironed jeans and a navy jumper that looked posh enough to be Harriet's – and even wore a smile. She said she'd 'glided through' Jill's ironing and felt up to getting out. How could I say no?

'I'm really curious,' she said, as we spun off Burgess Drive and onto a dirt road, a cloud of dust in our wake. Being in the car made Mum breathless and shaky, so she always drove as if the world would end if we didn't get to wherever as soon as possible. On at least two occasions I wet my pants sitting in the passenger seat when she was driving. 'Aren't you?'

'A bit,' I lied, as the heavy feeling in my stomach grew.

Dad had been Crematorium Assistant for a few weeks by then and was still waiting for the town's anger to die down. As he stepped off the bus each morning, people yelled after him from the bus windows, many of them workers from Parsons Cigarettes.

'If anyone's job is killing this town, it's theirs!' Dad said.

When I asked him what they said, he just let out a tired sigh and covered his eyes with his thick, hairy fingers.

He knew they resented Greg for moving to Boorunga just a week after Raymond Miller'd fled, leaving a handwritten note thumb-tacked to the door of his funeral home: *'closed due to unforeseen curcumstances'*. (Mr Miller was renowned for his bad spelling, which'd resulted in more than one typo on headstones, 'CLIT SAMSON' being the most memorable – Mr Samson's wife scribbled an 'n' between 'i' and 't' but the damage had been done, and everyone still referred to the dead man as 'old Clit'.)

Welcome to Compassionate Cremations: a shiny white sign greeted us at the end of a long, pebbled driveway that snaked around a grey stone fountain before widening in front of a large, freshly painted white house. It was one of the few that'd stood up to the earthquake, though it had shaken its filthy-rich owners out and all the way to Melbourne, Dad said. It'd then sat there, empty, among the towering gum trees, until some man called Greg'd turned up out of nowhere to buy it. Although only fifteen minutes from home (twenty, if a normal person was driving), we might've been in the middle of nowhere.

Glowing white pebbles crunched under my sneakers and wind warmed my face, wind I hadn't noticed at home. It made me think of ghosts, which I didn't do often, but if they were real, like Katie insisted – apparently her dead mum visited her on July 8 every year to sing 'Happy Birthday' – this'd be the place to find them. But would a cremated person's ghost be white and translucent like the ghosts in movies? Or black as coal, a person-shaped mass of ash? These were the stupid thoughts drifting through my mind when I spotted a face in an upstairs window. It was girl's face, that much I could tell, and it was staring right at me.

'What is it?' Mum was frowning. I must've made a noise.

I shot another look at the window, but the face was gone. I stepped closer to Mum, and considered, for one irrational moment, holding her hand.

'What do you make of your dad's office, Miri?' Mum pressed one nicotine-stained finger on the doorbell, which played the slowest rendition of "Greensleeves" I'd ever heard, its battery soon to join the deceased. 'Bit of a step up?'

Creepy came to mind, just as a giant opened the door and gave a giant smile, first to Mum, then to me. My skin tingled with goosebumps. I wasn't sure if it was because he owned a crematorium and he was the biggest man I'd ever seen, or because his moustache looked like a thin, brown caterpillar asleep on his top lip.

'Good afternoon, I'm Greg Parker.' American accent. Dad hadn't mentioned that.

Greg offered Mum a large, pale hand, covered in tiny cuts. Thankfully, he didn't expect me to shake it too. 'I do hope I can be of assistance.'

'Yes, you can.' Mum strained her neck to meet Greg's eyes.

'Lovely.' Greg's face rearranged itself into an expression of concern. 'Can I start by saying I'm deeply sorry for your loss. I can only assume it was someone very special to you. Your husband? A parent?'

'It's my husband. But he was in pretty good shape this morning.' Mum nodded towards the dark hallway behind Greg. 'He's in there!'

Greg frowned. 'Um, madam, I'm not sure I …'

'Dad works here,' I butted in. 'Jim Jamieson.'

'Oh, Jim's family!' Greg flashed his teeth again. 'How lovely to meet you. Henrietta? And you're the Miracle he's so proud of? Caused the earth to shake, I hear.' Greg looked down at me as if I was a cute puppy.

I stared at the doormat, worn thin, I presumed, from the shuffling of mourners' feet.

'He didn't mention how pretty you were.'

Pretty? I frowned. The man obviously wanted to make me uncomfortable.

Following Greg down the dark hallway, I rubbed my bare arms. I'd imagined the crematorium to be more like a giant oven than a fridge. The air was laced with the Dettol smell Dad had been bringing home. It must be a smell you get used to because Greg didn't mention it, but I wanted to retch so badly my eyes watered. Greg ushered us into the 'lunch room', and said he'd find Dad.

On one side of the room was a tiny kitchen and, on the other, a table with three brown plastic chairs, like the ones stacked around the edges of our school hall. Next to a glass ashtray sat Dad's lunchbox, empty except for crumbs and a wad of Glad Wrap.

'It'd be gross eating lunch in here,' I whispered.

'Why?' Mum hoisted her foot onto one of the plastic chairs. For a moment I thought she was about to escape out the small window. She adjusted the strap on her sandal. 'It's cleaner than our kitchen.'

'But the dead people are …' I nodded at the hallway. 'So close.'

Mum smiled. 'I don't think they'd be too fussed about your peanut butter sandwich.'

But it'd taste like death. A peanut-butter-and-death sandwich.

A fly was throwing itself against the window. Had it been exploring the crematorium? What had it seen? Or landed on? It was slow and fat. Full? Was it was trying to escape from the horrors of the place? Or did it get a buzz (ha ha) out of banging its head on the glass?

'Hey!' Dad, surprised to see us, was wiping his hands on a black apron. 'Having a good day?'

'Good enough.' Mum's expression was half grin, half grimace. 'Going to show us around?'

'Um, yeah, I suppose I could take you into the charging room, but …' Dad looked at me. 'Maybe just your mum, this time, eh? It could be a bit …'

'She can wait with me,' Greg said.

'Doesn't bother me,' I said, but I did wonder what was in the 'charging room' that he didn't want me to see. Was he going to set a body on fire in front of Mum? Give her a go with her Bic lighter? I shivered as Greg hunched over the tiny sink, filling the kettle, clanging cups in the narrow cupboard. The kitchen hadn't been designed with him in mind. Nor had Boorunga. Somehow he seemed too large, too loud, too …

'So, now, Miracle.' Greg turned to me. I wondered if his teeth were real. They seemed too clean and white for his face. Could he have … stolen them from one of the 'clients'?

'Ever seen a cadaver?' he asked.

I gazed at him, shaking my head, trying not to think about his – or someone else's! – teeth, trying not to look shocked, which probably made me look more shocked. *Cadaver*. Dad used that word too; I thought it was so he could pretend that the bodies hadn't actually once been people.

'Would you like to?' he probed.

A dead body! That was something I'd only ever seen on TV: a pale-faced (sometimes white, sometimes powder blue), purple-lipped, person lying flat, eyes rolled back and arms outstretched. Did I really want to see a real one? Would it stink like a dead wombat and make me want to vomit? What if I recognised the person, well, the person the body used to be? Would its empty eyes haunt me in my nightmares? I stared at the floor, at the shiny blue tiles, and concentrated on slowing my breath like Miss Jay taught us in health.

On the other hand, I wouldn't have to touch the body, to feel its cool skin. I could keep my distance and peek at it through half-opened eyes. I felt a tingle of excitement. Who else had seen a dead body? Probably no one at school. I could see Seth and Oli elbowing other kids out of the way so they could hear every detail – about the eyes, the colour of the skin, the clothes it'd been dressed in. Oli had boasted about watching the three *Omen* movies on his own, one after the other in the middle of the night. He'd be blown away!

'I think.' My voice wobbled. 'I would, please.'

'Sorry?' Greg's head was buried in the fridge. 'You drink tea?'

'No … I'd like to … see a … cadaver. Please?'

For a few moments Greg froze. Then he stepped away from the fridge with his back to me, placing a carton of milk on the bench. His body was shaking. With laughter.

'Oh, you're really cute!' He turned, wiping his eyes. 'Did you think I was serious?'

I shrugged, looking away, my face hot.

'Come on, Miracle. That wouldn't be very respectful of me. Would it?'

40

Too humiliated to agree, I said nothing. Greg hummed and clanged the teaspoon loudly in the chipped mugs.

Mum was still smiling as she and Dad appeared in the lunchroom, obviously not fazed by the morose surroundings and seeing disturbing things, whatever they were.

'Very impressive,' Mum said to Greg.

'Thank you for saying so. All our facilities are state of the art, and we're doing very well for a business that's just seven months old.' Greg passed Mum her tea. I wondered if it'd been a deliberate decision to have only black mugs. Would it be disrespectful to drink out of a pink mug or one that said 'I heart Boorunga'?

'You know, Jim, I think we've found another assistant.' Greg nodded at me. 'When's she going to give up the books and come work for us?'

Mum and Dad glanced at me, eyebrows raised.

'I don't want to work here.' My voice was sulky.

'Got a bit of a gothic streak in you, though.' Greg slowly sipped his tea while Mum and Dad waited for an explanation. 'She wanted to see a cadaver. Made an ever-so-polite request. Can't fault her manners, but I'd keep an eye on her.' He winked.

'But you. You …' I started, but something in his eyes stopped me. Never mind the cadavers; Greg belonged in *The Omen*. Satan was alive and living in Boorunga with a dead person's teeth. I turned to Mum. 'I'll wait outside. Can we go soon?'

'Sure. I've finished up, so I'll drive.' Dad looked baffled. 'We'll be out in a bit.'

I headed down the hall, as fast as I could without running, the floorboards groaning with every step. But before I reached the front door, Greg called, 'Whatever you do, don't turn left! Unless you want nightmares for the rest of your life.'

I ran the last few steps. In a nightmare the front door would be locked, my family trapped inside. So I almost cried out with relief when the handle turned easily. Outside was the same ordinary sunny day it'd been when we arrived.

The comforting warmth of the car brought tears. I tightened my seat belt and tried to calm myself with slow, deep breaths. I was never going to visit Dad's work again, no matter how cheerful Mum was feeling.

'So do you see now why you should give up the smokes?' Dad was saying to Mum when they finally came and folded themselves into the front seats.

'Why do you say that?'

'Well, as I said, a lot of them …' he looked towards the crematorium, 'had shoddy lungs.'

'Well, Janet never smoked.' She dug around in the glovebox. 'Seen my lighter?'

Dad drove us home at a more comfortable speed and I was relieved no one asked about my cadaver request. There was no mention of anything; just the sound of Mum's long, raspy breaths over the rumble of the engine. We were turning into Burgess Drive, me still too humiliated to speak, when I remembered the girl peering out the window. Did I imagine her? She can't have been a ghost. I always struggled to keep a serious face when Katie said stuff about her mum's ghost. If ghosts were real, Boorunga would be full of them. During the earthquake, two people were crushed to death in Woolies after thousands of tins of spaghetti and baked beans came crashing down on their heads. I'd studied the shelves later, the scuffed lino floor, the laminated $2.99 signs, for hints of death and found nothing eerie. I didn't believe in ghosts; the face must've belonged to someone as alive as I was. So who was she?

7

The following night I was sitting at the kitchen table, staring at my maths textbook, when Mum and Dad's voices rose above the TV noise and floated in from the living room.

'So Ray what's-his-name, with the pet kangaroo, must've shown up. Ray Peterson?' Mum was saying. 'But who else?'

'Hen, I've had numerous clients.'

'Clients? They're dead, Jim. D-E-A-D! So, what do you think's killing them?'

'It varies, of course, but you'd be surprised at the number of respiratory and gastro problems.'

'Meaning what?'

'Well, don't repeat this, but it's one of the reasons Greg moved here.'

'You said he'd heard Miller's Funerals shut down.'

'That was definitely a factor.' Dad lowered his voice.

I sat up straight, stretching my neck, straining my ears to hear.

'But he also knew about Boorunga's death rate. That's what made him close his other business and buy up here. Must be something in the air. Compared to other towns, it's unusually high.'

The numbers on my page blurred into each other. What was Dad saying?

'He was prepared to move his young girl here to capitalise on a high death rate? He's crazier than I am!'

Young girl. Greg had a daughter? Was she the 'ghost' in the window?

'Both he and his daughter are very healthy. He didn't see it as a risk.'

'Well, you know what Jill says?' Mum said.

'What *doesn't* Jill say?'

'She says it was the other way round: people only started dying once Greg opened for business.'

'Henrietta!' Dad's voice made me jump, but he sounded more shocked than angry.

'Her words were, "that crook is speeding up the living process to make a fast buck".'

'That's total bullshit!'

'Maybe, but why else do you think everyone's so against the crem? Raymond wasn't exactly a charmer. I think people miss his dog more than they miss him, and that Baxter's a mongrel – remember he bit you, right through your good socks?'

'But *speeding up the living process?* Killing people? Jill's been watching too much TV! Anyway, not everyone's against the crem. They still come to us.'

'Only through lack of choice. Who wants to bury their parents over in Aston?'

I stared at the table, at my exercise book, at the jumble of crumby plates, dirty mugs and junk mail around it. The numbers I'd scrawled seemed more pointless than ever. Who cared what equalled what?

'Well, Jill is full of it,' Mum said. 'And so are you. It's all nonsense. Lots of old people live in Boorunga, Jim. And that's what happens when you get old. You die!'

'Yeah, so thirty-five is old is it? Nina Simpson was thirty-five, bless her sweet soul.'

'Her *sweet soul*? I always knew you fancied her! I saw you wink at her at the butcher's.'

'Huh?' A pause. 'I don't remember that, but she was friendly. I like people who smile at me. Guess it makes up for –'

'So how often did she smile at you? This *sweet* young thirty-five-year-old? Did you stop off at her house on your postie round?'

'No! Look, I'm not going to argue about a dead pretty woman. I'm knackered and I'm going to bed.'

'Pretty? Okay, so you thought she was pretty? Pretty enough to –'

'Good night!' Dad said.

'Jim!' Mum called after him. 'What about Julian's vomiting? You don't think …'

Another pause.

'Julian's fine. He's just got a bug or something.'

'It's only April,' Mum muttered, but by then Dad had stomped into the living room, hindered somewhat by his floppy Kmart slippers.

'Good night, Miracle.' Dad kissed my cheek. 'It's a bit late to be solving more fractions tonight.'

'They're called equations, Dad. G'night.'

He rested a heavy hand on my shoulder. He scrubbed his hands after work – he sometimes stayed in the bathroom for half an hour, the hot tap running and the ghosts he'd brought home fogging up the mirror and floating out the window – but I still couldn't help wondering what (or *who*) his hands had touched that day. I hoped he was too distracted to notice me flinch.

I gave up on my homework and, too tired even to unzip my tunic, slid under my doona in full school uniform minus shoes. But, lying down, my brain went into overdrive. *Boorunga's death rate … It's unusually high.* I thought about that first dead possum I'd seen lying in the gutter, its filthy matted fur, soggy with drain water. It was the stench that hit me first, drawing my eyes downwards, before I could look away, shielding my nose and eyes with my arms. I'd seen plenty of dead possums and rats since, so I barely even noticed them anymore. Kids kept blabbing on about death at school, too. It led to more talk about Boorunga's curse. The general agreement was that those who didn't cop it in the quake all those years ago were going to die in another unusual way.

I thought about what happened to Big Bobby Sanson. Our class was on an excursion to the Twirly Swirl factory, and was standing in line to sample the biscuit mixture. We were all hot and bored, waiting to be rewarded for listening to one of Katie's dad's slaves drone on and on about the biscuit-making process. For some reason, those minutes Big Bobby spent waiting for his spoonful of compensation were just too much. He started coughing. Then his body decided enough was enough – it simply wasn't going to continue standing, breathing, *living* any more. What pushed it over the edge?

Then my mind settled on my biggest fear. Julian. He'd been sick for days, his skin the sickly yellow of our living room walls, grey shadows under his milky eyes, a cough like a seal's bark. At least that's how Mum described it to Harriet, and it was easy enough to imagine a seal making the strangled sound that escaped from Julian's throat. But he'd already suffered; he'd already used up a lifetime of bad luck. Surely he wasn't going to … No, I couldn't even think it.

'Julian's a survivor,' Dad'd promised me when I asked why he was still sick. 'Nothing can knock him down for long.'

I wanted to say, 'Yeah, well what about Big Bobby Sanson? He was three times my size, and he was knocked down by a cough', but I nodded, wanting to believe that Julian would soon get better, and life in our house would return to normal. Well, normal for us.

Mum'd once said that in a way Julian had died in the earthquake, that he was no longer 'all here'. 'Is that why he looks like an angel?' I'd asked, but Mum just shrugged, sadness tugging down the corners of her mouth. Still, the part of him that was here I loved more than anything, and if I tried to imagine him not being around, my mind went blank.

I could probably live without my friends, I decided. At school, someone was your best friend one day, yet the next, they were telling everyone you'd had it off with Warren Taylor, the ugliest boy in Year 9 who also, according to the boys, only had one testicle. Either that, or they said your clothes stank of piss, or you were a virgin, which was a bad thing, possibly even worse than having it off with Warren Taylor. Ironic. We were all virgins, or so I assumed. I wasn't the only one who was picked on – we all took turns in being 'Warren's girlfriend'. I could be as horrible as the rest of them, I admit, but I didn't enjoy it like the others seemed to. When 'Warren's girlfriend's' eyes watered, mine did too and I turned away before someone called me a 'pathetic drip', a sign that I'd soon take over as 'Warren's girlfriend'. If they died – Katie, Pheebs and the others – I reckoned I could handle it. I even thought I could cope if Oli died (in his sleep); at least then I'd be free from worrying about what he thought of me. But if my brother died, I was pretty sure I'd want to be dead too.

I don't know how many hours drifted by, but I must've fallen asleep eventually because when my alarm went off, my dream-self was crouched on a stepping stone in the front yard, paralysed in fear as a brown snake slithered across the lawn. It was a relief to wake up, to see an ordinary sunny day forcing its way through the gap between my curtains.

8

I had Miss Jones to thank for distracting everyone from the latest and most distressing rumour about Dad (I'd never even heard of 'necrophilia'). Not that her distraction was good news for me. She had called a special assembly to announce that Year 12's controversial debate: *Did the quake cause the curse – or the curse cause the quake?* was going ahead after all. I couldn't believe Miss Jones'd given in on the topic, especially after Simon Winters heard her say 'Over my dead body!' in the staffroom. She'd even suggested a compromise – *Would Boorunga have enjoyed such economic prosperity had there been no earthquake?* – but it'd been shot down by the prefects. 'We've got a right to free speech!' Josie Lockery, the school captain, was heard yelling from the Year 12 common room. She and Josh Henderson drew up a petition and marched around the playground like mini politicians, collecting signatures from almost all 288 kids on the roll (Sonya Edwards declined because of her earthquake phobia).

Apparently a new boy, James someone, only signed the petition after having his egg sandwich rubbed in his face, and several other Year 9s and 10s were blackmailed into submission, but most kids were actually excited by the idea, if only for the reason that Miss Jones wasn't.

Head of English, Miss Cluff, signed too, adding that 'never

before in the school's history has there been such an interest in debating'. Even Head of History, Mr Johns, supported the debate, and he was against most things that'd happened since the Industrial Revolution. 'We can't hide from our past,' he said from behind hundred-year-old spectacles as he carefully wrote 'Harold P Johns' with his gold fountain pen.

'Miracle Jamieson – Year 9' was the last signature on the second page. Katie'd passed me the clipboard, and to resist would've drawn attention to myself – and possibly an egg sandwich to my face. If anyone noticed I was shaking as I wrote, they didn't say so. But I would've preferred egg in my face than have the debate go ahead. If *The quake caused the curse* won, would people start saying I was part of the curse?

I hadn't believed the petition would work, or that Miss Jones would back down, until the words slid from her mouth just now. I sunk low into my plastic chair.

'I want you all to think of it as a bit of fun. Let's keep it light-hearted please.' As if 'fun' was something Miss Jones knew about. 'And under *no* circumstances will any betting take place. I'll repeat that *loudly* and *clearly* for the boys down the back, there's to be no *b-e-t-t-i-n-g*! Boorunga High School does not condone gambling of any form.'

She then announced that the Great Quake Debate would take place after lunch on Friday 12th July, and we could go straight home afterwards if we had written permission from our parents.

There was no way I could be at school that day. I'd fake a stomach-ache or something. The odds on the '*The quake caused the curse*' team winning were already six to one.

When I got home from school, there was more big news. Mum's first words when I entered the living room were, 'Guess who's going to be on the news?' Julian then croaked the answer – 'Dad!' – before I'd taken off my shoes.

Dad hadn't done anything heroic or admirable; he was just being interviewed about the crematorium, but still, it wasn't every day you saw your dad on TV. And it would help take my mind off the impending doom at school. I made popcorn without burning it and sat with Dad and Julian on the couch, waiting for *Simon Townsend's Wonder World* to end.

Dad shook his head when I passed him the bowl of popcorn. His whole face frowned, which made me nervous. Dad was the strong one. He kept us going on the days when the iron was too heavy for Mum to lift and she could do nothing but lie on the bed with a cold flannel over her eyes. I'd always thought that even if another quake struck and our whole house fell down around us, Dad would still think of something funny to say, something to make Julian and me smile.

'You're going to be famous!' I tried to lighten Dad's mood.

'You're right. Your nana always said I should be on television.' His mouth formed a weak smile. 'This could be my lucky break, Miri.'

'But you look like the Liberal Party's just got elected,' I said. 'Are you worried about the crem?'

'Yeah, well, those bloody vandals. I just can't –'

Dad was cut off by a knock at the door.

'Come on in, Worm,' Mum called.

My five-year-old cousin shuffled in and stood in front of the TV, blocking my view. It's unclear exactly when William became Worm, but he used to have trouble pronouncing 'William'. If he'd been named for his looks, 'Duck' would've been more fitting: he had fluffy white hair, and his belly hung over his little grey school shorts as he waddled around on two stumpy legs. Worm was the only one in our family with any fat on him that couldn't be attributed to beer (as in Dad's case), perhaps simply to defy his nickname. I was just happy that someone else in the family had a ridiculous name.

'Come to give me a hand with the ironing, have you?' Mum asked.

Worm shook his head. 'I'm watching Uncle Jim on the telly!' Still staring at it, he dropped onto the carpet and crossed his legs as if sitting on a mat at school. 'And Mum said to tell you Julian should drink lots of fluid.'

Mum pressed the iron down hard, her mouth forming an 'f', before she somehow composed herself and said, cheerfully, 'Julian, drink up!' She hated it when Harriet told her what to do.

I passed Julian his glass of flat lemonade and he took two loud gulps to satisfy her before laying his head back down on a cushion.

When the news finally started and Peter Finlay introduced James Jamieson from Compassionate Cremations, Dad appeared, his head bigger on the screen than in real life. I felt like reaching through the glass and straightening his collar, but he did look quite handsome. He still had hair, plenty of thick dark curls, and he was looking at the camera straight on so you couldn't see how long his nose was.

'It's been going on for a while, since before I took on the role of Assistant Manager,' Dad was saying to the microphone. 'But over the past couple of weeks it's got worse.'

Worm kept looking from the TV to Dad as if he couldn't believe Dad could be in two places at once.

'I was about ten metres away from the gate when I noticed. There's a sign out front that says, "Welcome to Compassionate Cremations".' He scratched his nose. I glanced over at the real Dad and he was scratching his nose too.

The sign filled the screen, black letters smeared with pink.

'Someone messed with it,' Dad said. 'Pretty late it must've been, Greg didn't lock up until around seven. They'd painted "Go to hell" right there!' He pointed at the pink smear.

'And you still don't know who?' the newsman asked. 'Surely you've got some ideas.'

'Not a clue,' Dad said. 'Greg dug out a leftover tin of white paint from the store room and I slapped it on so thick you'd hardly notice anything'd happened. Problem solved! Or so we thought. Until Tuesday – then the words were back again! Next day, same thing. Now I start each day by painting over the … abuse.' Dad flexed his wrist to indicate that it was sore from all his painting. 'Greg's even written "removing obscenities from front sign" into my job description.'

'There's no alarm system?' the newsman said.

'There's never been a need. I mean, who'd want to break into a crematorium?' Dad smiled at the camera to show he was joking. 'But we got one from Mitre 10 just last week. It did the trick for a couple of nights, but then … Wednesday, I think it was, Wednesday morning I got here to find the sensor smashed. Glass everywhere, and the footpath was spray-painted red.'

'You think it's the same person?'

Dad shook his head. 'There's more than one. The police are certain. The style changes, as does the method. Sometimes the words are in thick Texta – probably the work of a kid.'

'And you don't know what's provoking it? Why everyone's so against Compassionate Cremations?'

The real Dad's face wore the same expression as the TV Dad's: like he was about to cry. I glanced at Mum but she was focussed on Mrs Stanger's hem steaming under her iron. Or seemed to be.

'Compassionate Cremations offers a truly unique service for loved ones –' Dad said, before the newsman butted in.

'Can you give us a bit of background, James? Why did Greg Parker, an American businessman, decide to open the business in Boorunga?'

My stomach tensed. I willed the interview to be over.

Dad looked directly at the camera. 'Compassion is behind everything we do –'

'Thank you, James. That's all we have time for.'

'Bloody unbelievable,' the Dad on the couch growled. 'That wasn't how it went! I said much more than that! I even talked about our special two-for-one urn offer, though I know I shouldn't have – I got carried away. But he shook my hand – they didn't show that! He smiled and said how perfect I was on camera.'

'That was boring,' Worm said. 'You didn't get to do anything!'

'You did well, Jim,' Mum said. 'Never trust the media. They tried to make you look bad, but we weren't fooled.'

'The police don't care either,' Dad said. 'No one does!'

Dad then told us the police only got as far as the crematorium lunchroom before turning to leave.

'No offence, mate, but this place gives me the heeby jeebies,' Constable Kelly'd said to Greg. 'Full credit to any kid with enough guts to come out here at night.'

Dad and Greg had looked at each other. *Full credit* to vandals?

'Just pulling your leg!' Constable Kelly said. 'We'll catch those sneaky bastards.'

'Yeah, don't you worry,' Constable Avery added. 'We'll give them a good hiding.' He turned to Constable Kelly, 'Ready, Nige?'

When Dad finished talking, Mum spoke the words I was thinking but was too scared to say. 'You could just leave, Jim.' She lit a cigarette and sucked on it deeply, waiting for Dad to say something.

'I can't. Not now.'

'Why? Because you bet me a six pack you'd stick at it? We'd survive. The kids've lived on cheese jaffles before. Something else will come up.'

'No. I'm good at what I do.'

'Jesus Christ, Jim. Anyone can light a match.' She flicked her lighter.

'You know that's not what it's about. Greg says I've got a real knack for the business. I'm respectful of others, Henrietta. I really care – and our clients' families appreciate that. And that's why … It's why Greg's offered me shares. In the crematorium. In the business.' He looked from Mum to me to Julian. 'This is why I don't want vandals to stuff things up. It's why I put my hand up to go on TV. This is me. My career.'

'Get a grip, Jim,' Mum said after a moment, after the news sunk in. 'It's not like you've been voted Australia's next Prime Minister.' But I detected something in her eyes which just may have been pride.

'That's good, Dad,' I said, though in my head I was swearing at myself for suggesting the stupid job in the first place. Dad wanted to make a *career* of working in the crematorium?

'Can we watch *Dr Who* now?' Worm asked.

'I always wanted to do something with my life,' Dad said quietly.

'I'm allowed to,' Worm added.

'I bet you're not, Worm, but go ahead and turn it over,' Mum said. 'If you have nightmares, your mum can blame me.'

'Like I said earlier, my mother thought I should be on TV,' Dad continued.

Mum laughed. 'Your mother was addicted to soap operas. *Days of Our Lives, The Young and the Restless* and Earl Grey tea – that was her life! She probably didn't know there was another world outside her telly. Anyway, we can't buy shares. You need money for that!'

'It's all taken care of.'

Mum raised her eyebrows. 'Really? How?'

'The bank,' Dad said. 'I got a loan.'

'A loan? Okay.' Smoke escaped Mum's nose as she nodded.

'You must be serious.'

'This is a once-in-a-lifetime opportunity. I'd be a mug not to take it.'

'You could've asked me first.' Mum propped up the iron. 'But … you might be onto something. I'm never going to get rich doing lazy people's laundry.'

'Thanks, Hen. I knew you'd understand.'

'I suppose we should be celebrating,' Mum said. 'This is the kind of thing people celebrate, isn't it? Can you grab your dad and me a beer, Miri? Jim, I think you should invite Greg – your *business partner* – and his daughter over for dinner. Might have to spruce the place up a bit first. So maybe in a couple of weeks?'

I stared at Mum. She wanted to invite that man to our house? To eat 'dinner' with him? For a start, we didn't even call it 'dinner' like Katie's family, we called it 'tea' like Mrs Jensen-from-across-the-road and other people who lived in houses with cheap net curtains and Formica kitchen tables. That was the first time Mum'd said 'dinner', as if she imagined we'd be sitting down to something more sophisticated than a plateful of something she'd tried to cook.

Dad smiled at the suggestion – the big, genuinely happy smile that belonged on his face – so I knew it was pointless protesting. But now I had another event to dread. First the debate, then dinner with the most evil man in the world. Year 8 had been bad – I'd had a fight with Katie and Pheebs that stretched out for most of Term 3 *and* I got my first-ever period on our school trip to Canberra – but now those seemingly catastrophic events looked like minor inconveniences. Year 9 was going to be the worst year ever.

9

We were watching the news again, staring at the TV in silence. This time Worm wasn't with us. If he had been, Mum would've sent him off to play in Julian's room. I hadn't made any popcorn – I'd only managed to eat half a floury apple since breakfast – and instead of standing at the ironing board, Mum sat slumped in her armchair. She said she couldn't be stuffed finishing the Henrys' sheets.

We watched, stunned, as Ian Boston, Seth's dad, a tank of a man with flat, squashed-in ears, rubbed his eyes with the back of his hands, like a baby, before speaking into a microphone with the Channel 9 logo.

'There was no warning.' His chin quivered like Grandad's after he got Parkinson's. 'Jill talked about having a tickle in her throat – yeah, *tickle* was the word she used. But the night ... before ... she was fine. She had one or two glasses of wine ... and maybe a Pimm's because it was Thursday and she takes four dance classes of a Thursday. Deserves a little extra! But nothing out of the ordinary. And, yeah, I do remember now she'd been coughing quite a bit during the week, but not badly. She also vomited one morning but said it must've been something she ate. Apart from that she was fighting fit – inside and out. Of course anyone who knows my wife knows she was a health nut. She never smoked so much as a single fag in her whole life.'

'That's true.' Mum spoke in a whisper, as if she didn't want to upset Jill's husband by talking over him. 'Remember when she caught Reginald tossing a butt out his car window?'

I nodded. Katie'd told me Jill posted the butt to their house, along with a note, on fancy Japanese paper and in beautiful handwriting, telling her dad to put his filthy rubbish in the bin. When Katie told me at school, we laughed so much, Katie had to run to the loos before she wet her pants. Good thing Jill didn't know her son held the school record for the number of smoke rings blown from one cigarette (twelve).

'… she had a business to run,' Ian Boston was saying. 'She just gets … got … on with stuff … with life and her studio and everything … She was happy, Jilly was. On Wednesday night, she looked at our son Seth, while he was watching the box, and said, "Isn't he the most beautiful boy?" Those were the … they were the … the last words, well, she may have said good night to me or nagged me about picking my jeans up off the floor or something, but they're the last words I can remember, the last words she …'

I pictured Seth, his blond flat-top and big, greeny-blue eyes, lashes longer than Katie's. *The most beautiful boy?* Maybe, if he never opened his mouth or fixed his angry eyes on you. He'd been a no-show in roll call that day and Miss Jones interrupted our PE class to explain why. She'd stood in front of us on the netball courts in her knee-length flowery dress, her hairy legs on full display.

'I have some very sad news.' She paused to glare at the Goal Keeper and Goal Attack, who were whispering near the goalpost. 'One of our pupils – Seth Boston – has lost his mother. She passed away suddenly overnight. This is a difficult time for Seth, and I'd like you all to give him your full support.'

She asked if anyone had any questions. I wanted to ask whether Tommy and the other kids Seth tortured in the boys' toilets would be expected to offer their support, but I knew

Miss Jones's answer would be 'Go to my office', so I stared at the grass and kept quiet like everyone else. It's true, that's what actually popped into my head before I thought about Seth himself – before I imagined what he'd felt when he found out, and what he was doing at that exact moment, while we were boiling to death in the sun.

And what was he doing now, while the *Six O'Clock News* was on? Was he sitting on his couch watching too? I couldn't picture Seth crying. I'd heard him scream once, when a Year 12 stubbed a cigarette out on his wrist. His face turned the colour of the basketball he was clutching and his eyes watered but he didn't actually cry.

'Julian, how much lemonade have you had today?' Dad's words brought me back to the room. 'You need to drink more.'

'Here.' I put Julian's glass in his warm, clammy hand. He lifted his head and sipped, wincing as if the flat lemonade was acid. He even smelt like he'd gone off, like the black bananas and wrinkly apples in our fruit bowl.

'Give your nose a wipe too, son.' Dad dug his red hanky out of his pocket. 'Don't worry – it's clean.'

'Jill had a good heart.' Mum fanned herself with the *TV Guide*. 'Figuratively speaking, anyway. She was the one who suggested I work from home when I couldn't face going back to the shop. I thought it was a joke at first. *Ironing?* I was the Manager of Women's Wear! If a garment needed ironing, I told someone else to do it.'

'She's always looked out for you, hasn't she, love?' Dad said. 'I knew you didn't mean all those things you said about her.'

But Mum'd gone deaf. 'Jill convinced the customers to use my service, even delivering and picking up their baskets herself to save me the ordeal of leaving the house, or of talking with people. Ironic if you think about it. Jill talked more than the lot of them put together!'

Jill Boston. I think of her whenever I get a whiff of lavender. She was probably the most popular person in Boorunga, and the sweet scent of lavender went wherever she did.

'What didn't she do?' Mum was saying. 'Started up Boorunga's Ballroom Dancing Studio, Secretary of Boorunga High's Parents and Friends ...'

I remembered Jill's high heels crunching on the gravelly asphalt as she marched across the handball courts, cradling an armful of school fête leaflets.

'... practically every social event in town.' Mum hadn't finished. 'Started up two book clubs and a mums' coffee group, and still had the energy to herd all the cats involved in putting on the Christmas party at the fire station. She was bloody fit too!'

I nodded, picturing Jill jogging along the footpath in shiny black shorts and a 'Boorunga Festival' singlet the same shade of pink as her face. She'd beat our bus from one end of the main street to the other, despite Leon having been voted the school's fastest bus driver.

The news reporter said that Jill was crowned 'Miss Boorunga' six years in a row. Mum told me Jill'd proved unbeatable until 1970 when Laura Jackson stole the title within six months of moving here from Coongahoola. Whether or not this was because of Laura's affair with Mayor Parks (Mum was dead-sure it was), Laura held the crown until two years later when she had a car accident and ended up in a wheelchair. People argued about whether or not Jill was involved in the accident, but by then she was no longer a 'Miss', and even if she hadn't been pregnant with baby Seth, the creases in her 29-year-old face took her out of the running.

With Jill's 'passing' (Dad's word: before working at the crem, 'dropped dead' or 'carked it' would've been fine), the town lost its greatest celebrity. Despite her bossiness, everyone in Boorunga had loved her. Or maybe it was because of her bossiness; she didn't give anyone a choice.

I wiped my eyes on my sleeve. I didn't know whether I was crying for Jill, or for Seth, or because here was another person to add to the long list Katie and I were compiling of 'weird deaths'.

'Probably all that dancing – and running and carrying on. She did enough exercise for half the town,' Mum said. 'Even so, dying at forty-three is pretty out there.'

'It's what I've been talking about.' Dad lowered his voice, as if that'd stop me and Julian from listening. 'With no disrespect to Jill, how are people going to see this? Another … passing so soon is a bad look for the crem.'

I glanced at Julian, but his eyes were closed. Was he really asleep? I wondered for the millionth time if he knew more than he let on.

'Everyone knows you're as harmless as a house fly, Jim,' Mum said. 'But I can see how some would be wary of Greg.'

'Don't tell me you –'

'I don't suspect him of anything. If he was up to something you'd know about it. But others mightn't feel the same way. You said Greg called Ian. How did Ian take that?'

'He was bloody rude! Ian said Jill was going to have a *traditional* burial with Packer's Funeral Homes – a good twenty k away in Aston – and that Compassionate Cremations was the last crowd he'd consider using. Greg swore he heard Ian spit before slamming down the phone.'

'Seth spits,' I said, without thinking. 'But mostly just on Tommy Winterson.'

'Jill didn't choose Ian for his manners – or for those cauliflower ears,' Mum said. 'But there's something about Greg that gets up people's noses. I don't know, but I think he looks …'

'Creepy,' I jumped in.

'Not you as well, Miracle?' Dad stood up, angry. 'This is insane. Whose side are you on?'

'Yours,' I said. 'But I don't like Greg.'

'And I'm looking at things from other people's perspectives,' Mum said. 'Try it.'

'I'm going to *try* a beer,' Dad said. 'Then I'm going into the garage to *try* to relax!'

'Jill was a gossip and a know-it-all,' Mum said when Dad had left the room. 'And she was a bit of a tart. But she was my friend. I'm going to miss her.'

10

The first alarm bells went off in my head during roll call when Mrs Holland called out, 'Katie Heller. Katie? Has anyone seen Katie this morning?' and the only sound in the classroom was Joey Quin sniffing. Where was Katie? She always turned up at school, even when she said her ears ached like hell or her nose was dripping more than our leaky kitchen tap. I scanned the room. Oli was down the back on his own, kicking the table leg with his Dunlop Volleys. All term Katie'd spent more time pashing him behind the boys' loos than sitting with Pheebs and me on B Block. Lately she'd sat with him in roll call too. When he glanced up and caught my eye, he looked away.

At that moment, I was too busy thinking about Katie to give Oli much thought. Until the end of lunch when he called out from the lockers: 'Hey, Miracle!' Just like that, but in Oli's husky boyish voice. My heart beat a million miles an hour.

I walked over, hoping Oli and Seth didn't notice the slight wobble in my legs. It was the day after Jill's funeral and Seth's first day back at school. Despite Miss Jones having gone on and on about Seth needing everyone's support, he was acting like nothing happened, as if he had two perfectly alive parents like most of us. I'd been sneaking glances at him during maths. He frowned a bit more than usual, but his hair was still perfectly gelled into a flat-top and he seemed like the Seth he'd been before his mum died. At the lockers now, he stared back at me, and my knees almost buckled. His eyes were full of anger. Was he still pissed off about Pheebs breaking up with him? She would've noticed that ugly hickey on his neck even if I hadn't pointed it out in front of everyone. Or was this to do with his mum dying?

'How's it going?' Oli's face was washed-out and he seemed on edge somehow, but he grinned at me. The lettuce stuck between his teeth didn't detract from his looks.

'I'm … okay.' My mouth was dry. 'You?'

Was he only talking to me because of Katie? He'd been with Katie for so long they were practically husband and wife. If I went out with him, my mind started reeling, what would we talk about?

Oli passed me a brown shoebox with CLARKS stamped across the top. 'For you.'

'What is it?' A stink was reaching my nose.

'A present for you, Miracle. Open it.' He didn't look at me.

Something slid around inside the box, lighter than a pair of shoes. I didn't want to know what. I carefully placed the box – men's size 8, tan – on the concrete floor. I should've walked away too.

'Maybe we should just leave it,' Oli said to Seth. His face was pink with … what? Shame?

But Seth kicked the lid off the box. Inside: a shrivelled body, matted fur, empty black eye staring into nothing, and next to it, two tiny babies.

They weren't the first dead rats I'd seen; I'd witnessed one slowly decaying near my bus stop, and Dad'd found at least three in our backyard. The horrible thing about these ones, what made my stomach heave and my eyes water, was the fact that Oli Harrison had given them to me. *A present for you.*

Oli stared at his shoes. Seth stood sneering. Kids came closer, surrounding me, their breath hot. Pheebs and Sall were among them, laughing. I bowed my head to hide my tears.

'Can you give them a *compassionate cremation*?' Seth asked.

So that was it.

'For the dearly departed rats,' someone else said. Laughter rang in my ears.

'I don't know anything about my dad's job.' I kept my eyes on the dirty concrete floor.

'Here.' Seth held up a box of matches. He took out a match and struck it. 'I'll show you how it's done.'

Before the end of Spanish, our classroom door opened and a familiar-looking woman with long legs and hair cut short like a boy's stepped inside and excused herself to Mr Hanson. Oli's mum. So Pheebs was right; Oli and Seth were being suspended. While they opened and closed their desk lids, making as much noise as possible as they stuffed books into their school bags, Oli's mum scanned the classroom for the person responsible. For me. I stared at my desk, graffiti blurring through tears, until Oli and Seth trudged out behind her.

'It's not your fault.' My body froze as Pheebs rubbed my shoulder. What did she care? I'm sure she'd found Oli humiliating me more gripping than anything on TV.

Soon after, Rachel Napper knocked on the door. She gave me a cruel smile before announcing in her goody-two-shoes voice, 'Miss Jones wants to see Miracle Jamieson in her office. Immediately.'

I half walked, half jogged across the quad; when Miss Jones said 'immediately', she meant 'an hour ago'. 'Punctuality is my middle name,' she once told our class. ('Mary Punctuality Jones' – Katie whispered). If we weren't sitting in the hall for assembly by 9 am, we'd have to melt in the hot sun until kids poured out forty minutes later. That's how I'd known she'd never give Dad the caretaker job when he turned up so late to his interview. *Two hours* late! I'm surprised she didn't call the cops.

Miss Jones's office smelt of oranges and was as immaculate as everyone said. Kids reckoned she'd long given up trying to control the school, and had devoted her days to organising and reorganising her office, the one small area she could keep on top of. They said that after Big Bobby died, she'd become so obsessed with cleanliness she'd stuffed her briefcase with tissues for wiping door handles and anything else that could carry kids' deadly germs. It wouldn't be long, Pheebs joked, before she got three words added to the 'Boorunga High School' sign: 'No children allowed'.

'Please sit.' She pointed to a brown plastic seat in front of her nearly bare desk.

I slid into the chair, tears stinging my eyes.

Miss Jones studied me for exactly five seconds – each announced by the clock above her head – before her face softened and she tilted her head.

'How are things at home, Miracle?'

My mind went blank. What did *home* have to do with anything?

'Uh … it's …'

'Your mum's coping all right? Can't be easy with a disabled child.'

'Julian? He's not … he's okay. Well, he's a bit sick at the moment, but Mum's the same.'

'And your father?'

I shrugged. Why was she asking about my parents?

Miss Jones shifted in her seat. 'I do feel a little responsible for his current situation. But Rodney Barret was a more experienced candidate, and I had to think about what was best for the school.'

'That's okay. Dad got another job soon after. It's more money too.' I wasn't sure about the money but Miss Jones's pity was making me squirm.

'Yes, I'm aware of his new job.' Her smile was sickly sweet. 'Boorunga is a small town and I've always taken rumours with a grain of salt, but Raymond Miller was well liked, so the backlash against the crematorium isn't surprising. Did you know Raymond was a former pupil of Boorunga High? Well before my time, but –'

'Seth and Oli gave me a box full of dead rats!' My anger surprised me. 'I thought that's why you wanted to see me.'

'I was getting to that, Miracle.' Miss Jones put on the expression she wore at assembly when kids ignored her call for silence. 'It was a nasty prank, and I was sorry to have to suspend them, especially considering what Seth's been through. The reason I wanted to see you was to make the suggestion that you keep your dad's *business* under your hat. You can't win friends by associating yourself with that place, regardless of whether the rumours are … just that.'

She might as well as have whacked me with a wooden spoon. I'd heard she kept one in the second bottom drawer of her desk, and I'd seen the evidence of it in the form of a purple bruise on each of Benjamin Rowen's hands.

'But I don't.' My brain was scrambled. 'My dad didn't –'

'These are unsettling times, Miracle. We've had poor Bobby and Joanne pass away recently, and a very high absentee rate.' She picked up the single pile of paper on her desk, presumably listing those absent (including Katie, I remembered with a pang), and fanned her face. Her freckled arms made me think of salami.

'Boorunga High hasn't had this many absentees since after the earthquake in 1972,' Miss Jones said. 'People are scared, Miracle. So if you don't want to be the scapegoat, I'd keep my head down if I were you.'

'I never talk about Dad. This wasn't my idea! Why would I –'

'I'm trying to help you, Miracle.' Miss Jones stared pityingly through her thick glasses.

I stared back, wondering what she'd looked like at fourteen. If she'd worn those glasses then, she wouldn't have had any friends. Was that how she wound up being an unmarried school principal? 'But Miss Jones –'

'You can return to your classroom now. But just remember.' She held her fingers to her mouth and closed it with an invisible zipper.

'I didn't even …' My voice trailed away as I stood up. What was the point?

Miss Jones picked up a pen and started writing in a small, black diary, as if I wasn't there.

I shut the office door, hands shaking. I heard the scrape of Miss Jones's chair and her footsteps. No doubt she was wiping my germs from everything I'd touched. I leant against the door, took a few deep breaths, and urged myself to hold it together until home time.

11

The afternoon dragged on forever. When the bell rang, the relief teacher looked almost as relieved as I felt. She let her copy of *Pride and Prejudice* fall onto her desk with a thud and said, 'All right, off you go then.' I was first out, even beating the two ADHD kids. I bolted across the playground and all the way home, without getting a stitch or feeling puffed, without feeling anything at all. The hot air dried out my tears.

I headed straight to my room, ignoring Mum's soft crying from along the hall, and kicked the door shut. I flopped onto my bed, and shut my eyes, trying not to think about the dead rats. *A present for you.*

When Julian opened my door, I wiped my eyes on the pillow slip. He never knocked; the sound of a fist pounding on wood could send him into a panic, even when it was his own fist doing the pounding. But I'd known it was him by the soft sound of his feet. He wore size 10 sneakers, but his footsteps were as light as a ghost's.

'Hello.' He had his sketchpad under his arm.

I didn't have the energy to say anything. He didn't seem to notice I was upset and there was no point telling him. Whenever kids picked on him – called him 'spastic' or 'quake boy', jumping around as if electrocuted – he just pretended they weren't there. As if the part of his brain that worried about what other people thought had been damaged too. I envied him; I'd kill to have an off switch, to turn my worries off like my bedside lamp.

'From Worm.' He tossed me a tiny green banana, then stretched out on the floor and opened his sketchpad. I peeled the banana, which Worm must've climbed his back fence to snap off the vine, and, though my stomach felt full of concrete, ate it in two bites.

As I watched Julian draw, I started to forget about Oli and Seth, the dead rats, everything. A few faint lines became a soft, round baby-face: bottom lip, fat and sulking; large, sad eyes. Even though Mum said Julian'd never really grow up and I couldn't imagine him as an adult, I was sure that one day he'd be up there with the world's best artists. He was already as good as Sidney Nolan and all the other dead Australian artists in the book Harriet had given him for Christmas. Drawing relaxed him, transformed him. When he held a felt pen or pencil, and *only* when, his right hand was completely steady. His tongue poked between his teeth and sweat shone on his forehead as he concentrated on perfecting a nose, eye or cheekbone, but his drawing hand didn't tremble at all.

When the front door clicked shut, I snapped out of the trance. I listened to heavy footsteps creaking down the hallway and into the bathroom, to water pouring out of the tap and hands lathering up.

Then Dad's face was in the doorway. 'What are you kids doing holed up in here?'

I shrugged.

'What's up?' Dad stepped inside. I noticed splashes of red paint on the black shoes he'd bought with his first pay.

'Nothing.' My voice quivered. How could I tell him without blubbing like a ten-year-old?

'*Nothing* doesn't make you cry.' My bed sighed as Dad sat

down. 'Is it Mum? She misses Jill more than she'll admit. She can't help flying off the handle at every –'

'It's not Mum.'

'Well, what? What happened? Something at school?'

I stared at Dad's shoes, the paint like blood.

'Miri?'

'Some boys.'

'Okay.' Dad nodded slowly. 'What did *some boys* do?'

I took a deep breath and told Dad what Oli'd given me, what Seth'd said.

'Those little bastards!' Anger made the veins stand out on his forehead. 'Oli *Harrison*, did you say?'

'I don't think he wanted to. I think Seth made him. He was the one with the matches.'

'Jesus! I mean …' Dad rubbed his eyes. 'Seth's probably not in his right mind with his mum just buried yesterday. But … bloody hell! What did Oli say? "Can you give them a cremation?"'

'A *compassionate* cremation,' I said. 'Maybe he watched you on the news.'

'It's none of his bloody business what I do! It's certainly got nothing to do with you. I'll have a word with his dad. Steve will make the boy see sense.'

'No! No way.' My head throbbed. 'Oli's been suspended for it. He's already in trouble. You saying anything'd make it worse.'

'He was bullying you!' The bed groaned as he sprung up. 'I can't let that go.'

'Don't, Dad. It's embarrassing.'

But he'd already left the room, returning with the phone book.

'If I don't make this call, they'll think they're free to treat you as they please, they'll think I'm weak. Well, I'm not. At least, not

70

when it comes to my kids.' He flicked through the *White Pages*. 'Hark, Harley, Harrison!'

He stormed back into the hall and I heard him lift the phone.

The taste of bitter, unripe banana rose in my throat. Julian was sketching a sleeve on the baby's arm, as if nothing was going on, as if Dad wasn't about to humiliate me.

Dad dialled the number more slowly than anyone in human history. My heart pounded and I fought the urge to scream.

The silence after he'd dialled the sixth and final number was even more unbearable. I buried my head under my pillow.

'Yes. Can I speak to Steve please?'

I pictured Oli's mum holding the phone in the Harrisons' kitchen, her face folded in a frown.

'Jim Jamieson. Steve? Yeah, ah hey. Look. Ah, you would've heard what happened today.'

My cheeks burned with shame. I'd never live this down, never. I tried to think of something that could possibly be worse. Dad telling Oli off … in front of my whole class … wearing just his undies …

'Yeah? But, this isn't about me. Listen, *mate*, if your son … Well, fuck me, I know where he gets it from! If he does anything … if your boy BULLIES MY DAUGHTER again I will –'

'Fucking fuck!' Dad slammed down the phone.

'Fucking what?' Mum's tired, muffled voice wafted down the hallway.

'I've made the call.' Dad stood at my door. As if I didn't already know, as if Mrs Jensen-from-across-the-road wouldn't have heard his 'fucking fuck' over the theme music to *The Love Boat* or whatever crap was on her TV.

'The mug hung up on me,' Dad said. 'Reckoned Oli'd been punished enough. God damn it!'

'Oli?' Mum sounded she was sleep-talking. She leant against the wall, her eyes still closed. 'Punished?'

'It's okay, Dad,' I said. 'I'm okay. Just forget about it.' No way was I was going to tell him what Miss Jones had said. I didn't need him going off at her too.

'But it pisses me off,' Dad said. 'Who the hell do they think they are?'

'It's fine. I'm starting to feel better already.' It was a lie – in my head, I was stuffing all my things into my school bag and fleeing Boorunga – but the veins on Dad's forehead were pulsing and I worried he'd try to talk to Oli's dad in person. Oli's dad played rugby league and his arms were the size of Muhammad Ali's.

'What am I s'posed to do?' He rubbed his face, then called after Mum, who'd disappeared back along the hall. 'I'll come and see you soon, Hen.'

'Nothing. Thanks for sticking up for me. Oli won't be at school to bother me now anyway.'

'He'd bloody better not,' Dad said. 'Or he'll have me to answer to.' He sighed, sitting down again on the end of my bed.

We both looked down at Julian, at his perfectly steady hand etching a tiny buckle on the side of the baby girl's shoe.

'Wow, Jules!' Dad leant forward. 'That's so real. Who is she?'

'Baby,' Julian said.

'Baby,' Dad repeated, eyebrows raised. 'Looks like the Johnsons' little girl.'

'But they don't have kids,' I said. The Johnsons walked their border collie past our house most nights with matching red and blue velour tracksuits and sad faces. I'd never seen them to talk to each other, just to 'Cindy' the border collie.

'No, not now.' Dad spoke softly, as if they were walking by at that very moment and had supersonic hearing. 'But they did. A girl. Isabelle? Something pretty like that. She was still a baby when she died. In the ...' He glanced at Julian. 'E-a-r-t-h-q-u-a-k-e.'

Dad was always forgetting Julian could spell.

'How was work today, Dad?' I wanted to change the subject.

Dad leant back on the wall. He'd calmed down at least. 'Well, I had an interesting discussion with a bloke who's convinced the ashes we gave him aren't his wife's.'

'What? Whose would they be?'

'He doesn't know, but he's adamant they're not Ida's. He's convinced he'd recognise her smell.'

I winced. An urn of ashes smelt like an actual person? Like BO? Or farts? 'Doesn't she just smell like ash?'

Dad nodded. 'Some people are just … I'm putting it down to grief. Poor old bugger. On the plus side, there was no damage to the crem last night. Lightened my workload a bit.'

'Have they been caught?'

'No, probably having a rest, scheming something new. Sometimes they leave it three or four nights. Then they're back, bolder than ever, sometimes smashing windows too. Cheeky bastards!'

Julian shivered at the 'smashing'. I reached over and put my hand on his shoulder, holding it there until I felt his breathing slow, his body loosen.

'Don't think your mum'll be joining us for tea.' Dad stood, stretching his arms. 'Reckon you can go to school again tomorrow, Jules? You're looking a bit better.'

'Maybe,' Julian said.

Just as Dad left my room, I heard a car engine purring up our driveway.

'Thanks, Harriet. You're a gem.'

When I reached the door, Harriet was handing Dad a washing basket of clothes she'd collected from her book club. Mum always grumbled when Harriet dropped off her friends' clothes, even though she was afraid her work would dry up now Jill was gone.

'Want to come in?'

'I would, Jim. But I've got to get dinner on the table.'

'We could order Chinese,' Dad said. 'I don't feel like cooking.' It was hard to believe that just a few minutes earlier he'd been yelling at Oli's dad. 'Invite John and Worm too, of course.'

'Sounds lovely, but another night? I've got piles of marking to do.'

'Okay.' Dad's tight smile didn't disguise his disappointment. It made my chest hurt. Since his friends had turned against him he probably didn't have anyone to talk to. 'Another night.'

'Tell Henrietta there's no hurry on these.' Harriet glanced at the basket. 'Just whenever she can.'

Dad and I watched from our veranda in the dark as the shape of Harriet's car disappeared down Hays Street.

'I'll help you cook, Dad,' I said.

'Think I'd rather starve.' He managed another stiff smile. 'Just joking. That would be good, Miracle. Let's see what we can scrape together.'

A couple of days later, I'd remember this moment: Dad's words, the look on his face when I offered my company (I'm sure it wasn't the thought of my scrambled eggs that made him smile), his heavy hand resting on my shoulder as we walked inside. I'd remember this and burst into tears.

12

27 June 1986

I heard the *ring-ring, ring-ring* in my sleep, which at first didn't seem strange at all, even though I was speeding across the Sydney Harbour Bridge on a motorbike as wide as an elephant. But then I realised I was in my bed, not on my way to claim a free ticket to Luna Park, and it was dark and … why was the phone ringing? My clock said 2:52 am. I lay there, flat on my back, stunned.

Ring-ring, ring-ring.

The last time the phone rang in the dark it was to tell us that Nana Jamieson had suffered a stroke on the toilet. She'd died three days later, while watching *The Young and the Restless* with a plate of Iced VoVos on her lap. (I always think of Nana when I spy Iced VoVos at the supermarket. And, as much I love that pink icing, I'll never be able to bring myself to eat another one.)

Just like that night, I heard Dad silence the phone in the hallway with a half-asleep 'Ughh-o.'

I wondered who was on the other end, and if they were wearing pyjamas. Not that it mattered, but it was better than wondering if they were naked. Had someone died? We didn't have many relatives left, thanks to Nana Jamieson's genes, and I was sure nothing had happened to Harriet, John or Worm.

75

They were the kind of family nothing bad ever happened to. Unlike ours.

I sat up. Dad usually spoke so loud on the phone I could follow the conversation from my bed, but now I could only make out the words 'shit' and 'incinerator'.

I slid out of bed and opened the door slowly so it wouldn't creak.

'I just don't understand how.' Dad's voice was soft, but urgent. 'What time was Mrs Olsen delivered? I just can't … What a bloody nightmare. I just want to –' Dad's eyes found mine in the dark.

'I'll come as soon as I can,' he said to the phone. 'Hang in there, Greg.'

As Dad put the phone down, I stepped into the hall. 'What's happened?'

'Go back to bed.'

'Why? What's happened?'

'Nothing for you to worry about, big ears!'

Even though I knew what he meant, I touched my ears, reassured by their small, soft lobes.

The hall light flashed on, and there was Mum, her face wrinkled with sleep, her hair in a big, tired heap on top of her head.

'Greg rang and now Dad's going to work!' I said.

Mum's eyes were glazed. 'It's two-fifty-six.'

'Yeah, and Dad's going to work!'

I could've told her anything. Her face was as blank as a piece of paper, as it always was after she'd taken one of the tiny blue pills she kept in her bedside drawer.

'Christ, Miracle! Just go to bed!' Dad said.

I slunk back to my room, shutting the door behind me. I didn't wanted to push him. What if he had a stroke like his mum, my poor Nana? Even though she'd always looked like she'd been born centuries ago – with grey hair and olden-day glasses – Dad said she was young when she died. Though how anyone with grey hair could be considered young baffled me. He must've just meant she was young for a really old person.

I lay in bed, my mind racing. I wanted to hear what he was whispering to Mum, but I couldn't risk him flinging the door open and finding me standing there. *Big ears!* The crem must've been damaged again, or maybe Greg'd accidentally cremated Miss Jones. I closed my eyes and imagined I was back on the motorbike I'd been dreaming about before the phone woke me, and Oli was struggling to keep up on a PeeWee 50.

When my alarm jolted me awake, Mum and Dad's bedroom door was still closed, but our car wasn't in the driveway. I found Julian on the couch in the dining room, a bowl of shredded Weet-Bix on his lap. His face was pale; grey shadows dulled his eyes. My chest tightened. I'd thought he was well again.

'Jules!'

He didn't take his eyes off *Breakfast*, Mum's morning TV show on the days she got out of bed. A man was talking about Lindy Chamberlain and the new evidence that got her released from prison on parole. She'd already been stuck in there for four years.

'Did you know Dad went to work last night?' I plonked down next to him, sloshing the milk in his bowl. 'Something happened at the crem.'

His eyes didn't move.

'Something pretty bad,' I added, but I may as well have told him Dad had blown his nose. Julian wasn't fazed.

'Did you hear the phone in the night?'

Julian shook his head.

Most of the time I envied him. If only I too could be oblivious to the world. How much easier would life be if it was like watching *Neighbours*, witnessing pretend people's problems instead of having your own. This time I wanted to grab him; how could he not care? *You might not be normal, but you've got a brain, you've got feelings!*

But Julian dropped his bowl, cold milk splashing on my nightie, and dripping down my leg onto the carpet. A soggy mush of Weet-Bix lay in his lap like spew.

I leapt up, looking around for something to soak up the milk. Mrs Stanger's blouse? The Burgess's tablecloth? I grabbed a tea towel from the kitchen. Then I noticed the spoon in Julian's trembling hand, whacking his leg. His body jerked and his face twisted in a grimace, like it did on fireworks night. Maybe he *did* care.

'It's okay, Jules.' I held his arms. They were wiry but strong, too strong for me to still. 'I'm sure it's okay. Dad's sorting it out now.'

Julian, still shaking, stared at the TV, at an ad for margarine, a movie-star mum with white teeth being congratulated, as I mopped up the mess on the carpet. A tear slipped down his cheek.

'Better get changed before Harriet gets you for school,' I said. 'You look like you've pissed your pants.' It wasn't a kind thing to say but it got Julian off the couch.

School was the last place I wanted to go, but a day at home with my thoughts would be more tortuous than a year's worth of science. I couldn't think clearly; I'd attempted to iron my dress without realising the iron wasn't plugged in, and the only socks I could find were the clammy pair from the day before. I had to sprint down the road. Leon saw me in the rear-view mirror and jerked the bus to a stop halfway down Hays Street.

I wasn't ready to forgive Pheebs and Sall. I walked straight past them to the back of the bus. I was pretty sure they hadn't actually been in on the rat thing, but I'd heard their laughter. Why hadn't they stuck up for me? I didn't want to think about them. But I didn't want to stress about Dad either. I could hear his voice, feel his worry. *This is a bloody nightmare.* What was? What had happened?

I rifled through my bag for *Brave New World*, a distraction if I could possibly concentrate. That's when I saw it poking out of my pencil case. A folded piece of lined paper, torn from an exercise book. I thought it was rubbish, so I'm not sure what compelled me to open it.

I felt like the breath had been sucked out of me.

Lo siento.

Sorry. In scratchy handwriting, handwriting I'd recognise anywhere.

Oli was sorry for what he'd done. So sorry he'd gone to the trouble of writing me a note and sneaking it into my bag. He'd felt bad about upsetting me. Oh my God, and then Dad caused a big fuss by calling his dad.

When did Oli put it in my bag? Obviously yesterday, before his mum interrupted Spanish. I stared at the words until my eyes watered.

Stepping off the bus, my legs were jelly. I stumbled over to the school fence and grabbed the cold wire to steady myself.

'What's your problem?' The voice belonged to a bony girl with brown hair hacked short like a boy's. She was sitting on a bench with two other girls, swinging their legs.

'You.' I was so overwhelmed with emotion no one could upset me, especially not a Year 7 girl with bad hair. 'What's with the pegs?' Each of the girls had a plastic clothes peg clamped onto their nose.

'What do you think?' the boy-girl asked, in an ugly, nasal voice. 'Boorunga stinks like shit!'

I shrugged, walking away in case they actually meant me. I'd had a shower so there was no reason why I'd smell. I sniffed the air; it was thick and smelt like … well, like the stink of our rubber spatula after I'd put it on a hotplate. *Boorunga stinks like shit.* They were right, I'd just gotten used to it. The air'd been turning our snot black for yonks. All that factory chimney smoke had to go somewhere. But that was Katie's dad's fault, not mine. And at that moment, I had bigger problems.

As it turned out, I'd picked the worst day to be angry with Pheebs and Sall. If I'd talked to someone, anyone, even just some loner during roll call, I wouldn't have been the last person in the world to find out what was going on.

When I opened the door to the science lab it was dead quiet except for the tick of the clock. There were no kids. The lights were on, but Mr Knowles wasn't on the platform shaking his head, looking at the clock or muttering under his breath. The bench tops were bare and I couldn't see any bags on the floor. I checked the scruff of paper my timetable was printed on, even though I could recite it in my sleep. *Double science. English. PE. Social science. Maths.* I couldn't think of any reason why science would've been cancelled – that only happened in my dreams – so I sat on my stool, opened my text book and willed Mr Knowles to get there soon. That way at least one tiny good thing would come out of the day: he'd witness me being the first person to start work. That was like winning an Olympic medal in his books.

The lab felt like Antarctica with just me inside it. I was hugging myself to keep warm by the time four of the nerdy girls arrived: Janey, Kass, Adrianna and La. They all gaped at me – surprised I'd beat them to class, I guessed – then dropped their bags on the floor and sat in the front row without saying anything.

Then Barb Davidson sailed through the door, followed by Angie Granger, both born-again Christians, a species my friends and I mostly ignored. Instead of sitting down, they hugged each other, which normally wouldn't make me blink, but Barb was crying, actually sobbing, and Angie mumbled what sounded a lot like 'Not him'. Something was going on.

The other born-again, Sean Buchen, was next, his shirt hanging to his knees. What was happening? Sean was OCD when it came to neatness. He sometimes wore a tie, even though it hadn't been part of the uniform since our grandads went to school. He caught my eye and sneered. What? Sean was always friendly. I looked away, tears burning my eyes.

Joey and Steven – normal, non-Christian boys – followed Sean in, both looking at the ground, shirts out, hands stuffed in pockets. Steven started coughing, a barking cough like Julian's, until La whacked him hard on the back.

'Fuck it.' Sean kicked over a stool.

I jumped up as it crashed to the floor.

Sean had wanted to be a priest since primary school. Now he was acting like he was possessed by Satan. I shoved my books and pens into my bag. Perhaps I shouldn't have come to school after all.

I kept my eyes on the door, willing Katie to walk in. Surely she'd be back. Surely she wouldn't have *two* days off school. And where were Sall and Pheebs? I'd forgive them, forget their betrayal. I just needed to know what was going on.

I slung my bag on my shoulder and stood watching everyone as if they were putting on a play, just for me. The room now felt warm. Or was that just me? The stuffy air was thick as tar.

More kids arrived, watery eyes gazing at me before turning away. I struggled to breathe. What did this have to do with me?

Then, finally, Pheebs! I knocked over a stool as I raced towards her, the clang of it barely audible over the sounds of kids coughing and consoling each other.

I stopped when I realised that Pheebs was with Sall and they were holding someone up, someone doubled over.

'Katie?' By now my eyes were full of tears too.

'I can't!' Katie wrestled free of Sall and Pheebs and disappeared back out the classroom door.

'What is it?' I grabbed Pheebs's hand.

She snatched it away, as if I had AIDS or something.

'Please,' I said. 'Why … what's wrong?'

Pheebs opened her mouth, but spun around, and raced out the door after Katie.

That left Sall. She had no choice but to look at me – finally, someone was – her eyes pink and swollen, tears pooling in the creases of her fat cheeks. 'You really don't know?'

'No!'

She shook her head, as if baffled by my stupidity, then said, in a half-whisper, half-growl, 'Go ask your fucking dad!'

13

Your fucking dad?

I felt like Sall had punched me. Time seemed to slow as I turned and walked back to the tables, tears spilling.

I picked up the stool from where it lay near Steven's feet and sat down, my bag still on my shoulder. There was no point going home. Mum would still be burrowed deep in her bed and I'd have to wait for ever to make sense of this. Even so, I had a feeling I wouldn't be staying long. I wiped my eyes on the back of my hands. I didn't even know why I was crying, apart from the fact Sall had growled at me. Obviously something really bad had happened. And worse still, it was to do with Dad.

When Mr Knowles finally walked in, his grey hair standing up in clumps, sniffs replaced sobs. We were teenagers, not six-year-olds. But even Mr Knowles wasn't quite Mr Knowles. He'd run his hands through his hair so many times gravity had given up.

Mr Knowles dropped his briefcase onto his desk with a thump. I sat up straight and clutched the strap on my schoolbag.

'By the looks on your faces, you've all heard.' He snapped open his briefcase, then clicked it shut.

'I, for one, am feeling completely bloody shocked and just really sad. I s'pose.' He paused, licked his lips, waited for Steven to stop coughing. 'There doesn't seem much point in being here today. I don't feel like teaching and, well, you lot never feel like learning, but even less so today. I mean, who among you really gives two shits about acids and alkalis?'

He looked around the room, but everyone was too shocked to even shrug.

'But what else are you going to do?' he continued. 'Down a few wine coolers behind the hall? Sniff a bit of glue? Smash a few windows? Make your mark someplace with a can of spray paint?'

Snap click went his briefcase.

'I think we'd better carry on, don't you? Sometimes that's the only thing to do.'

The clock ticked, a few kids sniffed, coughed. Everything was wrong. Mr Knowles didn't normally swear. And how did he know about the wine coolers behind the hall?

'We need to establish some normality.' Mr Knowles snapped his briefcase open again.

'But Mr Knowles.' It was Sall. 'Things aren't normal!'

'No, they're not, no.' *Click*. 'But there's nothing you can do, Sally, and nothing I can do. It's up to the police now.'

My cotton tunic felt thick and heavy, sticky with sweat. I knew kids were glancing at me – I could feel their eyes – but I looked straight at Mr Knowles. I wanted to go, to sprint right out the door, but for the moment the safest thing – the *only* thing – I could do was look at Mr Knowles.

'That's why it's best to try to get it out of your mind. But if you can't, Sally, I understand. Mrs Hanson has come in specially and is providing counselling throughout the day. You can book a time with her at the office – anyone can.' His eyes skittered over mine. 'Now, if you like.'

Sall slid off her stool. She grabbed a tissue from the box on Mr Knowles's desk and walked out the door whimpering.

'I need to too,' Angie said. 'Or I'm gonna have nightmares.'

'Me too!' Samantha jumped to her feet. 'I sat next to him in English.'

'Go … Go, if you have to,' Mr Knowles said. 'Otherwise, turn to page two-forty-three.'

I sat next to him in English. I was in Samantha's English class. She normally sat next to … Oh God!

'Miracle?'

Lo siento.

'Miracle?'

I opened my mouth to answer, to say 'yes', but the word was stuck at the bottom of my throat.

Something had happened to Oli.

'Perhaps you should go too.' Mr Knowles's eyes couldn't meet mine. 'I suggest you go and see Mrs Hanson.'

I nodded.

What was going on? I slipped off my stool and crossed the lab, as thirty pairs of eyes watched on, as the clock ticked and my shoes squeaked on the wooden floor.

But I didn't go to the office, I didn't even pretend to head in that direction. Who would've cared where I went anyway? I ran down the corridor, across the playground, and out the school gate. Then I sprinted, walked, stumbled through town and over Boorunga Bridge, tears gushing and the cold air burning my throat.

14

When I opened the front door and heard Dad's voice, I'm sure my heart stopped. I stood frozen for a few seconds before charging down the hall to find him sitting at the kitchen table, staring down at a plate of Twirly Swirls. Mum, a cigarette squashed between her lips, was making two cups of tea, a worrying sign meaning that today she was the more capable one, that she was consoling Dad. I tossed my school bag onto the couch.

'Is it 3.30 already?' Mum often talked with a cigarette in her mouth but watching her with the grey stink pouring out her nose almost made me retch.

'What, Dad? What's going on?'

'The crem is closed.' His eyes were buried under his frown.

'You went there in the dark!' My school tunic clung to my skin. 'Why?'

Dad bowed his head.

'Tell me!' I wanted to shake him. 'Tell me what happened! Why is everyone bawling? What happened to Oli?'

Dad held his head in his hands and said nothing. I was ready to scream.

'What happened was, Oli …' Mum removed the cigarette from her mouth, and let out a long, steady stream of smoke, as if I had all day to wait, as if she was a fucking steam train, travelling from one side of Australia to the other, with all the time in the world. 'Was attacked. Last night.'

Attacked. That's the way she said it. *Attacked.* Calmly. Not *Attacked!* Mum loved drama – *Prisoner* was one of her favourite TV shows – she was down-playing things for my benefit.

The room was spinning. I sat on a chair next to Dad, gripping the seat to stop myself from falling. 'But is he …'

'It's serious.' Mum picked up a teaspoon, stirred her tea. 'He's in an induced coma.'

My body relaxed slightly. He wasn't dead. People came out of comas. Not only in TV shows, when they woke up after thirty years to find their girlfriend had married someone else. *Julian* had come out of a coma.

'That's what they do when someone has a serious head injury,' Dad said. 'They put them in a coma to stop the brain swelling.'

I remembered what Dad'd said about Julian: all you had to do was peer into the baby's vacant blue eyes to know something had happened to him, and he'd never be the same again. Would Oli still be Oli? My mind started spinning.

'But what's it got to do with *you*?' I said to Dad.

'Your dad has done absolutely nothing wrong.' Mum paused before adding, 'Oli was found outside the crem. Unconscious.'

The crem? My heart pounded. 'What?'

Dad released a long, tired sigh. 'Looks like he was one of the vandals.'

I stood up. It was too much to take in. Oli was in a coma. Oli was a vandal. 'So, what –'

'Look, I don't know!' Dad banged his mug on the table. Milky tea splashed over the edge and soaked into a stack of bills. 'Greg's talking to the police at the moment.'

'Greg's a vandal too?'

'Don't be stupid! Greg found him.'

I felt dizzy, but I was too hyped up to sit. 'But yesterday you called Oli's dad and –'

'Miracle, please!' Dad stood. 'It doesn't matter about yesterday. A shocking thing's happened. I don't know how. It's just – it's all – a horrible fucking mess.'

I watched him disappear down the hall. His bedroom door creaked open, then banged shut. I felt a surge of anger. I'd told him not to call Oli's dad. Why hadn't he listened?

'It's okay.' Mum rubbed my arm, her skin as rough as the sandpaper we used in woodwork. 'Oli will be okay. I'm sure of it.'

I sat down, wanting to believe her. Maybe he would be okay, maybe this was all a big over-reaction.

'I hated Oli yesterday,' I said, wiping my eyes. 'I even wished he was dead, just for a few minutes. But most of the time, he's nice. He's kind, much kinder than Seth. He thinks up really witty things, right on the spot, not hours after the moment's past, like I do. I really like him. Everyone does. I don't want him to be in a coma.' I sobbed.

'Course you don't. Have a good cry, Miri.' Mum's hand was so bony and light I could barely feel it, but she touched me so rarely, I was very conscious of it resting on my shoulder. 'Get it out of your system.'

I can't remember much else about that day. I don't remember Julian getting home, but Harriet would've dropped him off and she must've heard about Oli, so surely she would've come inside. Perhaps I was in bed. I remember kicking off my school shoes and pulling the doona over my head. I couldn't get Oli out of my mind. Or the thought that people believed Dad was responsible. I buried my face in my pillow.

Go ask your fucking dad! Sall obviously thought he hurt Oli.

Did Katie? Did everyone else? Was that why Dad was so angry? He'd never hurt anyone. He'd never even touched me. Mum'd whacked me with the feather duster after I'd tried to smoke a cigarette in the laundry cupboard when I was nine, but it was Dad who told her to stop. 'For Christ's sake, Hen, leave her alone,' he'd said, even though there was metho in that cupboard and I could've done worse than singe my lungs. I could've set myself on fire.

But if everyone thought Dad did it, how could I ever go to school again? If there was an Oli vs Miracle poll, well, that would be a waste of paper because everyone knew he'd win. In Year 8 he'd been voted both 'Best kisser' and 'Most likely to become famous'. What was I voted? 'Most unusual name' and 'Freakiest birth', both of which categories had been created by Katie and Pheebs just for me. I flung off my doona, suddenly burning hot.

I saw Oli's face, his messy hair and those eyes. The shoebox – *a gift for you, Miracle* – the shrivelled rats, the stench of death. And then, the note! *Lo siento*. I felt cold, so cold my teeth started chattering.

That's when the knocking came at the door.

15

Mum and I stood on the front doorstep as Constable Kelly led Dad across the stepping stones, down the driveway and to the cop car. The street light shone on Constable Kelly's bald head, turning him into an alien and making everything more sinister than it already was. My heart was beating so fast I struggled to breathe. A braver me would've yelled 'Go, Dad!', urging him to make a run for it. An even braver me would've sprinted across the lawn and tackled the alien before he guided Dad into the car. I just stood there, as useless as Mum and Mrs Jensen-from-across-the-road, whose short, round body was pressed against her living room window.

The three of us watched the car with Dad inside slowly edge out of the gutter and creep down Hays Street. Its lights were flashing, but there was no siren. Was Constable Kelly scared that if he turned it on Dad might freak out and reach into the front and strangle him? Or had he left it off because he didn't really think Dad was a criminal? Maybe the siren had just run out of battery.

We must've stood there for ten minutes, steam coming out of our mouths instead of words. I think we were waiting for Constable Kelly to realise he'd got the wrong man, do a U-ey halfway up Hays Street, and drop Dad home again.

Mum broke the silence by whistling. It was a horrible sound

– a sound that'd given Dad a migraine the Christmas she'd joined us for Carols in the Park – but I resisted the urge to cover my ears. It took me a while to recognise the tune from *Life of Brian*. I stared at her. Was she having a nervous breakdown? Or was she whistling "Always look on the bright side of life" to convince us both that Dad being taken away by a cop wasn't such a bad thing? Her face didn't answer my questions.

'They'll let him go, won't they, Mum?'

She nodded, then stopped whistling. 'A few words with him and they'll realise he's a big softie.'

'What if they don't?'

'If they don't … well … then … I need a cigarette! Blow Mrs Jensen a goodnight kiss and come inside.'

I waved at Mrs Jensen-from-across-the-road, who quickly stepped away and disappeared behind her curtain. I felt mean – she'd probably just had the most exciting few minutes of her life – but it wasn't our job to keep her entertained.

It'll be fine, I told myself, as I sunk into the depths of our couch. I'd always tried to look on the bright side. Miss Stewart had described me as an 'optimist' in my Grade 6 school report – possibly because I'd been the slowest person in the class at long division but had always finished my tests without bursting into tears or throwing my textbook at the window like Timmy Hancock did – and I'd loved the sound of the word. *Optimist.* After I'd looked it up in the dictionary and found out it was a good thing, I decided to make it mine.

The bright side of having a mum like Mum, for example, was knowing I didn't want to be anything like her when I grew up. To make sure I'd never end up with agoraphobia, I'd been stepping outside our house at least twice a day since I was seven, even on weekends. On freezing or wet days I settled for touching the cold, prickly doormat with my toes, but still. It was *outside*. Dad warned me I was developing a phobia about getting agoraphobia, but I knew I could stop if I wanted to. I just didn't want to. Ever.

But the bright side of everyone thinking Dad'd attacked my best friend's boyfriend, a boy I'd been in love with since the moment he'd stood on that mound of dirt in our backyard and taken the blame for something we'd both done? Even an optimist struggled to see that.

'Dad?' Julian croaked. I hadn't heard him come into the living room. He now stood in front of the TV, in his striped pyjamas with holes in the knees.

I looked at Mum, waiting for her to explain.

'I'll make tea.' Mum stubbed out her cigarette and stood up. She disappeared into the kitchen, and we heard the *tap tap tap* of her trying to use the can opener.

'He's gone to the police station,' I told Julian. 'They're asking questions about Oli.'

Julian nodded. He didn't look surprised, but then he never did. He just stood there, arms hanging by his sides, until Mum returned carrying three bowls.

'Soup,' she announced before we could get our hopes up.

I don't know if Julian even tasted it. He placed his bowl on the table, spilling a brown splotch on the *TV Guide*, and mumbled about bed.

Mum said, 'Your dad's just helping the cops do their job', but she didn't try to stop him.

That left Mum and me again. We sat in front of the TV, bowls burning our laps, not eating, not knowing what to say. My mind was spinning round and round – Oli, coma, Dad, police, jail – unable to settle on one, like a chocolate wheel that never stops spinning.

I should've known better than to switch the TV over to Channel 9. There was Oli filling the screen: his scruffy, dark hair; his perfect nose; those eyes that made my stomach flip; and his smile, the same smile he'd given me in ancient history, which'd made me feel like the luckiest girl in Year 9, even though he was sitting next to his girlfriend at the time, and he was only smiling because I'd said he could borrow my notes on Pompeii. My eyes filled with tears.

'… fourteen-year-old Oliver Harrison, discovered in the early hours of this morning by Director of Compassionate Cremations, Gregory Parker,' the TV-voice was saying. 'Police are still investigating the cause of his injuries but an unconfirmed source says they've arrested someone in relation to the attack …'

'*Arrested* him? Jesus!' Mum slopped soup on her tracksuit pants. 'I thought they just wanted him to answer a few questions.'

'But it's been ages.' I reached for Mum's cigarettes and removed one from the pack. I'd been practising with Katie and she'd taught me how to inhale without coughing my lungs up. 'Are they making him write an essay?'

'Oliver's parents, Steven and Judith Harrison,' the TV-voice went on, 'were too upset to comment. Oliver is their only child …'

'Dad called Oli's dad.' I stared at the TV, at the montage of Oli. I lit the cigarette and sucked lightly on it, waiting for all my worries to drift away. 'They yelled at each other.'

'He told me.' Mum didn't even notice the cigarette. 'Bad bloody timing.'

'They'll think it's Dad for sure.' I coughed. I needed more practice.

'Well, they can think whatever they bloody well like. Can you imagine him attacking anyone?' Mum picked a bit of something, corn it looked like, from between her teeth. 'I mean, I still can't believe he works at a crematorium. Remember when you broke your arm and it looked a bit floppy? He had to lie on the couch to stop himself from fainting. I had to call John.'

'I can't imagine him *doing* it. But.' I swallowed. My mouth tasted worse than Mum's ashtray. I had to say it: 'He did get really angry with me. Twice! In two days.'

'It's a bit of a leap – from telling off your daughter to putting a kid in a coma!'

She was right. There's no way he would've.

'Well, if they *think* he did it, will they still bring him home soon?'

'Do I look like a detective?' Mum frowned. 'Sorry, I just don't know. And put that bloody thing out before it kills you!'

Smoke had wafted up my nose and was burning my nostrils. I stuffed the cigarette into the ashtray. It hadn't worked anyway. I was as worried as ever.

One of those overly happy ads – with a smiling mum and a dad who'd never be accused of beating up a kid – filled the TV, and then the phone rang. We both jumped.

Could it be the police saying they'd made a mistake? Or Dad asking us to pick him up?

But no, it was Harriet. I handed the phone to Mum.

'Yeah, we've been watching … around five-thirty, I suppose. It'd just gotten dark. No, no handcuffs. He's not a bloody crim! I was hoping this'd be him … I'm not getting a lawyer – not after what that nasty piece of work did to Aunty Violet … Do you know how much they charge an hour? I've got no idea either, but I'm sure it's more than Jim makes in a year!'

Mum talked to Harriet for nearly an hour, which must've been some kind of record, while I stared at the TV, trying to make sense of her end of the conversation while waiting for the front door to open and Dad to lumber down the hall.

I don't know what time I finally gave up and lay on my bed, but I must've been exhausted because I went to sleep without even trying. I was woken by painful cramps. The clock said 8:15 am. I lay there holding my belly, as all the dread of the previous day crept back.

'Don't touch the curtains!' Mum's words came out of nowhere.

She was standing in my doorway, looking tiny in Dad's brown dressing gown.

'Unless you want to end up on the front page of *The Boorunga Times*,' she whispered.

'Huh?' I sat up.

'There are people out there.' Mum nodded at my window. 'Waiting.'

Mum's eyes didn't seem any crazier than normal, so I knew she wasn't imagining it. But it was hard to believe anyone would go to the trouble of hiding out in our yard. I tried to picture it: a man with a Hitler moustache flashed into my mind, crouched in the wattle bush, pointing a camera at my window, waiting for me to show my face.

I heard a voice. And another. Someone *was* outside. Two someones. Maybe more.

'You and Julian better stay in today,' Mum whispered as I crawled back under my doona. Cramps gripped my belly. I groaned. Dad was in jail. Cameramen were in our front yard. And I had my period. I wanted to sleep, to never wake up.

'Jules is crook again, anyway,' Mum said. 'It's a good thing your dad kept our earthquake supplies well stocked.'

'You hate tinned rice pudding,' I said, but Mum had already left.

I thought about spending the whole day at home, hiding from the world, waiting waiting waiting for Dad to open the front door. It'd be worse than being in a coma … but that wasn't a good thing to think. On the other hand, I had my period; I was allowed to be grumpy and think bad thoughts. Surely there was something we could do. Something *I* could do. So much of this was my fault. I should sort it out, sore belly or not.

I jumped out of bed and ran along the hall.

'Let's ring Constable Kelly!'

Mum dropped her lighter.

'Ask him what's going on,' I said.

Mum shook her head. 'Harriet says we shouldn't do anything without talking to a lawyer first.'

'Then call a lawyer!' I was aware I sounded more like an actress than a fourteen-year-old girl from Boorunga who was still in her school uniform from the day before, which was now stained with blood. But somehow our lives had turned into a TV drama. Just ask Mrs Jensen-from-across-the-road.

'I don't trust them. Your Great-Aunty Violet ended up living on potatoes and two-minute noodles because of a bloody lawyer.'

'They can't all be like that. You believe all dentists want our teeth to decay. And doctors want to make us sick. You can't believe everything you hear on talkback radio!'

'Well, I know two lawyers and they both belong behind bars. And anyway, what would we pay a lawyer with? Your Donald Duck piggy bank?'

It was Mickey Mouse, actually, and it'd been empty since I'd donated all my money ($26.50) to helping save the Gouldian finch from extinction.

'What about Harriet?' I asked. 'She'd help us.'

'This is not her problem.'

'But what if –'

'No! She and John have put all their money into that house in Lawson's Bay.'

'Jason, over here!' A loud whisper from outside, followed by the sound of feet running across the lawn.

'This is nuts!' I nodded at the window. I felt thankful for the extra locks on our front door.

'It's not good for my nerves.' Mum stood up and stretched her arms. 'I suppose we *could* call Constable Kelly – that's not a crime, is it? *I'll* call him. Okay?'

'Thanks, Mum.'

She headed towards the hallway, then stopped and turned. 'What will I say?'

'Just ask him when Dad'll be home. And tell him there's people in our yard who probably want to kill us. And ...'

'And?'

'Please don't swear.'

'I'll do my best.'

'You can do it, Mum.' I took a deep breath, hoping I was right.

'It's Henrietta Jamieson speaking. I'm calling about my husband, Mr James Jamieson.' Mum was using her politest voice, the one she saved for parent teacher interviews. It made her sound like she thought she was the Queen. But at least she wasn't yelling.

Yet.

'You've got the wrong end of the stick,' Mum yelled. 'He was just doing the right thing, helping you lot by answering a few questions. He didn't even pack his things! He uses a special soap because he washes his hands so ... you bloody ... Someone's screwed up. I'm sure our lawyer will sort you out!'

She slammed the phone down. She'd forgotten to mention the newspaper people outside, but I could hardly get her to call back now.

She shuffled back into the living room, tears smudging the dark rings under her eyes. 'It's true. They've arrested him. They're holding him until he can go to court.'

I imagined Constable Kelly with his arms around Dad, *holding* him. 'When will that be?'

'He said there's no sessions on the weekend. So Monday. But even then ... The bastard said there's no guarantee he'll get bail. He even told me not to get my *hopes* up.' Mum rubbed her eyes. 'As if hope is something I've got a handle on.'

16

'The cop said *I hope you've got some savings put aside for a rainy day*,' Mum said. 'A *rainy* day! What does that even mean? It's always bloody raining.'

'To pay for a lawyer?' I said.

'No, I think he just meant in case your dad can't go to work for a while. Apparently he can get free legal aid. But what if we have to pay to get him out? Bail can be thousands of –' Mum's face froze.

'Mum? What's wrong?'

'Your dad gave all our *rainy day* money to his *business partner*. To Greg! And … and he took out a bank loan for God knows how much.'

'Oh. We can always ask Greg for it back.' Even as I said the words, I knew it wouldn't be that simple.

'Well, I hope I can keep up the mortgage payments.' Mum was tying Dad's dressing gown cord into a giant knot. 'It won't be easy, but I can do some sums and see what I come up with. I certainly don't want to be out on the street. I can't even leave the house.'

'We have to ask Greg. He must know Dad didn't do it. And he owns the crematorium, so it's his responsibility.'

'You reckon?' Mum's eyes looked heavy, her face pasty.

'We have to do *something*.' Although I felt like crying, I tried to sound calm, sensing Mum was about to slip inside herself. 'We need to ask for our money back.'

She sighed. 'All right. We'll talk to Greg, but we'll do it in person and not here. Not with bloody *Jason and co.* hiding in our bottlebrush. I'll ask him to suggest a café.'

Mum stuck her head out the front door and scanned the yard before pulling it back in, her face pink from the cool morning air. 'Maybe this rain has scared them off,' she whispered. 'Ready? Go!'

I crept through drenching rain across the stepping stones to the lawn, crouched low like a crab, Mum and Julian following my lead. But once we'd locked the car doors and I peered out the window through dripping wet hair, I realised no one was in our yard to see or not see us sneak past. Three empty foam coffee cups stuffed in the lavender next to the front steps were the only evidence anyone had been there at all.

'Stop breathing, you two!' Mum fumbled with the key in the ignition. Our panic was fogging up the windows.

As we sped across town Mum muttered to herself, something about Mary Mother of God. Mum was praying! In the rear-view mirror, Julian's head was bowed and his eyes closed. He was praying too, as if it was something he normally did in the car on a Saturday morning. We never said prayers. Dad said religion was for people who had nothing better to do with their weekends. What was happening to my family?

At the traffic lights, we pulled up next to Leon the bus driver, who looked out of place in his tiny blue Mazda. I waved, relieved to see a normal person, someone who didn't want to interrogate us. He gave a nod and looked away. Was he shy when he wasn't working? Or embarrassed to be caught driving such a small car?

Across Boorunga Bridge, Mum drove the back way – through Anders Drive and down Henderson Way – her chin practically on the dashboard. She turned too quickly on the corner of Henderson, knocking over a metal garbage bin, so white plastic bags spilled their guts onto the footpath. I felt like we were in a movie car chase, except the only thing chasing us was our imagination. It didn't help that Julian, perhaps out of fear, spoke more words than he had in all of 1985, when he chanted, 'Go go go go go.'

'Duck!' Mum shouted when we were at the intersection near school.

Julian and I pressed our faces to our knees.

'It's okay,' she said a few moments later. 'Thought a man in that taxi had a bloody camera.'

My heart didn't slow down until Mum drove into the deserted car park and pulled up with a jolt in front of the giant pink biscuit. I guess the four-metre replica was meant to showcase the nearby Heller's Plastics' glossiest, pinkest plastic, but I probably wasn't the only one who tasted and smelt plastic when they bit into a Twirly Swirl.

Greg had suggested the Twirly Swirl factory café because it'd be empty on a Saturday, so we could 'meet away from prying eyes and ears'. Its usual customers were factory workers or kids on their way home from school, too starving to be put off by the stink of plastic.

When the waitress spotted us through the glass door, she clutched her chest as if we'd given her a heart attack. I wasn't sure if she was shocked to see us in our rain-soaked clothes and dripping hair or if she just wasn't expecting customers.

'I was about to close,' she said. 'Please take a seat. Anywhere you like.'

'By the door, please.' Mum's voice was shaking. The shine

on her face could've been rain or sweat. This was the first place she'd visited since the crem.

'Of course.' Magda – as per her biscuit-shaped badge – pointed to the table closest to the door. 'On a weekday, I sit there and people-watch. The only people to watch are dressed in overalls and face masks, so they're not great for fashion tips or anything, but still. I've filed my nails down to their cuticles and there are only so many crosswords you can do, if you know what I mean. My gosh!' She touched Julian's arm. 'Are you all right?'

Julian recoiled, looking away.

'Poor boy's shaking like a leaf!' She frowned at Mum. 'Didn't bring a jacket, love?'

'He's fine,' Mum said. 'It's just him.'

Magda kept frowning, as if trying to work out whether Mum was a child abuser. 'I'll put the heating on. Reginald says to only use it when the temperature drops below fifteen degrees, but we can't have our patrons shivering. It'll help you all dry off. Can I get you a blanket too, lovey?'

If Magda saw Julian shake his head, she pretended not to. She disappeared through a curtain of colourful plastic strips before returning with a red blanket, which she draped over him.

'I can't put my finger on it, but there's something special about you,' she said to Julian. 'You look like a saint or something. I haven't been to church since Dad dragged me there for my Holy Communion as a child, but I can't have a saint catching a cold in my café, can I?'

It made me wonder about Mum's agoraphobia. Was it really a condition? Or had she just met too many people who went on and on about nothing?

I felt a mixture of panic and relief when a black car pulled up next to ours, with Greg's face in the windscreen. The car was shinier than our Hyundai had ever been, even though we'd bought it new from Kingford Motors with Granny Holmes's inheritance. His wheels looked like they were real silver. Each one probably cost as much as our house.

Greg was already out of the car, tucking in his red checked shirt, when I noticed another face in the windscreen. A girl's. My heart sank. His daughter? Why was *she* here? This had nothing to do with her. If she went to my school, she could add 'beggar' to the long list of names kids would soon be calling me.

When she stepped out from behind the big biscuit, and I recognised her long, white-blonde hair, I shrank in my seat. This was 'Livvy, the new girl' in Year 12! Though she'd started at Boorunga High the year before – she'd worn her old school's green tartan dress to her first assembly, which proved she had guts – she was still known as 'Livvy, the new girl' or 'Livvy from Sydney'.

Livvy's hair wasn't plastered to her head like mine was. It must've stopped raining before they left home, or their garage wasn't so full of junk you couldn't actually fit a car in it. I combed my curls with my fingers.

Greg's smile revealed all his shiny white teeth.

'Good morning, Henrietta, Miracle.' He nodded. 'You must be Julian?' He offered his giant hand to Julian, who dropped the pencil he was doodling with to take it. 'This is my daughter, Livvy.'

'I know *Miracle*.' Livvy smiled at me, as if knowing me wasn't a bad thing, even though she was: a) in Year 12, b) part of the popular group, and c) on the 'affirmative' team of the Great Quake Debate, which believed the quake caused the curse. Maybe she'd already planned to weave me into her argument.

'There's only one Miracle at Boorunga High,' she said. 'Well, apart from the fact that anyone shows up each day.' She laughed. 'And this is your brother?'

'Julian.' His face went pink, clashing with the red fleecy blanket wrapped awkwardly around his neck. Obviously his selective mutism excluded pretty, blonde-haired Year 12s.

'I *don't* know you. I'd remember if I'd seen you before.' It was impossible to tell whether she noticed Julian's shaking. Her eyes were fixed on his face. My friends had similar reactions the first time they met him. Sall'd started choking. 'He looks like a doll,' she'd said, clutching a handful of coughed-up apple. 'Was he adopted?'

'Julian doesn't go to our school,' I started. 'He –'

'Okay.' Magda stood before us, rubbing her hands together. 'So bickies for five – they're on the house with the beverage of your choice. Hot chocolates for the kids? Coffees for adults? Black for you, Greg?'

'That would be brilliant, Magda,' Greg said. 'You take yours black too, don't you, Henrietta?'

Mum nodded. 'Good memory.'

'Sorry to hear about …' Livvy sat in the chair opposite mine. 'It really sucks.'

I bit my lip hard. 'Sucks' was for when you only got 49% in a maths test or when the school athletics carnival didn't get rained off – it wasn't an adequate word to describe your dad being accused of beating up the most beautiful boy at Boorunga High, or possibly in the world – but I wasn't about to argue about verbs with someone in Year 12, especially not someone in the debating team. We were going to ask her dad for money. That was humiliating enough.

'Yes, condolences to you all,' Greg said, as if someone'd died, which in a way Dad had. We all had. Greg looked uncomfortable in a flannelette shirt and dark denim jeans instead of his usual black suit. He took Mum's hand, something he had a lot of practice doing with the hands of dead people's wives and mothers. 'If there's anything we can do …'

Mum eyed me through strands of wet hair, pleading.

'Yes, please.' My voice wavered. 'There is something.'

Greg's smile looked faked, forced. *Cadaver*, I thought, then pushed the memory away.

'That's why we needed to see you,' I said. 'Because we, Mum and me and –'

'Look, we need money. The money Jim gave you when he bought into the business. Even if he's allowed to come home, he mightn't be allowed to go to work. Not until this is sorted out, and who knows how long … how long that will take.' Mum slumped against the wall, squashed by the weight of her words.

'You're asking me for money?' Greg let out a deep sigh and then chuckled, as if Mum'd told him a joke that he'd only just understood.

I glared at him, willing his chair to collapse.

'*Our* money. We need it back.' I crossed my arms. This was his fault. He was sitting here ordering coffee in a café while Dad was … what? Answering Constable Kelly's ten millionth question? Sitting, shivering in a cell in his blue undies? (Or had he put his jeans on before he left home? All I could remember was his hairy white legs walking along the hallway). At least Livvy wasn't laughing. I snuck a look at her face and was surprised to see watery eyes.

'Jesus Christ, it's hot in here!' Greg dabbed at his face with a paper serviette. 'Or is it the fact that I've just been asked for something I *don't* have?'

'Dad!' Livvy's hands were fists, pressed against the table.

'My apologies, Greg.' Magda appeared from behind the counter. 'The boy was shivering. I'll turn the heating down a notch.'

'Dad gave you all our money,' I said quietly, though I could tell Magda was listening because of the angle she was holding her head at, as if her neck'd snapped. 'He gave you the bank's money too. He got a loan from the bank and gave it all to you.'

'He *invested* in shares,' Greg said. 'You think I have that kind of money at my disposal?'

Magda cleared her throat as she approached with a tray. 'Here you go, sweethearts. Two black coffees, three hot chocolates and your complimentary bottomless plate of Twirly Swirls.' She arranged everything on the table in front of us, careful not to spill our brimming hot chocolates. 'I've started you off with our new caramel toffs – just shout when you're ready to try something else.'

I waited until Magda was sitting back on her stool, pen in hand, frowning at the magazine in front of her, pretending not to be completely focused on us.

'I think …' My voice was shaking. I took a deep breath to compose myself, and looked away from Greg and Livvy. I stared at the steaming mug and the table in front of me, but that was a mistake because I spotted initials scratched into the wood: *O.H.*

I squeezed my eyes shut. This wasn't the time to cry.

'*We* think Dad wouldn't be in trouble if it wasn't for you, so you need to help us get him out of it.' My heart thumped against my ribs.

'Hold on a minute. *I* got him into this mess?' Greg pointed at himself.

I felt like punching him, knocking the big white teeth right out of his mouth.

'It's *your* business. He's *your* partner.'

Greg laughed, shaking his head. He muttered something that sounded like 'unbelievable'.

'Dad, you're being rude,' Livvy said. She turned away to look out the window.

Greg picked up a caramel toff and used it to stir his coffee. The melted chocolate on his fingers made me want to gag.

'You must know the full story.' Greg locked eyes with me. 'This isn't about the crematorium.'

'It is! They found Oli there! We know the cops talked to you.'

'Settle down.' Greg pointed at me as if I was a dog.

'Dad!' Livvy said. 'Why do you have to be so –'

But Greg pretended not to hear. 'Henrietta, did you know Jim called the boy's father last night?'

The boy. Oli.

'Steve. Of course. Oli had been a prat at school.' Mum's voice was soft, her battery running low.

Lo siento.

'Did Jim tell you he harassed Steve?'

Livvy was leaning on the table stirring her hot chocolate, clanging the teaspoon, sloshing froth into the saucer.

'He told me the words he used,' Mum said. 'Steve was unreasonable.'

'Nothing justifies attacking a child, Henrietta.'

Livvy dropped her teaspoon. 'Why did you even bring me here?'

'He didn't do it!' I said, my fists clenched.

'Of course we'd all like to think that, but –'

'I don't want to be any part of this.' Livvy pushed back her chair, which screeched on the wooden floor. I glanced at Magda, now chewing on her pen and staring right back. This was 'people-watching' at its best. I wouldn't have been surprised if she'd started clapping.

'You really think Jim would …' Mum either couldn't think of the words or couldn't bring herself to say them. 'Just because he had an argument with the kid's dad?'

'I was shocked when I heard. Shattered to be honest. He'd sounded dead to the world when I called that night. But he must've just got home.' Greg looked at Livvy, but her head was bowed. 'I really thought he was a top bloke. Not the sharpest, perhaps. But solid. Reliable. But they've got evidence –'

'What evidence?' Mum asked.

'Well, his handkerchief. Red, tartan. You know the one?'

Mum and I looked at each other. Was my face as white as hers? The hanky he wore in his suit pocket.

'It was found not far from Oliver. I couldn't deny it was his. And then, after seeing those words on the wall, I –'

'What words?' Mum and I, at the same time.

'The words.' Greg spoke slowly as if Mum and I also weren't *the sharpest*. 'That were spray-painted on the wall.'

'The cop didn't –' I started.

'No one mentioned any bloody words!' Mum jumped in.

'There was a message on the back wall of the crematorium, near the shed,' Greg continued, eyeing me, 'behind where the boy was found bleeding.' Was he enjoying this?

'Jim said Oli Harrison was one of the vandals,' Mum said. 'He didn't mention any damage caused that night. It would've seemed beside the point.'

'Julian, are you okay?' Livvy said. 'Dad, you're upsetting him.'

Julian's pencil lay snapped in two on his saucer and he sat slumped, his head in his hands. His face was tinged green as if he was going to puke.

'Can you take him outside, Liv?' Greg said. 'Sorry, matey. I'm as upset about this as you are.'

'Here, take this.' Magda jumped up from her stool and followed them out the door, waving the red blanket Julian'd let slip to the floor.

'Oliver didn't write the message,' Greg continued. Had he deliberately waited until Magda had settled back on her stool, ready for the next instalment? 'It wouldn't make sense for him to write it.'

'What did it say?' Mum asked.

'I liked Jim,' Greg said. 'I haven't known him long, but long enough to … Can I be blunt? To be bloody gobsmacked that he'd be capable of such –'

'What was the message?' I stood up. 'Tell us!'

'Well, I'm amazed you haven't heard. But I guess Jim was hardly going to tell you, was he? It was written with spray paint probably snatched from the kid's hands.'

I could hear my breathing, Mum's breathing.

Greg licked his lips. 'The words were, "Stay away from my girl".'

17

I felt Greg's eyes on me as I tried to make sense of what he'd just told us. Thankfully Livvy was still outside with Julian, so she didn't see my face redden.

Stay – away – from – my – girl.

Dad wouldn't say that, he wouldn't use those words. He wouldn't paint them on a wall for the whole world to see. Why would he create a mess he'd later swear about having to clean up? Anyway, he wasn't even there. He was at home with us until the phone woke us up. He must've been.

'That doesn't prove anything,' Mum said, but doubt crept over her face. I could tell she was sifting through her memory, searching for something, anything to stop Greg from looking so smug. She wouldn't find much. I remembered her stumbling down the hall that night, still half-dreaming, to see why Dad was yelling 'Fuck!' I saw her later too, just a glimpse of her floating past in her pink dressing gown on the way to the loo. But that was all.

'It makes him more of a suspect, Henrietta,' Greg said. 'And he has been acting out of character lately. Surely you've noticed?'

Mum's eyes met mine. Had we noticed? On the phone to Oli's dad, he'd sounded like he was about to morph into the Incredible Hulk, but he'd calmed down afterwards. Watching

Julian draw had seemed to help him relax. By the time Harriet stopped by with the basket of ironing, you'd never have guessed that minutes earlier he'd been so angry. Dad and I'd then made dinner together – grilled cheese on toast – a meal usually saved for pub nights when he was too wobbly to chop up veges. He'd sliced the cheese into paper thin slivers because after he'd cut the mouldy bits off, only a small lump was left.

I'd only managed a couple of bites; the cheese tasted like glue and I couldn't get Oli's voice out of my mind. And that look on his face, like he didn't want to do what he was doing, he didn't want to be handing me the *present*. Men's. Size 8. Tan. I'd watched Dad devour his toast in big bites and Julian peck at his like a tiny bird, willing myself not to cry.

'He's not the same bloke who turned up for an interview a good twenty minutes early, the tiny piece of newspaper in his hand,' Greg continued. 'Maybe he wasn't ready to take on the role – not everyone reacts well, being exposed to so much death. And, I am aware of his *background*. He confided in me early on.'

'That was a long time ago.' Mum's face flickered with fear. 'And it was *not* his fault.'

'And so he told me,' Greg said.

What were they talking about? What wasn't Dad's fault?

'I don't know what you're saying, but I *know* he didn't hurt anyone! I know that for a fact!' My head was throbbing.

'Do you?' Greg asked.

'Yes,' Mum said. 'She does. He was home all night! Lying next to me.'

'Are you one hundred percent sure about that?' Greg leant towards Mum. His face was full of tiny potholes.

'I am.' But her voice wavered and she stared down at her lap.

'Well, not meaning to be rude, but aren't you on some kind of medication?'

'Beg your pardon?' Mum's head shot up.

My mind jumped back to that night. I'd set the table – just four plates, no need for knives and forks – and called out, 'Muuuum', but the only sound from the other side of the door was a muffled song on Radio B1. I remembered Dad saying, 'There's only one thing worse than cheese on toast, and that's cold cheese on toast,' which was our cue to give up on Mum and start eating. Julian's sketchpad lay open on the table, at the drawing he'd just finished of the baby girl. She had those eyes that seem to follow you wherever you go. When Julian went into the kitchen for a glass of water I quickly turned the page. I couldn't stand her watching me.

'I'm just saying,' Greg's voice snapped me out of my thoughts. 'It's highly probable that you didn't notice Jim vacate the house – if you were sedated at the time.'

Mum closed her eyes, her face red with anger, embarrassment, or both.

'I knew this was a bad idea.' She slid her cup across the table with a shaky hand, black coffee filling the white saucer. 'Let's go home.'

'I'm sorry I've upset you,' Greg said. 'Look, I don't think Jim was of sound mind at the time. A father's love for his daughter is a very powerful thing.'

I avoided his gaze. Guilt washed over me in waves. If it wasn't for me, this would've been an ordinary Saturday, with Dad sitting in his chair watching TV.

'I'd like to support you, but I'm not in a position to help out financially,' Greg said. 'I went through a messy divorce last year and my wife cleaned me out.'

'Why did you even move here?' Mum mumbled, still not looking at Greg. 'You heard the town was dying? Fancied yourself as some kind of superhero?'

Greg chewed his lip. '*Dying* is an overstatement, Henrietta.

Don't buy into the gossip. But if you must know, things weren't going so well for us in Sydney. My wife suddenly got it into her head that she was … well, a lesbian. So she packed up half our house, well, more than half really because the Arthur Boyd prints were actually mine, and moved in with the librarian from Livvy's school. This was very difficult for Livvy, as you can probably imagine. So when my good friend Reginald told me about the funeral business closing down here –'

'Forget I asked.' Mum pushed her chair out with a screech. 'Come on, Miracle. Before someone else ends up in a coma.'

'So I take it the caramel toffs aren't a hit?' Magda's wide hips, wedged between our table and the next one, suggested she was more of a fan than we were. 'I admit they're a little on the sweet side. I prefer old-fashioned chocolate chip myself. Can I get anyone a choc chip?'

'That will be it for now, thanks Magda,' Greg said. 'How much do I owe you?'

Livvy was watching us through the glass. She slid the door open, carrying the blanket. 'Are you leaving?'

'We certainly are.' Mum squeezed past her. 'Thanks for keeping Julian company.'

'He didn't say much, but I guess he's not well. He's got a wicked cough!'

Much. So he must've talked a bit.

'See you …' I was going to say 'at school', but how could I ever go back to school?

Livvy touched my arm. 'Hey, sorry this didn't work out. Call me if you want.' She smelt like the cinnamon johnny cakes Granny Holmes used to make.

'Uh, thanks,' I stammered, knowing I'd never have the guts to call her, that I'd have no idea what to say. I didn't want to talk to her anyway. Unless Greg suddenly changed his mind and gave us our money, in which case I'd forgive him for everything, even his big teeth, I never wanted to see either of them again.

'Take a deep breath, Henrietta.'

Greg had followed us outside the café, and was sliding his wallet, which admittedly looked pretty thin, into his pocket.

'And perhaps something a wee bit stronger for your nerves.'

Mum answered by slamming the car door so hard I was surprised it didn't fall off.

18

'Bastard!' Mum's eyes flicked between mine in the passenger seat and Julian's in the rear-view mirror. 'What's the bet he set your dad up? He probably wrote that graffiti himself.'

The car lurched and screeched as Mum nearly missed the turn-off into Anders Drive.

'Maybe he made that part up.' I spoke slowly to calm her down. 'The words. He could've just said that so we'd think it was Dad.'

Mum answered with a grunt, and for the rest of the drive she was quiet, her face as white as her knuckles on the steering wheel. Her anger slowly leaked away, taking her with it, like a punctured bike tyre, the air slowly escaping until it was just a piece of empty rubber. By the time we'd turned off Boorunga Bridge, the car was practically crawling.

Although I didn't believe in God, I thanked him for letting us make it across our squelchy lawn without anyone jumping out from behind a bush. Mum used her last ounce of energy to pass me the house key. She mumbled to me about Julian's medicine before slinking off to her bedroom, and pulling the door closed behind her.

Julian turned on the TV and stretched out on the floor in front of a movie so old it was in black and white. What would our lives be like in black and white? Things would be simpler.

We'd just be a normal family – two normal kids with two normal parents – and the only people who got dragged off to police stations would be normal 'baddies', the kind with Ned Kelly beards.

I sat on a kitchen stool, staring at the table, listening to the clock tick and the tap drip and the dull sounds of the black and white people talking on TV, trying to imagine Dad in a police cell. By himself. The thought of someone else, a real criminal with massive tattooed arms and fiery eyes, lying on a bunk above him, made my chest ache. I remembered the crushed look on Dad's face when he walked past my classroom back at the start of Term 1. My stupid plan had worked. Well, now I'd have to come up with a smarter one.

I needed a rich person to help us, but the only one I could think of was Katie's dad, Reginald Heller. The gold-trimmed black leather wallet he carried in his suit jacket had paid for practically half of Boorunga. He'd even forked out for the wooden benches that lined our school playground, as Katie was quick to remind us if we refused to share chips or lollies with her. He probably carried thousands of dollars on him in case he spied a business he liked the look of on his way to work. But he was the last person I'd ask for money.

When Katie'd introduced our dads at the Boorunga High fair, Reginald said, 'ugh' through a mouthful of sausage, and Dad told me later that his handshake was as icy as his grey eyes. If Mr Heller considered Dad less important than a fifty-cent sausage, he was hardly going to help us out, especially since Dad was accused of beating up his daughter's boyfriend. Besides, Katie would probably rather her dad killed mine than give him any money. Not that I was going to think about her. If I did, as well as everything else, my head was likely to explode.

Without Dad around, I realised, it was up to me to look after Mum. I had to be the adult. It could be hours, days or weeks before her fog cleared, before she dragged herself out of bed and into the shower, and pasted a lipstick smile on her mouth. I went in and placed a warm flannel on her forehead like Dad had done for Julian the days his cough pinned him to his bed.

Mum's eyes sprang open.

'Sorry,' I said. 'Didn't mean to scare you.'

'Thought you were a bloody photographer!'

'A photographer with a flannel? Is it warm enough? I put it under the hot tap.'

'Thank you.' She tried to smile. 'You know … your dad did a lot for me.'

'He'll be home soon,' my adult voice said. 'Maybe tomorrow. Or the next day.'

'I probably don't always seem grateful.' Mum's eyes were wet. 'I mean, his snoring drives me mad and he's always had trouble with his feet. His left foot stinks worse than his right – he doesn't believe me, but I'm sure of it. But he's a good man. God knows where I'd be if he hadn't talked me into marrying him.'

I nodded. Dad'd always told me Mum was the one with smelly feet – he'd even sprinkled Gran's Remedy Foot Care in her shoes without her knowing so's not to upset her – but I knew better than to mention that.

Mum sat up to clear her throat. 'He needs me – *he* needs *me*! But this problem … this nightmare … I can't see a way out of it.'

Again, I saw Dad walking past my classroom, hunched over, dejected.

Tears were spilling down Mum's face, making shiny squiggles on her dry, paperbark cheeks. I took a step back. This was the same feeling I got seeing the homeless lady cross-legged outside Coles in her long flowery dress caked in dirt, collecting coins in an old cat food tin. I was ready to turn and bolt. I'd rather see Mum's face tight with anger than saggy and sad. Then I wouldn't be expected to do anything except leave her alone. I wouldn't feel so powerless.

'Do you want anything else? More water?' I nodded at her glass. It was a cop-out, but I had to escape before I started blubbing too.

'No, you go. I'm all right.' She sniffed and reached for a tissue.

'You look … not very well.'

'Enough of your flattery.' Mum grimaced. 'Don't worry about me. Go on.'

'I've got a biology thing to do.' I backed away. 'Call out if you need me.'

I'm not sure why I ran – to get away from Mum or because I sensed something was up? I saw my reflection in the blank TV screen and looked around. Julian was folded up in the corner, under the windowsill.

'Jules? What's wrong?'

'Out there.' He pointed a trembling finger at the window.

What now? My heart thump-thumped as I lifted the edge of the curtain, just enough to see two men beside our wattle tree, holding brown paper bags to their mouths. Pies. Men were eating lunch on our lawn! One was bald and dressed in black, the other had a ponytail and ripped jeans. Both looked like they'd already eaten too many pies.

Then I spotted the camera. A monster on a tripod, facing our front door, waiting for my family to step out and onto the front page of *The Boorunga Times*. I dropped the curtain.

A roar of laughter sent goosebumps crawling up my arms. Were they laughing at us? How dare they stuff their faces and make fun of us – in our own yard. What if they wandered around the back where a week's worth of my undies hung on the clothesline?

117

I felt like opening the window and hurling something out – the TV would shut them up – but that was probably what they wanted me to do. And photos of me going crazy certainly wouldn't help Dad. Nor would me killing two fat men with a TV.

It was too risky to sneak down the back steps and grab the undies off the line. Making it into the newspaper with an armful of underwear would kill whatever chances I still had of living a proper life. So I sat at the kitchen table with my biology text book, desperate to ignore them, to do something normal.

But homework seemed more pointless than ever. Would I ever be able to step inside Mr Knowles's classroom again, anyway? Maybe I'd have to go to St Margaret's, the all-girls Catholic school. Judging by the 'St Maggies' on the bus, they only let posh girls in. Then it struck me that everyone in Boorunga would know about Oli and Dad anyway. The St Maggie's snobs were probably already pissing themselves with laughter.

I slammed my book shut. I needed a Plan B.

Katie. Katie was Plan B, my only hope. If she didn't actually hate my guts, if she realised what happened to Oli couldn't possibly have been my fault, perhaps she could talk her dad into lending us some money. For *my* sake, if not Dad's. And if she didn't, if she hung up on me and told the rest of Year 9 I was a filthy beggar, would that be the end of the world? The world had practically ended already.

As I dialled the number I'd known since we became friends in Mrs Hayden's class in Grade 2 – 306 457 – I pictured Katie, her short spiky haircut, her face, as pretty as Molly Ringwald's, except when she did that annoying thing with her tongue when she was thinking. On sticky summer afternoons we'd played hide and seek in the shadows of her enormous house, with her brothers, Kurt and Kyle (the three of them together were 'KKK'

– I never knew if it was a coincidence or her dad's twisted mind). I could only remember one huge argument, about who killed Azaria Chamberlain (Katie swore it was the mum, I blamed the dingo). We gave each other the silent treatment from halfway through recess until the end-of-school bell, but that was the only fight I could think of. Lately though, Katie'd been spending more time with Oli than me, so we didn't share as many secrets as we used to.

'Hello? Katie Heller speaking.'

I swallowed hard. 'Hi … Katie … It's me.'

19

'What do *you* want?' It was Katie, but her voice was wrong. It was the voice she used for shutting up bossy Year 10s or smart-arse boys, not the voice she saved for someone who knew everything about her, including that she wet the bed until she was nearly nine.

I'd deliberately avoided thinking about what Katie'd been going through, or remembering the last time I saw her: Pheebs and Sall holding her up, stopping her from collapsing on the classroom floor. I'd always felt like my brain could only handle so many worrying thoughts before it started shrivelling up like Mum's. But when I heard Katie's voice, her *wrong* voice, a flood of thoughts came rushing in. She'd been Oli's girlfriend for over a year, which is a lifetime when you're forced to sit through six periods of school a day. If she'd been at school on the day of the Rat Incident, she would've taken his side. She would've done anything for him.

'I need to talk to you.' I braced myself.

But then ... nothing. I could hear breathing – did Katie remember Miss Jay's breathing technique too? – but she didn't speak.

'I'm sorry,' I said. 'About. You must ... be ... I should've called before.'

Still nothing. Was she crying?

'But. Well, there's a lot …' My thoughts came out scrambled. 'Oli was, he *is*, he's just so … I mean, I like Oli, I really like him … not like you do, of course. I just –'

'Bitch.' It was just one word, whispered, but it stung like a slap.

'You might. You.' I tried again, struggling not to cry. 'You might think I've got something to do with … *it*, but I –'

'Leave me alone!' Katie spoke louder this time, and in case I didn't get the message, slammed down the phone.

Beep. Beep. Beep. Beep. Beep.

I dropped the phone and leant against the wall, the *beep beep beep* still ringing in my ears.

Then I started laughing. I giggled like the crazy homeless lady who sat outside Coles had done when a man gave her a packet of cigarettes. I let fat tears roll down my cheeks. It felt good to laugh, to be crazy. My best friend hated me. And Plan B had failed. What was going to happen to my family? To me? Would I end up like the homeless lady, pinning all my hopes on a rusty old cat food tin?

'It's over,' I said to the empty hallway, to the faded wallpaper, to the bald patches on the carpet. 'See you later, life.'

I was resting my head on the kitchen table when I heard a knock at the door. The sound of it in our silent house made me shiver. What now?

'Hello, Miracle.'

When I saw Harriet, heard the warmth in her voice, my eyes welled up again. Her smile was enough to make me feel like there was something worth smiling about, that good things might still happen.

'No one's out there?' I looked past her.

'Two men were playing cards in a white van,' she said. 'But

I gave them the look I save for my naughtiest pupils, and they sped off. Were they from the paper?'

I nodded. 'I guess we're famous.'

'Don't waste your twenty minutes of fame on that rubbish paper.' Harriet was carrying a *Choy's Chinese* bag. She stepped inside, the smell of fried rice making my stomach growl.

'It's like an icebox in here!' Harriet shivered. I breathed out a cloud of mist – my own fail-proof temperature test. She was right; it was freezing. I hadn't even noticed.

'Have you been smoking?' she asked. 'You reek.'

'Um, just one.' Actually I'd stubbed it out after a couple of puffs. It made my mouth feel dirty.

'One too many, Miracle. Honestly. Didn't you win the school cross-country?' Harriet gave me one of her concerned looks.

'I didn't know what else to do.' A few tears spilled out. 'Everyone hates me.'

'It might seem like that, but I'm sure they don't.' She squeezed my shoulder. 'I certainly don't!'

'You're not in Year 9 at Boorunga High,' I said.

'Well, I've got an idea that should cheer you up. Your mum's in bed?' She handed me the heavy bag. 'You and Julian start eating. I imagine you're starving.'

While Harriet was in seeing Mum, I called out to Julian then peeled the plastic lids off the hot sticky containers, faint with hunger. I filled a plate with spoonfuls from each and bit into a piece of sweet battered pork, listening to the voices from Mum's bedroom.

'We can sell the cottage,' Harriet was saying. 'That will give you enough –'

'You're not selling your house!'

'I mean the house in Lawson's Bay,' Harriet said. 'We can go without –'

'Don't you dare! I don't need your help.' Mum's voice sounded as weak as her argument.

'Come on, Henrietta. We *want* to help. Why are you being like this?'

'Because I already owe you everything!' Mum shrieked. 'Don't burden me any further.'

'Everything?' Harriet was quiet for a moment. 'Oh, Hen. You would've done the same for me.'

'It would never have happened to you! I was the weak one, *Number Two*.'

Harriet lowered her voice. 'It was a horrible thing – the worst! – but it was a long time ago. You can't let it define you. You can't let *him* win.'

It was a horrible thing? What were they talking about? Who was *him*? And what did he do?

'Don't touch me! I'm not a pet dog,' Mum was saying. 'You can't pat me better!'

'Please don't think you owe me. You need to move on, Hen. It affects everyone when you behave like this, especially now, with this dreadful mix-up with Jim. Did you know Miracle smokes? She was –'

'I'm just saying you're not selling anything on my account. Not over my dead body – and, even then, if you bloody pay for my funeral, I'll come back and haunt you.'

'Stop punishing yourself for –'

'Food.' Julian's voice made me jump. He was wrapped up in his blanket like an Eskimo.

'Have some,' I said. 'I feel sick.'

Julian had nearly finished eating by the time Harriet returned, mascara streaks on her cheeks. She sat in Dad's chair, and made herself smile at us, while her naked lashes blinked away tears.

'Can you both pack some clothes, lovelies?' She snapped the lids back onto the plastic containers.

'Where are we going?'

'You're coming to Lawson's Bay in the morning. With John, Worm and me. Get away for a few days. The fresh air will be good for Julian – and it'll do you good too.'

'What about Mum?' My stomach felt bloated and heavy even though I'd only eaten a couple of mouthfuls. 'And Dad?'

'You can't do anything for your dad right now. If it goes well on Monday he'll be home waiting for you when we get back. I'm sure he'd agree this is a good idea. Your mum wants to stay here. But she'll be fine. It's you who need looking after.'

'I can't go with you.'

'You can, Miri.'

'She needs me.'

'You're fourteen and *you* need someone to look after *you*. Your mum will be fine.'

'How do you know?' Part of me wanted to ask about the *horrible thing*, but the more sensible part really didn't want to know. Not then, anyway. Not with Dad gone, and me being the only 'adult' in our family. What could I do about it anyway? I wasn't especially grown up. I still couldn't shave my legs without nicking myself. I wasn't ready for any more of Mum's problems.

'We'll call her each morning,' Harriet said. 'And I'm sure Mrs Jensen will check in on her if I ask.'

'We can't just leave her!' I looked at Julian to back me up, but he was staring at the table, his mouth stuffed with rice.

'Just until Wednesday, Miracle. John and I can only get a few days off. Otherwise you'll end up as miserable as she is. And how's that going to help anyone?'

'But,' I said, though I couldn't think of any 'but'. Harriet was right. I didn't want to be stuck at home. And we'd never been to Lawson's Bay. Harriet'd invited us every summer since they bought the house, but Mum always said no. She couldn't cope with sleeping in a different bed in a different house, and she hated the ocean. She said the sound of it, the depth of it, the way it stretched out for miles and miles, made her question everything, including the point of her 'tiny life'. I could count the times I'd been to the beach on one hand, and that didn't include my thumb. 'Does she know?'

'Yes. Go on, pack your things. You too, Jules.'

I headed to my room before Harriet saw my eyes and started thinking I was weak too. Although I felt bad for Mum, I wanted to go. Who wouldn't? Being trapped in our house was almost as bad as being stuck in jail, maybe even worse. In jail you wouldn't be surrounded by endless piles of wrinkly clothes waiting for someone to work up the strength to sort, iron and hang on coat hangers. I needed to get out so I could breathe. Besides, Dad would be home on Monday, I was sure of it. The judge would take one look at him and say it was a stupid mistake. He'd yell at the cops for wasting his and Dad's time, and tell Dad how sorry he was about the mix-up. Everything would be back to normal by the time we returned. Oli would be out of hospital and Katie'd be feeling sick with guilt for hanging up on me. One day, maybe in a month or so, I'd even forgive her.

20

'I need to pee,' Worm said, squirming in between Julian and me on the back seat.

Harriet had just announced that we were 'halfway there' – halfway between Mum and Lawson's Bay – and we'd already run out of things to spy with our little eyes.

'Dad, hurry!' Worm's voice was thin.

'I told you not to gulp down the lemonade.' John spun around to glare at Worm, his thick, school principal's glasses slipping down his nose.

'I was thirsty!' Worm started kicking the back of Harriet's seat with his tiny Lightfoot sneakers.

As John pulled over onto a patch of dirt on the roadside, I shuffled away from Worm just in case. I held my breath as he wriggled across my lap and leaped out the door.

'Not on the electric fence, son!' John called, before turning to wink at Julian and me. 'Poor boy will get a shock he'll never forget.'

John's warning backfired: Worm was so scared of the fence he went in his trousers. We had to stop at McDonald's to relieve Worm of his soggy pants and the rest of us of their stink. Because our town didn't have a McDonald's of its own, the Golden Arches had legend status in the school playground. So when John gave into my pleas to stay for lunch, I told him he was my favourite uncle. His face glowed. I didn't have the heart to remind him that he also was my only uncle.

Even Julian's eyes were nearly popping out of his head as he surveyed all the lunch options. While John was helping Worm in the loos, we carried our trays up the sticky stairs, found a table with six stools, and Harriet removed all traces of the previous families' Happy Meals with tissues from her handbag. She sat and stared out the window at the people wandering along the main street below, while Julian and I unwrapped our cheeseburgers with as much enthusiasm as we did our Christmas presents.

'I'm glad you've come away with us.' Harriet looked from me to Julian. 'Even if circumstances aren't … the best. I know it's easy for me to say, but please try to put everything out of your minds. I'll check up on your mum – don't you worry about her – it's far more important that you relax.'

We both nodded, relieved to have her speech out of the way. My burger had a disappointingly rubbery taste, but I told myself it was delicious anyway. Apparently Seth could eat four cheeseburgers, large fries and a chocolate thick shake without throwing up.

'I've got to think about Dad, though.' I flicked two pickles onto the tray. 'We need a plan if they send him to jail.'

Harriet frowned. 'I think it's best if you give yourself a complete break. You'll find it easier to think once you've had some space. Besides, this isn't your problem to fix.'

I shrugged, my mouth full of rubber. To have a 'complete break' I'd need a lobotomy. She also didn't realised that it *was* my problem – that I was responsible for everything.

Once we arrived in Lawson's Bay though, I reckon I went whole hours at a stretch before the bad thoughts came creeping back.

The town – a 'tidy town' a blue sign told us – looked like the setting of an American TV show. Enormous palm trees stood along the centre of the widest main road I'd ever seen. I'd think about those trees later, the way their long, lazy, holiday leaves instantly made me want to kick off my sneakers and socks, stretch out in the sun, and forget Boorunga ever existed.

Harriet and John's 'cottage' was around the same size as our actual house, but the floors were wooden and creaky and there was barely any furniture, so Worm's laughter bounced from room to room. When I stood on tippy-toes on the front veranda, I could see a twinkle of ocean through the gums across the road. I could also sprint from the lawn to the sand without getting a stitch, so the beach couldn't have been more than 200 metres away.

Even though it was winter, my sloppy joe and jeans stayed in the bottom of my backpack. The sun was so bright I was always squinting, and the sharp, salty air stung my nose and made my eyes water, but in a good way. We flip-flopped to the beach each morning, flicking our rubber thongs off when they started sinking into the sand. Diving under the waves sucked our breath away and gave us ice-cream headaches, but that didn't stop us from swimming until our fingertips shrivelled up like sultanas.

In the afternoons, we walked to the Bay Bakery to buy hot meat pies and cream buns, which we ate at the wooden table on the back veranda, without knives and forks. Once we were stuffed full, Worm'd either disappear up the willow tree or to the house next door to play with twin girls who dressed him up in their clothes and tied ribbons in his white curls. Harriet and John stretched out on matching banana chairs, sipping gross-smelling tea and reading books that would've made Mum roll her eyes. Any book that wasn't Mills & Boons made Mum roll her eyes, but these were by Tolstoy and Kafka so her eyes would've practically rolled out of her head. She was like that with things she didn't understand. Unlike Harriet, she'd left school the day she turned fifteen, preferring standing behind a shop counter to sitting behind a desk, so there was a lot she didn't understand. She'd been rolling her eyes at my maths homework ever since I'd learned my twelve times table.

Julian and I stayed inside, usually lying on the sandy rug on the living room floor. I mostly read – I'd started *The Bell Jar* in the car on the way there – while Julian drew. He carried his sketchpad and pencils in a small canvas bag with a skull and crossbones on it to ward off thieves or nosy adults.

When Harriet suggested he draw the view from the veranda, Julian either didn't hear or ignored her. His favourite subject, his *only* subject, was people. Although they all looked as real as him and me, as Harriet, John and Worm, I never recognised a single one. Not back then anyway.

'Who's she?' I asked, as he dotted freckles on a horse-thin face.

'Someone,' Julian said.

'And him?' I pointed to a man with a mullet like Johnny Farnham.

'Someone else.'

'But *who* are they?'

Julian frowned, as if my questions were giving him a headache.

'Do you *know* them, Julian?'

A slight nod, a deeper frown.

I never understood how he invented all these people. Mum said he must've seen them on TV. 'Unless there's a secret life you and I are missing out on.' But I watched many of the same shows as Julian – *Blake's 7*, *V* and *The Goodies* were our top three – and I didn't recognise any of the people he recreated. I decided they must be from his dreams. It was the only explanation I could come up with.

While Julian was giving life to a whole new world, I tried not to let my mind drift to the one we were pretending didn't exist. But the afternoons were too still and quiet for me to keep the thoughts out. There was no TV in the cottage and all of Harriet's phone calls to Mum were made in whispers in the kitchen, so I didn't know what was going on. When I asked Harriet about Dad on Monday night, she said there was 'no change in his situation' after his court appearance, so he was still stuck in the police station. She promised me everything would work out though, and begged me not to think about it until we'd left Lawson's Bay. But that was easy for her to say. She hadn't seen Dad walk down the hall when Constable Kelly came to take him away. She didn't have his crumpled shirt and bare legs – those pale, hairy *guilty*-looking legs – imprinted on her mind. She also said Mum hadn't heard any news of Oli. What if he was awake, and lying in Boorunga Hospital blaming me?

On Monday afternoon, I asked Julian to tear some pages from his pad and pass me a pencil.

Dear Oli
~~I don't know what to say, except that I'm so so sorry about~~
~~I'm so sorry about what~~
~~I didn't find your note in my bag until~~

Julian looked up when I scrunched up the piece of paper. Even if Oli was awake, would he be well enough to read? I pictured his mum frowning, jaw clenched, as she glared at my handwriting, at my weak attempt to explain myself. She'd probably rip the letter into a thousand pieces – or send it to Miss Jones to read out at school assembly. I decided to try Katie instead.

Dear KT,

Before you chuck this in the bin, remember these things:

- *Even though you've spent most lunchtimes with Oli this year, we've been best friends since Mrs Hayden's class, which was 7 years ago.*
- *We only let Pheebs and Sall hang out with us so we could read Pheebs's Dolly magazines at recess and we didn't want to discriminate against Sall because she's fat.*
- *I've always kept your secrets to myself (even the one about you know who).*

So you owe it to me to read this! I need you to understand that Dad had nothing to do with what happened to Oli. He'd never hurt anyone – surely you know that?

Also, you must've heard what Seth and Oli did to me? Pheebs and Sall thought it was the funniest thing ever, which made me question the value of Pheebs's Dollys in the first place. Where were you that day anyway? You're never sick!

I'm writing this from Lawson's Bay – long story – but I'll be back on Wednesday, so please write back and put it in my letter box. I'm begging you – literally (I'm actually writing this on my knees!).

Love from your friend always,
Miri xxxxoooo

'Come for a walk to the post office, Jules?'

When Julian didn't answer, I realised he was asleep, his head slumped over a half-finished face. I crept out of the room, borrowed a thirty-three-cent stamp from John and walked to the post office alone.

That wasn't the first time Julian had fallen asleep mid-person. He'd done it a few times at home too. He'd then wake with a jolt, pick up his pencil and take up where he'd left off. I'd thought he was just tired, that the sickness was still sapping

him. On our last night in Lawson's Bay, I discovered the real
reason.

Julian and I were sharing Worm's bedroom, and Worm was
in with Harriet and John (Harriet said he was always 'worming'
his way into their bed at home anyway). We'd gone to bed late,
after John and Worm won Monopoly. They didn't deserve it –
we'd busted Worm stealing money from the bank twice – but I
knew better than to argue with a five-year-old.

That night a scraping sound woke me. I propped myself up.
The window was gaping open like a giant yawn. A cool breeze
floated through the bedroom, as the plastic blinds flapped and
scraped against the window frame. I made out a mound of
blankets and sheets on the other bed. But no Julian.

'Jules,' I whispered, leaning out the window into the dark. In
daylight, you could see the ocean stretching out forever, maybe
as far as New Zealand. But now, swaying willow branches
formed tree-ghosts and the sea was slick, black, menacing. As
the town slept, the ocean was more alive than ever, with the roar
of waves smashing over rocks. I shivered in my thin nightie.

I climbed back into the warm bed and waited, listening to
the rage of the waves. I'd give Julian time – a few minutes, then
a few more – before waking Harriet and John. They'd freak out
for sure.

I must've fallen asleep because then I heard Julian wheezing.
He tiptoed across the floor, unzipped his Adidas tracksuit top and
peeled off his jeans. Underneath were his blue striped pyjamas.

'Shhh,' he said when I sat up.

'Where were you?'

'Walking.'

'Weren't you scared?'

'No.'

'But it's creepy out there.'

Julian yawned.

'Have you done it before?'

'Yes.'

'Where do you go?'

He shrugged. 'Anywhere.'

'Well, you shouldn't. Not in the dark. In the dark people get murdered.'

He shook his head. 'Peaceful.'

He'd turned his back to me, blankets pulled over his head. *Peaceful*. That made sense. While some kids had problems with peanuts or eggs, Julian was 'allergic' to loud noise. On his first day at preschool, he found 'dance time' so terrifying he climbed out the classroom window. When Mrs Muir finally found him in the trike shed twenty minutes later, he was curled up behind a plastic tractor, still shaking and wheezing. Boorunga Preschool was probably the only preschool in the world to ban "Dinosaur Stomp".

I was the opposite; silence scared me. It made my thoughts too loud. I'd rather do anything, even kiss Seth Boston, than walk the streets on my own in the dark. How come Julian was so brave? Was it because he'd practically died once already?

The dread I felt that night didn't spoil the magic of those few days. I daydreamed about staying in Lawson's Bay forever, and becoming the mysterious 'new girl' at Lawson's Bay High. A school by the sea could never be boring. Even maths might be interesting. Besides, the only thing separating its sun-drenched classrooms from the beach was a small metal fence, which you could easily jump over. Even though I hadn't got beyond catching knee-high waves on Worm's boogie board, I imagined myself becoming a champion surfer. I'd win a medal, be on the *Six O'Clock News*, and all the kids from Boorunga High would wish they'd been my best friend.

I knew Julian wanted to stay too. I lost count of the times I caught him smiling. It was as if the sun'd dried out his lungs, the waves swept away his cough, as if he'd never been sick at all.

But on Wednesday it was back to reality: time to tidy the cottage, sweep the sand out the back door and off the veranda, cram our bags into the car boot. I climbed on the veranda railing and took photos of the sea in my mind to look through when I got home.

Once the palm trees were reduced to tiny specks in the car's back window, I was ready.

'Can you tell us about Dad now?' I asked. 'What happened in court?'

Harriet looked over at John, whose nod told her it was time to spill the beans.

'Your mum didn't know all the details.' Harriet strained her neck to look at me. 'But he's been remanded in custody until the next court date.'

'So … he's already in jail?' My heart was pounding.

'No, they're just keeping him at the station.'

'Because they don't really think he did it?'

'Because … the remand centre in Henley is too full,' Harriet said. 'But only until the ninth. Then he goes back to court.'

The *ninth*. A whole week away.

I stared out the window, no longer able to look at Harriet's face, at the pity in her eyes.

As we approached the 'Boorunga 20 km' sign, I noticed the dark grey cloud ahead, like a big smudge of dirt in the sky. My heart sank at the thought of returning to a dreary, wet day.

'I spy with *my* little eye.' Worm touched his eye. His nose had a new set of freckles and he smelt like the sea.

'Something beginning with … s.'

'Sky,' Julian whispered.

'No, dummy!' Worm pointed at the grey cloud with one hand and dug his asthma inhaler out of Harriet's handbag with the other. 'Smoke.'

'They're just clouds.' I elbowed Worm.

But when we drove into Boorunga, past the BP and Shell stations, the tile shop and Plumber's World, the roads were dry, the footpaths dusty. I spun around and looked out the back window, searching for the brilliant blue sky we'd left behind, but it was gone. As if God had thrown a blanket of dreariness over our town. Welcome home, I thought, closing my eyes so I wouldn't cry.

21

It hit me as soon as I opened the car door.

Harriet screwed up her nose as she stepped onto our driveway. 'Unbelievable. We should just move to Lawson's Bay.'

Julian inched across the back seat with about as much enthusiasm as I felt, tossing his satchel out of the car ahead of him. It landed with a *pfft* on our shaggy lawn.

'Poo-ey!' Worm said, throwing Optimus Prime – his latest toy and best friend – into the air. 'It stinks!'

'Jump back in, Worm,' John said from the car. 'Keep me company.'

'I don't want them to go!' Worm scooped up Optimus Prime from the grass. 'I want to beat them at Monopoly.'

'Hop in now, son, and put your seatbelt on. You'll see them again soon.'

'Bye, Worm.' I tucked his feet inside the car before shutting the door.

I wanted to climb in after Worm and tell John to drive away to the furthest place he could think of. The only thing stopping me was the thought of what might be waiting for me in our letter box. If Katie was a true friend, she would've quickly scribbled an answer to my letter and delivered it herself before I got home.

My fingers shook as I pulled out the wad of paper wedged between Stan's teeth. (Dad'd built our letter box with beer bottle top eyes, painted giant teeth around the slot, and called it Stan.) I separated the letters from the Kmart brochure, Twirly Swirl discount vouchers, and a flyer for Year 12's Great Quake Debate, which I screwed up and shoved in my pocket.

There were several of the long, important-looking envelopes Mum usually tossed onto the kitchen table as if they were paper-thin bombs, but my heart still ba-boom ba-boomed as I flicked through them. *Mr and Mrs James Jamieson. Mr James Jamieson. Mr and Mrs James Jamieson.* Nothing in Katie's handwriting, nothing for me. I punched Stan's wooden head before stuffing everything back inside it. Katie wasn't going to help me.

'They've been here again.' Harriet reached into the lavender bush and pulled out a yellow Chicken Twisties packet. 'How dare they leave a mess! I should write a letter to their silly newspaper.'

'They're pigs,' I said, remembering the two fat men in black, stuffing their faces in our yard as if we'd invited them to a barbecue.

Stepping into the dark hallway, I choked on another smell: a combination of cigarette smoke, rotten fruit, bed breath, and something else, something sour. Vomit. I leant against the wall, readying myself.

'We're fine now.' I stepped in front of Harriet, blocking her path inside. 'Thanks for taking us on holiday.'

'I'll say a quick hello.' She gently pushed past me and into the stench.

Although it'd only been a few days, it was like seeing our house for the first time. Most of our furniture once belonged to Granny Holmes and might've even been modern when she was alive, but now every chair had at least one wobbly leg and practically every flat surface had the shape of an iron burnt into it.

Cupboard doors creaked or hung off their hinges and the sad, saggy brown couch had dips in it from the hours, days, years Mum and Dad had spent sitting, staring at the tiny black and white TV, or 'idiot box' as Dad fondly called it. There were bald patches on the carpet from Mum's constant pacing, the green wallpaper was curling back at the edges, and stuff was everywhere – magazines, Mills & Boons, tools, old irons, ironing board skeletons – all of it covered in dust because Mum'd broken our feather duster in half, yelling that the damned thing made her sneeze.

I yanked open the heavy living room curtains, which Mum liked to keep closed, saying the sun bored through her skull, and swept a thick layer of dust off the windowsill with my fingers.

'Henrietta?' Harriet tapped lightly on Mum's door. 'We're here. We were lucky with the traffic.'

Julian and I stood in the living room, strangers in our own house. Mrs Taylor's cream slacks lay crumpled on the ironing board. I hated those slacks; Mum'd ironed them each summer for as long as I could remember. One day I'd drawn a star in blue Texta on one of the legs, and Mum acted like I'd burnt the house down. She didn't care that I was just trying to brighten them up; she said I could bloody well count my lucky stars that they were inside out. She didn't even smile when I pointed out the 'one lucky star'.

'They know!' Mum's voice made me jump.

'Sorry?' Harriet was still outside Mum's door. 'Hen, your kids are home. Julian is looking so much better. You should've seen him in the ocean. Swimming like –'

'They'll never let him out.'

'What are you saying? Why?'

'They know what he did before.'

'Oh Hen, that was a long time ago and –'

'He'll go to prison. We'll never see him again.'

'Hen, how much have you had to drink?'

'We'll lose everything – the house, my *bed* …'

Harriet opened Mum's door, went in. 'He hasn't been found guilty,' she said quietly. 'Aren't you going to say hello to Julian and Miracle?'

What was a long time ago? I looked at Julian, but he was staring at the floor. What had Dad done before?

'What do you want me to say to them?' Mum said. '"Hello, kids. Don't bother unpacking your bags, we're homeless now"?'

'Calm down, Hen! Did Joan pop in? She assured me she would.'

'Joan? Oh yes, indeed.' Mum's voice changed. 'Joany Joan brought me vodka, but she was very upset about it – said I *pressured* her – and that I'd better not tell you. Oops.'

'Okay, well. I'll take the kids home with me for now.' Harriet spoke gently but I could tell she was angry. 'I'll get you a drink and let some fresh air in. Honestly, Hen. This place is … Well, right now, it's a bloody dump.'

Harriet didn't look at us as she marched past and into the kitchen. I tried to open the living room window, but it wouldn't budge. I guess it'd just got used to being shut.

'My husband's a bloody crim and he's abandoned me,' Mum called out. 'What do you expect?'

Harriet carried Dad's beer glass, filled to the top with lemonade, towards Mum's room. Her face was wrinkled with worry.

'Drink this and get some sleep, Hen,' she said. 'We'll see you soon.'

We picked up our bags and followed Harriet back out into the hazy, grey day. I did my best to ignore the sick feeling in my stomach, the hot dread that moved up my body when I thought about Mum staying on alone in the house. I didn't even poke my head in, or call out on my way past. What was the point of saying goodbye if I hadn't even said hello?

Instead, I filed Mum's words to make sense of later. I didn't know whether it was tiredness from the long hours in the car squashed up with Worm asleep on my lap, hearing about Dad being stuck at the station until God knows when, the disappointment of not finding a letter from Katie, or the shock of seeing our house with fresh, holiday eyes, but I just didn't have the energy to care.

Harriet was looking over at Mrs Jensen-from-across-the-road's house.

'Poor Joan,' she said. 'I never should have asked.'

This time Mrs Jensen's round outline wasn't visible from behind the curtains.

'Yippee!' Worm said, as we climbed into the car. No one else said a thing.

John and Worm were the only ones to leave the house the next morning. I overheard Harriet on the phone, asking if she could take a day's 'compassionate leave' to look after her niece and nephew. She sounded annoyed when adding, 'Yes, Liz, my sister's children. Please mark Julian absent too.' She then rang my school and said I needed to stay home 'for family reasons'.

Harriet didn't think the photographers would bother us, but asked us to keep the drapes closed and not leave the house, just to be safe. Dull clouds sulked over the skylight in the bathroom anyway, so I didn't mind being trapped inside. I'd also been awake until after 1 am, rewinding and replaying Mum's words.

'What was Mum talking about yesterday?' I asked Harriet as she handed me a plate of Vegemite toast. 'Why was she saying they'll never let Dad out?'

'She was talking nonsense, Miri,' Harriet said quickly. 'I guess you know she'd been drinking?'

I nodded, tearing the crusts off my toast.

'She was catastrophising. Don't take any notice. Jim will get out – I'm sure of it.'

'But he won't be able to keep working at the crem. Greg thinks he did it.'

'It might be a while before things go back to normal, but it'll be okay.'

Harriet had a way of making me feel everything was going to work out. I decided to believe her for now.

'What about Oli?' I asked. 'Have you heard anything? Is he out of hospital yet?'

Harriet looked up from *The Sydney Morning Herald* and poured milk into her cup of tea. 'I'm sure we would've heard if there'd been any change. But I have a good feeling about him too.'

That was all I needed to hear. I could park my worries about Oli for a while and concentrate all my energy on Mum. I'd make a plan in case it was a while before Dad was released. Katie had deserted me, but I wouldn't think about that. I'd focus on developing Plan C.

Morning drifted into afternoon. Julian and I were flicking through magazines from the stack on Harriet and John's glass coffee table.

'Dad could be stuck at the station for a while,' I said. 'We need to do *something*.'

Julian looked up. 'Break in?'

He often surprised me, and this was one of those times. To look at him – at his wide, blue eyes and angel face – anyone'd think he was a goody-two-shoes. Suggesting we break in to the cop station wasn't the first time I wondered what was really going on inside his head.

'People only do that in movies,' I said. 'And they usually get caught.'

Julian shrugged, kept staring at the magazine on his lap.

I studied the photo hanging above the TV: Harriet, John and Worm when he still had all his baby teeth. I searched my memory for a photo of our family sitting together, all smiles, but I didn't find anything. Maybe that was something we could do when Dad came home. Harriet could bring her camera to our house and I'd say something to make Mum laugh, so she'd show all her teeth in a big open-mouthed smile. I probably should buy her some smoker's toothpaste first though. Or get Harriet to use her black and white camera.

I sighed, stretching out on the couch, and knocked Julian's sketchpad onto the carpet. My mind wandered back to Mum's words: *Don't bother unpacking your bags, we're homeless now.*

'We need money. Jules, where can we get money?'

'Harriet?'

'Mum's already said no. We need to get it another way.'

I looked at Julian's open sketchpad, at a man's face, at his beard and frowning mono-brow.

'There has to be another way,' I said, studying the face, the nose squashed like a pug's.

That's when the idea crept into my mind. 'You've got a special talent.'

Julian pretended to be deaf.

'Everyone thinks your drawings are amazing.' The room tilted, as I quickly sat up. 'What if … we sold your drawings?

Julian turned the page of the magazine on his lap.

'We could set up a stall.' My mind started racing. 'Not in Boorunga, not where the photographers are – and kids from school. We could go somewhere else. To … Henley? That's not far. On the train … so Harriet and John won't know.'

'Mine.' Julian pointed his foot at the sketchpad.

'We won't sell those,' I said. 'You can draw people who walk past. People do that. I saw it in Sydney, on our school excursion to The Rocks. You draw portraits of people, and they pay you for it.'

Julian looked down at the carpet, his long dark eyelashes resting on his cheeks.

'You're not keen?'

He shrugged.

'We mightn't make much at first, but if it works, we could go to other towns, build up a bit of a business. Then maybe a bank will give us a loan.' I'd heard at least some of what Mr Borris tried to teach us in commerce.

Julian nodded, still avoiding my eyes.

'Well, unless you've got another plan, this … this could work. You're a better artist than the hippie in Sydney and you're fast too … what's wrong?'

Julian lifted his legs, hugged his knees.

'Don't be scared. I'll be there too. I'll organise everything – I'll talk to the people and handle the money. All you need to do is draw.'

'Miracle? Julian?' Harriet called from the front door. 'Can you give me a hand with the groceries, please?'

'Tomorrow?' I said, getting up. 'If Harriet goes back to work?'

Julian nodded as he dropped the magazine and climbed off the couch. It was a slow nod – a nod that suggested he hoped I'd forget all about it – but still a nod.

I was so relieved I could barely eat lunch, even though it was bacon, tomatoes and scrambled eggs on toast with orange juice. Bacon only ever made it onto Dad's shopping list at Christmas and Mum always said only rich people bought orange juice.

While I was washing the dishes, Harriet dialled our phone number. She didn't ask if I wanted to say hello and I didn't ask if I could. I was so excited about my plan that I didn't want to hear Mum's voice; I didn't want to risk her bringing me down.

Afterwards, Harriet hung up. 'Your mum says hi.'

'She okay?'

'Well, she's not a ray of sunshine, but at least she's talking sense. She's had a shower.'

I pictured Mum in Dad's old brown dressing gown, with a musty stink from being stuffed at the back of the wardrobe all summer. She wore it draped over her shoulders, her hair fluffed up like a cloud. *Hang in there Mum. I'm going to help you – just hold it together for a bit longer.*

'She said Greg Parker's daughter rang,' Harriet added, pulling a tea towel out of a drawer.

'Livvy?' Livvy had called! She didn't think we were a bunch of freaks?

'Yes, Livvy – pretty name, isn't it? I was going to call Worm – *William* – Olivia if he was a girl. Your mum said Livvy apologised for Greg's rudeness. She said he gets like that when he's stressed, but she felt awful. Couldn't sleep apparently. What did he say exactly?'

'Um.' I didn't want to revisit our meeting at the café. 'Well, he thinks Dad … did it. And he said Mum wouldn't know because of those pills she takes. Something like that.' The words he'd accused Dad of spray painting – *Stay away from my girl* – swam around in my head. I didn't want to say them out loud, to make them real.

'He's obviously a poor judge of character, and very cruel.' Harriet shook the suds off the fry pan. 'I met him at the P & F Christmas function. He was very friendly – almost *too* friendly. Can't say I warmed to him. His handshake was a little … off.'

'I don't know how Dad works for him. He gives me the creeps.'

'Livvy sounds nice though,' Harriet said. 'He must be doing something right.'

Thinking about Livvy made my breathing speed up, like I was having a heart attack, but a good one, if there was such a thing. She thought well enough of me to call our house? I wanted to hold that thought and turn it around in my head, to look at it from all angles. Did she actually think I was okay? Even after meeting Mum and attempting to talk to Julian? Even after we'd practically begged for money, all three of us looking even more pathetic than usual, rain dripping from our hair and our cheap Kmart clothes clinging to our shivering bodies? Even after her evil dad threw back his head and laughed at us? Maybe I'd call her back. Would I have enough guts to do that? Perhaps once Julian and I had been to Henley and made some money. I'd have something to impress her with then. She might see that I wasn't quite as mental as the rest of my family.

'I'll need to go to school tomorrow, before Mrs Dodd has a nervous breakdown,' Harriet said. 'But your mum agreed it's best you two stay here until things die down a bit. That okay with you?'

'Yep, we'll be fine on our own.'

'If Julian has a … funny turn, you'll call the school immediately?'

'Yes, yes. I know what to do anyway. He'll be okay.'

I tried not to sound excited. At last, things were going my way.

22

As soon as we heard the Mazda reverse out of the driveway, we leapt into action, grabbing my backpack stuffed with Julian's art gear, our sneakers, jackets and beanies. We sprinted up the road and across Boorunga Heights Park, running side by side, hoods over heads, eyes on the ground, Julian wheezing in whispers. Crazy Joey, Boorunga's homeless man, tried to catch up to us for a while, waving his holey Australian flag as he wobbled along on drunken legs, but by the time we made it to the train station, he was just a blur of blue and red.

Although Henley was only half an hour away by train, I'd gone there only three times before – twice for interschool cross-country and once to see an old school friend of Dad's whose wife'd died in the earthquake. The town was considered 'blessed' in the earthquake, with only a few houses collapsing, all on the same street (Dad's friend was one of the unblessed ones). At school we learned that the mayor had declared it a 'pornography-free zone', even though it had more strip clubs than corner shops, and that it had a big problem with heroin.

As soon as we jumped onto the platform at Henley station, a man stepped in front of us.

'Got any spare change?' His warm breath in my face.

His T-shirt and jeans looked like they'd never seen the

inside of a washing machine, and dirt lined the cracks in his dry, bare feet. I felt my breakfast rising in my throat.

We shook our heads and quickly walked away, crunching through broken beer bottles. The picture I'd built up in my mind – of us catching the train home with a backpack full of five-dollar notes – quickly faded. But the next town was an hour away, so there was no way we could make it there and back before Harriet and John got home. I gave Julian what I hoped was a smile. I wasn't giving up.

The last time I'd been to Henley with the cross-country team, we'd raced out of the train station and up the road to the steps of the church hall. I remember leaving Jessie Smith for dead on the steps, then leaning against the hall doors to catch my breath.

As Julian and I walked past the church hall, a few empty two-dollar shops and 'everything half price' chemists, I noticed the blue of the sky, a proper blue, the colour of Julian's eyes, and his 'azure' pencil. The sun was up – right in the middle of it – but it wasn't strong enough to reach through my jacket. I walked faster to stop my teeth chattering.

When I saw the Henley Mall sign, my hope surged. The glass doors slid open and welcomed us with warmth. Inside was a Woolies, Grace Bros, Fosseys, Best&Less, food court and, best of all, people. People who wouldn't know us.

'This is perfect, Jules.' I threw my jacket onto an empty bench outside Woolies. 'What do you think?'

He shrugged, sliding the backpack off his shoulder.

We ignored the stares as we propped up our '*Your portrait – just $5*' sign on the bench, and, next to it, two of Julian's drawings glued onto black cardboard, one of a boy wearing an Adidas cap, the other an old lady with heavily lined skin.

Then we sat, waiting for customers to line up. I studied the white speckled floor, dirtied by the soles of thousands of strangers' shoes. I breathed deeply, trying to kill my nerves.

People, mums mostly, walked in and out of Woolies, some looking at us like we'd escaped from the zoo, others too busy reading shopping lists to notice us. I guessed buying a portrait wasn't at the top of anyone's list. Or even at the bottom. Tourists were the kind of people we needed. Loads of tourists lined up for portraits in Sydney. But tourists were even less likely to holiday in Henley than to spend a week running from Crazy Joe in Boorunga. Why did Henley have to be our closest town? It had a high unemployment rate. If I'd thought about that properly I would've realised that anyone lucky enough to have five dollars in their pocket probably needed it to buy bread and milk. Or Diet Coke, as one woman had – I counted five bottles in her trolley as she passed us, saying, 'You should be in school!'

'Do your parents know what you're up to?' an old man asked. His voice was friendly and he winked, but didn't stop to ask for his portrait.

'Aren't you the girl who …?'

I slowly lifted my eyes from the floor and saw a woman spilling out of a denim mini skirt.

'Didn't they take your daddy away?' she continued. Her hair was a replica of our cobweb broom, dyed pink.

How did she know? Was she from Boorunga? Surely the people of Henley weren't so desperate for something to do that they read *The Boorunga Times*?

I glared at her. 'Aren't you the woman whose skirt is too tight? *You* should be put away.'

She looked down at her skirt, at her enormous, white, jelly legs.

'Sorry.' I'm not sure she heard me. I almost wish she'd yelled something back instead of slowly turning around and lumbering away, leaving me with a heavy feeling in my stomach.

'What a beautiful boy. Is he real?'

This came from a woman around Mrs Jensen-from-across-the-road's age, which was somewhere between eighty and one hundred and fifty. Julian focused on chewing his fingernails, but I smiled, ignoring her question.

'Would you like to see him draw?' I stood, wiping my sweaty palms on my jeans, preparing to deliver the sales pitch I'd rehearsed in bed the night before.

'Thanks, love. I'd rather just look at him if you don't mind. He's pretty as a picture.'

I couldn't decide whether she was slightly mental or creepy, but I felt light with relief when she finally shuffled away. We didn't need her scaring off real customers. I checked my watch and tried to calculate how long it'd take to make enough to cover our monthly mortgage payment, which I guessed was around five-hundred dollars. 'A million years' was my answer. I was as bad at maths as I was at making money.

My stomach rumbled with hunger as half an hour crawled past.

But then, just as if we'd said a prayer and God'd actually listened, a woman walked up to us, and not by accident. Our first customer! She wore enough make-up for ten customers, her lips thick with hot pink lipstick, which might've looked passable if she wasn't wearing a beetroot-coloured lacy top. She chewed gum like it was her first meal in days, and held the hand of a girl younger than Worm. I wondered if she was a stripper from one of the clubs Henley was famous for. I'd be okay with that. Strippers needed money too, and maybe taking her clothes off was the only thing she was good at.

'You can draw like that?' She pointed a sharp, black fingernail at our display.

'He's very talented.' I tried not to sound desperate.

'We've got ten minutes before my ex picks her up.' She pushed the girl forward. 'Can you draw Maddison? It'll keep me company while she's gone.'

'Not going!' Maddison screwed up her face, wringing tears out of her sulky eyes.

'Yes! Julian can draw her in nine minutes, maybe eight,' I said. 'Can you sit down here please, Maddison?' I took the girl's warm, sticky hand and sat her on the bench facing Julian. I hoped he wouldn't draw her too accurately. She badly needed a nose wipe.

'How come youse aren't at school?' the woman asked, as Julian studied Maddison, twiddling his pencil.

It was a question I'd prepared for. 'It's our commerce project. We've turned art into a small business.'

'They never let us out of the gate when I was at school.' The woman chewed noisily, as she tried to think back a billion years. 'Probably knew what we'd get up to … hey? What's wrong with your boyfriend? He got the DTs?'

'He's not my – Jules? What's wrong?'

Julian's face was as white as the paper, and his whole body was shaking, his HB pencil scribbling all over the page.

'What's he doing?' The woman stepped towards Maddison. 'He having a fit?'

I grabbed Julian's arms, holding them tight, trying to still them.

'No, he has a … condition. He's okay. Aren't you, Julian?' My mouth felt dry, and the mall's fluorescent lighting suddenly seemed too bright. I stared at the sketchpad, at the 'portrait': a tornado of grey circles leading to a black hole where the pencil had stabbed through the paper.

'Come on, Jules.' I released his left arm, then the right. 'That was a practice. Have another go.'

Julian bowed his head. A tear dripped onto his jeans, then another and another.

'You're taking the piss! He can't draw for shit!' Maddison's mum said. 'He on drugs too?'

'No! He *can*. He just hasn't done it like this before. I'm sorry.'

'*School project*, my arse! You're con artists. I'm not paying you a cent.'

Maddison's wet eyes were now almost as wide as her gaping mouth, as if this was the most fascinating thing she'd ever seen. But then her mum grabbed her arm, practically pulling it out of its socket, and she blubbed, 'No no no!' as she was dragged towards the food court.

I'd love to say I ran after them and yelled, 'Dirty stripper!' so loudly everyone in the food court looked up from their greasy, plastic plates. But I did nothing. I felt too angry to move. I was angry at Maddison's mum, angry at my plan, angry we'd spent more money paying for the train (total of six dollars) than we'd made (none). I wanted to scream at the people walking past with nothing better to do than look at us, at the boring mall with its filthy floor, at the world. Instead, I took a deep breath. *In out*. Another. *In out. In out.*

'Okay.' I stood. 'Want to go?'

Julian nodded, big tears now plopping onto his sketchpad, soaking into the paper.

'Audrey!'

An old man in a black hat stood stooped in front of us. He seemed to be talking to Julian's drawing of the old lady with the crinkly face.

'There you are, Audrey!' He *was* talking to the picture, I realised, goosebumps spreading up my arms. 'Have you seen my keys? They were in my suit pocket this morning, but now I can't find them.'

The man noticed Julian and me. 'You've met Audrey?' His eyes looked empty, like a blind person's. 'I can't find my keys.'

Julian handed the drawing to him.

'You can keep her,' I said.

'Yes, yes, Audrey's mine.' The man tucked the drawing under his arm as if he'd been carrying it all along. 'You haven't seen my keys?'

'No, sorry.' I scanned the floor in case he'd just dropped them.

'Audrey?' I whispered to Julian, as the man hobbled away.

Julian shrugged, not looking at me.

'This was a really dumb idea.' I started stuffing our things into my backpack. 'Let's get out of here.'

23

We were watching TV when we heard Harriet's car in the driveway. Car doors banged, the front door flew open, and Worm raced in, jumping into the beanbag next to me.

'Monkey magic!' he said to the TV.

'Made it home before the rain.' Harriet's voice came from behind a stack of coloured manila folders. 'I hope you didn't get too bored?'

I shrugged. 'It was okay.'

I think we did a convincing job of looking relaxed, but my heart was thumping so hard Harriet had to ask me twice to help her get tea ready.

I should've been relieved we'd made it back without getting busted. But my plan had been a big fat failure. A demented old man had ended up with Julian's picture of 'Audrey' and we'd ended up with nothing.

Half an hour later, I carried the bowls to the table, one at a time so my hands didn't burn, Harriet turned the TV off and we all sat at our places.

'Where's Dad?' Worm asked, nodding at John's bowl, covered with a saucepan lid.

I knew John was late because Harriet kept looking at her watch, but she said she was sure he wasn't far away, and asked me why I wasn't eating my spaghetti bolognaise.

'Sore stomach.' It was true and I didn't even have my period. My stomach felt heavy. Worm and Julian's slurping made me queasy. I stirred the spaghetti and mince around my bowl.

I wondered what was going on at home, imagining our house, cold, dark and silent, except for Mum's cough and her slippers scuffing along the hallway.

'Mandy Jarvis has nits,' Worm said. 'She got them off Tom.'

'Again?' Harriet bent for a piece of spaghetti Worm dropped on the floor. 'Does Miss Kelly know?'

Worm shook his head. 'Mandy said not to tell.'

By the time John walked in, Julian was spooning more ice cream into his bowl and Worm's face was more chocolate ice cream than skin.

Worm leapt off his chair and wrapped his pudgy arms around John's legs. 'Dad! Dad!'

'Hey, son. Please keep your face off my good suit.' John lifted Worm and carried him back to his chair. John's head was shining and his jacket was rain-splotched.

He dried his glasses, put them back on and looked at me and Julian.

'I've just been to see your dad.'

'He's home?' I jumped up, my heart nearly bursting out of my chest.

'Ah, no. I've just been to the police station.'

'Oh.' I sat back down. Of course.

John loosened his tie. 'But he's fine. He's doing remarkably well. When I arrived, he was sharing a pizza with another bloke. They offered me a slice but I knew better than to ruin my appetite.' He winked at Harriet.

'John. Please be serious,' Harriet said.

John rubbed his head; it looked slippery in the yellow dining room light and I found myself wanting to touch it. 'I'm just reassuring you all that Jim's holding up well. The room he's in,

154

I guess you'd call it a cell, but it's clean and quite homely. He's sharing with a half-decent bloke who hasn't paid his parking fines for thirteen years – figured he'd rather do time in a cell than pay six hundred dollars.'

'When's Dad getting out?' It was great news he wasn't sharing a bunk with a mass murderer, but he was still locked up.

'I can't answer that, love,' John said. 'He's going to court again next Wednesday. They may well say he can go home that day.'

'But what if they don't?' I asked.

'Well, at the moment …' John removed his glasses. His eyes looked exposed, naked. I turned away. 'I'm thinking he might be better off in there.'

'How can you say that?' Harriet folded her arms, her classic school teacher pose.

'Just for now. For his safety. Harriet, this is bigger than … It's huge! People are outside the station, and they're angry. You should hear what they're saying. It's ugly out there.'

'I overheard talk in the staffroom.' Harriet clipped the lid back on the ice cream. 'Some of the younger teachers. I hoped it was just gossip. How did you get past? You didn't get … they didn't say anything to you?'

John sat down at the table, even though his clothes were still wet. 'One young man – not the brightest of sparks – told me I should be ashamed of myself for visiting, and there were one or two nasty comments, but many of them were former students. I'm pretty safe.'

'So what can we do?' Harriet said. 'What can I tell Hen to get her out of bed?'

John sighed and lifted the lid off his bowl. 'I'm not sure. She could visit, but she'd probably need a police escort.'

Harriet winced. 'I doubt she'd be up for that.'

'Us?' Julian said.

'Yeah. Can we go?' I asked. 'Can we visit?'

'Me too!' Worm said. 'I want pizza.'

Harriet and John looked at each other in that way adults do when they're about to say no.

'It's not a good idea.' John patted Julian's shoulder. 'Not at this stage. The atmosphere out there – it's no place for you two.'

'But he is their father,' Harriet said.

'Yes, and believe me, it'd break their hearts,' John said softly. His words made my eyes fill up, but I blinked back the tears. I wasn't going to cry, I was going to do something. Anything.

'I want to see Oli then. Can I go to the hospital?' Even as I was saying the words, they surprised me. Where did they come from? Did I really want to see Oli? To look at him in a hospital bed?

As I was speaking, Julian's glass tipped over, a tidal wave of juice flooding the tablecloth.

'He's having an earthquake!' Worm cried.

Julian was shaking, worse than he had in Henley, worse than I'd ever seen, the legs of his chair thumping like our washing machine stuffed with too many sheets. I watched, too scared to react, to move.

Harriet and John both froze for a few seconds too – as if someone'd pressed pause on the world – but then they leapt up, chairs squealing on the floorboards, and they grabbed Julian, Harriet holding his shoulders and John his wrists.

'It's okay, Julian,' Harriet said. 'Everything will be all right. Your dad will be fine.'

But Julian was staring at me and I got a feeling it wasn't Dad being in jail that was bothering him. I searched his face, but his wide, blue eyes might as well have been made of glass. They didn't tell me anything.

'Sweet boy.' Harriet kissed Julian's head. 'He'll be home soon. Just you see.'

Julian's shaking gradually slowed, and then, finally, he was calm again, his breathing steady. He wiped his forehead with his sleeve. His skin was so pale and perfectly smooth, like Harriet's porcelain tea cups. There was no hint of fuzz on his top lip like other sixteen-year-old boys had, no freckles or pimples like the ones I swore at in the mirror. That crazy old lady in the mall was right – sometimes he did look too good to be real.

He stood up and stepped away from Harriet and John. 'Bed,' he whispered.

'Good night!' Harriet called after him.

'Night, Julian,' John said to the table. 'Poor kid.'

'My head's itchy!' Worm said. 'Can I have more ice cream?'

'No, you can get ready for your bath,' Harriet said. 'We'll give your hair a wash.'

'But why can't I have a shower?' Worm whined, sliding off his chair.

'That gave me a fright,' Harriet said, once Worm was out of earshot. 'No wonder your mum's so … on edge.'

'He's not usually that bad.' I wondered again what the trigger was. Did the word 'hospital' set him off? Did it remind him of what happened when he was a baby?

'I need to go to the hospital,' I said. 'I've known Oli since preschool.'

Harriet and John made eye signals at each other, signals I couldn't understand.

Harriet took my hand and squeezed it. 'Love, I don't know if that's a good idea.'

'Why not?' I snatched my hand away. 'I didn't do anything to him. And neither did Dad.'

John sighed. 'I think she's right, Harriet. And if Miracle hides away, Jim looks more guilty.'

'Oli might wake up,' I said. 'He might tell me Dad had nothing to do with it.'

'Miri,' Harriet said. 'I think the chances of him waking while you're there are very slim.'

'But people wake up from comas all the time.'

'Julian's coma was different. And he was lucky.'

John cleared his throat. 'When he wakes up, assuming he does, and God willing he will, it'll probably be a while before he remembers everything. If ever. But I'll take you.' His eyes met Harriet's. 'She'll be safe with me. No one's going to attack a school principal.'

'Really, John? Are you sure … she'll be okay?'

Harriet twisted her tiny gold horseshoe earring.

'I'll make sure she doesn't come to any harm. I think it'll be good for her.' John crossed his arms. 'It's not healthy hiding away here – any more than it is her hiding away with her mum. How about tomorrow afternoon, Miracle?'

'Yes. Thanks.' I forced out a smile, but felt hot and fuzzy-headed. I'd got what I'd asked for. But did I really want to go? Why not just focus on helping Mum and Dad? Why go anywhere, or do anything, if I didn't have to? I didn't know what I felt; what was going on inside my head. How would I feel when I saw Oli? And how would Oli and his family feel when they saw me?

But deep down I knew I had to go. I'd be brave. I needed to know Oli was going to be okay. And maybe, just maybe, he'd wake up and I'd finally find out what went on that night.

24

The next day dragged. Julian couldn't be bothered changing out of his pyjamas and I caught him drawing a sad face on the bathroom mirror with stripy toothpaste before rubbing it off with toilet paper. He wasn't the only one acting strange. Harriet dropped a plate, then threw her tea towel across the room and swore at the plate for breaking. I couldn't imagine what my visit was going to be like – the thought of walking through the hospital doors made me panic – and I knew John was the only person who thought I should be going.

By the time we drove into the car park, I was sweating in my tracksuit top, and my T-shirt was damp and clingy. I'd borrowed some of Harriet's 'Mum' deodorant, and was now worrying that it only worked on actual mums. But Oli was hardly going to notice BO, unless it was bad enough to wake him from his coma, which he'd thank me for anyway. I had bigger things to worry about. Like Oli's parents. What would they do when they saw me? Would they yell at me? Scream at me to leave?

John was humming the theme song to *Minder* as he undid his seatbelt and adjusted his tie. I guess he was nervous too.

Walking across the soggy hospital lawn, we passed a small crowd of adults rugged up in parkas, scarves and beanies. It was like we'd walked into a movie set, without cameramen.

They held up placards that screamed ABORTION IS MURDER! and LIFE BEGINS AT CONCEPTION in angry black letters and chanted like they were possessed: 'A heartbeat is a life.' Those who weren't carrying signs held their hands together as if they were in church. A man with thick glasses glared at me as I walked past, my sneakers squelching in the mud.

I hadn't thought much about abortion, and I had no idea why they were kicking up a big stink about it outside a hospital. An abortion was only what bad Year 12 girls had, or were rumoured to have had, the kind of girls who got called a *dirty slut* or a *filthy scrubber*. I hardly knew what an abortion involved, and I took no notice of the rumours about rusty coat hangers and girls bleeding to death, especially when the girls who supposedly had had abortions turned up at school as usual on Monday. I hadn't actually realised abortions were a proper operation people went to hospital for.

John and I climbed the steps in silence. I stared at my muddy sneakers, mortified by the thought that the man glaring at me might've imagined I'd come to the hospital for an abortion. Luckily, the idea that the man might've assumed that John was responsible for me getting pregnant didn't occur to me until later.

Boorunga Hospital had been rebuilt after the earthquake, and was still called the 'new hospital' even though it was practically as old as me. The foyer smelt a bit like the crem, like disinfectant and medicine, masking the stink of something else. Cancer? Death? Rows of people – mainly coughing kids and their red-eyed mums – sat in school chairs, facing the reception desk.

I covered my nose, trying not to breathe in sickness, as John talked to the nurse – 'Celia' her badge said – behind the glass window.

'I'm sorry, sir. Oliver's in ICU. Family only.'

'I understand.' John scratched his ear for a moment. 'But you see, this is a unique kind of a situation whereby my niece –'

'She's most welcome to leave a note, card or flowers.' Nurse Celia looked bored, as if a hundred other visitors had dropped in to see Oli that day and she was sick of repeating herself. 'But she cannot go into ICU. Sorry.'

I probably should've sprinted to the car with relief, but I was psyched up and ready to see Oli. My mind was also dizzy with thoughts of foetuses, heartbeats and coat hangers, and of me being pregnant.

'Can I just look through the door? Or a window?' I asked. 'I really need to see him!'

Nurse Celia frowned. 'We have our policies. I can't let in every girl who has a crush. This is a hospital and Oliver is in a *very* serious condition.'

I felt my face flush. 'I don't have a crush!'

'Are Oliver's parents here?' John said. 'Please. We wouldn't be here if it wasn't important.'

Celia rolled her eyes. 'I'll check. What's your name?'

'Miracle Jamieson.' I was expecting the usual look of surprise when I said 'Miracle', but the nurse was more interested in my second name.

'*Jamieson*, did you say? You're not Jim's –'

'She's a friend of Oliver's,' John said.

Nurse Celia nodded but it was obvious she was dying to ask me what the hell I was doing there. 'If you can take a seat and wait. Please.' She gestured towards the rows of people studying their hands or the magazines on their laps, all pretending not to be fascinated by me demanding to see a boy in intensive care.

John and I sat in the front row so Nurse Celia couldn't ignore us. She spoke to another, younger nurse, who shot me a look that said 'Really? You think Oli's going to want to see you?', before her shoes squeaked off down the corridor.

A few minutes later, Mrs Harrison's familiar figure came towards us. Long, skinny legs, and a tiny head. *Pin head,* I thought. Had it always been so small? Or could sadness make you shrink? Her hair was flat, as if she'd been standing in the rain. Puffy face and crooked lipstick.

I stood up, hoping to feel braver. John stood too, like a stake supporting a young tree. I felt a strange urge to curtsy, it must've been my nerves. Luckily I was also too scared to move.

'We are so, so sorry about your son –' John started.

'Miracle?' Mrs Harrison didn't take her eyes off me.

'I just … I want to see Oli.' It came out as a squeak. I could sense everyone – the sick kids and their mums, the old couple, the man with the sling – watching me.

'You've got some nerve!'

'I feel sick … about what happened.' My voice trembled. It was the truth; when I pictured Oli lying unconscious outside the crematorium – which I saw glowing brightly, obscenely, in the dark – my head felt hot and heavy. 'I'd really like to see him … please.'

'*You* feel sick? That bastard. Your father –'

'Enough!' John held up his hand.

Someone behind me called out, 'Mind your language!'

Mrs Harrison seemed to shrink, like a kid in trouble for something they haven't done.

'Sorry, Judith, isn't it? I didn't mean to be rude,' John said. 'This is a terrible terrible thing, and you have our deepest sympathy. But Miracle isn't to blame. Irrespective of what they're saying about her father, my niece is a kind-hearted girl who has suddenly been ostracised for something she had nothing whatsoever to do with. And she feels deeply saddened about Oliver.'

Irrespective of what they're saying about her father. Why wasn't John defending Dad? Surely he didn't think Dad was guilty?

My teeth started chattering. It now felt icier inside the hospital than it had out on the lawn.

'She had everything to do with it.' Mrs Harrison spat out the 'she'.

'I didn't do anything,' I squeaked.

'Judith, I don't think you've heard the full story.' John realised he was pointing at her, and quickly dropped his hand.

'Don't lecture me!' Mrs Harrison snapped. 'I'm not a schoolgirl.'

'I was upset about what he did. Him and Seth.' My voice shook. 'But I never wanted anything to happen to him.'

Mrs Harrison's tiny eyes glassed over.

'Please let me see him.'

'Why? Can you perform *miracles*?'

'I can't sleep.' It was all I could think of to say. 'I think about him all the time.' I think about Dad, too, I thought, but she wouldn't give a stuff about that.

'You think seeing Oli will help you sleep? I haven't slept since … since …' The skin around her swollen eyes looked bruised, even under the foundation.

'But I also thought … maybe … it could help … Oli,' I said. 'If I saw him.'

'This isn't a fairy tale.'

'Please.'

Mrs Harrison stared into my eyes until I looked away.

She then turned to John. 'You're a good teacher. Oli really responded to your teaching style in Grade 5.'

'He's an intelligent boy.' John paused for a few moments. 'Please let her see him.'

By now her pain was leaking down her cheeks. 'You think it'll do any good?'

John shrugged. 'I don't know. But I'm sure it'd do no harm.'

'Steve'll be back in twenty minutes or so.' Mrs Harrison

looked at her watch. She dabbed her eyes with a clump of tissue from under her sleeve. 'You can come in with me.'

'Thank you,' I whispered. My legs starting shaking; I was going to see Oli.

'But only for a minute – and just so you can appreciate the seriousness of the situation.'

I nodded. I wanted to turn and run through the glass doors and down the stairs, elbowing the protesters out of my way, to the safety of the car.

'Steve won't be as understanding as me,' Mrs Harrison was saying. 'He won't want you here.'

'A minute will be enough.' John touched Mrs Harrison's shoulder. 'Thank you for being so understanding.'

'You're sure you can handle this?' Mrs Harrison faced me.

I nodded, but both of my legs were trembling; how could they not notice? How could they believe I could handle it? 'I think so.'

'You think so?' Mrs Harrison broke her stare. 'We'll see.'

25

Mrs Harrison charged ahead, glancing back now and then, as she followed the thick red, yellow, and blue lines on the shiny orange floor. We turned into another corridor, a copy of the first. Giant cartoon fish swam along the wall, presumably trying to tell kids that getting their tonsils yanked out or their bones bent back into shape was going to be fun. The yellow line took a sharp left turn, then the blue line turned right, leaving us with just the red line. Red, like a neat stripe of blood. Occasional black skid marks made me picture ambulance men racing stretchers down corridors, desperate to park patients in beds before their hearts went still.

Mrs Harrison stopped, and there it was in black capital letters: Intensive Care Unit. My heart was hammering. I'd watched enough TV to know that of all the wards in a hospital, this was where you'd least want to end up.

Mrs Harrison looked at me then sucked in her breath, as if to swallow her grief. She clenched her hands and pushed through the glass doors.

There were six beds, three on each side, all dwarfed by brightly lit machines like the ones at Game Zone. Intensive Care couldn't be more different from a video arcade, but I guess I didn't have anything else to compare it to.

Only three of the beds contained people-shaped lumps. Mrs

Harrison approached the first one – Bed 26 – and leant over it, so I could only see the bottom half. The safe half.

But it didn't seem right. The lump didn't look much bigger than Worm. Oli wasn't one of the biggest boys in our year – he'd only come up to Big Bobby Sanson's shoulders – but he never got called 'midget' or 'stumpy'. I'd never thought of him as small.

'I'm back, sweetheart,' Mrs Harrison murmured.

I focused on a tangle of wires stretching up to a giant machine that blinked and bleeped like something out of *Star Wars*. My eyes then crept to the end of the bed and landed on a clipboard hooked over the bedframe. I stepped back so I could read it: *Oliver Joel Harrison dob 13-07-1972.*

Joel. His middle name was Joel. I remembered the day in Ancient History when he told us his middle name was Aristotle. I knew he was bullshitting, but Katie believed him. She believed every word he said.

Mrs Harrison was still leaning over him, maybe stroking his face or sweeping hair away from his forehead. I always liked how his fringe flopped into his eyes, but his mum was probably annoyed by it, like Mrs Hall, who once tapped on Oli's head at the beginning of drama class, and said 'Come out, Oliver. I know you're in there somewhere'. I took a long, deep breath to stop myself from sobbing.

Mrs Harrison heard me choking. She turned and whispered, 'Hard to believe your father was capable of this.'

I shook my head. 'He's not … He didn't.'

She gave me a hard look, the sort that could shatter every window in the ward if she wanted it to, before her eyes welled up.

'Go on, talk to him.' She nudged me forward. 'They say he might be able to hear. Let him know it's you.'

I didn't want to say anything in front of her, but I stepped closer to the bed. I still couldn't see all of him. She was in the way of his head, his face.

'Oli? It's … Miracle.' My voice was barely louder than the hum of his machine.

My heart drummed as I waited for a croaky 'Hello' or 'What are you doing here?', my eyes still stuck on the bed's faded green blanket. But nothing happened. Neither Oli nor the machine that connected him to his life showed any sign of having heard me.

My eye wandered to the thin tanned arm that lay on the sheet, purple with bruises. It *was* Oli. I'd known that elbow and that small dark mole since we were four-year-olds fighting over a tricycle at preschool, a blue one with a red wire basket. I could see him in his Oscar the Grouch singlet and denim shorts. He'd won the fight, but I'd let him. I never liked seeing other kids cry, least of all Oli Harrison. Silly thing was, he then deliberately rode over my foot and I ran blabbing to Miss Carter.

I forced my eyes from Oli's arm to his chest, watching it slowly rise and fall. Up … Down … Up … Down … Up … Down …

It was then that Mrs Harrison stepped aside, and my eyes finally landed on Oli's face. Before I could help it, I made a sound. A cry? I don't know if you could even call it that.

'The scars will fade over time.' Mrs Harrison's voice was wavering. 'His face is still beautiful.'

I nodded, without taking my eyes off his face in the middle of the white hospital pillow. I let my tears spill; I didn't have the strength to hold them in. What'd happened? Who did this to him? It wasn't Dad. There's no way in the world Dad could've had anything to do with this.

I felt hot, and black splotches dotted my vision. I leant back on something, a trolley, and sent it whooshing into Oli's bed. The crash of metal on metal hurt my ears. But Oli didn't even blink.

I crouched down, my hands flat on the cold floor, and breathed deeply. I could taste the hospital smell.

'Bit hard to take in, isn't it?' Mrs Harrison held out her arm.

I took her rough, cold hand. 'I was going to faint.'

'Steve'll be back soon.' She dug the tissue out of her jumper sleeve and blew her nose. 'Let's go.'

She led me back out the glass doors, and I kept my eyes on her UGG boots as they followed the blood-red line back down the corridor.

26

'Miracle.' It was Harriet's voice.

I tried to lift my head, but it felt like it'd melted into the pillow. I'd only just shut my eyes; it was 3.46 am when I'd last checked the clock. Mrs Harrison had been right: seeing Oli hadn't helped me sleep.

'I'm awake.' This time I managed to sit up.

Julian's bed was empty, his navy blue doona a lake on the floor. The sun was beaming through the window.

'Someone's here to see you,' Harriet said from outside the guest bedroom door.

'Okay!' Panic pushed me out of bed and in front of the dressing table mirror. My hair was matted and tiredness ringed my eyes like a pair of swimming goggles. Who could it be? Katie? Pheebs? Sall? Oli's dad? It was Sunday – it could've been anyone. I wanted to lie down and crawl back into my dreams. But I pulled on yesterday's clothes and wandered out.

The 'someone' sat on the brown leather couch in the dining room, pretending to be interested in Worm's *Dr Who Annual*. I was shocked.

'The white doctor's my favourite, so that's me,' Worm was telling her. 'But Mum likes the brown doctor. See! He's got curly hair.'

'Oh, yeah. I like him,' she said. *She* was Livvy. Dressed in a fluffy black jumper, denim mini-skirt, black stockings and Doc Marten boots, she looked more like a pop singer, like Madonna or someone, than the daughter of a crematorium manager. She gave me a quick smile.

'So you're the brown doctor, too?' Worm looked up as I sat on the La-Z-Boy. 'Miracle's the brown doctor. She's got his mop.'

'I just woke up.' I smoothed my hair, annoyed that Worm had drawn attention to it. 'Why don't you get dressed? Livvy doesn't want to see your undies.'

'They're Speedos!' he said. 'I don't have *Star Wars* undies.'

'How are you?' Livvy smiled at me again, but she was chewing on her finger. Nervous? A row of silver bangles shimmered up her arm.

'Sleepy.' It was the only word I could think of. I desperately hoped more would follow.

Livvy picked up one of Harriet's good mugs and took a sip. The smell of coffee made me think of Dad sitting in his chair, doing the crossword.

'Come on, Worm. Get your towel!' Harriet stood in front of us, digging through her handbag.

'Julian's helping me with the groceries while Worm's at his lesson,' she told me. 'John's in the shed trying to get the lawn mower going. It's a stubborn old thing. Okay if we leave you two to it?'

Livvy was fiddling with her bangles, strumming them like a guitar. I nodded, though I didn't want to be left alone with her. Not only was she in Year 12, she was part of the popular group, and she'd had boyfriends. Loads of them. How was I supposed to talk to her?

'Sorry, this is probably a bit weird,' Livvy said after the front door slammed. 'I'm probably the last person you want to see after ...'

'No, it's … good. I couldn't sleep. And I'm a mess. Well, my hair's always a mess, but I washed it last night and it was still wet when I went to bed.' So much for my fear. Now I couldn't stop babbling.

'Last time I saw you,' Livvy said, 'it was pretty fucked up.'

'My hair?' She remembered how I'd looked in the café? 'Yeah, it was raining and we –'

'Not your hair! God, I didn't come here to diss your hair.' She shook her head. 'I mean the *situation*. My dad and your mum.'

'Oh, that.'

I remembered Greg's face, his laugh, my urge to knock his big teeth out of his mouth. 'It was a dumb idea to ask your dad for help.'

'I understand why you did, though. How are you meant to live if your dad's not making money? How's your mum?'

I never said much about Mum, not even to Katie. To confirm that she was as nutty as everyone thought would be like putting my hand up and saying *Tease me*. But I guessed Livvy'd already figured her out.

'We saw her last night,' I said. 'She doesn't have the energy to go anywhere. She's in bed pretty much all day.'

'What about you? This must be so hard.' Livvy reached for her coffee.

'Um.' To say I felt like the whole world hated my guts would make me sound like I was Worm's age. I didn't want Livvy to think any worse of me than she already did.

'I'm stuck in limbo,' I said. 'I don't know when I'll go back to school. Maybe not until Dad gets out.'

'Have they sent you work to do from home?'

I shook my head. 'My uncle says I could do revision, but school doesn't care, I haven't heard from them. Miss Jones probably wants me to leave.'

'She probably hasn't even noticed. She's too busy stressing about the Great Quake Debate. Can you believe she wants us to have a mock debate in front of her before the real one? Such a control freak! Sorry. You probably don't give a shit about that.' Livvy sipped her coffee. 'Do you know how your dad's doing?'

I nodded and repeated what John had told me about his visit. 'I wanted to go too, but the people hanging outside would probably beat me to death to teach Dad a lesson. Anyway, my aunty and uncle said no.'

Livvy was strumming her bangles again. She cleared her throat. 'Look, I really need to tell you something.'

'Okay.' I tried not to sound disappointed.

Outside, John chose that exact moment to yank the cord on the lawn mower. It coughed a few times before working up to a full roar. I stood up, ready to open the window and ask him to stop. But this was his house; I was just staying in the guest room. And, anyway, did I really want to hear what Livvy had to say? Why couldn't she have just wanted to visit me? To be my friend. Why did there have to be something she *needed* to say.

'I came here to tell you …'

'Sorry, I can barely hear you!'

'Sit here?' Livvy patted the couch. 'It's kind of private.'

'Your secret's safe with the lawn mower.' I moved Worm's *Dr Who Annual* and sat down.

'I haven't known your dad long,' Livvy said.

I leant in closer and smelt her cinnamony scent.

'But I know he wouldn't do –'

Just then the mower fell quiet and Livvy stopped talking. We heard John's faint 'Stupid bloody thing' and smirked at each other. I sat back, hoping it would be a while before he got the stupid bloody thing started again.

'He wouldn't do anything like that,' Livvy continued. 'I'd bet my life on it.'

Her words felt warmer than one of Harriet's hugs. My eyes filled up.

'I know too.' I wasn't going to cry. 'I did wonder whether he could've flipped out – just for a moment. You know how sometimes you feel so pissed off that … Well, I do – just for a minute – then it passes. But … there's just no way. He was angry about the rats, but not enough to … And he wouldn't have known Oli was at the crem that night.'

'It's bullshit,' Livvy said. 'Even if he has got a criminal record.'

'What?' It came out like a hiccup.

'Sorry, you didn't know?'

I shook my head, feeling my face redden.

They know what he did before. I recalled Mum's words.

'Dad told me,' Livvy said. 'He didn't say what it was for. It was probably something minor, like stealing a car or something.'

I looked away from Livvy. Dad would never steal a car. He wouldn't even let me take flowers from Mrs Jensen-from-across-the-road's garden when her face wasn't pressed against the window. Is this what Greg meant when he mentioned Dad's *background* to Mum? I'd file this, along with other hard-to-think-about things like whether Susan Singleton really did have sex with the caretaker in the PE shed, to process when I was ready. If I ever could be.

'Anyway, those words,' I said. 'The message about *his girl.* That's just not Dad.'

'He didn't write that.' Livvy shook her head.

'I saw Oli.'

'They let you in? I heard his mum banned everyone, even Seth.'

'His face … I nearly fainted.'

Livvy sighed, closing her eyes. 'That makes me feel worse.'

'Why? Do you ... Do you know something?' The words stumbled out.

Livvy's frown cut deep into her forehead, like Mum's when she was trying to answer a quiz question on *Sale of the Century*. 'I feel like I have to tell someone.'

'Did you tell Mum? Harriet said you'd called.' My mind was racing. 'You called my house and talked to her.'

'No, no. I was calling for you.' Livvy stood up. 'She wouldn't want to hear this.'

'What? Do you know who it was?'

Livvy picked up John's *Footrot Flats* birthday card from the bookshelf and read the front, before putting it down again.

'Was it ...' I didn't want to ask, but right then I knew it had to be Greg. How could it not be? He *was* the kind of person. And it would've been easy for him to make Dad look guilty. Why hadn't I seriously considered him?

'Did your dad say something?' I said.

'No. He didn't say anything. He ...'

Because of Livvy, because I liked her. Well, not *liked* like, just as a friend. And Greg was her dad. I'd suspected him at first, but when I found out Livvy was his daughter, I'd put him out of my mind. But now she was here telling me ... telling me what?

'... has a bad temper, really bad.' Livvy sat down again. 'He's not like your dad. He used to ... hurt my mum. That's why she left.'

This time I welcomed the sound of the lawn mower coughing back into action. Livvy closed her eyes.

'Want a juice?' I practically shouted, not knowing what else to say or do. 'Or anything else? Tissues?' I passed her the Kleenex box from the coffee table.

The sound of Livvy blowing her nose blended with the mower's rumble.

'What about you?' I leant in close so I didn't have to yell. 'Does he hurt you?'

Livvy looked down and brushed fluff off her jumper. 'No. Well, not yet.'

'Why don't you live with your mum?' I remembered what Greg said, about her being a lesbian.

'I want to.' Livvy played with her silver bangles, let them slide down her arm like a slinky. 'I miss her. He shoved her out of the car once.'

'What? Why?'

'Oh, I don't know, I don't think he liked her lipstick …'

The mower stopped again and we laughed. Livvy's face was lined with tears.

'Thank God!' I said.

'My ears are ringing.'

We were quiet for a moment, waiting for the mower to start. Silence.

'I don't know why your dad would want to hurt Oli though,' I said. 'Does he even know him?'

Livvy shook her head. 'I think catching him on the property was just the last straw. Dad was furious with me. And also with …' She took a deep breath. 'Your dad.'

'You and *Dad*? Why?' Heat crawled up my body.

'Well … my dad saw something.'

'But our dads got on well. Dad said he liked Greg, once he got to know him. He's had much worse bosses. This guy George was –'

'I did something really dumb,' Livvy blurted.

'What?' I couldn't imagine Livvy doing something really dumb. Or even just a bit dumb.

'Well, um. I can't believe I'm about to tell you this, but.' She took another deep breath, and aimed her words at the wall behind me. 'I'd just made your dad a coffee: Nescafé, two sugars and very milky, you know the way he likes it. And he said something really nice to me. Something about my earrings – I was wearing the dangly fake diamond ones Mum gave me for my fifteenth birthday.'

I nodded, praying for John to crank up the lawn mower again, to blast away Livvy's words.

'He said they looked pretty and he had this look on his face and I … well, until Boorunga High, I'd always been to girls' schools.' Livvy glanced at me, her face flushed, before talking to the wall again. 'I mistook his look for something else.'

I squirmed, wanting Livvy to both hurry up and to stop.

'I put the hot mugs on the filing cabinet,' she said. 'And I kissed him.'

'You *kissed* my dad?' It was worse than I'd thought. Much worse. My face was on fire. 'Just like … um … on the cheek?'

But Livvy wasn't listening, or was pretending not to. 'The worst of it is, Dad walked in before … Jim pulled away, before Jim had realised what I was doing.'

'What did he do?' I tried to focus on Greg, on what Greg did, rather than on Livvy's pretty Year 12 lips touching Dad's dry, old man's mouth, or Dad's eyes wide open in shock. I couldn't think about tongues. I'd only kissed two boys – both while playing 'truth or dare' – and both of them had tongues like dead slugs. I only hoped Dad's breath didn't stink, that he hadn't slipped a boiled egg into his lunchbox that morning.

'Well … he … *my* dad said, "Here's Harvey" and slammed down the urn he'd been carrying – Harvey Ward's ashes. He slammed it so hard on the lunch table it gouged the wood. I got such a scare I bumped into the filing cabinet and spilt the hot coffee all over myself. Look.'

She slid the bangles up her arm and showed me a red mark in the shape of Italy. I might've said 'ouch' or something, but I was still too shocked to take in what she was saying.

'He left the room, and Jim followed, trying to explain,' Livvy continued. 'But Dad shut himself in his office.'

I closed my eyes, trying to make sense of what Livvy was telling me. The week before I'd been told Dad was a violent criminal, now I was picturing him as a …

'Your dad wasn't to blame. It was all me,' Livvy said. 'He didn't know what was going on. I've told Dad that. But he wouldn't listen.'

'But I can't … It doesn't make sense. How does Oli come into it?'

'Wrong place, wrong time. Dad was in a bad state of mind, so catching Oli – or one of the kids who'd been pissing him off over the last few months – could've … could've sent him over the edge. And, of course, framing your dad for it – how perfect was that? It let Dad off the hook and made your dad pay for what he did to me, even though it was really me doing it to him. '

'So you really think it was him? What about the hanky? They said they found Dad's red hanky in the bush.'

'Dad must've put it there. Maybe your dad left it at work. But there's no proof and I can't say anything. I feel guilty for even telling you this. But even guiltier for what I did and how this all turned out for you and your family.'

So she did care about me. That was something.

'So the cops don't know any of this?'

Livvy shook her head. 'They asked Dad questions, of course. He was the one who found Oliver.'

'It was the middle of the night!' I remembered. 'What was he even doing there?'

Livvy sighed. 'The hospital had rung Dad and said some old lady's body was being delivered at four, so he had an excuse. Dad's pretty clued up. He had the police apologising for wasting his time with so many questions. Shit. I just don't know what to do.'

'You've got to tell them,' I said. 'He can't get away with it.'

'I can't.' Livvy sat up straight. 'I can't dob in my own dad.'

'He should be in jail! And my dad should be at home.'

'He'll kill me if he knows I've said anything.' Livvy bit her lip.

She was probably right. If he could do what he did to Oli, God knows what he'd do to her. 'I'll go to the cops then.'

'Really?' Livvy sat up straight. 'What would you say?'

'I'll think of something.' But what? And were people still outside the station? Harriet and John would try to stop me.

Livvy leant forward and held my wrists. I remember thinking how cold her fingers felt, and noticing her mauve nail polish, chipped at the ends where she'd bitten her nails. 'Promise you won't mention me.'

'Promise. They might tell me to go away, or think I'm lying, but I've got to do something.'

'You're braver than me. Police scare me. But so does my dad.' She let go of my arms, sat back in the couch. 'I hope they believe you.'

'I'll do it,' I heard myself say. 'I'll go to the police station tomorrow.' I stood so quickly the room tilted, so I sat back down again. I didn't want to talk to the cops, or risk getting attacked or abused, but I needed Dad to be free. And I wanted Greg locked up. I wanted him to be the one who was eating pizza with the man who never paid his parking fines.

27

On Monday I woke up sticky with sweat. I'd been dreaming about Mum wandering down our street in her striped flannelette nightie, the one with holes her bony elbows poked through. She kept turning her head, looking around, and whispering my name. I yelled out – *Mum! Mum!* – but she didn't see or hear me. I sat up, my heart still racing, tears wetting my face. I had to sort out our mess. I needed to be at home, and for Julian and Dad to be there too. For everything to be back to normal. Even if our family's normal was nothing like anyone else's in the world, at that moment, I couldn't think of anything I wanted more.

I felt cold, even though I was wearing Harriet's spare bathrobe and the heater was cranked up. Out in the kitchen, Harriet and John were talking in low, serious voices. I was halfway through my cornflakes before they seemed to notice me.

'Good morning,' Harriet said, though her frown suggested otherwise. She was scribbling a list.

'What's going on?' I wiped milk from my chin.

'Nothing to worry about,' John said.

'But what?'

'Just … my friend, Mia West, is in hospital,' Harriet said. 'She's one of John's teachers.'

'Did someone beat her up?' I asked.

'No.' Harriet's frowned deepened. 'She went for a jog this morning and then ... well, by the sound of it, collapsed at her front door. Probably just overdid it.'

'Hopefully it's something minor,' John said. 'I'm wondering who can take her class. 2B are a real handful.'

'How are you today?' Harriet forced out a smile.

'Good.' I took a deep breath, bracing myself. 'I need you to drop me off this morning. Please.'

Harriet put down her pen and reached for my hand. The bags under her eyes made her look more like Mum. 'But Miri, I thought you were going to stay with us a while longer.'

'Stay here!' Worm's voice came from under the table. I hadn't noticed him hiding there.

'I am, I will. I meant can you drop me at the police station? And pick me up after? I'm going to talk to them about Dad.' I paused to breathe. 'Make them understand it wasn't him.'

'No, Miracle.' Harriet let go of my hand. 'I don't think so.' She and John frowned at each other.

'Why not?' The cornflakes turned to sand in my mouth. 'I don't care about the people outside. I'm not scared about being *traumatised*. I can't be any more traumatised than I already am.'

'It's not the best thing to do,' John said.

'Why not?' I dropped my spoon. They'd been so nice to me and Julian and I was grateful they'd taken us in, but I was starting to feel trapped, like I was the one locked up. 'He's been stuck in there for days! How's he going to get out?'

'We'll see what happens in court next week.' John spread a thick layer of Vegemite on his toast. 'Unless other evidence comes to light before then.'

'You're happy for him just to stay there?'

'None of this makes me happy, Miracle,' John said. 'Worm, sit up at the table and eat your breakfast, please.'

'But you think he's guilty!'

'I've never said that.'

'You think he beats up teenagers!'

'Please don't put words in my mouth,' John said.

'You don't have to say anything. I can tell.'

'Well you're clever because not even I can tell what I think. I'm ninety-nine percent sure he didn't; it's certainly out of character –'

'You didn't see Oli! See what the person did to him.'

'Like I said, I'm ninety-nine percent sure you're right. I'm just waiting for that piece of evidence to put him in the clear. There's bound to be something. There always is.'

I was on my feet, and before I knew it, the words came spewing out: 'Livvy reckons it's her dad! Greg!'

'Oh my God,' Harriet whispered. 'Is that why she was here?'

'I wasn't meant to say anything,' I said, before relaying what Livvy had told me, leaving out the bit about her and Dad. I'd never be able to repeat that. Instead I told them about Greg's terrible temper and that Livvy reckoned Greg had no conscience so didn't think twice about pinning the crime on Dad.

'What makes her so sure?' John said. 'Did she witness it?'

'Greg's a creep! It was obviously him!'

'That doesn't necessarily make him guilty,' Harriet said. 'There are plenty of *creeps* in the world, but not all of them are dangerous.'

'But he's really violent! He tried to kill her mum – like he tried to kill Oli.' I hardly knew where the words were coming from. But once I'd said them, they made sense. I had no trouble picturing Greg as a murderer. He owned a crematorium! Why would you want to burn bodies for a living? Dad only did it because he was desperate. Maybe Greg'd killed other people and got rid of the evidence. Maybe that's why he moved to Australia in the first place. Perhaps he'd already killed people in America and had fled before he got caught.

'Calm down, Miracle. Oli is still alive and I'm sure no one meant to kill anyone,' John said. 'What exactly did Livvy say?'

I tried to repeat what she'd told me. I couldn't remember half of it and as the words came out, I knew they weren't doing her story justice.

'Miracle.' John was tearing his toast into strips. 'I didn't get a chance to meet Livvy. But how well do you know her? Can you really trust what she's saying?'

'John.' Harriet frowned at him, then looked at me. 'The poor girl. She looked haunted. I'd be inclined to take her word over his.'

'I don't care whose word you take, or what you think.' I banged my fist on the table.

Worm yelped like a puppy. I felt a stab of guilt but was too angry to say sorry.

'I'm going to the cops. You can't stop me!' I pushed my chair back.

'Tell her, Harriet,' John said quietly. 'There's no point prolonging it.'

Harriet hugged Worm and whispered in his ear. A tear slid off her cheek and disappeared into his curls. Then another and another. She looked up at me. 'Sit down sweetheart, please.'

I did as she said. I was still shaking with anger, but the only time I'd ever seen Harriet cry was when Molly died on *A Country Practice.* I knew it would be worth listening to.

'Miracle, we were going to tell you later, but …'

'What? What?' I wiped my sweaty hands on my pyjama pants.

'Don't panic. Everyone's okay, it's just that …' Harriet dabbed at her tears with the sleeve of her bathrobe. 'God – what a week! Well … your mum. Well, she …'

'What did she do?'

'She went there herself, Miracle,' John said. 'To the police. She went down there last night – walked the whole way.'

I blinked away an image of Mum staggering down the street in her nightie – thin, white elbows poking out into the cold night.

'To set things straight,' Harriet said.

'She gave them quite an earful,' John added.

'That's putting it politely.' Harriet closed her eyes and let out a deep sigh. 'She abused everyone in sight, called them every name under the sun. To say it didn't help is an understatement.'

'Mum made it worse?' It was a silly question. Of course she'd have made it worse. She always did.

'She was arrested,' Harriet said.

'She's in jail too?' My mouth dried up; I gulped down a glass of apple juice. Mum wouldn't be able to handle jail, being in a strange bed, being somewhere that wasn't our house, being told what to do and what not to do. Jail would kill her.

'Thank God it didn't come to that,' Harriet said. 'They let her go. They phoned here late last night. Your light was still on but I didn't want to give you something else to keep you awake, so I collected her and drove her home. But she might have to go to court and … it just doesn't look good.'

'But why? Why did she do it?' Mum would've hated going to the police station.

'Stress, I imagine. Fear – of living alone, of losing him,' Harriet said. 'And she'd been drinking.'

'We don't think she's been taking her medication either,' John said.

'God, it's all just … shit,' I said. Worm, now relaxed and leaning against Harriet, smiled. No doubt he'd be saying 'shit' for the rest of the day and blaming it on me. 'What else can we do?'

'Very little.' John wiped his hands on his napkin. 'I'm sorry. As hard as that sounds, we just have to wait. Now I'd better get a move on.'

'Worm and I'll get going too.' Harriet stood. 'If I stop by the hospital to visit Mia on the way home, I'll be back by four. Will you two be okay until then?'

I watched Worm drawing spirals in brown sugar on the tablecloth.

'Yes,' I said, because she wasn't asking me a question. I didn't have a choice. 'But I have to do something. I *need to*.'

'You *need* to relax, Miracle,' Harriet said. 'Be kind to yourself.'

'Shit,' Worm whispered to the sugar. 'Shit. Shit.'

28

Julian's mouth hung open. He lay on the couch with his head hanging off the edge and his long, bony toes splayed on the wall. The hairs on his legs were still blond and fine, like Worm's little-boy legs. When I asked if he was okay, he replied by opening and closing his mouth like a goldfish. Maybe he'd been absorbing all that'd been going on, after all. He'd said fewer words than normal since we'd moved to Harriet and John's, his sketchpad lay abandoned on the floor of our room with his dirty washing, and now he was a goldfish. Something was up.

I couldn't look at him any longer. I walked a lap of the house, trying to think what to do. I'd start behaving like him if I didn't act fast. I spotted the phone on the kitchen wall, the phone that had conveyed many whispered conversations between Harriet and Mum, and I stopped pacing. I could call the cops without anyone knowing. But what would I say? Explaining myself down a phone line was even harder than doing it while looking at a person's face. What if, like John, they didn't believe me? What if, like Mum, I made things even worse?

I needed a Plan D, if such a thing even existed. Plans A and B seemed to be enough for most people. I hadn't been able to pull off Plan C. I needed to make money myself. Selling Julian's drawings had turned out to be the world's dumbest idea, but there were other ways to make money. I'd get an actual job.

Apart from robbing a bank, which I couldn't even do in my dreams without tripping over or running straight into a cop, it was the only realistic way of getting money. Plenty of kids left school at the end of Year 10 and started working. I was only a year younger than them and definitely smarter. The boys leaving our school the year before had let a sheep loose in the staffroom on their last day. The sheep had to be put down and the boys were fined a thousand dollars each. I obviously had a higher IQ than all of them put together.

The Boorunga Times lay open on the kitchen table, the Sports section still wet with brown rings from John's coffee. I flicked through to the Classifieds, trying not to think about the last time I'd read those pages. CREMATORIUM ASSISTANT. NO EXPERIENCE NECESSARY …

This time was different. This time I was scanning the page for something *I* could do.

TEACHER'S AIDE. No. I'd probably be expected to know as much as a teacher. And what if a kid asked me to explain compound fractions?

WAITRESS. Yes! I could carry coffee to and from a table. Just to be sure, I took John's mug to the sink. I then carried it back to the table and carefully placed it on the tablecloth without spilling a drop. It didn't contain a drop to spill, but still. 'Your coffee, Sir,' I said. I could smile, too, if I had to. But then I saw the name – Twirly Swirl Café – and the person to call – *Magda Sudaka* – and felt like throwing the mug at the wall. Our family's conversation with Greg was probably her juiciest eavesdrop ever. Besides, her boss was Reginald Heller. Katie's dad. It definitely wasn't the job for me.

I wanted to screw up the newspaper or shred it to bits, and scream so loud the whole of Boorunga would hear. But I gritted my teeth and started at the top of the page again. There had to be something I could do.

BUILDING APPRENTICE. I'd helped Dad make our go-kart, back before I got bored with him explaining every step in a weirdly excited voice, as if he was the host of *The Curiosity Show*. He'd taught me how to hold a hammer properly, and how to hit a nail without flattening my thumb. It was worth a go.

Harriet and John's phone was shiny and white and attached to the wall, unlike the heavy old cream-coloured thing that sat on a chest of drawers in our hallway, with its long, tangled cord that was too knotted to stretch into my bedroom. The things in their house made ours look like the relics we studied in Ancient History. Even Mum looked prehistoric next to Harriet.

To 'dial' the number, I just had to press the keypad, instead of actually turning a dial with my finger. I listened to the tiny sound of the phone ringing down the line, my heart leaping.

'Morning, you've reached Steve Harrison Builders. Nathan speaking.'

I slammed the phone down. *Steve Harrison Builders.* Mum was right. If Boorunga was any smaller, we'd have to marry ourselves. Me, asking to be Oli's dad's apprentice! He probably would've had me arrested. I took a deep breath.

HAIRDRESSING ASSISTANT. The thought of touching other people's hair, their grease and dandruff and nits, made my skin crawl. But maybe I could wear gloves. I pressed the numbers. The voice that answered – Barbara's – was as soothing as our school librarian's, and I managed to answer all the questions without sounding too young and without revealing my intense dislike for nits. But then, just when I thought I'd passed the test and she'd be willing to give me a go, she asked me another question.

'What did you say your name was, love?'

'Um. It's … My name is … Miracle.' I closed my eyes. The trouble with having a name like mine is I never get confused with anyone else. This is especially unhelpful when your family is at the top of Boorunga's most-hated list.

'Miracle,' Barbara repeated.

'Yeah, Miracle Jamieson.' Saying my last name was unnecessary, but I had to fill the silence with something.

'Jim's daughter,' Barbara's voice was flat.

'I can start tomorrow, if you like.'

'I'm sorry, Miracle.'

I let the receiver drop, watched its bungee cord save it from crashing to the floor. Then I hung it up properly, but only because I didn't want to add a new phone to the list of my family's debts.

Getting a job was a waste of time anyway, I told myself. How could I earn enough money to cover the mortgage, bills and food, not to mention Mum's medicine, cigarettes and vodka?

I was leaving the kitchen when the phone started ringing. I stared at it. It wasn't until Julian called out 'Phone!' that I actually picked it up. Barbara's 'I'm sorry' had sounded so certain. Could she have changed her mind?

'Hello?' I said.

'Is that Miracle?' Not Barbara's voice, a boy's.

'Yes. Who's this?'

'Don't think we don't know where you are.'

This time, when I dropped the receiver, I left it hanging.

29

I didn't know who was on the phone – probably Seth or one of his friends – but the call gave me such a shock I burst into tears and fled out the back door. I climbed onto Worm's rubber tyre swing. The rope and the branch groaned under my weight. I breathed in the smell of freshly cut lawn, a smell that usually made me think of summer, but now made me feel sick. Anyone could've found Harriet and John's number in the phone book, but how did they know I was here? And why were they trying to scare me? If it was a joke, they obviously had no idea what I was going through.

I didn't tell Harriet when she and Worm came home. I just sat there and watched her sit down at the kitchen table to write in her notebook. I didn't want to give her another worry to add to her list.

I felt as if my insides had been wrung out. I was tired of thinking the same thoughts over and over, thinking I'd let Livvy and Dad down if I kept Livvy's story to myself. I had to do something, go somewhere. The only place I could think to go was home. I'd been shutting Mum out of my mind, her all alone in our dark house, so when I did let her in, I realised how much I missed her. Her visit to the police station would've sucked up a year's worth of her energy. If I could make her feel better, even just a little bit, that'd be something.

To my surprise, Harriet didn't say no.

'Does she still like macaroni and cheese?' she asked. 'She loved it when we were growing up.'

'I think so.' I couldn't remember Mum ever mentioning it. She wasn't really a 'food' person. Not when there were cigarettes to smoke and pills to swallow and vodka to drink.

'How about I cook some now and we take it over? I'll make enough to leave some for John and the boys.'

'I think she'd like that.'

I'd been mentally preparing myself as we drove over, but I still felt a wave of nausea when I opened our front door. The air inside was stale, cold, damp. The musty smell bothered me more than the drowned cockroaches in forgotten cups of coffee. I'd grown used to the scent of Harriet and John's – a spicy, firewoody kind of smell – and to Harriet opening the 'drapes' (we called ours 'curtains') each morning to let the light in.

A stack of clean plates – three – sat on the kitchen table and, on them, a handful of cutlery. Mum'd listened to Harriet at least. She'd registered that we were bringing dinner.

'Mum?' I knew she'd be in bed, but I felt like I should warn her. To give her time to … make herself normal?

'You go, love.' Harriet opened the living room curtains. 'I'll heat up dinner.'

I turned on Mum's light and blinked in the sudden brightness.

'Mum? We're here.'

A few seconds passed before she moved, before she revealed her face. I took a step back.

If she didn't have a twin, the sight of her wouldn't have shocked me so much. I thought about Oscar Wilde's *The Picture of Dorian Gray*. Mum was like a portrait of Harriet, except, of course, Harriet had nothing to do with Mum's sunken face, her shrink-wrapped skin. I held my mouth and blinked hard.

'You okay, Mum?'

'Huh.' She slowly sat up, rubbing her eyes, and reached for a mug that was fighting for space on her bedside table with a box of tissues, a glass of something brown and a KB ashtray filled with cigarette butts. 'I don't know … s'pose so. You?'

'I'm okay. Harriet's just about to serve dinner.'

'Serve? You gone all posh on me now?'

I smiled, despite the heaviness in my stomach. 'No.'

Mum groaned. 'Guess Harriet told you what I did.'

I nodded, looking away, as if I wasn't bothered, as if I didn't think it was the stupidest thing she'd ever done.

'Made a mess of everything, didn't I? I just thought that … well, it's so bloody wrong … I just had to tell them.' Mum's eyes flooded with tears, and I swallowed to stop mine from doing the same. 'It just makes me so angry! If they took five minutes to get to know him, they'd see what a big softie he is. If they put a funnel-web in his shoe or something – saw him shriek like a little girl – they'd see.'

'I was thinking of doing the same thing.'

Mum frowned. 'Shrieking like a little girl?'

'Going to the cops. Telling them they'd got it all wrong.'

Mum stared at me for what seemed like forever. I looked away, down at the new red Converse sneakers Harriet'd bought me. They were so new and clean, and so brightly red, they made the rest of me – my clothes, my skin, my self – feel faded and old.

'You would've made less of a mess of it than me,' she finally said. 'I was so angry my brain was about to burst. Hope you never feel like that – hope you've got more of your dad's genes than mine. I'm pretty sure I used the "c" word. More than once.'

'Oh, Mum.' God, she really had stuffed up.

'Yeah. Whoops.' She gave me an almost-smile.

I remembered the day she'd called our neighbour Mrs

Belkin the 'c' word. Mrs Belkin had been standing at the end of her driveway, bending to her letter box when Mum opened our front door and screamed the 'c' word – just that word, with no others around it – with the full force of her lungs. Mum then stormed out with Mrs Belkin's washing basket and tipped it upside down in the middle of the road. Mrs Belkin stood there, hands pressed to her cheeks, not moving even when the wind picked up an enormous blouse and blew it into the gutter. I never found out why Mum was so upset, but I never saw her ironing Mrs Belkin's size 16 Suzanne Grae dresses again.

'Harriet's heating up macaroni and cheese,' I said. 'She made it for you.'

When Mum smiled, her face creased like crêpe paper. 'Mac cheese – that's what your gran used to make for us when we were little. Harriet must remember that.'

'She said it was your favourite.'

Mum nodded. 'God, how I hated your gran's stews! I wasn't allowed to leave the table until I'd swallowed every last slimy mouthful. But her mac cheese was something else.'

I helped Mum onto her wobbly legs. She was like a newborn lamb, and I worried that if she fell she might never get up again. Goosebumps coated her skin. I grabbed Dad's dressing gown and helped her into it.

'Thanks,' Mum said, her voice dry and raspy. 'What would I do without you?'

I looked away, saying nothing.

The three of us sat down to eat. Harriet's attempts to get Mum to talk – Julian sends his love, he's looking after Worm … he has been a bit quiet lately, hasn't he, Miri?… I wonder whether the kids should start doing some schoolwork – were followed by the empty drip of the kitchen tap.

After a few mouthfuls Mum lay her fork down. 'Thanks, Harriet. It's good, but I'm full.' She patted her stomach.

I imagined the inside of her stomach, empty except for pills and beer and spirits that made my eyes water when I sniffed them. If you shook her, she'd probably explode.

Harriet put her fork down too. 'Hen, I'm sure you've heard about AA?'

'Alcoholics Anonymous?' Mum said. 'Of course.'

'Did you know a group meets in Boorunga Hall? Twice a week. Wednesday and Saturday. 12.30.'

'And why are you telling me this? Can they cure agoraphobia? Depression? Can they get your husband out of jail? And bring your kids home?' Mum glanced at me.

'They can help with your drinking.'

'I'm a lot of things, Harriet. But I'm not an alcoholic.'

'Maybe not,' Harriet said. 'But our father was – and apparently these things run in the family. And there are enough empty bottles next to your bin to make an entire university pass out. That's not normal.'

'It just helps. It quietens the voices. I'll stop. When the voices stop.'

'I think that's what a lot of alcoholics say,' Harriet said. 'How about a cup of tea? You can't be too *full* for that.'

I was still struggling to get through the macaroni and cheese. I didn't want to offend Harriet, but it kept sticking in my throat. How could Mum add *alcoholic* to the list of things she already was? And if *these things run in the family* I might as well give up living right now.

'How much tea do you drink a day?' Mum asked Harriet. 'Perhaps you have a little problem of your own.'

Harriet didn't smile. 'After that, we'd better head off.' She stood up, scanning the room for clean mugs. 'If I leave it to John the boys won't eat before nine.'

'Um.' I cleared my throat. 'I'm staying here.'

They both looked at me.

'I'm not leaving Mum.'

I knew I had to stay. I'd miss Harriet and John's – the house that was always warm even when the lawn was white with frost, the big, soft bed in the guest room, the choice of five cereals for breakfast, Worm's voice echoing from the toilet when he was 'finished!'. But this was my home. I couldn't stay in limbo forever. And, of course, there was Mum. She needed me. Maybe if I talked to her enough, she wouldn't be able to hear the voices in her head.

'But your things.' Harriet was now in the kitchen. I heard her fill the kettle, turn the tap off, place the kettle on the bench.

'Can you drop them over?' I asked.

'Yes, of course I could.' Harriet came out carrying a box of Homebrand tea bags. 'But are you sure?'

'She'll be fine,' Mum said. 'She's got me.'

Harriet raised her eyebrows, but said nothing as she searched the teabags for an expiry date, something she always did at our house. 'But Julian will stay with us for a while longer? This house is cold and a little damp. You don't want him getting sick again.'

Mum nodded. 'I miss Jules, but I know you take good care of him.' She chewed at her thumb. 'Better than I do.'

'Just till things get sorted out,' Harriet said. 'He misses you too.'

I felt pleased with myself. I'd just made a decision, not an easy one. And at that moment, with it out in the open, I felt I'd done the right thing.

30

Black stitches swayed down Oli's left cheek like a line of drunk ants. It looked as if he'd been sewn up by Worm instead of a doctor. His mouth hung open, and spit had soaked into his fat, white pillow.

All the other beds were now empty. It was just Oli and the machine he was attached to, its tiny lights frantically flashing to keep him alive.

'*Lo siento*,' I whispered.

Then, like magic, the black stitches disappeared one by one and the black-red gashes faded to smooth pink.

Oli opened his eyes, those beautiful brown eyes that always gave me butterflies.

My heart beat a million miles an hour as I breathed him in.

'Miracle.' His voice was rusty, barely there. 'Thank you.'

His machine bleep-bleeped, but when I glanced at it, it stopped.

'Thank me?' I winced at the clumsiness of my words.

'You brought me back.' He smiled, his teeth milk-white and perfectly straight, and his eyes locked onto mine.

I looked away, noticing the pale green hospital blanket, the picture of Oscar the Grouch embroidered on it – the same picture he wore on his favourite singlet back in preschool.

I started to feel woozy and reached for the bed frame. Oli's machine bleep-bleep-bleep-bleeped and was quiet again.

'I want you to be my girlfriend,' he whispered.

'Oh. I. Um.' I put a hand to my chest to stop my heart from exploding.

'I want to marry you,' Oli said. 'I'll even propose properly. You know, like they do in the movies. On one knee.'

'Um.' My face was ablaze.

'We'll just have to wait till we're … forty-four.'

'Forty-four?' I loved Oli's sense of humour.

'Well, if you want your dad to hand you over – you know, how they do – we'll have to wait till he gets out.' Oli smiled again, but his eyes'd lost their shine.

'Out?' I tightened my grip on the bed.

'Yeah. Well, if he gets out twenty years from now, we'd be forty-four.' Oli lifted his arms, placed his hands under his head.

'He's not going to jail,' I said firmly. *Bleep bleep* went Oli's machine, its lights flashing red. 'He's just being held at the station. They'll let him go.'

Oli sat up, as if he'd just woken from an afternoon nap, as if he'd been right as rain all along. 'You saw what he did to me.'

'You look okay now.' I swallowed my tears. 'And it wasn't Dad anyway.'

'I look okay because you're a miracle. But, face it, your dad's a fucking nutcase.' He was shouting to be heard over the machine.

'No.' I stepped back.

'So's your mum, to be honest. Lock 'em both up, I say.'

'No, Oli. You're wrong!'

The machine's bleep turned into the bleep of my alarm clock. I don't even know why it was set; I had no reason to get up, nowhere to go. I sat up, untangled myself from the sheet. I had a sour taste in my mouth. Of course Oli hadn't woken up. Of course he didn't want to be my boyfriend, or to marry me. I shook my head, shook the threads of the nightmare away. There was an ache in my chest. Where were my friends and why hadn't they called? Did they all hate me, like Katie did? What was going to happen to my family and to me?

31

I wasn't expecting to see the future *Miss Boorunga* when I looked in the mirror the next morning, but the miserable face staring back made me want to dive into bed. But I wasn't giving up. I searched my drawers for clean clothes, pulling out my denim mini-skirt, *Stop Making Sense* T-shirt and blue flannie. Today I was going to be strong.

I ploughed my comb through all the knots, forcing my hair into a ponytail. I rubbed moisturiser into my face. It didn't instantly transform me like the plastic-faced model in the TV ad promised, but I felt slightly less like a scarecrow, which was a definite improvement.

My first mission was the house.

I started by scraping one-hundred-year-old bolognaise sauce off the stove, and kept going – scrubbing, wiping, washing, sweeping, mopping – until the kitchen resembled a kitchen again, the smell of bleach and Jif so strong my eyes watered and a chemical taste soured my mouth. I worked like a robot, only stopping to eat spoonfuls of cold macaroni and cheese, and then to carry out an experiment with the Smirnoff Vodka I found under the sink with all the cleaning stuff. I gulped hot mouthfuls straight from the bottle until I spewed them back out onto the lino. Even though it meant mopping the floor a second time, I was relieved that both my taste buds and stomach were repelled by the poisonous liquid. It confirmed I wasn't an alcoholic.

After the kitchen, I attacked the bathroom, then the living room. I didn't even give up when Mum appeared, ghost-like with her nightie floating over her grey skin, searching for another packet of cigarettes, and told me I should be in bed, forgetting that a) I hadn't had a bedtime since I was five, and b) it was one-thirty in the afternoon. I kept at it until I'd used up every drop of bleach and Spray n Wipe, squeezed out the last blob of Jif, and the sponges had more holes than Dad's socks.

The result wasn't perfect. The black mould above the bath was as much a part of the bathroom as the brown wallpaper it was growing on, and it'd take a truckload of paint to whiten the walls yellowed by Mum's cigarette smoke. The stains on the carpet, coffee rings and scratches on the table were there before I was born and would remain until after I died. But the house was in a better state than I could remember.

My next mission was almost as daunting: to buy food from the corner shop. Mum would've tried to stop me, but she was snoring loudly when I removed the twenty-dollar note from Dad's wallet, which, thankfully, was still under his pillow where he always kept it.

The shop was only a kilometre away. I'd been keeping watch on our front yard through the living room window, and the only trespasser I'd spotted was Tibbles, Mrs Belkin's ginger cat. I convinced myself the photographers had got bored watching our weeds grow while waiting for signs of life from behind our curtains. They'd probably put their fat, hairy arms up for a more exciting job, like a silent reading competition at Boorunga Preschool.

It was cold outside but the gum trees' branches were still, and the street was deathly quiet. The end-of-school bell wouldn't ring for another half hour and then it'd be at least twenty minutes before Leon herded all the kids onto the bus, drove them across town and up Hays Street. I puffed out tiny clouds of steam as the stones crunched under my Converses. My body ached from all the scrubbing and mopping, and I guess I wasn't thinking straight. Perhaps it was the vodka, or all the chemicals I'd breathed in. I felt relaxed, too relaxed.

The rubber doormat ding-donged when I stepped into the shop. My heart was beating fast, though I wasn't sure who I was afraid of seeing. The boy who'd called me at Harriet's? The photographers? Oli's dad? But after a quick scan of the aisles my heart slowed again. No one was hiding behind the rack of dusty birthday cards. The shop was empty apart from the owner, Mr Butler with his wild, grey mono-brow, and the sickening smell of overripe fruit.

'Hello there, Miss Jamieson.' Mr Butler nodded at me when I emptied my armful of tins, bread, tomatoes and bananas on the counter.

'Hello.'

'I was very sorry to hear about your father,' he said.

'Thanks. It's a mistake.' 'Mistake' wasn't a strong enough word, but if I'd said 'fuck-up', Mr Butler probably would've clicked his tongue in disgust and charged me an extra two dollars. Everyone knew he went to church at least twice a week and believed swearing was a sin.

'Yes.' Mr Butler began packing my groceries into a plastic bag. 'I'm quite sure they've got the wrong fellow.'

Tears filled my eyes as I stepped out onto the street. Mr Butler was nothing more to me than someone to buy Kit-Kats and Violet Crumbles from, to count out my sticky handfuls of ten and twenty-cent pieces, but he was the first person I wasn't related to who'd showed me any sign of kindness. I'd sensed he was waiting for me to say more, to give him some goss to pass onto Mrs Butler, but he gave me a warm smile when I said goodbye and I knew he'd meant what he said about them having 'the wrong fellow'.

I let warm tears roll down my cheeks as I walked along Hays Street, the heavy plastic bag digging into my fingers. I only wish I'd held them in until I was safely inside. If my eyes weren't swimming in tears, I might've noticed the white combi van parked under the wattle tree near the Olsens' letter box. Their house was at least fifty metres away from ours, so if I'd spotted the van I could've turned around, or snuck home through the Clarks' and Lockerys' backyards. But I didn't. I was sobbing like a four year old, still thinking about Mr Butler, and about how his concern made his eyes disappear into his mono-brow.

'Miracle?' It was the man with the ponytail who'd eaten a pie on our front lawn the morning after Dad was taken away. He stepped out of the van and onto the footpath in front of me before I had a chance to wipe my eyes.

'Can I talk to you for a minute, please?' He had a lisp like Todd Walker in Year 9, who everyone said was a poof.

I pushed past him, bowing my head.

'Have you heard the latest on Oliver?' His voice followed me.

I kept walking, jaw clenched.

'Were you close? Boyfriend and girlfriend?'

I kept my eyes on the footpath, blocking him out.

'Did you hear his condition has worsened?'

I stopped, forgetting that this man was the last person in the world I wanted to talk to. *Worsened?*

'The doctors are saying he mightn't make it through the week.'

'I didn't know,' I said.

'How will your old man plead?'

Vomit burnt the back of my throat. The look on the man's face was incongruous with the words that'd just escaped his mouth. It was as if he'd just said Manly was playing Parramatta in the rugby league grand final and he was asking whether I thought Parramatta would win. I then noticed the camera in his hands. I don't remember hearing it click.

32

'I don't know what to say.' Mum slid her hand along the newly bare kitchen table, as if she couldn't believe it was real. 'If we weren't completely broke, I'd say "Here's some pocket money," but we are, so …'

'I've put everything in a box in the linen cupboard,' I said. 'There were quite a few letters and … bills that hadn't been opened.'

Mum scratched her head, frowning. 'You didn't happen to find my good lighter?'

It was the morning after I'd seen Ponytail Man, a cold, deafening-rain-on-the-roof day, and although I'd fessed up about going to the corner shop – I'd made us toast when I got home – I hadn't wanted to worry Mum by mentioning the white combi van. Or the man inside it.

I was about to reveal the stash of lighters I'd collected from around the house – I'd even dug one out of the soil of our only surviving pot plant – when there was a thump on the front door.

'God, what now?' Mum said.

'I'll get it.'

'Check first!'

There wasn't a person-like shape on the other side of the glass, so I unclicked the three locks and slowly pushed the door open. I scanned the yard. Rain was bucketing down, drowning the grass, drenching the bottlebrush, gushing down the driveway, turning each of the six concrete stepping stones into brown pools. It wasn't until I was closing the door that I spied the plastic-clad rolled-up newspaper on the door mat. We'd only ever bought *The Boorunga Times* when Dad was looking for a job, so I knew it wasn't ours.

'Who was it?' Mum asked.

'No one.' I waved the paper at her, dripping water across the lino. 'This was delivered by mistake.'

'That's never happened before.' Mum broke off the corner of a Cruskit and crumbled it into dust. 'You think it was a mistake?'

'Yeah, well, why'd someone give us one for free?' I ripped off the wet plastic sleeve, hoping I'd find out something about Oli. Something to prove Ponytail Man wrong.

I spread the paper on the table, ironing it flat with my hands. When I saw the large photo in the centre, my stomach lurched. I gripped the table.

'Jesus fucking Christ!' Mum leant over my shoulder.

Above the photo, above *my* head, were the words: 'MY DAD'S A KILLER!'. The giant letters bled into a blur of black. A black hole.

'Your face. You're … a mess.' Mum stared at the photo. 'But when? When did they take this?'

'He …' I wanted to disappear into the hole.

'Sit down, Miracle. Your face is as grey as … something.' Her voice trailed off as she helped me into a chair.

'I saw them on the way home. From the shop.'

'Bastards!' She picked up her glass of what I'd thought was water, but later realised was vodka, and gulped it down.

'I didn't want to tell you,' I said. 'I didn't see the van until he got out. That white van. He told me … He asked me about Dad. But I didn't say that!'

'Of course you didn't. They make things up all the time. They wrote that Jill was the Manager of Women's Wear, when she was *my* assistant. But this?'

'What am I going to do?' I stood up, panicking. 'Everyone will think –'

'Calm down, Miracle. Oliver didn't die. No one's killed anyone.'

I shook my head. 'The man said he's not getting better.'

Mum reached for my hand, and tears poured out of me.

'It's still got nothing to do with us,' she said.

'But people. People will think. They'll think I said this.' Now my nose was running too.

Mum ripped off a piece of newspaper. 'I wouldn't even eat fish and chips wrapped up in this trash. Give your nose a good blow.'

'You don't eat fish and chips.' But I blew my nose on the strip of paper, half an article about the quality of Boorunga's water. Then I reached for the rest of the newspaper, taking a deep breath. What else had they made up about me?

'Give me that!' Mum grabbed the paper.

She tore what remained of the front page into long strips, then ripped the strips into smaller bits, shredding it again and again, before throwing the lot up into the air. A confetti of lies floated down onto the table.

She nodded at me, so I grabbed the next page and tore it in half, ripping all the meaning out of the words. The paper disintegrated so easily in my fingers. I felt strong, in control.

'Complete crap,' I said, ripping up another sheet, and another, as Mum did the same. By now we were giggling, the way you do when everything is so wrong laughter is all you have left, like I'd done at Granny Holmes's funeral when I realised she'd never offer me another pink Iced VoVo. I guessed Mum was drunk, but I didn't care. Together we destroyed every word, every photo, every real estate ad and kids' athletics result, smearing black ink all over our fingers and hands.

We were shoving all the bits of paper into the kitchen bin, half giggling, half sobbing, when the phone rang.

'Can you get it?' Mum said, a bruise of ink on her cheek. 'Could be the cops. Harriet's warned me off speaking to them.'

I walked along the hallway as if marching to my death. Sideways rain pelted the front door. Would it be Livvy, wondering why I'd never talked to the cops? Or would it be Harriet? Please be Harriet. Or, the cops! Yes – let it be them, calling to say they realised they'd stuffed up and begging for our forgiveness. Please! Let it be good news. I grabbed the phone with my inky hand.

'Hello.'

'Miracle? It's Pheebs.'

'Pheebs?' I couldn't think what to say. I'd waited so long for a friend to call, I'd given up, accepted that everyone hated me. Then it hit me. Our copy of *The Boorunga Times* may have been unrecognisable, coated in tea and crumbs in the depths of our kitchen bin, but thousands of other copies lay spread out on thousands of other kitchen tables, each in one perfectly readable piece.

'Miracle, you've got to listen to me – please!'

'What is it?' This wasn't about me crying on the front page? Or calling my dad a killer?

'I need to tell you something!' She sounded breathless.

'Okay, what?' It could only be bad news. I held the phone away.

'Look … It's Oli's dad.' Pheebs spoke softly and I imagined her standing behind her bedroom door, the phone cord stretched so tight from the kitchen a loud word could snap it.

'Yeah, I know he hates us,' I said.

'Yeah. But he, um. Well, he …'

'He did it?'

'Did it? Oh, you mean he hurt Oli? No. Nothing like that. He's planning something. To do something to your dad.'

'Dad's done nothing wrong.' God, I was sick of saying that.

'That's not what they think. Oli's not getting better. He might even, you know …'

'I know.'

'Yeah, so his dad and Katie's dad – and a few others – well, I just heard. They want to get your dad.'

'They can't.' I tried to keep my voice from wobbling. 'He's stuck at the police station. He'll be there until after the next court session.' Knowing he was safe didn't stop me from shaking.

'All I know is they're planning to *get* him.' She whispered the 'get', and I knew then that she was on my side.

'How?'

'Katie only heard bits, and don't tell her I told you. She's acting *so* weird right now, but I'm sure she's not making this up. Cross my heart! They had a meeting about it and everything.'

'But what does "get him" mean?'

'I dunno. Hurt him or something. But you can't say I told you!'

'What can I –'

'Please don't say anything.'

'I won't, but –'

'I can't imagine your dad hurting anyone.'

'He wouldn't!' I choked. 'But thanks. For telling me.'

'I had to,' Pheebs said. 'I just can't … Fuck. This must be hell for you.'

'Yes.' I leant against the wall.

'I'm sorry. I thought you could warn him. Just don't tell anyone I told you. Bye.'

'Pheebs! Wait!'

Click.

Beep. Beep. Beep. Beep. Beep.

I slid down the wall, holding the phone to my ear, until long after the beeps stopped.

33

'Surprise!' Worm flung his arms in the air.

I jumped, almost wetting my pants.

Worm was hopping up and down on our doormat, dressed in a blue striped T-shirt, navy school shorts, and a smile that showed all the gaps where his baby teeth used to be.

Harriet and John stood behind him, each with a bag of groceries, and Julian was coming across the lawn with a backpack on each shoulder. It was late afternoon and the rain had finally stopped, leaving the world a washed-out grey, the colour I'd been feeling since Pheebs's phone call.

'Aren't you surprised?' Worm's bottom lip replaced his smile.

Another surprise was the last thing I needed, but Worm hadn't known that. Nor could he – or any of them – know that their knock on the door had made my heart race so fast I couldn't breathe, which was why I just stood there looking at them.

'Jules is homesick,' Worm said. 'Mum's making hamburgers!'

'Home.' Julian eyed his backpack.

'I thought we'd all come round and join you for dinner,' Harriet said. 'Bit later than I hoped. We stopped at the hospital to check in on Mia West, the friend I told you about.'

I'm not sure what set me off – Worm's excitement, the relief of seeing them all, or the warmth of Harriet's voice – but my reply was a sob that dredged up a flood of tears.

'It's all right, don't cry.' Harriet handed John her shopping bag so she could hug me. 'Mia's recovering well. Could be home at the end of the week.'

'I need her back at school. 2B are getting way out of line,' John added. 'I feel for the relief teacher.'

'It's not that.' I sniffed.

I felt Julian's eyes on me, questioning.

'Don't you like hamburgers?' Worm asked. 'You don't have to have pineapple.'

'Please don't worry about that ridiculous article,' Harriet said. 'Everyone'll forget about it soon enough.'

I knew they would've seen it. Although she and John said *The Boorunga Times* was rubbish, they still had it delivered to their house, along with *The Sydney Morning Herald*. It was a bit like Radio B1, our radio station: everyone claimed to hate it, but they still seemed to know what DJ Paula's top ten songs were each week.

I wiped my eyes. 'But it still makes me feel sick.'

The truth was, I'd managed to get the awful photo out of my head, along with the horrible words I hadn't said. I'd let Pheebs's warning gnaw at me instead, replaying her words over and over while trying to read *Lord of the Flies*. I'd decided to keep them to myself. What good would telling anyone do? Dad was in the safest place he could be and Mum seemed to have finally climbed out of the hole she'd sunken into.

'You've done wonders, Miracle,' Harriet said, looking around the living room. 'Want to start on ours next?'

I shook my head. 'My shoulders still ache. Your house is perfect anyway.'

'It would've been a challenging job.' John ran his fingers along the clean windowsill. 'If you'll forgive me for saying so, Hen.'

'Say what you like, John. But I can't say I've ever seen you with a mop in your hand.' Mum winked to show she was joking, though it was true. I'd never even seen John wash the dishes.

'Julian, give me a hug.' Mum wrapped her arms around him. 'I've missed you.' Julian looked at me over Mum's shoulder. Mum wasn't much of a hugger, but he didn't seem shocked. Had he missed Mum too? It was impossible to tell; he wasn't smiling and his eyes didn't tell me anything. He was almost the same height as Mum now. When had that happened?

'I'm hungry!' Worm said. 'Can I watch TV?'

'If Aunty Hen says yes,' Harriet said. 'I'll get dinner on.'

'Go for it, Worm,' Mum said.

Harriet turned on *The Wonderful World of Disney* for Worm before disappearing into the kitchen, and John sat on the couch next to Mum. He launched into a story about a relief teacher who'd burst into tears when he'd walked into her classroom, and Mum did a convincing job of looking interested, nodding and saying 'Really?' every now and then. I wondered whether, in reviving the house, I'd somehow revitalised her. I'd scrubbed off some of her anxiety, mopped up some misery.

Julian held out the backpack of stuff I'd left at Harriet and John's.

'Thanks.' I noticed he'd taken his sketchpad out of his own backpack. 'Going to draw something?'

He shrugged, his way of saying yes. I realised I'd missed him too. Watching him draw, seeing his right hand stop shaking and his body loosen, had always made me feel calm. I'd missed feeling calm. I dumped my bag in my bedroom before joining him on the carpet in front of the TV.

I tried to lose myself in the moment – in Julian's long, thin fingers pressing his pencil lightly on the paper, in the almost normal conversation Mum was fumbling through, in the chatter of American kids on Disney, in the comforting smell of fried

211

onions sailing from the kitchen – and to ignore Pheebs's urgent voice in my head. It was probably only talk, I told myself. What good would hurting Dad do anyway? Those men'd just end up in jail. Besides, as long as Dad was in a cell at Boorunga Police Station, no one could touch him.

But then. Julian's drawing. The eyes. He'd just finished the right eye, and a thick eyebrow, and had moved his pencil down the paper, thin grey lines forming cheekbones, creating structure, shape. But the eyes! I'd never recognised anyone in Julian's drawings, but now there was something familiar about the shape, the squint. I kept watching, deaf to Disney, to John's voice. The hair should've been the giveaway, the way it hid the left eyebrow, messy in a deliberate way. I must've known then, but it was like dreaming, watching from some faraway place. I kept watching, even as goosebumps crept up my arms. But then. Julian moved his wrist, revealing the lips – the lips curved into *that* smile.

I stood up so fast my head spun. 'What are you doing?'

'For you.' Julian smiled his angel smile.

'But that's …'

He nodded, touching Oli's pencilled cheek with his finger.

'Seems a good likeness from here,' John said. 'What's wrong, Miracle?'

'It's Oli Harrison!'

Mum stood and peered over. 'It does look a lot like him. He's a good-looking boy. Perhaps you could give it to him some day.'

I tried to breathe slowly, to calm myself. It felt like Julian'd done something wrong, but what? The picture was perfect, the likeness incredible. But why? Why had he suddenly drawn someone I knew? And why Oli? Julian would've remembered Oli from when he used to come to our place to play, but that was ages ago. He knew why Dad was at the station, of course. But like most things, what happened to Oli hadn't seemed to have bothered Julian.

Maybe Julian had missed me, I thought. Maybe the drawing was a special gift, a way of cheering me up. But I couldn't relax, couldn't be happy, not even when I sat at the table and saw that Harriet had stuck little toothpicks through our burgers as if we were at a restaurant, and that as well as sparkling wine for the adults, there was lemonade for us. Everyone said how yummy the burgers were, even Mum. I couldn't taste mine. Each mouthful sank like a rock in my stomach.

'This wine tastes a bit odd.' Mum reached for the bottle.

John glanced at Harriet. 'Ah yes, it's alcohol free.'

'What?' Mum read the label. 'I didn't know such a thing existed.'

I was swallowing a mouthful of lemonade, the bubbles burning my throat, when the phone rang.

'Answer that will you, Miracle?' Mum turned to John. 'What's the point of wine with no alcohol?'

'You don't answer your own phone?' Harriet asked.

'You said yourself I shouldn't talk to the cops. What if it's them?'

I sat stuck to my chair, terrified of who might be on the other end of the phone line, of what words they might force into my ear, into my mind. Would it be Pheebs scaring me with more threats?

Harriet watched me for a second, then pushed her chair back. 'I'll get it. Miri, you've hardly eaten.'

'Can I say hello to the cops?' Worm asked.

'You can eat your dinner, son,' John said.

I took another bite of burger and slowly chewed it. John tried to keep the conversation going, but stopped when Harriet's 'Thank you so much!' gushed along the hallway. Could it actually be good news?

Harriet came and stood at the head of the table behind John, who'd made himself at home in Dad's seat. 'What a wonderful coincidence we're here all together at this moment. Fill the glasses please, John!'

John reached and splashed more pretend wine into his, Mum's and Harriet's glasses, then more real lemonade into the three Vegemite jars that, in our house, doubled as kids' glasses.

'My goodness.' Harriet sat down, the excitement practically bursting out of her.

'Come on, spill the beans.' Mum elbowed her sister.

'Well, this is the best you could hope for – under the circumstances.' Harriet clasped her hands together and looked around the table. She couldn't stop smiling.

'We can't have won the lottery,' Mum said. 'We've never been able to afford a ticket.'

Harriet lifted her glass. 'To Jim! To Jim coming home!'

Dad was coming home? I jumped to my feet and might've even tried to wrap Mum in an awkward hug, but in a flash, I remembered. Pheebs. *They want to get your dad.*

I slipped back down into my chair.

'You're not joking?' Mum tilted her head at Harriet, her face, her whole self, lighting up. 'He's getting out? Even after what I did? What I said?'

'That's what the sergeant said. He'll be on a twenty-four-hour curfew until the next court date, but that's not far away. And they didn't actually press any charges against you. Said you were under *extreme* stress.' Harriet's cheeks looked so red, I wondered if some alcohol had accidentally got into her wine. 'Perhaps they realised Jim was needed here – to look after you! Miri, I just said your dad's coming home. Miracle, you look miles away.'

'I'm listening,' I said. 'It's really great. Fantastic.' I forced a smile then hid my mouth behind my glass and took a huge gulp. The lemonade went down the wrong way, and I spluttered. What the hell was I going to do now?

34

John stood as he lifted his glass, as if we were the royal family and Dad was about to be crowned King, but for some reason we were celebrating in the servants' quarters. 'To Jim. To Jim being reunited with his family.'

'Jim!' we chorused, our glasses clinking together, wine and Vegemite glasses alike.

'So who told you?' Mum sniffed her fake wine. 'Who was on the phone?'

'Sergeant Nick,' Harriet said. 'They've got a bit of paperwork to do. Goodness knows why that takes all night. Surely they've got an "innocent" stamp they can just whack on his file. But Jim should be free to go tomorrow.'

'Nick, the one with red hair?' Mum asked. 'Looks six months pregnant?'

'He's a bit overweight.' Harriet nodded, a smile spreading across her face. 'And I think you told him as much.'

Mum winced. 'I thought "Fat F-U-C-K" summed him up nicely.'

'I can spell!' Worm said. 'I know what F-U-C-K spells!'

'Shush, Worm,' Harriet said. 'You didn't hear that.'

But she laughed, and Mum laughed too. For the first time in ages, they actually seemed like twin sisters. Mum's laugh was deeper than Harriet's – was that her depression's fault? Had it dragged her voice down? – but they opened their mouths and tilted their heads in a similar way.

'I can't believe it, Hen.' Harriet dabbed at her eyes with a paper towel. 'I can't believe he didn't put you away too!'

'And be called a fat you-know-what all day?' Mum let out a snort. 'He couldn't get rid of me fast enough!'

'A fat fuck all day long,' Worm said, squishing a piece of pineapple with his fork.

'Worm!' John said. 'I think you've had enough lemonade.'

'So, anyway, tomorrow you'll put on your best manners, Hen,' Harriet continued. 'Sergeant Nick said he'll give Jim a lift home sometime before lunch.'

'My God.' Mum shook her head. Her eyes were moist too, like Harriet's. 'Can it really all be over?'

Julian chose that moment to slide off his chair, wiping his mouth on the sleeve of his flannelette shirt.

'Had enough?' Harriet nodded at the toasted bun, lettuce and pineapple still on his plate.

'Full.' Julian patted his stomach.

'Probably gets his poor eating habits from me.' Mum watched Julian walk away. 'We hardly ever sit together for our meals. Could barely even see this table until yesterday!' She turned back to Harriet.

'Did he say why they're letting Jim go now? Have they got someone else?'

'TV!' Worm leaped out of his chair and ran to join Julian.

Harriet sighed. 'No. Well, if they have, the sergeant didn't say. Jim's not exactly in the clear yet, but surely he will be after the next court hearing.'

'I wonder who spray-painted those words.' Mum picked up her wine glass. 'Some arsehole who wanted Jim to look guilty.'

'I'm sure they'll find out eventually, but you know what? I think that trashy article about Miracle helped.' Harriet smiled at me. 'A young girl left without her dad ... looking traumatised. Seeing Miracle might've made them realise he's just an everyday dad.'

'Maybe they'll put me in jail instead,' I said. 'For looking so ugly and stupid.'

'Sweets, what's wrong? I thought you'd be over the moon.' Harriet frowned at me. 'Surely you're not going to let that newspaper thing bother you. No one reads it! Except, possibly, the police.'

I realised I had to tell them what Pheebs said. If I kept her words to myself I was likely to explode into a thousand worries. I wouldn't mention her name, but I had to speak up. What if the second Dad stepped out of the station, he got ... what? What were they planning to do? Hurt him or kill him?

'... you think?' Harriet was looking at me.

'Think what?' I said. Mum's eyes were on me too.

'Perhaps your family should go away. Have a break,' Harriet continued. 'When the fuss dies down.'

I nodded, though I couldn't see it happening. I couldn't imagine the fuss ever dying down. The *fuss?* What kind of word was that anyway?

'You've hardly eaten anything either,' Harriet said. 'I thought you and Julian liked my cooking.'

'Yeah. It's just –'

'You don't look well.' Mum reached and touched my forehead. Her hand felt cold. 'You're burning up.'

'I'm okay.' But I didn't need to touch my forehead to know Mum was right.

'She's got a bit of a temperature,' Mum said to Harriet and John, as if they didn't believe her.

'There are a few bugs doing the rounds.' John stood and pushed his chair, Dad's chair, under the table. 'I'll go check what the boys are watching.'

'You're probably feeling overwhelmed too. Are you, lovey?'

'No. I'm … I've got something to say.' My mouth was too dry to swallow.

'What?' Mum said. 'What is it?'

I licked my lips. 'This morning. You know how Pheebs called? She wasn't just seeing how I was –'

'Oh bloody hell!' John's voice from the living room. 'Jesus!'

'What, John?' Harriet called. The three of us sprang up from the table. I was amazed at how quickly Mum moved.

On the TV screen was a photo of Oli wearing a dirty footy jersey, his face red and sweaty and his hair caked with mud. Then another: in his school uniform, arms folded, and staring away from the camera. Then: standing on a log with Seth, both holding fishing rods. And finally: at the school disco, his arm draped around Katie's shoulders. Perfect, unblemished Oli. Oli, before …

Then Oli was replaced with footage of his parents walking down the hospital corridor. Mr Harrison's mouth tightly closed as if he was struggling to keep it shut, and his eyes burning with anger. Mrs Harrison walking behind him, her short, boyish hair greyer than I remembered. There was a hole in the elbow of her red cardigan and, for some reason, it was this, Mrs Harrison's threadbare elbow, that triggered my surge of tears.

There must've been words, too, to accompany the images. The news reporter must've explained exactly what'd just happened. The time it'd happened. I didn't hear anything until Oli's story was over. And it wasn't from the TV. The only noise, the only words I heard came from Julian.

'Hello.' Julian was talking to the wall next to the TV, the bare wall. The TV screen was now filled with the bruised face of a little girl from Henley.

'Hello, Oli,' Julian said.

35

'Let it out, Miri.' Harriet sat next to me on the couch. I felt the weight of her arm resting on my shoulder, but I couldn't feel anything else, nothing from inside of me. 'Have a good cry.'

Even Mum's eyes were wet. She sat in the chair with her arms folded and an unlit cigarette between her lips. John turned the TV off and busied himself making cups of milky tea. I didn't normally drink tea, but I held the hot mug in my hands and let it burn my skin, let the sharp pain of it overpower the nothingness I felt inside. John also passed around a plate of caramel Twirly Swirls but Worm was the only one who took one.

Julian lay flat on his back with his belly button showing, humming. I didn't recognise the tune, but it made my skin tingle. If I could summon up the energy to move, I would've grabbed a Twirly Swirl and thrown it at his head.

'Julian, is that necessary?' Mum stretched out her leg and prodded him with her foot. 'Look around. Everyone's upset.'

Julian kept his eyes on the ceiling, still humming.

'Well, perhaps we should go now. Pack up your Lego, Worm.' Harriet tucked a tissue into her sleeve, picked up her handbag, stood and smoothed out her skirt. 'We'll stop in again tomorrow when Jim gets home.'

'No.' The word leapt from my mouth.

'What?' Mum said. Or was it Harriet?

'Maybe he won't come home now,' I continued. 'Cos of Oli.'

'I don't think that makes a scrap of difference,' John said. 'It doesn't make your dad more guilty. It just makes the crime worse. A lot worse.'

'Makes it murder,' Mum mumbled.

'Your dad *is* coming home, Miracle,' Harriet said. 'The sergeant is bringing him home to you.'

'But he can't!' I punched the arm of the couch. 'Not now.'

'He won't be allowed to leave the house,' Harriet said. 'But at the next court –'

'They're going to … they're going to get him.'

'Who is?' Mum leant forward in her chair.

'I was trying to tell you. Pheebs told me.'

Julian stopped humming, and sat up.

'She said they've had meetings and everything. It's all planned. She was ringing to warn me.'

'Who? Who's they?' Mum asked.

'Oli's dad. And some others. Katie's dad, I think.'

'What exactly did she say?' Harriet or Mum asked.

'That's all. Just that they were planning to do something to him. Hurt him or … She wanted to warn me.'

For a few moments everyone was silent, apart from Worm who was playing with his Lego spacemen.

'I wouldn't be too worried,' John said. 'Sounds a bit like a story a teenage girl might make up.'

'No.' I shook my head. 'I know she wasn't lying.'

'Did you see Steve Harrison? That look on his face?' Mum said to John. 'He'd be capable of anything.'

'He looked like he'd lost everything in the whole world.' Harriet dug another tissue out of her pocket and dabbed her cheeks. 'Understandably too.'

'Yes, but the anger!' Mum said. 'The rage in his eyes.'

'He's known for his short fuse,' John said. 'And that Heller is a nasty piece of work. He rules over his workers like a dictator.'

Harriet let her handbag drop to the floor and sat on the arm of the couch. 'So, what do we do? Let the police know?'

'We have to,' John said. 'And if Phoebe did invent the story, she'll learn an important lesson.'

'But you can't say she told me!' I'd only just discovered Pheebs was still my friend. I didn't want her to dump me. 'I wasn't meant to say her name.'

'The police are going to ask, lovey,' Harriet said. 'If they're going to investigate, that'll be the first question they ask.'

'But I said I wouldn't say.' Pheebs could also be scary when she was angry.

'If this isn't a prank, it's pretty serious,' John said. 'We're going to have to be completely honest with the police. Your friend'll forgive you. She'll understand it's the best thing for your dad.'

I pictured Dad – a sad, lonely, stuck-in-a-prison-cell version of Dad, his hairy white legs still bare, though surely they would've given him some prison pants to put on – and my chest heaved.

'Okay,' I said. 'I get it.'

'Leave it with me,' Harriet said. 'I'll call Sergeant Nick first thing in the morning.'

After they'd said goodbye and closed the front door behind them, there was another ring from the hallway. I froze.

'Bloody phone,' Mum said.

When I didn't move, she said, 'Oh, I'll get the damn thing.'

I covered my ears, not wanting to hear what she was saying, but she was back within a minute.

'It was Greg's daughter,' Mum said. 'Wanted to talk to you. I said you're not up to it right now.'

'Thanks. I'm not.' Was Livvy calling to ask if I'd watched the news? To tell me the cops had finally got Greg? I didn't really care what happened to him anymore, as long as Dad was off the hook. But remembering Livvy's visit, her sitting next to me on the couch, bangles twinkling up her arm, reminded me of what I'd been storing at the back of my mind.

'Mum? Is it true Dad has a criminal record?'

The look on Mum's face answered my question. 'Who told you?'

'Livvy. What did he do?' I tried to sound casual, as if I was asking about something normal like what subjects Dad studied at school.

'It was a long time ago. And it wasn't his fault. It's certainly none of Livvy's business.'

'What happened?'

'He saved me. And he didn't even know me from a bar of soap.'

'Saved you from what?'

Mum stared at her fingers, her lips twisted, as if she was trying to trap the words inside her mouth. In a voice so soft I strained my ears to hear, she told me it happened back when she was the Manager of Women's Wear at Grace Bros. She was tidying up the changing rooms and Dad was sitting in a chair outside, waiting for his mum, Nana Jamieson, to decide what to put on lay-by. She'd tried on three dresses and two blouses. Mum remembered this fact because Dad'd repeated it in court.

'And?'

'Well, there was another man there too, but he wasn't waiting for his mum. Or wife. Or anyone else. He was hiding in one of the changing rooms.'

I held my breath, scared for Mum, for the person she was previously, when she was someone who left her house to go to work each day. I was also scared she'd stop talking before the end of the story.

'I've never been able to say his name,' she said. 'I'd never seen him before that day, before he grabbed me as I reached into a changing room to collect the coat hangers, and pulled the curtain shut. He was a strong man, much stronger than me, and he pressed his greasy hand over my mouth so I couldn't breathe. I'm not sure how long he held me like that, but it felt like a lifetime. He started … touching me … I was completely powerless and utterly terrified. Somehow I managed to whimper and your dad heard me. One thing you can't fault about your dad is his hearing.'

'So Dad rescued you?'

Mum nodded. 'He knocked the other bloke out. Didn't know him, didn't know me. But he hit that bastard so hard he was hospitalised. And your dad got charged for it. The other bloke walked free. I can't remember whether I trusted cops before then, but I certainly haven't since.'

Was this also the *horrible thing* Mum'd talked about with Harriet? The thing Mum owed her sister *everything* for? I waited for Mum to say more, but she stood up and looked around the living room as if she'd lost something.

'So that's how you met Dad?'

'Romantic, isn't it?' Mum tried to smile. 'You won't find a love story like that in a Mills & Boon.'

'What did Harriet do?'

'Harriet.' Mum frowned. I could tell she was wondering how much I knew. 'Well, she helped me get back on my feet, encouraged me to get out of bed, and when I was ready, out of my flat and back into the world. She was very patient. She and John took me in, invited me to live with them. They'd come here after John was posted to Boorunga Primary; he was just a teacher back then. That's why we ended up in Boorunga. Your dad eventually followed me here.'

Nightmares plagued my sleep. In the first dream, Dad was

hitchhiking around Australia trying to find where Mum'd gone. He kept running into random houses opening cupboard doors, calling out 'Henrietta!'. But a worse dream, the one that finally woke me, was about the night Oli was attacked. I was at the crem, in the kitchen, doing my maths homework at the tiny lunch table, when I heard Oli call 'Help!'. I'd leapt out of the chair, yanked the front door open and ran outside without being scared of the dark. Somehow a torch was in my hand, and I shone it at the ground where Oli was lying, his blood blackening the white pebbles. 'It'll be okay, Oli,' I whispered. I then raised the torch and flashed it in the face of the person standing over him. I let the torch drop from my hand.

My scream was powerful enough to jerk me awake. I was shaking and my sheets and Boy George nightie were sticking to me. For a moment I thought I'd wet the bed.

I lay awake in the half-dark, too scared to go back to sleep, but not ready to face a new day. By the time the sun finally appeared, I was exhausted.

Mum was in the kitchen, slathering a burnt piece of toast with margarine. She said that Harriet had already talked to the sergeant. He hadn't been surprised by Pheebs's warning. When he'd turned up at the station a few minutes before her call, he'd seen graffiti on the brick wall of Milson's Pharmacy, opposite the station.

'What did it say?'

Mum cut her toast in half then into quarters. 'It was serious enough to make them agree to keep your dad in for his protection – and for our safety.'

'They're going to keep him in?' Thank God for that. '*Our* safety? So what did it say?'

'Harriet wouldn't tell me.' Mum dropped the knife into the sink. 'I told her I could handle it – they're just bloody words! – but she cut me short. Said she had to get ready for school. Honestly, that sister of mine! She treats me like a kid.'

36

A doctor from Boorunga Hospital was interviewed on the breakfast news, her lips painted bright pink. She explained what'd happened to Oli's brain after the swelling had gone down, but I can't remember any of it. All I remember is her lips and knowing she'd looked in the mirror and taken care to choose a lipstick – *bright pink* – and carefully painted it on. I guessed she didn't get to go on TV very often so she wanted to impress the other doctors, but to me it made her look like she didn't have a heart.

Mum tried to make me feel better by saying if Oli had woken up from the coma, he might've been severely brain damaged, so 'going peacefully in his sleep' was probably a blessing.

'Isn't it better to be alive?' I said, knowing that someone who spent half their life wishing they were dead wasn't the best person to ask.

'That's a matter of opinion. His parents probably wanted him alive regardless, as most would. But I think that's a bit selfish. What do you reckon? What kind of life would it be for him, being retarded?'

I knew she was just being honest, but I didn't agree. 'What about Julian? Should he've died?' I spoke quietly even though Julian was out of earshot.

'No, of course not. Julian's not retarded. He's special. And you know what? I reckon he knows a lot more than he lets on.'

'I know he does.'

'Sometimes I look at him and wonder what's going on in his head. A hell of a lot more than we give him credit for, I'm sure. He could hold a pencil before he could talk. He's kind of a genius.'

I nodded, thinking about his latest drawing. He'd finished it before we heard the terrible news. Did he already know Oli had died? How could that be possible?

I was about to ask Mum when something went *thwack* against the living room window. Mum and I leapt off the couch. The curtains were closed because Mum was convinced the photographers would come back. I decided it must've been a bird, and was sitting back down when there was another thump. And another.

Thwack. Thwack. Thwack. Thwack.

'What the hell?' Mum grabbed my arm. 'The window could smash.'

Then, silence.

We waited a few minutes. My heart hammered. Mum's breath came short and raspy. Then I carefully pulled aside a curtain and peered out. Yellowy slime with shards ran down the window.

'Eggs?' The gobs of goo made me nauseous.

'Better than stones.' Mum joined me at the window. 'Much better than bullets. But what a bloody mess.'

My nausea turned to burning anger. Who'd thrown them? Not the photographers – they'd never *deliberately* messed up our yard. Who else'd been hanging out on our lawn?

'Come on, Mum!'

'Where? We can't go outside.'

'Someone's got to clean it up.'

'Not now. They could still be out there!'

'If they're dumb enough to stick around, they can help.'

I did most of the work, wiping off the slime with an old towel, spraying the glass with Windex and rubbing it clean with scrunched up pieces of *The Boorunga Times* from the bin. Mum and Julian picked up all the sticky eggshells and stuffed them in a Woolies bag. Twenty eggs, Julian reckoned.

I was about to put the eggy towel and paper in the outside bin when a car drew up. It was almost as fancy as Katie's dad's car and definitely a rich person's: red and shiny with dark windows so you couldn't see inside.

Mum was crossing the lawn with the bag of eggshells.

'Oi!' A man's voice. 'Gonna give yer old man a cremation?'

'Shut your mouth and piss off!' Mum yelled. 'Jim's done nothing!'

Laughter spilled out of the car. Men's laughter. They were laughing at Mum in Dad's dressing gown, tiptoeing so she didn't get bindis in her bare feet, the plastic bag ballooning beside her.

I ran towards them, yelling, the sticky towel still in my hand. I screamed that they'd nearly given us heart attacks, nearly killed us. Before I got near the car, it roared away. Thank God. I don't know what I would've done otherwise. Thrown the towel at the windscreen?

'Well done, Miracle.' Mum was sitting on the plastic bag, pulling bindis out of her feet.

I smiled, shocked by my own behaviour. I'd scared them off!

Sometime before dark, Harriet dropped in to give me *The Boorunga Times*, the paper she'd tried to assure me that no one ever read. She said I might be interested in that day's issue.

Oli, or 'Oliver' as he was now called, took up the whole front page as well as pages two and three. Through watery eyes, I read about his hobbies (swimming, fishing, *Star Wars*), his latest achievements (winning the regional schools' one-hundred metres freestyle, coming third in our school's cross-country), and that his goal was to be the first person to kayak solo across the Tasman Sea. The article described him as 'high-spirited', 'popular', 'cheeky' and 'fun'. It was obviously written by someone kinder than the person who'd made up all those lies about me.

I flicked through to the end of the Classified pages, the obituary section, and found a small notice Harriet must've missed. If she'd seen it, she would've made sure I didn't:

'Oliver Joel Harrison. Oliver was the light of our lives, our only son, the best son parents could hope for. He was stolen from us and his murderer will be brought to justice. Rest in peace, our precious boy. Steven and Judith Harrison.'

Brought to justice. What did that mean? Was that another threat? Would it ever be safe for Dad to come home?

37

Oli's funeral was being held at St Peter's Anglican Church. The day was Friday, 12 July, a date I'd been dreading ever since Miss Jones'd called that special assembly a lifetime ago. I could still see her on the stage in front of us, on tippy-toes so her words didn't get lost on the way to the microphone: *The debate will take place here in the hall after lunch on Friday 12th July.* It was hard to believe I'd cared so much about brainbox Year 12s arguing about something there was no answer to, and that I'd imagined my life'd be over if *The quake caused the curse* won and kids thought I was somehow part of it. Little did I know then that I'd end up being known as the daughter of a murderer. How much more cursed could I be?

Anyway, the debate must've been canned or postponed because there was no school that day. For as long as I'd been at school, I couldn't remember it closing on an actual *school day*. When Big Bobby and Joanne died, some of us were bussed to the funerals, but we were bussed back again before the end-of-lunch bell rang. For all the kids who didn't give a crap about Oli and just wanted to get out of double maths, the day off would've seemed like a gift from God. But for practically everyone else, it would be a day spent mourning the loss of the boy whose face they'd seen in the news for nearly three weeks.

'Ready?' I called from the living room. I was shivering in my denim skirt and red Sportsgirl top, but I had no 'good' warm clothes, and, as I told myself, being cold was a privilege. Oli wouldn't feel anything at all. 'It's nearly one o'clock!'

'Is this okay?' Mum was wearing a navy blue dress which hid her bumpy white knees and had her hair in a bun.

'You look like a school teacher,' I said.

'You mean like Harriet?' Mum studied her reflection in the TV. 'Well, I probably could've got into teachers' college if I hadn't dropped out of school.'

'Ready,' Julian said. His effort to dress up meant turning his white T-shirt inside out so it looked clean. His sketchpad was tucked under his arm.

'There are few children I actually like, though,' Mum was saying.

'Okay. Let's sit down,' I said.

We sat in our usual chairs at the table, at the centre of which was a dusty white candle I'd dug out of our emergency kit and forced into the empty fake wine bottle Harriet and John had brought round.

The memorial service was Harriet's idea. There was no way I could attend the real thing. Mum'd told me to put the idea out of my mind before I'd said a thing, and I didn't argue. Even if the cops didn't think Dad was guilty, it seemed the rest of the town did. I couldn't imagine anyone pelting eggs inside a church, but having the whole town's angry eyes boring into us would be a hundred times worse. It made me sad, though; I'd known Oli longer than Katie and there was no way she could've loved him more than I had. I'd never seen her face turn pink when he smiled at her.

Instead, Harriet and John promised to say goodbye to Oli for me. They'd never even met him, but I liked the thought of them being at the funeral, in the church, singing the hymns and saying the prayers.

I was about to start our service when Julian sneezed. The candle's flame flickered then died.

'That was symbolic.' Mum passed me her lighter. 'Oliver went out peacefully.'

'Can I start now?' I was desperate to get the service over and done with.

I launched into the only prayer I remembered from the few Religious Instruction lessons we'd had at school before someone's parents complained and had them banned. 'Our Father, who art –'

'Can we skip the religious claptrap?' The sharp smell of alcohol hung on Mum's words.

'Um, okay.' I couldn't remember the whole thing anyway. 'We're sitting here now to … remember Oli.'

'Oli,' Julian repeated. He opened his sketchpad to the picture he'd drawn the day Oli died and lay it flat so the three of us could stare at it.

We sat in silence, our eyes floating between Julian's drawing and the thin yellow flame as we remembered Oli. Well, God knows what was going through Mum and Julian's heads, but I was thinking about Oli. Until the smell of burning candle dust dredged up images of the crem. Even though there was no way on earth Oli's parents would've handed him over to Greg, I couldn't remove the thought of Oli lying behind one of Compassionate Cremations' closed doors.

'Hey,' Mum said. 'Things will get better, promise.' She reached out from her chair and gave me a half-hug. I felt her bony ribs, but her body was warm. The deep purple pools under her eyes glistened. Was she crying for Oli too?

'Oli's okay.' Julian clasped his hands together, trying to keep them still.

'He's not really,' I said. 'He's dead.'

Then I realised Mum was crying actual tears. 'What's wrong, Mum?'

'I'm sorry. Not much help, am I?' She sniffed. 'I think I need a nap.'

'Please stay,' I said.

But she'd already pushed her chair out and was on her feet, her sudden movement blowing out the candle again. There was nothing I could do but watch her go, and hope she went to sleep before refilling the mug she'd been pretending was full of tea.

I hadn't even liked the idea of a memorial service. I wanted to get Oli out of my head, not obsess about him even more; I'd only gone ahead with it as a way of holding on to Mum for a while longer. I could tell she was trying hard to be strong for me, but I also knew she was drinking from the stash in her cupboard and that this would eventually take her away from us. I wasn't sure how she'd been stocking up her supplies, but Mrs Jensen-from-across-the-road must've been involved. Until then, I'd conveniently assumed the shopping bags she left for Mum at our front door were cartons of Parsons cigarettes.

'Rest in peace, Oli,' I whispered.

Julian had obviously finished mourning Oli, if he'd been mourning him at all. As soon as I said, 'I think that'll do', he walked straight to the TV and sprawled in his beanbag in front of *Days of Our Lives*. Mum often watched *Days* while she was ironing, and Pheebs and Sall sometimes skipped school after lunch to find out who was sleeping with who, but even its dreary theme music made me want to bang my head against the wall.

I looked at Julian's portrait of Oli on the table and felt crushed with sadness. The drawing was now more alive than Oli was.

'Julian? I need to ask you something.'

Julian didn't move, his mind too deeply submerged in the TV world.

'Marlena, we can't go on long like this,' a man with a black eye-patch was saying to a woman with big hair. 'Something's got to give.'

I jumped up, stormed over and turned the TV off.

Julian blinked at me, stunned.

'Why'd you draw Oli?'

He chewed on his bottom lip.

'Please don't sulk,' I said. 'Talk to me. Why'd you draw him on the day he died?'

'I saw,' Julian whispered to his knees.

'You saw him? At the hospital? How?'

'Here,' Julian tapped the side of head, just above his ear.

'In your head?'

He nodded, eyes scanning the room.

'Did you know? Did you know he was dead?'

'Yes.' He was still looking everywhere except at me.

'But how could you know?'

'See.' Julian tapped his head again.

'See what?' I was trying my best to stay calm.

'Dead.' Julian's voice croaked.

'Dead? Ghosts? You see ghosts?'

'Dead.' Julian nodded.

I stared at him, trying to read his eyes. He wasn't joking, Julian never joked. Was he crazy? How could he see ghosts? But then. Then it struck me.

'Wait!'

I rushed to the table for the sketchpad. I knelt next to Julian, and flicked through the pages, through all the faces that'd come before Oli's, none of which I recognised. 'These people. Are these people all dead?'

He nodded again, this time his clear, blue eyes met mine.

I pointed at a girl whose plaits were coming loose. 'Who is she?' When Julian said nothing, I turned to another page, pointed to the face of a man who looked around Dad's age. 'And him?'

He shrugged.

'When did they die?'

Julian started shaking violently, the beans in the beanbag swooshing like a rushing river. 'Nineteen ... seventy ... two.'

I grabbed his shoulders to hold him still. 1972? The year I was born. The year Julian was ...

'You see the people who ... were in the earthquake?'

'Dead.' A tear slid down his cheek.

'That's unbelievable. You've been drawing them all this time. Dead people.'

'I,' he whispered to his knees. 'I died.'

'But only for a few seconds. They brought you back!'

'I died.' Julian buried his head in his knees.

38

'It's okay.' I hugged Julian. 'If you really did die, then you came back to life, which means you're special. It means you're kind of magic.'

I held him until his shaking slowed to a tremble and he pulled his arm away to dry his eyes on his T-shirt. I turned the TV back on. Staring at the screen was his way of relaxing and Mum said it was cheaper than a shrink. He often stayed up watching it until the test pattern came on, long after Mum and Dad had gone to bed.

Surely what he'd told me was impossible. I thought about the ghost of Katie's mum, who Katie swore was always watching over her. Apparently, whenever her dad gave her 'the strap' (it was actually the leather belt that held up his huge trousers), the ghost of her mum appeared, sat at the end of her bed, and whispered, 'There there, my Katie bear'. Katie's mum'd died in the house they still lived in, while giving birth to Katie in an inflatable pool her dad'd bought so they could avoid going to hospital. 'Mum took her last breath the moment I took my first,' Katie'd said. 'How could she "rest in peace" leaving me here?'

I'd always loved the idea of having a ghost to look after me. I'd even wished my own mum would die (painlessly, of course) just so she could appear at the foot of my bed, but, even so, I'd always thought Katie'd made the whole thing up.

If ghosts were real, how come I'd lived for almost fifteen years without seeing one? People had lived and died in Boorunga for over a hundred years, thousands of years if you consider the Aboriginals who inhabited the land before the Town Hall was built. Other families had lived in our house before Mum and Dad moved in. Wouldn't ghosts be everywhere?

I had to do something with what Julian'd just told me, but what? My watch said 2.05 pm. I guessed the funeral would be over, that all the people would've poured out of the church and spilled over the road to the community centre, where, according to Harriet, they'd talk about Oli's life 'over tea and cake'. If anyone was truly sad about losing Oli, how could they eat cake? Even a lamington would get stuck in my throat. I was glad I wasn't there, hiding in the shadows, unable to talk or eat cake.

'I'm going for a walk,' I told the back of Julian's head. If practically everyone I knew was crammed inside the community centre, I could go anywhere without being seen. I could be free.

As I stepped outside, I was shocked to see the sun trying to force its way through Boorunga's grey sky. It felt wrong; it should've been bucketing down for Oli's funeral. There should've been lightning, thunder, hail the size of tennis balls. If God was real he obviously hadn't been watching the news.

I'd reached the end of the driveway when a flash of blue caught my eye. Blue, billowing out of Julian's bedroom window. My first thought was: ghost! But of course it wasn't a ghost proving its existence; Julian'd left his window open and the curtain was flapping in the breeze. That was all. But I stood staring, my heart racing.

I don't know why the sight made the hairs on my arms stand up. Maybe because Mum never opened our windows, not even on suffocatingly hot February days. It was part of her quest to keep the world out. Or perhaps it reminded me of that night in Lawson's Bay, the plastic blinds flapping and scraping, the window open like a giant yawn. Mum'd have a panic attack if Julian ever snuck out of our house, if she found out he was walking the streets of Boorunga in the dark. That's what made me wonder. What if Julian had … He wouldn't have. But what if … I turned and raced back down the driveway.

I grabbed Julian's sketchpad and flicked through it until I found Oli. I then turned off the TV and stood in front of Julian.

'Do you sneak out at night?'

He frowned, wrapped his arms around his knees.

'Like you did in Lawson's Bay. You said it was *peaceful*. You also said you'd done it before.'

He looked at the blank TV screen, and started chewing his thumbnail.

'I'd never thought about you doing it *here*. What about Oli? What happened to him?'

'Shut up!' Julian stuck his fingers in his ears.

That's when I remembered my nightmare: Oli lying on the ground, his blood on the white pebbles, my torch, the face. But that was just a dream.

'Were you there *that* night?' I wanted Julian to shake his head, to say no, so I could turn the TV back on and leave him alone.

But he didn't. He curled into a ball and started rocking from side to side.

'Were you there? At the crem? When Oli –'

'Stop!'

'You were?' I felt a stabbing pain in my chest. 'What happened?'

Julian stopped rocking and climbed to his feet, holding on to the bookshelf to steady his shaking body.

'Is *that* why you can *see* him?' I asked, holding up the sketch of Oli.

I'll never forget the sound of his scream, like an animal's. I stood there, frozen, my ears ringing. I still couldn't move when he grabbed the sketchpad out of my hands and tore out the Oli page, ripping it into pieces. He flung the sketchpad and it bounced off the ironing board and hit the wall. The screaming went on and on. This was *Julian*. My angel brother.

Mum's voice drifted out from the bedroom. I yelled something back: 'We're okay' or 'Don't worry', I can't remember what exactly. I should've been honest, I should've cried 'Help!'.

'What's wrong? Why are you so upset?'

When I think about it now, I see it in slow motion: Julian reaching up to the shelf above the TV and grabbing the snow globe, that crappy souvenir John'd brought back from the Gold Coast. But, of course, it happened very fast. I'll never know if he actually aimed it at me because before it left his hand, I'd shut my eyes.

It sounded like a cricket ball hitting a bat. *Thwump*. That's all I remember. The next thing I knew, Julian was leaning over me, shaking and blubbering, snot pouring out of his nose. My head was throbbing and I felt like I was going to puke.

'Sorry,' Julian was saying. 'Sorry sorry sorry.'

I touched my forehead. The sight of blood on my fingers made me feel hot and sleepy. The snow globe lay in the middle of the floor, upside down, the 'snow' still trapped inside the glass. It must've been the base – the words 'Gold Coast, Queensland' – that cut into my skin.

More muffled words from Mum's bedroom. I think she was saying 'I'm trying to sleep', but this time I didn't have the energy to reply.

'Help me,' I said to Julian.

He sprang into action, running to the kitchen for a tea towel. I lay there, holding it against my forehead as the urge to throw up came in waves.

'It's ruined.' I passed the bloodstained tea towel back to Julian. 'Can you get my hat?'

I held on to the coffee table and pulled myself up, my head throbbing and the taste of vomit in my mouth.

Julian was still sniffing. He held out two caps and a beanie. I took the beanie and put it on, flinching as the prickly wool grazed my forehead.

'Hug.' Julian dropped the caps onto the couch and held out his shaky arms.

'I'll be back later.' I pushed past him.

39

I'd heard about concussion. I knew I should go straight to bed rather than out the front door, but too many thoughts were fighting in my head. If I'd stayed still any longer I would've gone mad. Besides, I couldn't tell if it was my swelling forehead making me so shaky, or the thought of what'd just happened. Julian obviously had been at the crem that night. But why? I thought back to that day, *the* day. When I told Dad about what'd happened at school, about the rats, the stupid bloody rats. Julian was lying on my floor, drawing a baby girl – a dead baby girl? But my story hadn't seemed to bother him. He hadn't looked up or lifted his pencil off the paper. Things like that never got to him. Or did they? What did Julian know? What secrets was he hiding?

My head kept thumping. I made it to Johnson Avenue, then crouched over and retched, but nothing came out. Why hadn't Julian thought to give me a drink? I needed water. I needed sleep. But I'd walked too far to turn back.

Crossing Angus Street, I spotted a sign hanging off Boorunga Bridge:

RIP Oli

Love you always

The 'o' in 'love' was a heart. Katie's handwriting. I swallowed a sob and quickened my pace.

I hadn't been looking for the graffiti the cops'd told Aunty Harriet about. I'd actually forgotten all about it. But the thick, red paint smeared on the side of Milson's Pharmacy was impossible to miss. Whoever'd tried to cover the words hadn't finished the job. I didn't need to step any closer to make out the black letters underneath:

Bang Bang Jim's Dead!

So now I knew. Why Harriet didn't want to tell Mum what it said. And I knew what Pheebs meant by *'get'*. I ran straight across the road without checking. Not that it mattered. There were only two cars parked on the main street. All those people John'd said had been hanging around the station must've been at the community centre, probably helping themselves to a third piece of cake.

I can't remember if I actually decided to go to Boorunga Police Station or if my legs just took me there. I slowed at the steps and walked up one at a time, so the cops wouldn't think I was about to drop dead. Then, before I could change my mind, I pulled my beanie down to my eyebrows and pushed the heavy glass doors.

I'd always thought the police station's windows were tinted black to protect the world from all the bad stuff going on inside. So even though I still felt like puking, I was disappointed to see desks and grey metal filing cabinets. There were no more guns or criminals in handcuffs than you'd see in the post office. At first I thought the water cooler was a mirage – my vision was slightly blurry – but the cups were real plastic, and the water made a real bubbling sound when I filled one up. I drank it too quickly and started coughing.

A row of orange plastic chairs told me I should wait, so I stood in front of them. Spotting a stack of pizza boxes on one of the filing cabinets made me relax a bit. Cops were just normal people; they ate ham and pineapple pizza.

Three men and one lady, all wearing blue shirts with NSW Police badges on their sleeves, sat around a table, one scribbling notes, the others talking in serious voices. I looked down. The carpet was the speckled brown of our older classrooms at school, a pattern perfect for camouflaging stains. I wondered what kind of stains were hiding in the carpet under my sneakers.

A cop heaved himself out of a chair and waddled over to me. He must've been the one Mum'd said looked six months pregnant, the one she'd called a Fat F …

'Can I help you there?'

'Yes, um, I just wanted to …' My mind went blank. What did I want to do? Did I want to tell them my brother maybe knew something about what'd happened that night? What I really wanted to do was lie down and sleep.

'My dad's in here,' I said. 'I want to see Jim Jamieson, please.'

'You Jim's girl?' The cop sounded friendly at least. 'He talks about you a lot. Magic, isn't it?'

'Miracle.'

'Sergeant Nick.' He held out his hand.

It was surprisingly small and soft.

'You been in an accident?' He leant in close, and I noticed hairs growing out of tiny holes on his nose, like miniature pot plants.

I pulled my beanie down, wincing as the wool pulled on the drying blood. If I threw up, I reassured myself, it'd blend into the carpet, so I wouldn't be arrested for damaging police property. 'Just tripped. On the footpath. It doesn't hurt.'

He frowned. 'Your mum know you're here?'

I shrugged, looking at the clock on the wall behind him, at the second hand slowly ticking.

'Well, you'd best tell your dad then.'

I glanced at him and he smiled. 'Come on.'

I followed Sergeant Nick through another glass door and

down a long corridor. The walls were so white they were almost blue in the bright light, and the floor was bare, shiny concrete. The further we walked, the cooler the air. I zipped my parka right up to my neck.

Sergeant Nick stopped in front of a grey door near a No Exit sign, and panted, like a tiny dog that'd just sprinted across a park.

'We'll see if he's in, shall we?' He took a silver key from a ring of keys attached to his belt and unlocked the door. I could tell by the way he leant against it to open it, his face the colour of tomato sauce, it was no ordinary door.

I covered my nose as I followed him inside. As much as I'd missed Dad, I didn't miss the smell of his socks.

I saw a small man hunched over on a bed, and gasped. Dad? But then I saw the man on the bed opposite: Dad! Apart from the grey prison tracksuit and the extra hair on his face, he looked the same as ever. And surprised to see me.

'Miracle!' He leapt to his feet.

'Hi Dad.'

'What happened?' He pointed at my forehead.

'Nothing. Just tripped.' I pulled my beanie down again, without letting myself wince.

'Does it hurt? I can see blood.'

'No,' I lied. 'It did, but it's okay now.'

'What are you doing here?' He frowned. 'Are you on your own?'

I nodded. 'Just ... visiting.'

'It's great to see you,' Dad said. 'But your head's bleeding. I think you need to see a doc.'

'It hardly even hurts.'

Dad smiled, though the frown was stuck on his face.

'Might as well stay for afternoon tea,' Sergeant Nick said. 'Raspberry buns?'

'Sausage roll?' the man on the other bed said. He had a beard like Worzel Gummidge.

'Right you are. Jim?'

'Whatever you're having's fine.' He turned to me. 'Is everything okay? Where's Mum and Julian?'

'Home.'

'She holding up?'

A nod seemed like less of a lie than actually saying yes.

'They were about to send me home, d'you hear that?'

'Yeah, we know.'

'Safer in here for now, they say. I'd kill to get out, though.'

'Not literally, of course.' The small man laughed. 'Eh, Jim?' He winked at me.

'Miracle, this is Bruce,' Dad said. 'My, ah, room-mate.'

'Hello,' I said.

'Heard lots about you,' Bruce said. 'Saw you in the local rag too. Must be hard on you, but don't waste any worry over your old man. He's done nothin' and the coppers know it.'

'I know too.' I didn't add that I knew he'd once hit a man so hard the man ended up in hospital. But Dad'd hit him for a good reason so it didn't count.

'Relieved to hear it,' Dad said. 'It'd break my heart if you thought I was capable of anything like that.'

I wanted to tell Dad that Julian knew something. Well, that I was pretty certain he knew something, that he was there that night. But really, I didn't know anything for sure. And if the cops heard, wouldn't they want to question Julian? What if they locked him up too? I couldn't picture him here, in this room that reeked of socks and boredom. Between the two beds was a wooden table with 'Darren', 'Jonno', 'Mikey', 'Pete' and other names scratched into it, and a pile of falling-apart magazines lay on the concrete floor. The room was slightly warmer than the corridor, thanks to the fan heater whirring in the corner, and it had a skylight to remind you how grey and miserable the world was outside. But it was smaller than my bedroom. It was still a cell.

'It's not so bad, Miri,' Dad said. 'If I'd done something wrong, the guilt'd gnaw away at me. I'd be unable to sleep, unable to eat. But the only thing I'm guilty of is losing my temper with the poor kid's dad. That I can live with.'

'So you're okay in here?'

'Yeah, don't you worry about me. My mattress is lumpier than your mum's porridge and Bruce snores like a machine gun.' He grinned at Bruce. 'But I get six or seven hours' sleep on average. We get two hours' exercise each morning, walking the corridor – helps tire a bloke out. I don't like what this is doing to your mum and God only knows how we're going to keep food on the table, but I'm not losing my head. I worked out quickly that anger gets you nowhere. Not when the whole thing's out of my hands.'

I managed to forget about my head for a while, to concentrate on distracting Dad from asking about Mum. I was telling him and Bruce about the waves at Lawson's Bay, and about how Worm cried every time they swept his legs out from under him, when Sergeant Nick returned.

'Here you go.' He clutched two white paper bags. 'One sausage roll and the last three buns in the bakery. Almost everything else'd gone. Marge did the catering for the wake.'

He handed a paper bag to Bruce, before passing Dad and me a raspberry bun each. His round fingers were almost the same pink as the icing.

I looked at the sticky bun in my hand, and my stomach heaved.

'Strangely quiet out there.' Sergeant Nick eased himself down onto Bruce's mattress. 'You could go for a walk, Jim, or streak naked down the main road, no one's there to see you. 'Cept Marge of course.'

'Don't think I'll take my chances, thanks,' Dad said. 'Anyway, this is my first visit from Miracle. I'm not going anywhere.'

I'd been right not to say anything, I told myself. I'd talk to Julian again once he'd calmed down, and find out exactly what he knew. My nightmare of Oli being attacked, of Julian standing over him, was a stupid dream, nothing more.

'You're looking after your mum?' Dad asked.

'Yeah, but I'd better go soon. She doesn't know I'm here.' I felt embarrassed admitting that in front of a cop, but Sergeant Nick didn't look bothered.

'Give her a call on your way out.' He dropped the last of the bun into his mouth. 'Tell her I'm giving you a lift.' He looked at Dad. 'If there's booze at that wake, it'll be chaos out there. I'll drop her to her door.'

I remember the tug of sadness as I hugged Dad goodbye, and the awkwardness of giving Bruce a quick hug too. I remember dialling our number on Sergeant Nick's desk phone, knowing no one would answer it, and to keep Sergeant Nick happy, pretending to tell Mum I was just five minutes away. And I remember how important I felt as I climbed into the cop car – not in the back where criminals sat, but in the front seat.

But that's all I remember. When I came to, I was in Boorunga Hospital.

40

I saw Oli's face, and sat up. The *Six O'Clock News* was on the TV hanging above my bed. I couldn't hear much over the voices of the Chinese family crowding the bed opposite mine, and it was probably just as well. If I could make out the words or hear the background music, I probably would've bawled loud enough to wake the whole hospital.

Without sound, the funeral didn't seem real. All the kids from Boorunga High stood together in school uniform, most in proper school shoes instead of sneakers. They formed a guard of honour just as we'd done for the school caretaker who died when the gum tree he was lopping fell on him and broke his back. I spied tiny puffs of smoke coming out of a Year 12's mouth. Normally smoking was a crime that'd cost you at least four demerits, but Miss Jones's head was bowed. If the smell had reached her nose, she was obviously beyond caring.

When I recognised Seth, standing at the end, closest to the church, I had to prop myself up for a better look. He and Oli'd been best friends for as long as I could remember, and Katie and I'd rated him the second hottest boy in our year after Oli. I don't know whether what Dad said about the TV making you look worse was true, but today Seth wouldn't have made the top twenty. His face seemed to be covered in a red rash, his chin was quivering, and his hair lay lifeless on top of his head. He can't have had the energy to smother it with gel.

Then there was Katie. A black AC/DC hoodie swallowed up her uniform and hung almost to her knees. She must've wanted to look sadder than everyone else and maybe her brother's top was the only black thing she could find. She'd always said she hated AC/DC.

When I saw Oli's parents, I sank back into my pillow. Close-ups of tightly held hands, of heavy frowns, of eyes on the ground. Seeing them there, looking so grim, made me want to cry. I understood for the first time why they hated Dad, why they wanted to *get* him. They just didn't realise they were blaming the wrong person.

I was still staring at the screen when I heard a very familiar 'Excuse me, please.'

Harriet was threading her way through the Chinese family. She was dressed in a navy skirt and matching jacket with unnecessarily wide shoulders, the outfit she'd worn to Big Bobby's funeral.

'Miracle. What have you done to yourself?'

I touched the bandage on my forehead. 'How did you know?'

'Sergeant Nick. There was no answer at your house, so he called me. What happened?'

'I was running, and tripped. A crack in the footpath or something.'

Harriet frowned. 'And landed on your forehead?'

'Yes.' I squirmed.

'Sergeant Nick had his doubts – and I don't believe it either. You're not a very good liar.'

I shrugged.

'You can't have just *tripped*. What really happened?'

'It was an accident.'

'Of course. I wasn't thinking you'd hurt yourself on purpose.' Harriet pointed to a spare chair near the window. 'I'll just grab that. My feet are sore from standing all day.'

'So?' She sat beside the bed and pulled her skirt over her knees.

'Well, I didn't want to say anything. Because it *was* an accident. But it was sort of Julian's fault.'

'*Julian* did this?' Harriet's eyes were wide.

'He didn't mean to.'

'But how?'

I shrugged again. 'It's a bit complicated and I'm too tired.'

Harriet twisted her pearl earring. 'And so you ran away?'

'I needed to get out of the house. I didn't plan to go to the station.'

'Lucky you were in the car when you blacked out. The sergeant said you'd talked to your mum before you left.'

'I pretended. It was just easier. The whole police station was listening.'

Harriet looked around, before whispering, 'Was she drinking?'

When I nodded, my head throbbed like hell.

Harriet shifted her chair closer to the bed. 'And you didn't run into any trouble visiting your dad?'

'No. Everyone must've been at the funeral. The cop didn't mind – he even gave me food. Dad's good too.'

'That's great to hear. And if you're wondering about today, it was a lovely tribute. So sad, but touching.'

'I saw it on the news.'

Harriet sat with me for ages. She talked me into trying the watery pumpkin soup and promised me fifty cents if I drank a full cup of juice. She reckoned the hospital food was bad for a reason – to make patients want to get out of there as soon as possible.

After the nurses changed shift, the new one, Anna, suggested Harriet come back in the morning. We realised she thought Harriet was my mum, but we didn't bother correcting her. Neither of us wanted to explain that my mum was probably more zonked out than I was.

At 10 o'clock, Anna switched off the main light, and blew each of the four girls in my ward a kiss goodnight.

I wondered how we were supposed to sleep with the corridor light shining in and nurses rattling trays and pulling curtains, and girls moving around trying to get to sleep with drips in their arms or their legs in the air. Suzanne, the girl next to me, was the worst. Her bed was squeaking so much I wondered if she had the world's worst case of worms as well as a broken pelvis and wrist. She was probably only around ten, and had been hit by a car while riding her BMX to school. Or so she told me. I also heard her tell one of the Chinese ladies she'd been hit by the school bus.

'I can't sleep in this place,' Suzanne said.

'Didn't they give you painkillers?'

'I've got this tube.' She held up her wrist in the half-dark. 'But I want to go home.'

'Try to think about something else.' I wished I'd closed the curtain between us before Anna turned off the lights. My eyes felt heavy.

'I can't!' She whacked her good arm against the mattress. 'I can't go to sleep in here.'

'Why not? These beds aren't so bad.' I'd actually been thinking how much softer the mattress was than mine at home.

'Cos of the boy that just died in this hospital.'

I chewed on my thumb. There was no getting away from Oli.

'Someone bashed his head in,' she said. 'He never woke up.'

I didn't say anything.

'Didn't you hear about it?'

'Yes. He was my friend.'

'Liar!'

'He was.' She made me angry.

'You're lying.'

'It's true. *And* my brother was there when it happened.' I don't know why I told her that, but it felt good to say it out loud, to get it outside of me.

'What?' Suzanne's bed squeaked as she turned on to her side. 'Did your brother bash him?'

'Course not! He just saw it.' I saw the flash of panic on Julian's face, seconds before he hurled the snow globe.

'I heard weird noises last night.' Suzanne rolled onto her back. 'If you feel anything – like hands touching your neck or something – that'll be him. It'll be his ghost getting revenge.'

'Ghosts aren't real.' Again, I saw Julian.

'You're just saying that.'

'Why would I?'

'How would I know? You're probably a zombie. You look like one. I saw the hole in your head.'

I touched the bandage Anna'd wrapped round and round my forehead. I thought I looked more like Mr Bump from the *Mr Men* books. 'You'd better be nice to me then. Goodnight.'

Suzanne sighed and shuffled over so her back was to me. I knew when she was asleep because her bed was finally silent and she started whimpering like a kitten.

41

The night stretched for an eternity, the sounds of nurses' shoes squeaking in and out of my dreams. I woke to find my blankets in a mountain on the floor and my hospital nightie halfway up my stomach. My forehead only hurt when I pressed hard against the bandage, but I felt shaky when I lifted it off the pillow, and my hips ached from being in bed for so long. After a man-nurse took my half-eaten breakfast away, I stared at the weak blue sky through the window above Suzanne's bed and imagined how many bones I'd break if I climbed onto the wooden sill and jumped to the car park below. It was weird to think that other people were having an ordinary day, that Katie, Sall and Pheebs were at school, in the back row of 7D, arms folded and feet up on their desks, waiting for Mrs Holland to say 'Quieten down everyone, please!' before taking the roll.

Suzanne's parents and two red-headed brothers with matching oversized *Ghostbusters* T-shirts arrived half an hour after the Chinese girl's family, so Suzanne told them they were late and to go away. Her mum handed her a lunchbox full of grapes and a paper bag with three *Richie Rich* comics inside it, all of which I would've been thankful for if I was still in primary school, but Suzanne folded her arms and said she'd asked for a *Dolly* magazine. I caught the brothers staring at me through purple bubbles of gum and remembered that I looked like an ancient Egyptian mummy. I shut my eyes and pretended I was asleep until Suzanne's parents kissed her goodbye and said they hoped she'd cheer up soon.

I was sitting up in bed, wondering whose head had last slept on my pillow, whether they were still alive, and whether they'd had nits, when the ward doors whooshed open. Mum appeared, her shirt collar tucked in and face pink with panic.

'Look at you.' She squeezed my hand with her cold, dry fingers.

'Mum?' I was still blinking at the unlikely sight.

'You're okay,' she asked. 'Not brain damaged or anything?'

'Not that I know of.' I glanced to see if Suzanne was listening. She was staring at the TV above her bed, her bottom lip stuck out in a sulk.

'I know you didn't trip over.' Mum looked over at Suzanne, too, then turned back to me. 'Something happened at home. I heard you two banging around. And I found the torn up drawing of Oliver.'

Her words sucked all the air out of the ward. I kicked off my blankets. 'What did Julian say?'

'Nothing at all. Harriet said it was something to do with him. He's hardly come out of his room. I found the tea towel in the bin.' Mum nodded at my forehead.

'Sorry.' I touched my bandage.

'I don't care about the stupid tea towel. What happened?'

Suzanne looked over, unfolded her arms.

'Was it *really* Julian?' Mum was obviously desperate for me to say no.

'He threw the snow globe.' It was out.

'The what?' I saw pain in Mum's bloodshot eyes. Suzanne's eyes were on me too.

'You know, that thing John got from Queensland, with sand inside it instead of snow, so it really should be called a sand globe?'

'The tacky thing on the shelf?'

I nodded. 'He chucked it, and it hit my head.'

'Why would he do that?' Mum raked her fingers through her hair.

I looked down at the blankets, which were now in a heap at the foot of my bed. One white, the other pale green. The same pale green as the blanket on Bed 26 in ICU, but also the same as the blanket on Suzanne's bed, and probably on all the other beds in my ward. The chances of me getting Oli's blanket would be very small. Would they even keep the blankets from a dead person's bed? Still, thinking about it made me hot.

'Miracle?' Mum started massaging her head as if she was washing her hair.

'I don't think he meant to hit me. He went a bit wild. I didn't see him aim.'

'Okay.' When Mum dropped her hands I saw they were shaking. 'So it was an accident?'

'Kind of.'

'Can you tell me exactly what happened?' She sat on the edge of my bed. 'What upset him so much that he went a *bit wild*?'

How could I tell her? She looked like she was about to slide off the bed onto the floor. Getting from home to the hospital would've used up a week's worth of energy. How could I cause her any more worry?

'We had an argument,' I said. 'I was angry so I slammed the door.' Since I was old enough to reach a door handle I was taught to close a door quietly so I wouldn't distress him.

'*Slammed* the door? Why would you do that?' Mum leant away from me.

I picked up my cup, swallowed a mouthful of warm juice, thinking fast.

'Why'd you slam the door?' Mum asked.

'I don't remember.' I put the cup down.

'Come on, you must!'

'Her brother killed that boy!' A voice called.

Mum jerked her head, saw Suzanne looking at us, wide-eyed, from under her blanket.

'Hello there,' Mum said. 'Who are you?'

'Suzanne Jenkins. The boy died just four wards away from here.' She spoke from under her blanket. 'Her brother was the one who bashed him. She told me.'

'You're a liar! I only said he was there.' I glared at Suzanne. 'Every word that comes out of your mouth is a lie.'

Mum stared at me, both hands clinging to the edge of the bed. I wanted to scream at Suzanne for being such a big-mouthed brat. I wanted to disappear.

'He was there that night, Mum,' I said. 'He went wild because I asked him about it. But he wouldn't say what happened.'

'What absolute nonsense.' Mum stood too quickly and swayed. 'I think I need to go. I need to lie down.'

'I'm sorry.'

'Get plenty of rest.' Mum leant over to kiss my cheek. Her lips didn't reach my skin.

42

'Do you want the good news or the even better news?' Anna started unwrapping my bandage.

'Um, both?' I breathed in her jasmine scent and realised I'd miss her.

'Your wound is healing nicely. You'll need to come back to get the stitches out, but Dr English said you can go home today.' She placed a breakfast tray in front of me. 'One last meal to make you appreciate your mum's cooking even more.'

I didn't bother telling her that Mum only ever made us boiled eggs and the white was almost always clear so I usually just plopped them into the bin when she wasn't looking. I was going home! The scrambled eggs tasted good now I knew they were my last.

I felt lightheaded when I slid out of bed, but my head didn't hurt. I dressed in the jeans and sloppy joe Mum'd dropped off, and folded up the blue hospital gown for the next poor kid who woke up in Boorunga Hospital. I grabbed my bag from under the bed, stuffed it with my books, Walkman, tapes, and the *Dr Who* card Worm'd made me at school.

I sat on the edge of my bed, trying to read *Emma*, but struggled to concentrate. I wanted to be out of there before Suzanne woke up and started telling more lies. I'd guessed Harriet would be picking me up – Mum would need at least a week to recover from her visit – so when the doors opened and I saw who walked through the door, I let *Emma* drop to the floor.

'Dad!' I leapt off the bed. 'What are you doing here? I'm going home.'

'Careful, go easy. I know you're going home. So am I.'

'Me too.' Sergeant Nick winked. 'I'm coming too.'

I waited for him and Dad to laugh.

'He is,' Dad said. 'Nick's staying at ours for a bit.'

I'd thought Dad got on well with the cop, but inviting him to our house? I was the one with the head injury.

'Just to keep an eye on things for a while,' Sergeant Nick said. 'It'll be like having your own body guard. Hey, Jim, how about we call me your bodyguard?'

'Yeah, I like it.' Dad picked up my bag. 'Makes me feel famous.'

Suzanne's bed squeaked. She lifted her head and squinted at me.

'Let's go.' I picked *Emma* up off the floor and looked at the pale green blanket for what I hoped was the last time, then I pushed Dad towards the door.

'She's a real firecracker, this one,' Sergeant Nick said. 'Can't get out of here fast enough.'

Mum raced down the front steps like an Olympic triple jumper and dashed across the lawn, as if the only way to get out the front door was to run like hell.

'What's going on?' She shielded her eyes with her hand. I'm not sure whether it was from the sun or the sight of a cop car. 'I was just on my way to see you.'

'Dad's out!'

'I can see that,' Mum said. 'What happened? You both do a runner?'

'She got the all-clear.' Dad rested his hand on my shoulder. 'And I wanted to surprise you.'

'You did. My heart nearly gave out when I saw the car.' She stuffed her keys into her jacket pocket. 'Welcome home, Jimmy.'

'Thanks.' Dad kissed her cheek. 'God, am I happy to be here.'

Sergeant Nick coughed, scratched his ear.

'Good morning, Officer.' Mum faked a smile. 'Thanks for dropping them home.'

'It's Sergeant, if you want to be picky.' He heaved a black Nike bag out of the car boot. 'But I don't, so you can call me Nick.'

'That Jim's stuff?' Mum eyed the bag as Nick lifted it onto his shoulder.

'His? Nah, all his belongings fitted into an A4 envelope. Returned it to him this morning, didn't I, Jim?' Nick said. 'This is mine.'

'He's stopping a while, Hen,' Dad said.

'He's stopping?' Mum shoved her hands into her pockets. 'What, with us?'

'It's the least I can do to guarantee your family's safety,' Nick said. 'Just while we wait for the judge to clear Jim. A formality really. But please don't go to any trouble. The couch will be fine. I've slept in worse places.'

Mum opened her mouth and closed it again. She turned to Dad, but he'd crouched down in the garden.

'Could've at least warned me.' Mum pointed at the cop car parked metres away from Stan. 'What'll the neighbours say?'

'Hen, there's nothing left for them to say. They already think I'm a cold-hearted killer.' Dad stroked the lawn. 'Jesus, the grass … how soft is this grass? And smell the air!'

We all inhaled. I looked at the grass, long overdue a mow, the dull green bushes which'd lost their bottlebrushes, and the baby gum trees.

'I can smell Heller's Plastics.' Mum wrinkled her nose. 'And just a hint of the Johnsons' compost.'

'Beats smelling your own sweat.' Dad sniffed. 'And the sweat of the bloke sleeping a metre away from you.'

'Come on in, then,' Mum said. 'Good thing Miracle thought to clean the house.'

'Is that why they call you Miracle?' Nick followed us up the front steps. 'I could do with someone like you around. Do you cook, too? What's your signature dish?'

'Um. Tomato on toast.' Would having a cop stay be worse than being in hospital? Was he going to interrogate me every time I opened the fridge? Arrest me for staying up past midnight?

I waited until Dad and Nick were in the living room before opening Julian's bedroom door.

'I'm home,' I said. 'Weirdly enough, so's a *cop*.'

Julian lifted his eyes from his desk and clocked the plaster on my forehead, the damage he'd done.

'Sorry.'

'I know you didn't mean it,' I said. 'But I'd like to know why you were so angry.'

'Shhh!' Julian squeezed his hands over his ears.

'Can you just tell me why you were there, Jules?'

It was like I'd pressed his 'on' button. Julian's body went from lightly trembling to shaking so hard I thought the chair legs would break.

'Please, Jules?'

But he'd slid off the chair and curled up.

'Go!' He sobbed, rocking side to side.

'Sorry,' I said, even though I didn't know what I was sorry for. I left his room before Nick could arrest me for harassment.

I then picked up the phone to do what I'd been planning on the way home.

'Hello?' It was the voice I'd known since it asked me if I wanted to play elastics in Grade 2, the voice of the person I'd called my best friend.

'Katie? It's Miracle.' I held my breath, preparing for a phone slamming in my ear.

'Oh. You're not in hospital?' Katie, back to her usual self. I exhaled.

'It was just for two nights. They let me come home.'

'So you're okay?'

'Yes. But listen.' I had to tell her before she remembered she hated me. 'You probably still think I'm a bitch, but Dad's out now and he'll be let off soon – a cop told me. So you were wrong. And before you blab to your dad, we've got protection, around the clock, so we're totally safe.' Saying that the cop was actually sleeping on our couch would be too much information.

'I knew it.' Katie's voice was quiet, as if she was half asleep. 'I knew it all along.'

'Huh?' I rubbed my eyes, forcing away the tears.

'I'm sorry. He shouldn't have got the blame. He's way too ordinary.'

'Ordinary' probably wouldn't be flattering if I didn't know what Katie's dad was like.

'Dad's not violent,' I said. 'He's never even hit me.'

'I know. He didn't even lose it when he busted us with your mum's pills.'

So Katie hadn't completely erased the memories of our friendship? I remembered the day Dad found Katie and me giggling at the *Playboy* calendar in the toilet, after daring each other to swallow one of Mum's little blue pills. It was probably the worst thing I'd ever done, worse than setting the tablecloth on fire when I was practising lighting matches to rid me of my fear of Bunsen burners. Katie'd come up with the idea when

Mum was sleeping one afternoon and we couldn't find her cigarettes.

'He was fuming,' I said. 'He just has a different way of showing it. He didn't yell. But the look he gave me was heaps worse.'

'Not worse than having the crap beaten out of you. Seriously, if that was my dad, I wouldn't have been able to sit down for a month.'

Knowing Mr Heller, this probably wasn't much of a stretch. I'd heard plenty of stories about his temper and I'd seen the bruises on Katie's arms and legs. I felt a pang of pain for Katie. But I couldn't forget how badly she'd treated me. The letter she'd never bothered to answer. Those things she'd said. *Get out of my life*.

'Why have you been so horrible to me?'

'I'm sorry. I didn't really think it was your dad, that he could do *that*, but I had to be angry with someone. Sorry, that sounds lame. It felt good to be angry. With him. And with … you.'

I picked at a piece of wallpaper that'd come unstuck, my eyes filling with tears.

'I'm sorry, Miracle. I know it makes no sense. Nothing makes sense. Now they're saying it was probably your dad's boss. His own daughter dobbed him in. But I don't even feel angry with him. I don't feel anything.'

I knew she was crying. I could hear her sniffing. I stood there, leaning against the wall, letting my tears run all over the phone.

I wanted to say something else. To tell her I'd missed her, to ask her to come over or to meet up somewhere, but the words didn't come.

'Bye.' I winced. That wasn't what I wanted to say.

'Okay. Bye.' Katie hung up, leaving me with a sick feeling that she had something else to tell me.

43

I couldn't imagine what my friends would say if they knew a cop was having a sleepover at our house, but having Nick staying was better than I'd expected. He wore tracksuit pants instead of his uniform, so he seemed like a normal type of visitor, like an uncle or a friend of Dad's, if Dad's friends didn't all hate him. You could tell which side of the couch was his favourite by the sprinkle of biscuit crumbs he left when getting up to check the window or 'duck to the loo'. He had a stash of Twirly Swirls in his bag, which he said Reginald Heller gave him for keeping a close eye on the factory at night. Our living room smelt like a combination of vanilla and cop's BO, but after a couple of days I barely noticed it.

If Nick didn't move from the couch to the window during ad breaks, we probably would've forgotten he was there to protect us. His officers were 'investigating' the threats against Dad, but until anything actually happened, we had to 'hold tight and play it safe'. We didn't even know if anyone still wanted to *get* Dad. I was hoping they'd focused their anger on Greg instead.

I don't know whether it was me he was trying to avoid, or Nick, but Julian spent most of the time in his bedroom, only skulking out when Dad or Nick yelled, 'Grub's up!' So he avoided walking laps of our yard with the rest of us. 'Exercise time' was Nick's idea. He said it was for our mental health, but

I reckon it was also because if he got any fatter he'd struggle to do up the fly on his navy work trousers. We started in single file: Nick first, then Dad, me, and lastly Mum, who was whispering directions to her legs so they didn't turn and carry her back into the safety of the house. Nick's pace was too slow though, and the sound of his breathing made me feel like he was going to die right there on our lawn, so on our second lap, I overtook him and Dad before breaking into a run.

'Come on,' I called to Nick. 'You said we need *exercise*.'

'Should've named her Cheeky,' I heard him say to Dad.

As I sprinted past the baby gum trees in our front yard, I spotted Mrs Jensen-from-across-the-road. I couldn't make out the look on her face through her curtain, but I pictured her taking off her glasses and rubbing her eyes in confusion. *Pull up a chair*, I wanted to call out, *we're going to be here for an hour*. I imagined her thinking about calling the cops to say we'd gone mad, but then realising that not only was a cop car still parked outside our house, the fat man waddling between Dad and Mum must be a cop. I hoped her heart was strong enough to cope.

I slowed down to a jog, but kept running until I lost count of the number of times I touched the clothes line. My mind kept drifting towards Livvy. What had she said to the cops? Was she angry with me for saying nothing? What did Greg do after she'd dobbed him in? Partly I wanted to check she was all right, but more, I wanted to get her face out of my head. There was nothing I could do anyway, so what was the point? If Greg got the blame for Oli, no one would need to know Julian was there that night. As soon as Nick decided it was safe enough to leave our couch, life would go back to normal.

If only.

Two days later, I was lying on my bed rereading *The Bell Jar*, when I heard a knock on the front door. My heart leapt into my throat. I was reacting like Julian, I realised, and I forced myself to breathe deeply until my heartbeat slowed down. A cop car was parked out front and an actual cop was in our garage learning how to make a go-kart for his nephew. We couldn't have been safer if our house had been patrolled by the army. I picked up my book and made my eyes follow the words.

'Miracle, Katie's here.' Mum's voice slid through the crack in my bedroom door.

I sat up and closed my book. Even though I'd been aching to see Katie, my heart sped up again and my tracksuit suddenly felt too thick. I couldn't remember the last time she'd come to my house, or we'd even just had a proper talk without Pheebs, Sall or Oli listening in. Even so, after the way she'd treated me I didn't feel ready to see her, to have her in my room.

'Hi.' Katie gave me a half smile.

I tried not to stare at her – the new, shrunken version of her. She looked like she'd swapped her school tunic for Sall's size XL one. When she sat on the edge of my bed, the mattress barely moved.

'Hey.' I pulled my knees up to my chest.

'Looks sore.' Katie's eyes were on my forehead. 'Did the cops do it?'

'The cops?' I tried to imagine Nick punching me, his soft, pink hand clutching a Twirly Swirl. 'No, it was an accident.'

'I heard it was the cops.' Katie looked down at her Doc Martens.

'Why would they beat me up?'

'Dunno. Kids just make shit up.' She picked at a thread on her tunic. 'Look, sorry about … for being such a bitch. I was just so, you know, traumatised.'

I swallowed, determined not to cry. 'I haven't been feeling on top of the world either. And what happened to Oli had nothing do with me.'

'I know.' Katie was struggling not to cry too. 'I'm really sorry ... got a fag?'

I shook my head. 'I don't do that anymore. Don't want to turn into my mum.'

Katie shrugged, blinking away tears.

'You're lucky to have her,' Katie said. 'Your mum. And your dad.'

'Yeah.' I'd always envied other people for their normal parents. Never Katie though. I never wanted Mr Heller to be my dad, even if he had the fattest wallet in Boorunga.

'He hit me with the ironing cord. Used it like a whip.' Katie pressed her school uniform tight against her legs. 'You know the plug bit? It left ugly little holes in my thighs. Twenty-one of them.'

'Why? What'd you done?'

'That's what I need to tell you.' A tear rolled down Katie's cheek, then another and another.

'What happened?'

'I got ...'

'You what?'

'I got ... pregnant.'

'Pregnant?' If she wasn't crying, I would've laughed. Surely it was meant to be a joke.

'Yeah. Hard to believe.' Her tears were streaming down.

'For real?' I was still struggling with knowing I was going to bleed every month until I was older than Mum. Getting pregnant was something women did. Well, women and, every now and then, one of the Year 12 girls who snuck into the PE shed after school.

I crawled across the bed, put my arm around Katie. She still felt like my old friend, a shrivelled version, but also she was a stranger. She'd grown up and left me behind.

'But you're skinnier than before,' I said.

'Yeah, cos I'm not … any more.'

Oh God. 'The ironing cord?'

She shook her head. 'Abortion. He made me.'

'Your dad?'

Katie nodded, wiping her eyes. 'He took me to the hospital.'

I thought about the angry protesters standing on the wet hospital lawn, and their placards: ABORTION IS MURDER! LIFE BEGINS AT CONCEPTION.

'They just sucked the baby out … with a … kind of like a vacuum thing. Then when I got home … the ironing cord.'

My stomach churned at the thought of a baby being 'sucked out'. 'When?'

'Two or three weeks ago? Before Oli …'

'That's …' I couldn't think of the right word. Katie's life was a whole new level of hell.

'And now I feel worse! I feel even worse … Since O –.' Her tongue got stuck on the 'O'. 'Since he … died.'

She started blubbing, snot bubbling out her nose.

'Wait a minute.' I ran and grabbed some toilet paper. 'Here you go.'

I looked at my fingernails while Katie blew her nose once, twice, three times, thinking how much she must've liked Oli – maybe she had *loved* him? – how much she must've missed him. That was when I finally made the connection. I'd been too shocked, my head spinning too fast, to think about how she'd actually got pregnant.

'Oli was …?'

'Who'd you think?'

I opened my mouth, then closed it. I didn't know what to say.

Katie folded up the toilet paper, stuffed it in her pocket. 'Oli was the only one for me.'

44

I lay back on the bed, my head ready to burst. It was no secret that Katie and Oli used to pash behind the tuckshop, and a couple of times Oli'd turned up to Social Science with his shirt untucked. Both times Katie'd given me a bet-you'd-love-to-know-what-I've-been-up-to kind of smile, but my jealousy always stopped me from asking. She may even have tried to tell me, but whenever she talked about Oli I'd quickly changed the subject.

Oli, a dad! I struggled to picture Katie changing a stinking nappy, ploughing a pram through Woolies, or flopping her milky boobs out for the whole world to see. But the idea of Oli with a baby was even harder to grasp. Perhaps because I'd known him since we were practically babies ourselves, or because I'd secretly believed that all those wishes I'd made – on every birthday candle, every dandelion – would come true and we'd end up together. The thought of him holding a baby instead of a soccer ball made my throat tighten.

'One day I had a boyfriend and a baby,' Katie was saying. 'The next, I had nothing.'

I sat up. 'Did … he know?'

'Oli? Yeah. That's how come my dad, um …' Katie stared at the wall. She looked so sad and small, like a girl, not a … mum.

'Your dad what?'

'It's how Dad found out. Oli'd come around to ask me why I'd been acting so weird.' Katie chewed her lip. 'So I told him I was pregnant and felt like shit because I was puking up my breakfast each morning, and I was bloody scared – of getting fat, of leaving school, of never being able to get drunk at a Year 12 ball. But I was a teeny bit excited too because … it was *his* baby.'

I nodded, though I was dreading what was coming.

'Should've been more careful – we were talking about it on the front veranda. I thought Dad'd already gone to the factory. But then, he was there. God, Miracle, the look on his face …'

'What'd he say?'

'Nothing at first. He was too angry to speak. He walked back and forth on the veranda, massaging his head with his hands. Then he went really quiet and said, "How could you?"'

I dug my fingernails into my palms.

'I said "Sorry Dad" or "We hadn't meant to", something like that, but he waved his finger in my face, and said, practically spitting, "You, of all people".'

'Because of … your mum?'

'Yeah, I guess so. It feels better to think he was angry because he didn't want me to die. But the dumb thing is, it was his fault Mum died. He made her have a home birth, wouldn't let her go to hospital, not even when she was howling with pain. Kurt still has nightmares and he'd only just turned two. Dad was fucked up even before she died.'

I could believe it. I couldn't imagine him ever having been any different.

'Um. What was I just saying?'

'Your dad'd heard you … telling Oli.'

'Yeah, he went ballistic! Screamed at Oli, "I'll break your bloody neck, you little bastard", stuff like that. Oli took off as fast as he could …' Katie sobbed quietly. 'That was it. That's the last time I saw him.'

Break your bloody neck. I closed my eyes, picturing Mr Heller screaming at Oli. I couldn't imagine Oli scared, but if it was me I'd be traumatised. I was even terrified when Mr Heller answered the phone.

'Had the abortion the next day. Dad said he pulled a few strings to get it over and done with fast.'

My mind was racing, struggling to put everything in the right order. So that's why Katie wasn't at school on the day of the Rat Incident. And that same night was the night Oli was attacked. *Break your bloody neck.* Did that mean …? My God! Could Mr Heller have attacked Oli?

I stared at Katie, waiting for her to blurt it out, to say, 'My dad did it'. But, although she kept talking, she didn't mention him again. Was she too sad to think clearly? Or did she know? Was she telling me all this for a reason? This Katie was so different to the Katie of a few weeks ago, I couldn't tell.

I got her more toilet paper, then held her cold hand and said the things I thought I should say, that things would be all right after a while, and one day she'd meet someone else like Oli. But I wasn't really thinking about Katie anymore. I wasn't even thinking about Oli and the poor dead baby they'd created together. I was thinking about her dad.

Stay away from my girl. Were they Mr Heller's words?

Before she left, Katie kissed me on the cheek, something I don't think she'd ever done before. I would forgive her, I decided. We'd be friends again after all this, after what I was about to do. I headed straight for Julian's bedroom.

'Jules. I need to ask you something.'

Julian was lying on his bed. He didn't look at me.

I closed his bedroom door behind me.

'Julian.' I pulled out the chair from under his desk and sat down. 'You didn't mean to hurt me, did you?'

He shook his head.

'I think I know who did it. You must too!'

'Scared,' Julian whispered.

I jumped up and went to him, held both of his hands to control the shaking. It was going to be tough for him, but there was no other way.

'You were at the crem that night, weren't you? You know something.'

He looked away, up at the pictures – his portraits of ghosts – on his wall, then at the ceiling. He nodded.

'You need to tell me what you saw.'

Tears streamed down his cheeks and he started shuddering violently. I put my arms around him, held him tightly, breathing in his musty boy smell.

'Take your time, Jules. But I really need to know.'

'Dad. I went. I –'

'What? Dad was there?'

He shook his head. 'I went. For Dad.'

'You went to the crem to find Dad – in the middle of the night?'

'To catch. For Dad.'

'Catch what?'

'Bad.' He freed one of his shaky arms, pretended to paint in the air.

'Catch the vandal?'

A nod.

'And did you see the vandal?'

'Oli.'

'So it was Oli? He was spraying graffiti?' Tormenting my dad? How dare he! They were my first thoughts. Before I remembered what had happened to him. That he was dead.

'And was he on his own?'

Julian held up two fingers.

'Oli and someone else?'

He nodded.

'Who was it? His friend?'

He shrugged, biting his bottom lip.

'Was anyone else there?'

He nodded slowly. 'Big.'

Big. A big man. Katie's dad? It must've been.

'Did you recognise him?' I asked. 'Was it Mr Heller?'

A slow nod, shallow breaths.

'And this man hurt Oli?'

Julian nodded again, tears still rolling down his cheeks. I took a deep breath to stop my own tears. I needed to hear everything, I had to stay in control.

'What about the other boy? What'd he do?'

'Scream. Run.'

'So Oli was left behind?' I asked, thinking I never would've left him behind, never would've abandoned him. 'Oli was left with the man?' Katie's dad, I was sure of it.

'Loud.' Julian clutched his ears. 'Scream, scream.'

'Did anyone see you?'

Julian shook his head. 'Spiky bush.'

'God, what a thing to see.' Then I remembered what Livvy'd told me.

'What about Greg? Was he there?'

'No.'

So Livvy was wrong too.

'We need to tell them what happened.' I didn't like Greg, but I hated Mr Heller more for what he had done to Katie. I also owed it to Livvy to get the real story out there.

Julian shook his head. 'Trouble.'

'Sergeant Nick's not like a proper cop, so it's okay. You liked his hamburgers. There's nothing to be scared about.'

Julian chewed his thumbnail, frowning.

'I know it must've been a hellish thing to see. But I need your help to make sure they believe –'

The door burst open, cutting me off. Julian pulled his doona over his head.

'Julian?' Worm stood in the doorway with Nick's police hat on his head.

'Julian! Can we play? You can have Optimus Prime.' Worm looked at me. 'Why's he hiding?'

'He's probably scared you're going to arrest him,' I said. 'Officer Worm.'

Julian lifted the doona. 'Soon,' he said to Worm. 'Play soon.'

45

Julian followed me into the living room where Nick was waving his arms around, telling one of his many cop stories to Mum, Dad, Harriet and John, maybe the one about him chasing two guys who broke into the school, back before his legs got too heavy for running.

'It's Twiddlydum and Twiddlydee,' Nick said.

'It's Tweedledum and Tweedledee, I think.' Dad hadn't stopped smiling since he'd settled into his favourite armchair, the first thing he'd done when he got home. I'd just be watching TV or reading a book and he'd keep looking at me like I was a new-born giraffe or some fascinating thing he'd never seen before.

I wondered if being stuck in a cell would have a similar effect on Mum. Or would it take a lifetime in prison to make her feel good when she came out?

'We've got something to tell you,' I said. 'We know what happened to Oli. We know who did it.'

Dad's smile faded (so that's all it took: a mention of the case). 'You're not mucking around are you? Cos if you are, I don't want to hear it.'

'Dad, we're serious.'

'Wait just a sec.' Nick reached into his bag, revealing his hairy back. 'I'll get my notebook.'

Worm ran in, skidding on the carpet, holding the police hat on his head with both hands.

'Can I've your gun?' he asked Nick. 'I won't pull the trigger. Promise.'

'I'm sorry. It's not a toy, little man.' Nick reached back into his bag.

'Worm, can you go play in Julian's bedroom, please?' Harriet said.

'Here.' Nick passed Worm a Twirly Swirl. 'From my top secret police supplies.'

Worm shoved the biscuit in his mouth before running back along the hall.

'Julian was there,' I said. 'He was there that night.'

'Julian?' Dad placed his coffee mug on the carpet. 'Julian?'

'Got a pen?' Nick asked Dad. 'Can't think where my one got to.'

Dad lifted the couch cushion, digging around until he found a pen for Nick, while Mum and Harriet gaped at Julian, who stood next to me, his head bowed.

'He was at the crem.' I nodded at Julian.

'I thought that was nonsense,' Mum said. 'I thought that was something to do with the knock on your head.'

'He saw Oli and another boy. And he saw the person who did it. He knows who it was.' I spoke fast, not wanting anyone to butt in, not wanting to get my words mixed up. I had to be clear, I had to be believed.

'Julian was here, in bed,' Mum said. 'I hope you're not wasting Nick's time.'

'True,' Julian said, staring at his shoes, the crisp, white Reeboks Harriet must've bought him.

'Rubbish. Has she talked you into this?' Mum covered her face with her hands.

'How'd you end up at the crem at night?' Dad asked. 'I'd have heard you. We'd have heard you open all the locks.'

'Window,' Julian whispered. This time his eyes met Dad's.

'He was trying to find out who the vandals were,' I explained. 'He was doing it for you, Dad. He just wanted to help.'

'So what are you saying? You climbed out your window and just walked there?' Mum whispered through her fingers.

Julian nodded.

'Oh Julian.' Dad stood up, started pacing.

'That was a very dangerous thing to do.' Harriet glanced at Sergeant Nick.

'You're a fine boy all the same,' Dad said. 'You're a braver person than me.'

'So who did it?' Mum asked me. 'You said you know.'

'We do,' I said. 'It was Katie's dad. Mr Heller.'

'Jesus Christ!' Mum slid a cigarette into her mouth, looked around for a lighter.

'You're sure?' Dad shook his head. 'Why would he? Why'd he want to protect the crem?'

'I reckon he'd be capable,' Mum said. 'He's a total nutcase. He works people to the ground, fires them without a second thought. But, your dad's right, why would he care about the crem?'

'It wasn't about the crem,' I said. 'It was about Oli and Katie. He must've followed Oli.'

'He probably would've been at work,' Dad said. 'He works about eighty hours a week, doesn't he?'

'He's the boss,' Harriet said. 'He can leave whenever he wants.'

'I can check that,' Nick said, before turning to me, waving his pen. 'Okay now, Miracle. What exactly did he see at the crematorium? Tell us everything you know. And then I'll get a statement from Julian.'

'Hey Jules, you didn't have my hanky with you?' Dad asked. 'My lucky red one?'

Julian shrugged. 'Maybe.'

I watched Nick write LUCKY RED HANKY!!! and draw a big circle around it.

I don't know how long we talked, but by the end of it we had wet faces and dripping noses, well, all of us except Dad who'd probably never cry again after his lock-up experience, and Nick who was paid to hear stuff like this. He struggled to get Julian to say much, which wasn't a surprise, and said it was crucial we find out who the other boy was before he did anything else.

'No offence, but someone with a disability could be considered an unreliable witness,' Nick said before continuing to chew on the end of Dad's pen.

It wasn't much of an obstacle. I was pretty sure who the other boy was. I dug out my school year books, primary through to high school, until I found the most recent. Then I sat with Julian at the kitchen table, examining each class photo, studying the face of each boy.

'Anyone here?' I asked. We were looking at Mr Marsden's Year 7 class – Pheebs's old class. Julian shook his head as I ran my finger across the back row of boys.

'There,' Julian said after I'd turned to my class photo. 'Him.' He pointed to a face with a fuck-you smile.

'Seth Boston.' I let out my breath. Seth and Oli. I'd guessed it was Seth – who else would it be? – but now Julian had confirmed it. I went and showed Nick.

'Oli's best friend. Well, he was.'

'Boston?' Nick circled the face and underlined his name. 'Any relation to the lady who died? Jill?'

'Yes. He's the son,' Dad said. 'Poor kid.'

'Right. I'm onto it,' Nick said. 'Might question him myself, if you don't mind. I could send Constable Hammer round here while I'm out?'

'We'll be fine,' Dad said. 'Thanks.'

'If you're sure.' Nick reached into his bag, pulling out a crumpled blue police shirt and bunched-up navy trousers. 'I guess that lady across the way will be keeping an eye on things too.'

'Joan?' Dad smiled weakly. 'She won't miss a beat.'

'I won't be long anyway,' Nick said. 'Three, four hours tops.'

'Here,' Mum said. 'Let me iron them for you.'

'Thanks, Henrietta.' Nick handed his uniform to Mum. 'That's very kind of you.'

'Not really.' Mum shook out the shirt. 'I can't stand the sight of wrinkles. I'm OCD, on top of everything else.'

'Nick?' Dad said.

'What is it?'

'Please don't charge him. The boy, Seth. Find out what he knows and let him go. Enough pain has come out of this already. He's been through enough.'

'I'll see what I can do, Jim. The main thing is we get him to verify the story so we can get the person responsible.' Nick frowned, looking around the room. 'Now where'd little Worm get to with my hat?'

46

Sergeant Nick later told us that as soon as Seth opened the front door and saw him standing on the doorstep in his neatly ironed uniform, Seth's face crumpled and he clutched the door frame. All Nick'd said was 'Hello, Seth', but Seth was too rattled to reply.

If you believed Nick, which I did because he's a cop and why would he lie, Seth cried all the way to the station, emptying the car's box of tissues and leaving a wet patch on the back of the driver's seat from where he'd buried his face. Mr Boston sat in the back beside him, struck dumb with shock. It took a cup of coffee and ten minutes of being shut inside a tiny room for Seth to calm down enough to be able to talk. But once he started, Nick had to scribble fast to keep up.

'Me and Oli'd been there twice since my mum died.' Nick later read us Seth's words from his notepad. 'I was angry and I dunno, attacking that death factory made me feel better. Kids said Livvy's dad put something in the water so he'd get more *business*. So, if that's true, maybe that prick killed my mum? It wouldn't surprise me. His daughter Livvy's so up herself. She pretended to like me, but she's just a user. She lies about everything. I hate her, hate them both. Why'd they even move here? To make money by wiping out a town? Me and Oli weren't the only ones. Heaps of guys trashed the joint. There's a stash of paint in a hollow paperbark tree in the bush for anyone who wants a go. But that night it was just me and Oli. Then the old bloke turned up.'

Seth told Nick that Mr Heller knew about Katie being pregnant, and he guessed her dad'd followed them there to 'scare the crap out of Oli'.

'He yelled out Oli's name,' Seth'd said. 'I didn't want to get busted – and I didn't want anything to do with Oli's shit. I've got enough of my own, y'know. So I just bolted. Before anything happened. Bolted all the way home. I just thought Oli'd do the same.'

Seth told Nick he'd nearly puked when he heard that Oli was in a coma. He was 'dead ashamed' he hadn't hung around to protect his best mate. But even after Oli's mum finally let him visit Oli in hospital and he saw how damaged his face was, Seth still thought Oli would get better.

'He was tougher than anyone,' Seth said. 'And he was my mate. I didn't believe a mate my age could actually die.'

Seth'd had nightmares since the attack. In his dreams he was beaten up for being a 'gutless wimp', punched and kicked by Mr Heller, his dad, teachers, kids at school, everyone. He knew he should've said something, but the longer he left it the worse he knew he'd look if he decided to talk. He was also 'shit-scared' of what it'd do to his dad – he'd suffered enough since his mum'd died. Besides, admitting he was there that night was hardly going to help Oli wake up, Seth decided. And everyone was too busy worrying about Oli to care about any damage they'd done to the crematorium. So after days of worrying himself half to death, Seth decided to keep his mouth shut.

'Did you know someone else'd been charged?' Sergeant Nick asked Seth. 'That someone else was being blamed for the attack?'

Seth shrugged. 'He worked there. I thought maybe he was up to no good anyway.'

'Jim Jamieson is a good man. His family has suffered because of this.'

'Yeah. I guess,' Seth said.

After Seth heard that Oli had died – Steve Harrison turned up to tell Seth himself – he hadn't been able to sleep at all, not even for a minute. His mind was too jumbled, his guilt too heavy. He knew who the murderer was, but because he'd kept quiet for so long he was too scared to step forward.

'The only answer I came up with was to top myself. Leave a note explaining everything, saying it was Katie's old man. I just couldn't decide which way to do it,' Seth admitted, in tears again.

'What would that achieve?' Nick asked him. 'Having the town mourning for two boys instead of one? Making your dad want to top himself as well?'

'I don't know,' Seth said. 'I just can't … couldn't live with all that stuff in my head.'

'You've got it off your chest,' Nick told him. 'You can live now, son.'

Seth wasn't charged. Nick agreed with Dad; he'd suffered enough. His only punishment was to apologise to Dad and Greg for any damage caused, get some counselling, and be a witness in court.

As it turned out, that wasn't necessary.

47

At around the time Nick was dropping Seth and his dad home, the red car showed up on our street.

Dad saw it crawling to a stop across the road. It was impossible not to. It was the shiniest red you've ever seen, and less than a hundred years old, so it stuck out like a sore thumb on our street. It was the car that'd sped past when Mum, Jules and I'd been picking up sticky eggshells. Through Julian's binoculars, Dad made out two men wearing sunglasses through a half-open tinted window. Dad kept peering between the curtains every minute or so as the men sat there, dark glasses facing our house. He'd stepped into Nick's role, acting like a cop himself. Until the fourth time he looked. Then he spun around. The binoculars went flying.

'Hide!' he said. 'Hurry!'

I froze.

'Jim, I'm too old for hide-and-seek.' Mum was on the couch, her arms folded. 'Invite them in so I can give them a piece of my mind.'

'One of them *is* coming,' Dad whispered. 'Hide!'

I scanned the living room for somewhere to disappear, but my feet were glued to the carpet. I couldn't move, couldn't think.

'Go!' Dad urged us. 'They could be dangerous. Get under the bed, in the cupboard, any bloody where. I'll call Nick.'

I sprang into action, sprinted to my room and slid under the bed, squeezing in among the soft toys, lost socks and wrinkled-up paintings I'd been shoving there since primary school. I breathed in dust and carpet fluff, my heart pounding. I could just make out Dad's voice from the hallway. He was on the phone, his delusions of being a cop having fled in fear.

When I heard the bash on the door, I actually wet my pants. Wet warmth filled my jeans, and I felt my face go hot with shame.

Another bash came at the door. Who was it anyway? And what did they want? Had Mum hidden? I hoped to God she hadn't just pulled the couch blanket over her head. And what about Jules? He'd be shaking like crazy.

'Jim!' A man's voice boomed, a voice I knew. 'I know you're there. I saw your nose in the window.'

'What do you want?' Dad's voice shook.

'A word with you.'

'I don't have anything to say to you.' Dad was trying to sound relaxed, but his voice was too high; he was nervous as hell.

'Come on, man up! Or would you prefer I come round the back way?'

Hearing that voice, knowing what he'd done – to Oli, to Katie, to Dad, to our whole family – made me so angry I couldn't keep still any longer. What gave him the right to screw up our lives? I slid out of the dusty dark, and crept down the hall, leaving my fear under the bed. I was so mad I forgot about my wet jeans.

'Miracle!' Dad yelled, but I'd already unlocked all three locks, already yanked the door open, already faced Mr Heller.

His eyes were cold. I took a step back, losing my nerve.

'Miracle! Get inside.' Dad was standing beside me. He nudged my arm, but I was frozen still.

'You sound paranoid, Jim,' Mr Heller said. 'Too much time in isolation?'

'What are you doing here?' Dad stepped towards Mr Heller. 'I can't think what you and I possibly have to say to each other.'

'We know who did it.' I sounded braver than I felt.

Mr Heller smiled, his fat face shining with sweat, black suit taut on his large body.

'The cops know too,' I said, noticing the Adidas bag on his shoulder. Katie's PE bag.

'Miracle. Go inside, please.' Dad's voice broke when he said 'please'. I inched back into the hall to stop him having a stroke.

'Your blessed little *Miracle*,' Mr Heller said. 'She's corrupted my daughter – I'd put money on it.'

'I'd like you to leave.' Dad was trying to sound calm. 'Please just get out of here.'

'Have you been leading my Katie astray, *Miracle*?' The bag strap slipped off Mr Heller's shoulder.

'I said go! Please,' Dad said.

'This won't take long,' Mr Heller said. 'Thing is, you destroyed Steve Harrison's life, so I offered to help him out.'

'Help him out with what?'

Mr Heller unzipped the bag to show Dad what he meant. I stepped up, grabbing Dad's arm.

'He wants revenge for his boy's death.' Mr Heller nodded at the bag.

'Please.' Dad placed a hand on his chest. 'I understand Steve's pain, but he's got the wrong bloke.'

Mr Heller sighed and shook his head, as if he was a school teacher and Dad was lying his way out of detention.

'Why else would I be home?' Dad's voice was thin. 'I just need to clear my name in court and I'll be a free man.'

Mr Heller nodded at the car parked across the road. 'How do you think that makes Steve feel?'

'It should make him realise it wasn't me. It was someone else. And I'm pretty sure you know who.'

'Bullshit,' Mr Heller said, opening the bag. I'd only seen guns on TV, had never wanted to see one in real life, especially not in Katie's dad's hands. When Mr Heller pulled the gun out of the bag, I felt a weird sense of recognition.

'Shoot yourself,' I blurted. 'Blow your own bloody head off.'

'Miracle! Inside!'

'You killed Oli,' I said.

Mr Heller's grey eyes were like marbles. 'I thought Katie was lippy, but you!'

'You're going to jail,' I said.

'I wasn't planning to use this.' Mr Heller rubbed the gun on his suit jacket. 'My boy's. I just brought it with me to give you a good scare. Which has worked by the looks of it.'

I glanced down at my jeans.

'But if I shot the pair of you right now I'd be doing Boorunga a favour,' Mr Heller continued.

'How dare you!' It was Mum. The grey fluff in her hair suggested she'd been hiding under a bed too. 'How dare you threaten my family! You – of all people!'

'Ah, the crazy wife.' Mr Heller raised the gun again, this time pointing it at Mum. 'Should I put you out of your misery while I'm at it?'

'You two. Please,' Dad was yelling now. 'For Christ's sake. Go inside.'

But Mum was on a roll. 'Did it make you feel like a big man? Did you get a rush of power when you beat the life out of a teenage boy?'

'Hen,' Dad hissed.

Mr Heller growled. 'Why would *I* touch the boy?'

'Because of Katie,' I said.

Mr Heller faced me, his eyes so cold they were burning.

'Because Katie loved Oli,' I said.

The corners of Mr Heller's mouth started twitching.

'She loved him so much,' I continued, 'she got pregnant with –'

'Shut up!' Mr Heller whispered the words, but they carried so much fury that my knees went wobbly.

'His baby,' I finished.

'No.' Mr Heller shook his head.

'She told me everything.'

'My Katie's a good girl.' Were there tears in Mr Heller's eyes? 'Not like you.'

'Miracle,' Dad said. 'I don't think we have much more to –'

'Katie's *not* having a baby.' Mr Heller shook his head again.

'Not anymore,' I said. 'You put a stop to that. And to Oli. It was you! There's no point saying you didn't touch him because we know you did.'

Mr Heller lowered the gun. He looked away for a long moment, then turned to Dad.

'What would you have done, eh? My girl – she's just a kid. She doesn't need a baby – she's a baby herself!'

'I don't know, but –' Dad started.

'Shut up!' Mr Heller's temper fired up again. 'It was an accident.'

'But you did it,' Mum said.

'He fucked with me,' Mr Heller said.

'So you went after him?'

'Someone had to teach him a lesson,' Mr Heller said. 'The way I was taught.'

'By murdering him?' Mum said. 'Like you murdered Annette.'

He took a step back and made a choking sound. I remembered where I'd seen the gun before. If I wasn't standing in front of the man who'd killed Oli, I'd have burst out laughing.

'*That* was an accident,' Mr Heller said. 'I loved my wife. More than anything. You don't know what you're talking about.'

'Now look,' Dad stammered.

'This is your fault – *you* did it!' I said.

Dad grabbed onto my jumper, and tried to pull me towards him, but I wasn't finished. Mr Heller had killed Oli, he'd hurt my best friend, and he'd turned the town against my family.

'You're going to jail for the rest of your life!' Nick hadn't actually said that, but surely it was true. If not forever, for a very long time.

Mr Heller glared at me.

'Come on, mate.' Dad's voice was gentle. 'It's over.'

Mr Heller turned to Dad. For a while he didn't say anything, but then he took a deep breath and said, calmly, 'You don't understand.'

'No, I don't think I –'

'I was at the factory, trying to forget about … trying to forget … when I heard *him*.' Mr Heller talked as if me and Mum weren't there. 'I thought it was the Valium. I'd taken three to calm the hell down after the day I'd had. I thought it was the drugs screwing with my head. But no, it *was* his voice. Him and his mate, up to no good in the middle of the night, laughing and clowning about like it was an everyday thing to get a girl knocked up. *My* girl!'

He probably would've gone on, but then, as if we were in a movie, Nick was there, behind Mr Heller, his sweaty ginger hair sticking to his forehead, and with him were two cops I didn't recognise. I hadn't heard a car pull up. I looked across the road. A paddy wagon was parked where the red car had been.

'Okay, mate, lower your weapon,' Nick ordered.

I let out my breath thinking it was all over, thinking Nick'd handcuff him, tell him he had the right to remain silent – or was that something people just said in the movies? – and that'd be the end of it.

'It's not even real,' I said, feeling brave now that the cops had come to the rescue. 'I remember when Katie's brother Kyle got it for his birthday. He used to scare me with it. It only shoots ball bearings.'

'Fuck you all,' Mr Heller said.

I saw him look down at the useless piece of metal in his hand, and Nick take a step towards him. But that's all I saw.

Then I was lying on the cold concrete and someone was moaning.

48

A blast of pain raced up the side of my head. I touched my ear, expecting wetness, but my skin felt dry. I looked at my fingers: no blood.

'Sweetheart?'

I glanced up and saw Mrs Jenson-from-across-the-road, except she wasn't across the road, a shadow in her curtain, she was right here on our front veranda, leaning over me.

'You've had a bit of a knock,' she said. 'Can you stand?'

I thought about it. Could I stand? My body felt heavy, but I guessed I could. I stared at Mrs Jensen's wrinkled hand, but I wasn't ready to take it. I heard other voices, serious voices, car doors slamming, a police siren.

I lifted my head and saw Dad propped against the front door. There was no blood on his clothes or skin. But the look on his face was as scary as a pool of blood. I followed his eyes and saw Nick, crouched over. And that's when I realised where the moan was coming from.

'Mum!'

49

One by one, our family was falling apart.

The nurse, Anna, who'd stitched me back together had also sewn up Mum's cheek with the same black thread. I'd closed my eyes when she changed Mum's bandage, scared of what I'd see, but then I couldn't help myself. I saw a dark red hole surrounded by tiny black lines.

'I can see right inside you,' I said to Mum. 'Your secrets aren't safe anymore.'

Mum let out a small groan.

'Please don't make her smile,' Anna said. 'She needs to keep her face still.'

'Sorry, Mum.' I patted her hand.

Dad stood up and stretched his legs. 'Anyone would think my family was competing for the Head Injury of the Year Award,' he said. 'Jules, don't get any ideas.'

Julian looked from me to Mum and shrugged.

Mum wrote on the notepad she kept on her lap. 'I won.'

She was right. Her broken jaw and the hole in her left cheek looked way more painful than my snow globe scab. She couldn't talk, but she held up the word 'OUCH!', written on her notepad, whenever anyone asked how she was feeling.

The thing is, I should've won the award. That's what I learned when Dad made his statement to Nick. It was me Mr

Heller was aiming for, me he wanted to hurt. When he lifted his arm – the arm that held the gun Kyle used to keep next to a pile of *Phantom* comics near his bed – Mum knocked me out of the way. Instead of hitting me, the barrel of the gun struck Mum.

That made Mum a kind of hero. She wasn't the sort of mum who gave out big, warm smiles, wrapped her arms around me and said how much she loved me, but when it really mattered, she'd reacted in a split second. She probably saved my life!

Mum scribbled on her notepad and held it up. 'What are you staring at?'

I smiled and felt my cheeks burn. 'Sorry.'

'Do you kids want a drink?' Dad asked. 'I saw a machine.'

Julian and I stood up. I shook the pins and needles out of my legs.

'Coke?' Julian held out his trembling hand.

'Go for your life.' Dad filled Julian's hand with coins.

Julian and I walked down the corridor, following the thick blue line, which was soon joined by the yellow, and then the red line that'd once led me to Oli. The drink machine was new so I had to read the instructions out loud, and my Fanta got stuck so we had to thump the machine a few times before it whooshed down and fell, clunk, into the tray at the bottom.

'Katie was here,' Dad said, when we sat back down in the chairs next to Mum's bed. 'I told her where to find you, but she raced off the other way. Poor kid. She left these.'

On the table next to Mum's bed were a card and purple flowers which'd been squeezed into the vase with the pansies Nick'd dropped off the day before.

On the front of the card was a pink rose and the word *sorry*. Inside, in Katie's perfect handwriting:

Dear Mrs Jamieson,
We are so sorry for what he did. Please get better soon.
From Katie, Kurt & Kyle Heller

He – she couldn't even write his name. I swallowed another mouthful of Fanta. The bubbles stung my nose and the orange was too sweet. I'd got it all wrong. I'd been thinking we'd done Katie a favour, that her dad getting caught was a good thing. But I hadn't thought what else it might mean, that we'd be passing the position of the most hated people in Boorunga from my family to hers. And what else would happen? Would she be forced to live somewhere else now that she had no parents? Would the government let her stay with her brothers if they knew they wagged school and played on the Atari all day? Katie'd obviously felt too ashamed to want to see me.

'Time to go, kids?' Dad nodded at the 'Zzzzzzzzzz' Mum had scrawled on her notepad. 'Remember what Dr English said? Plenty of rest!'

Mum closed her eyes. Dr English had explained that Mum's jaw would have to be 'reconstructed'. I imagined him taking her whole face apart before piecing it back together, dabbing on super glue to stick the bones in place. He said after the operation she'd be 'right as rain'. The tube that was carrying pureed food to her stomach would be taken out, and she'd be able to bite and chew like a normal person. She'd be able to talk. She'd take off the hospital gown that's designed to let the whole world see your bum, and put on her jeans. She'd come home. We were incredibly lucky, Dr English had said, looking from Dad to Julian to me. A bit higher and she would've lost her eye. I'd nodded at the kind doctor with the smoothly shaved face, but I was stuck on the word 'lucky'. If we were really 'lucky' Mum wouldn't have been hurt in the first place. If we were *lucky*, Celia on the hospital reception desk wouldn't now know all of our names and sometimes even smile at us.

Outside the hospital, we were a new combination of Jamiesons: Dad, Julian and me. Dad's fake cheerfulness started draining away as soon as the hospital's glass doors closed behind us, and was gone by the time he unlocked the car. Mr Heller had shaken the smile off his face and left grey rings around his eyes. The wrinkles rippling his forehead – had they been there before Constable Kelly turned up at our house that night? – reminded me of the corrugated cardboard we painted in Miss Coles's art class.

'I should've listened to your mum,' he said, clicking his seatbelt. 'I should've thrown in the job at the first sign of trouble. What was I thinking, going into partnership? Now we're up to our eyeballs in debt. And I'm back where I started – without a bloody job!'

'It's not your fault, Dad.' I realised it was time to fess up. 'It's actually mine.'

Dad shook his head as he started the car. 'Your dad's a fool.'

'No, Dad.' I closed my eyes, not wanting to meet his. 'I didn't want you to get a job at my school, so I messed up your interview. You wouldn't have got the job at the crem if I hadn't interfered.'

'My interview?' Dad sounded confused.

When I opened my eyes tears spilled out. 'I'm really sorry.'

Dad pulled into another car park and stopped the car with a jolt. Was he angry? Was he going to ask me to get out and walk? But he leant towards me.

'Look, just forget about it.' He rubbed my arm. 'I couldn't have worked for that woman anyway. Okay?'

I nodded, wiping my face on my sleeve.

Dad turned on the radio and we listened to Cat Stevens sing "Where Do The Children Play?" as we drove out of the car park, all thinking our own thoughts.

It took me a few seconds to recognise the man sitting on our front steps wearing a Manly football jumper. Nick hadn't said he was coming over, but I think Dad and Julian were as glad to see him as I was. A Pizza Hut box lay on his lap and he leant on a box of Fosters.

'It's my day off,' he said, following us inside. 'I'm not here on business. I'm here as a friend.'

The four of us ate warm pizza in front of *Little House on the Prairie*. When Nick asked us about Mum, Dad started blaming himself again, 'like a bloody broken record' Mum would've said if she was with us and her jaw still worked.

'It could've been worse, mate. Much worse.' Nick tore the ring off a beer can. 'He could've had a real gun and shot the three of you.'

'Thanks,' Dad said. 'But that thought doesn't cheer me up.'

Even though we didn't need his protection anymore, Nick was still a giant lump on our couch the next morning.

'Drink driving is not a good look for a sergeant,' he said, shuffling out of his sleeping bag. 'Bags first shower.'

He was singing "I Did It My Way" so loudly in the bathroom that it took us a while to realise someone was at the front door. Dad glanced at me before I followed him along the hall. Who would it be? Katie or Harriet? I didn't have the energy to talk to Katie – and I was pretty sure she'd used up all our tissues the last time she was over – so I was hoping for Harriet.

Dad opened the door to a big bunch of flowers, and behind it, someone whose face we'd last seen on our TV screen – Oli's dad, Mr Harrison.

The three of us stood there, staring at the flowers. They were round like the sun with bright yellow and red petals, wrapped in the shiny purple tissue paper my birthday presents usually arrived in. They looked out of place in Mr Harrison's rough hand, shading his wrung-out face. He reminded me of a sad clown.

'Gerberas. For your wife,' Mr Harrison said. 'I'm … sorry.'

Silence. Nick had stopped singing, turned off the taps.

Dad opened his mouth, but said nothing.

'Everything okay, Jim?' Nick called out.

Dad cleared his throat. 'It's fine.'

I grabbed Dad's hand to show him I was standing next to him, keen to hear what Mr Harrison had to say.

Mr Harrison spoke to the flowers, to the yellow and red petals, instead of to us. He said he felt 'crook' at the thought of what Dad'd been through: being blamed for something bloody terrible that he'd had nothing to do with. He said 'um' and 'ah' a lot and kept scratching his chin.

'It's okay, Steve,' Dad said. 'It's all sorted now.'

'How have you been?' Mr Harrison's sad eyes caught mine.

I shrugged.

'Been a tough time for you too.'

'Yeah.'

'I don't know what else to say, Jim. I've been a bloody wreck. Still am. After you'd had a go at me on the phone that night … I was sure it was you. When I heard about the graffiti on the wall – well, to me it seemed obvious. I didn't know Oli … s'cuse me.' Steve handed the flowers to Dad and got a tissue out of his pocket.

I studied the flowers in Dad's hand while Mr Harrison blew his nose. A few of the yellow petals were already browning on the edges, as if Mr Harrison's slow, painful words were causing them to wilt. I wondered if they were one of the many bunches that must've piled up at Oli's house after he died, or had Mr Harrison actually gone to a shop and bought them? I decided it didn't matter. Surely second-hand flowers meant 'sorry' just as much as new ones.

Mr Harrison continued. 'I didn't know anything was going on with him and Katie Heller. And then … I was just so angry, so bloody sad and angry … I'd just lost my only son.' Steve's voice was wobbling. I felt like shutting the front door on him. Not to push him away, but to spare him having us see his pain.

'Yeah, mate,' Dad said. 'I know.'

'It's not an excuse, but I need you to understand. I've been a mess. Couldn't sleep, couldn't eat, nearly hammered a nail right through my finger.' He held up a finger wrapped in a dirty Band-Aid. 'I still lose track of time. I headed off to work the other day and couldn't understand why no other cars were on the road, then I realised it was Saturday. I can't think straight, Jim. I've been blind.'

Dad nodded at the doorstep.

'Heller played me. Kept coming around, stirring up trouble. Convincing me you needed to pay. But no one was meant to get hurt. He said he'd use his boy's BB gun to put the wind up you. But …' Mr Harrison dabbed at his eyes. 'Look, I'm just really sorry. So's my wife.'

'Thanks,' Dad said. 'I appreciate your words.'

Mr Harrison shook his head. 'Words aren't enough. I want to make it up to you. If you need any work, let me help you out. There's always building jobs going.'

'Yeah?' Dad said. 'I'll think about it.'

'Um. Well.' Mr Harrison held out his hand.

'I appreciate it.' Dad passed me the flowers and shook Mr Harrison's hand, being careful not to squeeze the Band-Aided finger.

'Hope Henrietta is back on her feet soon, I really do,' Mr Harrison said. 'Bye, Miracle. Take care of yourself.'

'Mr Harrison?' I felt like I needed to say something. 'I really liked Oli. He was kinder than the other boys and he made everyone laugh, even the teachers. I miss him too.'

He gave me a quick nod before turning away, probably so I couldn't see his tears.

Dad shut the door and leant against it.

'Well,' he said. 'Maybe we can move on now, Miri. Once your mum gets home. We can all move on, eh?'

'Would you work with him?'

'I don't know. I can forgive him, but I'm not sure I want to be his mate.'

'But if he's going to give you a job, it could be worth it,' I said. 'Better than the crematorium.'

'I'm not going back there. Maybe … Let's get your mum home first, eh?'

50

You might think that knowing no one wanted to kill my family any more would be enough to make me happy. But I felt the way I had on my tenth birthday when I asked for roller skates and instead got socks with tiny pairs of roller skates knitted into them. They were probably the best socks I'd ever owned – thick, and fluffy on the inside – and they were great for sliding on the kitchen lino. But whenever I saw them in my sock drawer, I felt a sting of disappointment.

After Nick cleaned up the mess he'd made in our kitchen – he'd cooked us sausages and eggs for lunch – stuffed his sleeping bag into his boot, and driven off to start his afternoon shift, Dad suggested taking me and Julian for a drive. We cruised across the bridge, past my school – which was deserted since it was after 3 pm – and then Julian's school – which always looked deserted because only seventy kids went there – and back over the bridge again, then into the Woolies car park.

If you didn't count the hospital, it was the first place we'd been with Dad since he became 'as free as a bird'.

Dad parked outside the glass doors, and we sat there for a lifetime, staring at the 'Specials' posters through the car's foggy windows. Twirly Swirls were half price. One dollar a packet. I don't know why that stuck in my mind. After our meeting in the Twirly Swirl café, Twirly Swirls made me think of Greg, the words that came out of his mouth. I never wanted to eat another one in my life. Not even if they cost twenty cents. Not even the chocolate fudge ones.

A lady walking past looked straight through our windscreen, then elbowed the man she was holding hands with. *It's him*, I guessed she was saying.

Dad sighed.

'This is too weird,' I said.

'Come on.' Dad unbuckled his seatbelt. 'We've got as much right to be here as anyone else.'

We walked through the sliding doors in a line: Dad, Julian, then me.

In the fruit and vege section, an old lady with a black scarf around her head backed away from Dad, making the sign of the cross with her broccoli.

Dad rolled his eyes at me.

'So I'm the devil now?' he whispered.

'Innocent,' Jules said, loudly enough for the old lady to hear from behind the tomatoes.

'Quake boy speaks!' a girl in a green skivvy said to another girl who looked like her sister.

I didn't realise I was glaring at her until I saw the fear flash on her face. She stood still, as frozen as the Paddle Pop in her hand, until her sister pulled her away.

'Hurry up, Dad,' I said. 'I want to go.'

'Jim!' A man pushed his trolley over to Dad.

'Mate, I always knew they had the wrong bloke.' He held out his hand.

Dad shook it, and said, 'Thanks, Martin.'

When we were looking for the Spray n Wipe, a boy from school, with a fluffy peroxided mullet and braces, headed along our aisle holding a tin of International Roast coffee and a Mars Bar. I didn't have time to spin around and flee, so I sucked in my breath as he approached in the hope that it'd somehow make me, if not invisible, at least less visible. It didn't. But he grinned a metal smile that said, 'I know who you are, you're weird, but I am too, so I don't give a shit'. I let out my breath, and half smiled back. I think his name was Peter Moon.

We were standing in a queue behind the Miller family when I spotted her on the other side of the checkout. No one else in Boorunga owned a Country Road sloppy joe.

'Livvy!' I called.

Her cheeks turned pink when her eyes landed on me. She gave a quick wave with her car keys, and ran-walked out the supermarket's glass doors, a box of cornflakes bursting out of her plastic bag. She couldn't have left any faster if she'd jumped into someone's trolley.

She must've heard what'd happened. About Mr Heller. About Mum. So why didn't she stop to talk to us? Was she too embarrassed to face Dad? Or did she feel stupid for blaming Greg?

On the drive home Dad started whistling. It was the tune Mum'd whistled the night he'd been taken away, only I immediately recognised it because Dad wasn't tone deaf. "Always Look on the Bright Side of Life." I tried to catch his eyes in the rear-view mirror, but they were glued to the road.

'Might duck down to the pub for a bit,' Dad said, once we were home and he was putting the milk into the fridge. 'The lads asked me to drop by.'

I was leaning on the kitchen bench, flicking through the phone book. 'Who?' I asked. 'Ted?'

Dad nodded. 'And Ray, Stuart, the others.'

'That's good, Dad.' I found Greg and Livvy's address – 72 Heller Close, Riverview Estate – and wrote it on my hand in blue pen. *Heller Close.* Would they change the name now that Heller was in jail?

'Yeah, well. Expect they feel lousy for turning their backs on me,' Dad said. 'I would, in their shoes.'

'They should!' I said. 'Anyway, I'm going for a walk.'

I could practically see a bubble pop up in Dad's mind with the words 'be careful' inside it, and then another bubble reminding him there was nothing to be careful about. He smiled. 'I'll tell Jules to hold the fort.'

'Okay, bye.'

I raced along the hall, grabbed my shoes, and sprinted out the door before he had a chance to ask me where I was going.

51

Walking down Mills Road, I felt like a stranger. The street I'd been falling off my bike and grazing my knees on since I was in primary school seemed like it belonged to some other town. And where was everyone? Why could I hear my sneakers hitting the footpath? I had a strong sense that something had changed.

When I got to the end of the skinny path that crossed Boorunga Bridge, I squinted up at Heller's Plastics on the opposite corner, painted in a rainbow, the red, blue, purple and orange of its lunchbox range, pretending to be something out of *Charlie and the Chocolate Factory*, desperately trying to be good. Then I saw the sky – as blue as Julian's eyes – behind the blackened chimneys growing off the factory's roof. I took a deep breath and smelt … grass. Then I realised what was different: I could breathe.

I ran across the road, towards the giant steel gates.

CLOSED UNTiL FURTHER NOTiCE, a handwritten sign told me. My mind reeled. Not only had I not considered what would happen to Katie now that her dad was locked up, I'd also forgotten about his factories. I guess I'd assumed they'd carry on, that, if anything, they'd be better places to work without him storming around, a cloud of anger in a black suit. From what Mum and Dad had said, he spent most of his time either threatening to fire people or actually doing it.

Further down the road, two men were unloading boxes from a truck outside the Twirly Swirl factory, so that was obviously still going. Thank God. There'd be a riot if the town's supply of Twirly Swirls dried up.

I pressed my face against the cold metal gate. It had to be a good thing, Heller's Plastics closing. We'd be able to breathe. Swallowing the smoke that spewed out of its chimneys was probably as bad as smoking entire packets of Parsons Reds at recess.

But the empty car park made me sad. I knew heaps of kids whose dads worked there and I knew what this would mean for them. They'd have to watch their dads cut out ads in the Classifieds, dress up in suits stinking of mothballs, rehearse job interviews in the mirror like little kids trying to get a part in a Christmas pageant. And how many of them would apply for the same jobs? I imagined Dad in a one-hundred-metre queue of desperate dads in too-big suits. Then I shook the image away. I didn't need anything else to worry about. Dad could work for Steve if he really needed to. Things were going to get better, they had to.

Always look on the bright side of life.

Then there was Katie, whose dad was to blame for everything. She must've known. How would she have felt? Especially when he was pretending to be friends with Oli's dad as a cover-up. I needed to thank her for telling me what'd happened, for dobbing him in. But that could wait. Katie had stuff to deal with, and so did I.

The footpath in Riverview Estate was so white and clean, I felt like the first person to walk on it. Standing on tippy-toes I could just glimpse the Boorunga River, so whoever called it Riverview must've been seven feet tall or drunk. Whoever designed the Estate must've been drunk too, because they'd knocked down all the trees and most of the front lawns were blankets of dry dirt. There were only four houses on Livvy's street, all exactly the same – wooden and on stilts like most built after the earthquake. I guessed if there was another quake, the people in these houses would carry on as usual, enjoying a view of everyone else's rubble.

'Please don't let Greg be home,' I said to the shiny pebbled driveway that led to number 72.

'Please don't let Greg be home,' I whispered to the doorbell as I pressed it.

But when the door opened, Greg filled the doorway, a carrot in one hand and a small knife in the other. He was dressed like an ordinary man in navy tracksuit pants and a brown flannelette shirt, but his eyes were as businesslike as ever.

'Ah, Jim's little Miracle,' he said. 'Should we have been expecting you?'

'No. I … I was just dropping in.' I tried not to look at the knife. 'To see Livvy.'

'How's Mum?' Greg's teeth closed around the carrot.

'She's getting better.' I hoped he couldn't hear my voice shaking.

'Good, good. You must be pleased to have your dad home too.'

I wanted to say, *Why do you care?* He hadn't given a stuff about Dad, even though they'd been business partners. Friends, too. Or so Dad thought. 'Is Livvy home?'

Greg took another bite of carrot and wiped the knife on his tracksuit pants. The blade looked sharp. He stared at me while he chewed, the crunching making my stomach turn. Then he shook his head and walked inside.

After a lifetime, Livvy came out in a white bathrobe and bare feet, her long, wet hair hiding her face.

'Hi.' I wondered if I'd said it loud enough because she didn't reply.

She led me to two cane chairs on the front veranda, sat down and stretched out her long barbie-doll legs. Her feet were narrow; her toenails painted hot pink.

Livvy sighed and glanced behind her to make sure the door was closed. 'If you're going to tell me off, get it over and done with.'

'Huh? I wanted to see how you were.' I felt my face burn. 'I was worried you were in trouble with your dad.'

'So you didn't figure it out?'

What was she saying?

'I know it wasn't your dad,' I said. 'But I can understand why you thought it was.'

'I didn't though. I made it all up. The stuff about him being so angry that night.' She talked to the sky, the blue, blue sky. 'And about me and your dad. Sorry. I feel stupid about it now.'

My mind was spinning. I thought back to her sitting on the couch at Harriet's, Worm's *Dr Who Annual* on her lap, the things she told me. How could she have made them up?

'The burn,' I said. 'You showed me it. You burnt yourself when your dad slammed down the urn, when he busted you.'

She held up her wrist, the shape of Italy faint but still there. 'I tripped carrying a coffee up the stairs. It had nothing to do with either of them.'

'So there was no …' I couldn't bring myself to say it.

Livvy shook her head. 'Your dad's not bad looking for an old man, apart from his nose anyway – you're lucky you didn't inherit it – but I wouldn't do anything like that. With someone his age.'

I nodded. I felt a bit insulted, but mostly relieved. Still, it didn't make sense.

'But why? Why would you want your dad to get the blame?'

'I hate him for screwing up my life,' Livvy said quietly. 'For bringing me here. I wanted you to tell the police so he'd get arrested. The graffiti gave me the idea. *Stay away from my girl.* It could've been Dad's message to your dad. I was using you. I'm sorry.'

'He could've gone to jail,' I whispered.

'That was the plan. I got so desperate *I* called the police on him. I can make up convincing stories. As you now know. Dad was furious! He threatened to send me to a shrink.'

'But why get him in trouble?'

'So I'd be sent to live with Mum. He took me away, said she'd never get custody of me because she's a *lesbian.* She's living with the librarian from my old school. *Elena.* He doesn't want me growing up in an *unnatural* environment.'

'And your mum wanted you to stay?'

Livvy nodded. 'She calls practically every day, tells me she misses me so much it hurts. It'd be awkward living with Elena, but I'd rather her than Dad. I wasn't given a choice.'

'But your dad pushed your mum out of the car!'

'I made that up,' Livvy said. 'He did threaten to though, and he's made worse threats. I don't blame Mum for turning into a lesbian – he probably drove her to it – though I would've preferred she chose someone who didn't work at my school and who shaved her legs.'

I looked down at my own legs, thankful I was wearing jeans. I made a mental note to steal one of Dad's razors.

'I know my dad comes across as all charming, as if he cares for people's *loved ones,* but that's not who he really is. He's very controlling. He says he's just *protective,* but I feel like a prisoner. He's told me to stay away from boys – which is why … It's why I've been with more than most girls at school.'

I thought about the rumours I'd heard, and that time I saw her compare hickeys with two other Year 12 girls at the bus stop. Then I remembered the dark purple one I'd noticed on Seth's neck. 'Even Seth Boston?'

'Oliver's friend.' Livvy nodded. 'He turned psycho when I refused to go out with him. But he's in your year, and I didn't even like him. I don't like any of them.'

'God. Your life is as mental as mine.' I watched a bee hovering over a bush before landing on a purple flower. A bee, getting on with its simple little bee life. I had a feeling Livvy wanted to tell me more about Greg, but I didn't want to hear it. I was content with knowing he'd had nothing to do with Oli – and that Dad had nothing to do with Livvy. I felt stupid for having believed that about Dad.

'I wouldn't blame you for hating me.' Livvy chewed on her fingernail. 'You probably think I'm a pathological liar. And a slut. Probably both. But I'm not. I'm just … messed up.'

'Yeah, well. Me too.'

She looked up, her eyes watery.

'Sorry about your mum. How's she doing?'

'She can't speak yet,' I said. 'But that's not necessarily a bad thing.'

Livvy smiled, so I let my words tumble out. 'It's the only time she's been away from home. That I can remember. She hates being out of our house. She kicked up a stink – banging a cup on the side of her bed – until the nurses moved her to a bed by the window. It's as if she needs to know she can do a runner if the urge to go home gets too strong. They had to swap her with a woman with a broken pelvis.'

A long shadow approached us, followed by Greg, carrying two white mugs.

'Coffee, girls?' Greg passed one to me, and the other to Livvy. I mumbled thanks as I took the hot mug with both hands, but was careful to avoid his eyes. Maybe one day I'd be ready to ask Livvy more about him, but at that moment I didn't want to know.

'Must run in the family,' Livvy said, after Greg'd closed the front door and we'd both taken a sip. I didn't normally drink coffee so I couldn't tell whether it was poisoned or if it was supposed to taste like dirt. I took tiny sips just in case.

'What? Agoraphobia?'

'Survival. Your mum's tough. So are you.'

I looked into my mug. 'I should go.' My heart was racing and I couldn't sit still any longer. Maybe it was Livvy's confession, maybe it was the coffee. Or poison.

I realised I didn't care that she'd lied. I'd lied as well – to Dad. We were as bad as each other.

'Will you come to school tomorrow? We're finally having the Great Quake Debate, after it was postponed for the funeral. We've stayed back every afternoon this week to prepare.'

I remembered how much I'd dreaded the thought of the debate. But who cared now if anyone thought I was part of Boorunga's curse? I didn't.

'Which side are you on?' I asked, even though I already knew.

'*The quake caused the curse*. We're going to win. The odds are now seventeen to one. Mr Henley decided to turn it into a maths project as well – using Monopoly money. He doesn't know the boys are using real money too. Please come.'

'Okay,' I said. 'I'll talk to Dad.'

'Great. Bring money to place a bet. On *my* team.'

I could feel her watching me as I opened the gate.

'Miracle?'

I turned to face her.

'I knew there was something special about you. I knew when I met you.'

'What?' I said. 'How am I *special*?'

'The way you handled everything. Most people would've gone to pieces. But not you – you helped put that creep away.'

'I keep thinking it was all my fault.'

'It wasn't. You must know that. You're actually kind of a hero.'

'I doubt it, but thanks.' I felt my face flush. 'See you tomorrow.'

52

I sprinted all the way from Livvy's, stopping only to catch my breath when I felt a twist of pain in my side. I liked the feel of cold air in my throat and the burn in my calf muscles. The streetlights were on when I made it to the finish line – the closest edge of our driveway – but it was still light enough to see the sign sticking out of Mrs Jensen-from-across-the-road's front lawn. *For Sale*. I stared at it, my breath coming out in little clouds. Of all the shocks I'd had in the last couple of hours – the factory closing, Livvy's lies, Greg being half human – this was the biggest. Why was she moving? Had she seen one thing too many from her window? Mrs Jensen had lived in her house for as long as I'd been alive. For me, she and her house were one and the same.

I headed straight for the bathroom, washed all the tiny ginger hairs out of the basin – cleaning up after himself obviously hadn't been part of Nick's police training – and filled it with warm water. I splashed water on my face, letting it drip down my arms and onto the floor. Through the splotches of toothpaste on the mirror, I studied the scar on my forehead, the scar that would always remind me of Julian's moment of madness. I'd get a haircut. Every few months, usually when Julian's eyes started to disappear, Mum'd get out the sewing scissors, and sometimes the results were just as good as a real hairdresser's. She could cut me a fringe to hide my scar.

Dad lifted his eyebrows when I sat in Mum's armchair, but he didn't ask where I'd been and I didn't offer any clues. I was practically fifteen; I needed to get my freedom back.

Still, I was keen to know how his evening had gone. 'Did you go to the pub?' I asked.

Dad nodded. 'Felt like a celebrity. Everyone wanted to buy me a drink.'

'How come you're home, then? We can look after ourselves. Can't we, Jules?'

'Huh?' Julian's head poked over a comic book.

'I wasn't really in the mood,' Dad said. 'It's hard to forget that they turned on me so quickly. Also, Harriet and John are coming over. There's a special on the plastics factory on *60 Minutes*.'

'I walked past it,' I told him. 'I didn't know it'd shut.'

'Yeah. Earlier in the week. Haven't you noticed the sky lately?'

'Why?'

'There's no smoke!'

'No, why did it close?'

'Dodgy practices,' Dad said. 'After they put Heller away, his workers must've spilt the beans. That man is rotten to the core.'

'What kind of *practices*?'

'Well, they're saying the factory's waste was leaking into our waterways.' Dad held up an invisible cup and tipped it towards his mouth.

'We've been drinking it?' I imagined a cup full of thick, black liquid.

'It could explain why so many people have been crook.'

Julian let the book fall onto his lap. 'Me?'

'I hate to say it, mate, but it could be,' Dad said. 'You've never been sick like that before.'

'So Harriet's instinct was right, then. She told me to boil water. But the factory's been there for ages. Why isn't *everyone* dead?'

'It's doubled in size over the years and changed hands a few times. All the owners can't have been crooks! But, know what the worst of it is? Your mum heard this in hospital. Might just be gossip, but it makes sense to me.'

Julian leant towards Dad. When did he start becoming interested in our conversation?

'Well, Raymond from Miller's Funeral Homes? He was onto them. He saw a pattern in all those deaths. Apparently he'd met with a couple of doctors to talk about it, too. Must be some truth to him liking the bottle – though he sounded pretty sharp to me – but more likely his leaving town had something to do with him cottoning on to Heller and trying to pull the plug on the factory.'

'So they made him leave?'

'Looks like it. He was here one day, gone the next. Just left a note on the funeral parlour door, saying "Closed due to unforeseen circumstances". They probably threatened him, maybe even with that BB gun of Heller's.'

'Does anyone know where he is?'

'I don't know.' Dad cleared his throat. 'Nick will probably try to track him down, ask him questions. He was a nice bloke, single, a bit shy. He always wore a tie, the same tie, black with tiny crosses on it. Religious. Not that it did him any good. You know, I reckon –'

But we never did hear what Dad reckoned because we heard someone tapping on the front door.

'That'll be them.' Dad pulled himself out of his chair.

Worm came sprinting into the living room and dove into the beanbag next to Julian. 'Fish and chips!'

'Joan Jensen is selling up?' Harriet placed the paper package on the table, a salty smell filling the room.

'Yeah,' Dad said. 'Says she's fed up with waiting for Bruce to come home, poor woman.'

'But … Bruce,' John said. 'Didn't he go to war?'

'He did. She forgot that around a decade ago. Forgot about the telegram too.'

I pictured Mrs Jensen-from-across-the-road standing in her favourite spot by the window. Is that why she was watching? She wasn't pressing her face against the glass to snoop on my family? The thought of her waiting for her husband hour after hour, day after day, made me sad. I should've visited, made her a cup of tea or something. Helped make at least twenty minutes pass by.

'Poor Joan.' Harriet unwrapped the steaming package. 'But good on her for starting a new life at her age.'

'Yeah, a new life,' Dad said. 'At the retirement home across the bridge.'

'Well, the company will be good for her,' Harriet said, before turning to me. 'Any thoughts on returning to school?'

'I'm going back tomorrow.'

'I thought you'd said Monday.' Dad started setting the table.

I shrugged. 'Tomorrow's a half day anyway. There's a Year 12 debate. Livvy's in it. She's really excited.'

'Good on you, Miracle,' John said. 'The sooner your life gets back to normal the better.'

'You'll be fine, love,' Harriet said. 'Help yourselves everyone, it's nearly seven-thirty. Here's yours, Worm.'

'More sauce.' Worm wrapped his hand around the bottle and blobbed half of it into his bowl.

Once we'd filled our plates, we all sat around the TV: Dad in his chair, Harriet and John on the couch, Julian, Worm and me on the floor. Boorunga was the first story on *60 Minutes*.

'Boring!' Worm said.

I poked a sticky red chip in his mouth. 'Shhh.'

'*The people of Boorunga, a town that was ravaged by an earthquake nearly fifteen years ago, and torn apart by the brutal beating of a teenaged boy, learnt today that, over the past twenty-four months, they've been slowly poisoned by their own town's leading industrial operation. A shocking report on Heller's Plastics, which, until it was forced to close this week, employed nearly five hundred locals, revealed practices that are thought to have led to the deaths of several residents.*'

'Unbelievable.' Harriet shook her head.

'I always knew Mr Heller was bad,' I said. 'He never let Katie –'

'Shhh!' Worm shoved a chip in my mouth. 'I'm listening!'

'Well, at least it's over,' Dad said. 'We can all get on with our lives.'

'The bridge!' Worm pointed to the TV, his stubby fingers coated in tomato sauce. 'And the library. And police station. And the … '

I stared at the screen, at the images – of Boorunga's main street, of inside and around the factory, of the 'closed' sign I'd read only hours before. The food in my mouth suddenly tasted like plastic. I spat it onto the plate, and pushed the plate away.

'Poor Raymond Miller must've figured out what was going on,' Harriet said.

Dad nodded. 'Yeah, I reckon so too. And Heller didn't miss a beat. He called up his mate Greg and told him there was a gap in the market.'

'So, you think Greg knew?' John asked.

Dad shrugged. 'I don't know. He could've been covering for them. But I dunno for sure. Don't know what to think anymore.'

'I suspected something was up with the water,' Harriet said. 'It tasted a bit off.'

'Yeah?' Dad said. 'I never really drink the stuff. I've always felt bad that I don't drink much water; who'd have thought it'd save my skin?'

'And did you know we took the kids to Lawson's Bay? That's when Julian got better,' Harriet said. 'I just thought it was the sea air that'd cured him. Worm, let me clean your hands!'

'Miri told me.' Dad nodded. 'We owe you a lot.'

I pushed my plate further away – the sight of greasy chips was making me queasy – and lay stretched out on the floor, trying to make sense of everything. So much had changed, and not just for me and my family. I felt like I did when I was seven and Katie told me Santa Claus wasn't real. Even though Dad'd already outed himself as the Tooth Fairy after he tripped over my slipper when swapping my front tooth for a twenty-cent piece, for some reason, I'd never doubted the Easter Bunny or Santa. The thought of Dad drinking the beer and eating the Twirly Swirls we left out for Santa, and in other houses, other kids' dads doing the same, felt so wrong. It was like for my whole life the world had been pretending to be something it wasn't.

But I wasn't going to let the feeling bring me down. I'd learnt a lot since I was seven – perhaps not as much algebra and statistics as I should've – but I was definitely smarter. And I had lots to be happy about. No one thought Dad was a psycho anymore. He was home where he belonged, sitting in his chair, wearing his old Kmart slippers, and Mum could now eat soup and pureed vegetables, and pronounce swear words clearly. She'd even given up smoking, saying she was sick of all the exercise, having to walk to the waiting room to have a fag. 'Next thing you know, I'll be fit!' she complained.

She promised to stop drinking too. 'If I'd been blind drunk, I couldn't have moved so fast,' she'd told me. 'I wouldn't have been able to live with myself if Heller had got you.' She also said that hospital was the best 'rehab' she could hope for because it was free.

Then there was Julian. He was lying next to me, leaning over his sketchpad, the glow of the TV turning his blond hair pink, his steady fingers sketching the curve of a neck.

314

'Who is it, Jules?' I tapped his elbow. 'Who are you drawing?'

'Wait.'

I knew who it was before he started on the eyes. I recognised the short, scruffy hair. According to Katie, it took two tubes of gel a month to perfect the messy hair look. After finishing the eyebrows, just visible under the floppy fringe, Julian drew the mouth, this time shaping it into a tight smile. I blinked back tears and bit my lip.

'*Lo siento,*' Julian whispered. 'From Oli.'

Acknowledgements

A big thanks to:

Tina Shaw, Dione Jones and everyone else at Cloud Ink Press, for bringing *Miracle* into the world.

To Penelope Todd, for editing *Miracle* with the same care and precision you brought to *All Our Secrets*.

To Damien Lane, for being the first person to read *Miracle* front to back (and for doing so twice).

To Janine Murray, for nailing the brief and designing another fantastic cover.

To Catherine Robertson, for reading a pre-edited draft of *Miracle* and still managing to say nice things about it.

To the New Zealand Society of Authors and Norman Bilbrough, for a comprehensive manuscript assessment.

To Nathan Blackwell, for answering my questions on the criminal court process (something I've thankfully never needed to know about until Jim landed in a police cell).

To my writers' group – Janis Freegard, Kate Mahoney, Jackie Owens, Annette Edwards-Hill, Phil Evans, and Mikael Aldridge – for your valuable feedback.

To the recently departed Alison Lane, aka Mum, who instilled in me a love of reading and writing.

To Allan, Tess and Tilly, for letting me shut myself away in my office for hours on end.

And to anyone else who has offered encouragement or took the time to read this book – thank you.

jenniferlane.co.nz